# CUTLASS

### TAMI FRANKLIN

Cover images by:
stock.adobe.com/©Alik Mulikov
stock.adobe.com/©theartofphoto
stock.adobe.com/©Photocreo Bednarek
stock.adobe.com/©Andrey Armyagov
stock.adobe.com/©lotus_studio
DepositPhotos.com/©katalinks

Cover design by T.M. Franklin

PUBLICATIONS
www.enchantedpublications.com

Visit the Author's web site at
www.TMFranklin.com
ISBN: 0-9985468-4-4
ISBN-13: 978-0-9985468-4-1

*For Kate and Susana, without whom this would never have been written.*

*And for all the wonderful readers who supported this story along the way . . . you are some seriously crazy people.* ☺

*October, 1745*

She clutched at his bloodstained shirt, her fingers slick and red as she knelt over his battered body. Her heart pounded, loud and fierce in her ears as she fought to stay calm—to do something other than give in to her rising panic, or collapse in devastated sobs and cling to her father as she did when she was a little girl.

"Papa? Dear God, no! What happened?"

In the wreckage of his ransacked study, she barely noticed the scattered piles of papers and books, the overturned chair behind his desk, or the cupboard door hanging crooked by one hinge. It swung slowly back and forth, revealing periodic glimpses of the empty space within . . . the space where her father kept the cutlass, wrapped in linen to protect it from dust and damage.

The hinge creaked—a countermelody to her father's labored breaths.

He opened his mouth to speak, but thick crimson strangled the words in his throat, bubbling out to drip down his chin and cheeks and seep into the threadbare rug.

"No, no . . . don't talk," she whispered through choked tears. She cast about for something to use to staunch the flow of blood and finally yanked a blanket off the chaise behind her and pressed it to his chest. "It'll be all right. Just stay calm."

Her father gasped in reply, eyes wide and searching. His lips moved frantically, but no sound escaped.

"Shhh . . ." she said, brushing the hair back from his face. His skin was cold and sickly pale, all color draining out through the gaping wound in his chest. He groaned, and with a rush of strength, he grabbed her wrist, his gaze suddenly sharp and focused as he opened his mouth again.

"Papa?" She leaned in closer to hear the words—the name that would haunt her for years to come. The name that would give her purpose, an avenue for her grief when her father's erratic heartbeat finally slowed, then stopped. The name that would allow her to forge the pain and loss into a weapon of single-minded furious determination.

"Tremayne," he whispered with his last, gasping breath. ". . . Tremayne."

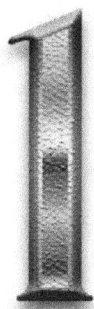

*Often when the sunlight wanes, I find myself perusing the vastness of the sea about me, and ponder the warnings of those who speak of the wildness of this place. Some fear the natives of the islands and their strange ways. Others, the dangerous creatures who dwell in the depths beneath me. I, however, have come to know that the true danger of these waters lies not with the savages, nor the beasties below. No, the true threat is the man without honor, without conscience.*

*He calls himself the pirate.*

*- The Journal of*
*Simon Alistair Mellick*
*6 October, 1664*

**May, 1748**

Only a handful of fluffy white clouds marred the wide expanse of blue sky as the *Black Arrow* sliced through the choppy waters of the Atlantic. Captain Jonathan Tremayne tilted his head, eyeing with approval the full sails billowing overhead and the full crew busily at work on deck. He stood, legs splayed widely, with a compass open in one palm, the fingers of his other hand wrapped lightly around the wheel. He allowed the ship its head more than trying to force it in a specific direction.

The wind was with them today.

The men knew not their destination, save Maxwell Baines, the captain's second-in-command and most trusted confidant.

*Only* trusted confidant, to put a finer point on it. Jonathan Tremayne shared neither his thoughts nor his faith easily, but over the years, he had grown to rely on his first mate and indeed trust him with his life.

That trust had been well earned. The captain, in fact, owed his life to Baines twice over.

But that was a tale for another day.

"Baines!" Tremayne bellowed, snapping the compass closed and tucking it into his coat pocket. "Assemble the men."

"Attend the captain!" Baines shouted immediately, the command echoing across the deck and down the stairs to the bowels of the ship, as well. Within minutes, the crew had assembled in a loose circle around the helm. The captain relinquished the wheel to his quartermaster, Crawley, and turned to address the men. He said nothing for a moment, just paced before them slowly, gripping the hilt of his dagger in his fist, the thump of his boot heels muffled slightly by the crash of the waves. A patch covered what remained of his left eye, a scar running from his temple to chin evidence of the injury that nearly claimed his life. His good eye glinted bright blue-green—the color of the sea—as he appraised each man before him steadily.

"I know there's been talk of our heading," he began, "and what booty lies at the end of this journey." He stopped his pacing, his gaze locking on each of his men in turn. "At morning's light, we will encounter the *Enchanted Lady,* and I plan to take her."

At the mention of the notorious vessel, a nervous murmur arose from the crowd.

"Avast!" Baines barked, silencing the men immediately.

"Now," Captain Tremayne continued, "there's treasure aplenty on board the *Lady*, and each will get his fair share. But somewhere on that ship is a chest that is mine and mine alone." He glared menacingly to emphasize his point. "Baines will give you a description of the chest. The man who brings it to me will earn a double share of the *Lady's* treasure." An excited rumbling rolled through the crew.

The captain raised a hand, silencing them. "And I need not tell you that anyone found to be keeping back a portion of the booty before it's duly divided by Crawley will find himself dangling from the main mast." His voice lowered to a threatening growl. "And any who might think to keep the chest for himself I'll see to Davy Jones myself, at the point of my sword."

A collective gulp resounded across the deck, and Tremayne turned abruptly on his heel. A flash of movement to his left caught his eye and he paused, seeking out the source. A young boy he didn't recognize huddled behind the massive hulk of Sam Hutchins, the master rigger.

"Boy!" the captain called. "Show yourself!"

The crowd parted, all eyes following the captain's gaze as he took a step toward the boy.

"Don't make me ask again," he snarled.

The boy stepped tentatively out from behind Hutchins, his bowed head covered by a dark woolen cap. His breeches were torn at the knee, his body swallowed by a voluminous shirt and flapping leather vest. He wrung his hands nervously, and the captain frowned at the delicate bones, wondering how such a fragile creature could survive at sea.

"What's your name, boy?" he asked gruffly.

The boy mumbled an answer.

"Speak up!" Tremayne ordered.

"Smith, sir."

"Smith, eh?" He looked to Baines questioningly.

His first mate shrugged. "He came on board at Hispaniola. We needed another powder monkey."

Tremayne scowled at the information, for some reason uneasy at the idea of the boy serving on the gun crew. "How old are you, boy?"

The boy hesitated only a moment and the captain's scowl deepened. "Do not be lying to me, now."

"Seventeen," he replied quietly, his eyes still focused on the deck.

"Seventeen?" Tremayne repeated. "Mite small for seventeen, aren't you?" He eyed Baines, but the man just shrugged again in response. "I doubt he could even carry a half-empty powder barrel, if that," he muttered, half to himself.

"I'm stronger than I look," the boy said stubbornly, and Tremayne fought back a chuckle of surprise. The boy had spirit.

Still, spirit had its limits, and the captain quickly rearranged his features into his trademark glower. "Mind your place, boy."

"Aye, Cap'n." He wrung his hands again, the knuckles white with tension.

Tremayne's good eye narrowed as he came to a decision. "Baines, have you found a replacement for young Tom as of yet?" The cabin boy had jumped ship in Havana and had not been seen since.

"No," Baines replied, picking at his teeth with the tip of his knife. "Not yet."

The captain removed his hat, scratching at his scalp briefly before replacing it. "That settles it, then. Smith here will take his place.

"Boy," he said in a brusque tone. "You'll be seeing to my needs from now on. For now, I'll be wanting a shave and my supper." When the boy stood frozen in place, the captain planted his fists on his hips, raising his voice to a near roar. "Move it, Smith! Don't be keeping me waiting!" The boy rushed to the stairs, and the captain stalked after him.

"The rest of you—back to work!" he bellowed, the command echoed by Baines as the crew scrambled to return to their stations.

Nobody noticed the satisfied smile on the face of the boy named Smith.

Captain Tremayne wasn't exactly certain what compelled him to help the boy. Part of it was the fact he did indeed need a replacement for Tom—someone to keep his cabin in order and keep his things in repair. Despite his bloodthirsty reputation, Tremayne had a need for order and structure . . . discipline amidst the chaos. For in reality, his ship was a well-oiled machine, each crew member fulfilling his tasks with efficiency and pride.

But they also knew how to relax. Which led to the other reason he felt compelled to take young Smith under his wing.

His men worked hard, but they also played hard. After a long day of backbreaking labor, and a few jugs of rum, they were wont to take their pleasure where they could find it. Many would wait until they made port, finding relief in a willing female at a pub or a brothel—or in a dark alley, if the need be. But a few took what they could get where it was offered, opting for hard muscles instead of soft curves.

Jonathan had no problem when both the participants were consenting. But he'd already caught a few longing looks toward young Smith as he had charged him with his new post, and he wouldn't stand for anyone taking advantage just because he was smaller and weaker. If the boy chose to participate in some onboard recreation, that was his choice, but no one on his ship would live in fear of such a thing.

Abruptly, Smith halted in the narrow space, and Jonathan stumbled into his back, knocking the boy sideways into the wall.

Smith grunted as Jonathan leaned into him, gripping his hip to regain his balance.

"What the bloody hell?" the captain growled as he righted himself.

"I'm . . . sorry, sir," the boy said meekly, his eyes on his worn shoes. "I wasn't sure which way to go."

Tremayne adjusted the leather belt that held his flintlock across his chest and propped his hands on his hips. "To the right, boy. Through the door."

Smith nodded and hurried down the dark hallway, tripping slightly over his own feet. The captain followed behind, striding into his quarters and throwing his hat onto the massive bed—one of the captain's few bows to luxury. As soon as he'd taken command of the *Black Arrow*, he'd replaced the uncomfortable bunk with a feather mattress and silken coverings. His cabin was his sanctuary after all; filled with personal items and prizes from his many conquests. Few were allowed in his private abode, and even now he was nervous about allowing Smith entrance into his lair. He spotted the boy out of the corner of his eye, standing awkwardly by the door, waiting for instructions.

Tremayne sighed. He had no patience for training the boy, but there was really no alternative. Usually, he'd leave the task to Max or one of the cook's boys, but he was starving and filthy and had no time to wait.

"To the galley, boy," he ordered. "Fetch water for my shaving, then see the cook about my meal." When the boy hesitated, he added gruffly. "Be quick about it before I change my mind and have you swabbing the head."

Evidently the threat of having to clean up the toilet area at the bow of the ship was enough to spark Smith into action. He jumped and darted out the door, and Jonathan chuckled at the sound of his feet pounding toward the galley in the bowels of the ship. The captain shrugged out of his coat and pulled his weapons belt over his head before tossing them both onto the bed. Tugging his shirt from the waistband of his breeches, he reached for the jug of rum on his heavy wooden desk and poured a hefty dose into a tankard. His dagger belt stayed in place around his hips, a second pistol tucked into it and his jeweled dirk secure in his right boot. Captain Tremayne was always armed. Even in sleep, his hand gripped the dagger under his pillow; his flintlock tucked securely beneath the mattress.

Taking a long swallow from the tankard, he collapsed into a carved wooden chair he'd liberated during a raid the previous summer while rubbing a hand absently over his scruffy cheek. He could glimpse the blue sky out the porthole above the bed, the swaying of the ship bringing the deeper blue of the sea into view every few seconds. He was lulled by the hypnotic swaying of his ship, combined with the relaxing buzz of the rum. So much so, that at first he didn't realize his cabin boy had returned, a steaming bowl of water in his hands.

He waved a beringed hand at a small table beside him. "The soap and razor are on the shelf over there," he said, pointing across the room. Smith hurried over, setting the bowl on the table carefully, but still managing to splash a little on the polished wood. He gasped, using his shirttail to wipe up the water before retrieving the mug of soap and straight razor. Adding a little water to the mug, he began to swirl the shaving brush into the soap.

Jonathan eyed the boy carefully, noticing the nervous way he swallowed. He really was a little thing, practically skin and bones with wide amber eyes and cheeks smooth as a babe's.

"You ever shave a man before, Smith?" he asked gruffly.

"Aye, sir." His voice squeaked and he cleared his throat. "My . . . my father."

The captain nodded, leaning his head back on the chair. "Well, carry on then."

Smith reached for a strap attached to the side of the table and began to run the straight razor slowly back and forth before testing the edge against his thumb. He reached for the mug without meeting Jonathan's gaze, and the captain closed his eye and felt the soft sweep of the brush against his skin. He could hear Smith's shaky breaths and wondered why he seemed so terrified of him. When the boy set the mug aside and Jonathan felt the razor touch his cheek, his hand flashed up to grip Smith's wrist as his eye narrowed on the boy's reddened face.

"Take care," he warned. "I'd not like to have to gut you because your hand slipped." Tremayne's hand gripped his dagger, slipping it from the scabbard with a quiet hiss to emphasize his words before laying it across his stomach.

Smith swallowed thickly and nodded. "Aye, sir." He hesitated briefly before taking a deep breath and sliding the razor across the captain's skin with a gentle scrape. Jonathan relaxed, but his fingers remained wrapped around his dagger as the boy shaved him, dipping the razor into the bowl of water between each stroke, and finally wiping his face with a piece of rough toweling. Jonathan reached for a small tin of salve on the table, dipping in his fingers before smoothing it over his cleanly shaven cheeks. The spicy scent wafted in the air, and he felt Smith watching him carefully.

"An herbal remedy to prevent irritation," he muttered, not sure why he was explaining himself. He put the lid back on the tin and stood abruptly, before rounding his desk. "Deal with that," he said gruffly, motioning at the now soapy water, "and bring me my supper." The captain turned his attention to some documents on the table as Smith hurried to fulfill his wishes.

Jonathan examined the parchment that had led him this far. It was just a torn scrap bearing a few words and a portion of a pencil drawing, but it pointed to the *Lady* as the place to find the chest he sought. It was only a step on his journey, however, for inside . . . *inside* the chest was the answer he was looking for. Once he had it, he would have what he'd been seeking since he first took command.

Wealth.

Power.

*Vengeance.*

Jonathan smiled grimly at the thought, rubbing at his patch in remembrance. The man who took his eye—who nearly took his life—would pay. In time, he would pay.

"Sir?" Smith's quiet voice interrupted the captain's concentration, making him jump. The fact that he was startled irritated him more than anything else.

"Must you prowl about like a timid kitten?" he barked.

Smith started in surprise and before he schooled his features, Jonathan thought he might have spotted another emotion there.

Irritation? No, it was almost . . . *fury.*

But just as soon as it appeared, it was gone, replaced by the fearful hesitance the captain was rapidly growing accustomed to, and Jonathan thought perhaps he'd imagined it after all.

"Your supper, sir," Smith said quietly, and Jonathan realized he was holding a covered tray. He studied the boy's face for one more moment before he slid his papers into a drawer and waved him over. Smith set the tray on the desk, removing the lid and holding it behind his back. Jonathan saw his chest expand as if inhaling the scents released into the room—roasted sausages, potatoes, some fresh vegetables they'd obtained at the last port, and a small loaf of warm bread. Jonathan broke off a piece of the bread and popped it into his mouth, washing it down with a swig of rum.

The loud rumble of the boy's stomach drew his arched brow.

"Sorry, sir," Smith said, his face reddening again as he moved closer to the door. "Is there something else you need of me, sir?"

Jonathan chewed on another piece of bread. "When was your last meal, boy?"

He shifted nervously. "Uh, I had some hardtack and salted beef. A little ale . . . earlier."

"How much earlier?"

The boy's eyes circled the room, not meeting Jonathan's as he wrung his hands. "Uh, sometime . . . yesterday. I think."

The captain sat back in his chair, grunting in irritation. "Yesterday? Of all the . . . " He tore apart the rest of his bread, laying a few sausages inside before pressing it closed. "Here," he said, tossing the makeshift meal to the boy. "Eat that."

Smith crammed the sandwich into his mouth hungrily.

"And in the future, do not be missing meals," Jonathan added around a mouthful of potato. "You're skinny enough already, and you'll need to pull your weight on my ship. I will not have you interrupting my concentration with your growling belly or swooning like some blasted female!"

At that the boy choked, his eyes growing wide as he covered his mouth to keep his food from spraying around the room.

"Good God!" Tremayne growled, rolling his eye as he crossed to the boy and smacked him on the back soundly. Smith continued to cough and Jonathan reached for his tankard, holding it to his lips.

"Have some of this," he ordered. Smith grabbed at the mug, tilting it back and washing down the food with a large gulp.

Then he began a whole new round of coughing.

"What . . . what is that?" he asked on a wheeze, tears streaming down his scarlet face.

"Rum. What else?"

"I thought it was water."

The captain laughed. "What man in his right mind drinks water when there's rum to be had?"

"Captain?" Max appeared in the doorway. He looked confused at the picture before him but knew better than to ask any questions.

"What is it?" Jonathan replied, reaching over the desk and popping a sausage into his mouth.

"We're nearing Sav-la-mar," he replied. "Do you want to make port or remain offshore 'til dawn?"

"Any sign of the *Lady*?"

"None yet."

Jonathan rubbed his chin in thought. "They've been at sea for months, so they'll put in to Lucea tonight to take on supplies before making the run to Santa Marta. We'll stay here, hidden by the shore and set out to intercept them before first light."

Max nodded. "Aye, Cap'n." He turned to head back up on deck.

"Max, a word," Jonathan called after him, casting a glance behind him at Smith before following his first mate into the passageway. He closed the door quietly and lowered his voice.

"Keep an eye on Rafferty," he ordered. The master gunner had only been on board the *Black Arrow* for about a month, and although Jonathan didn't fully trust him, he needed the young man's expertise with weapons. "He's shown a particular interest in talk of the *Lady,* and I've heard rumors from his former crew that he's been known to line his own pockets before the loot has been counted."

"You think he'd dare after your warning?"

The captain shook his head ruefully. "There's no telling. Men can be foolish and greedy, men the most foolish of all."

Baines nodded. "I'll assign Jenkins to watch him," he said. "I trust him, and he won't let Rafferty out of his sight once we board tomorrow."

"Are the cannons readied?"

"Aye. We're short on musket balls, but we've plenty of chain shot."

Jonathan nodded in approval. "Good. Good. Don't let the men overindulge tonight. We'll need to be up before the sun."

"Aye, Cap'n." At that, Max walked down the dim passageway toward the deck stairs and Jonathan turned to re-enter his quarters. He grimaced in anger when he saw young Smith running his finger along the hilt of the cutlass he kept on the shelf behind his desk.

"What are you doing, boy?" he roared. Smith jumped, whirling about and tucking his hands behind his back.

"Sorry, Captain," he stammered, his eyes wide. "I didn't mean anything."

Jonathan crossed the room, catching the boy up by the collar of his shirt until his toes barely grazed the floor. "Remember, boy," he spat. "You are on this ship—*my* ship—at my pleasure. Anger me, and you'll be feeding the fish after a good flogging." He shook Smith like a rag to emphasize his point. "Do not touch anything in this room without my expressed permission to do so. Is that clear?"

The boy let out a strangled sound and Jonathan loosened his hold slightly. "I said, is that clear?"

Smith sucked in a breath. "Aye . . . Aye, Captain."

He released the boy with a shove toward the door. "Off with you, now. Be back at four bells. We set sail before the morning watch."

Smith ducked his head and ran from the room without another word. Jonathan shook his head in frustration at the boy's audacity as he turned to consider the cutlass that had held him so enthralled. With a small smile, he pulled it from the shelf, sliding the shining blade from its leather sheath. To most, it would seem like an ordinary sword, he supposed and—except for the single large sapphire set in the hilt—of very little value. Jonathan knew its true worth, however, and it was far beyond the value of the glittering blue stone. He studied the engraving encircling the gem, whispering the now-familiar words aloud.

*Dixitque Deus fiat lux et facta est lux.*

Latin for *And God said, "Let there be light, and there was light."*

The significance of the piece of Scripture, Jonathan was still unsure of. Yet he knew it was another key in the mystery he was endeavoring to solve. One that he would come a step closer to unraveling once he set foot on board the *Enchanted Lady.*

In the depths of the *Black Arrow*, the boy called Smith scrambled down the dimly lit passageway, ducking behind casks and into corners whenever anyone else came near. Eventually, he found the door he was looking for, and after a quick glance in both directions to ensure he was not being observed, he slipped silently through it.

The storage room was packed full, but there was just enough room behind a large pile of crates where he had created a small pallet to rest his head. Smith grunted as he shoved a wooden chest in front of the door, praying that it would be enough to deter anyone who might decide to enter. No one had tried as of yet, but he couldn't be too careful.

Once the door was barricaded, he padded quietly over to his pallet and lowered himself to the ground with a quiet sigh. He rested for a moment, his back braced against the cool wall. He was a bit lightheaded from the large gulp of rum that still burned his throat, and his hands trembled slightly in memory of his terrifying encounter with the captain. He knew, possibly better than anyone, that Jonathan Tremayne was a cutthroat and a barbarian, and Smith would need to be more careful in the future if he was going to stay alive long enough to complete his mission.

Bone-tired, Smith pulled off his cap and released his clubbed hair from its leather thong, running his fingers through the greasy brown strands before scratching at his dirty scalp. He slid the vest from his shoulders, and lifting his oversized shirt, picked at the knot that held the rags bound around his chest. When the cloths finally loosened, Smith unwrapped the rags with a relieved exhale and rubbed at the aching flesh underneath.

The flesh that—were it discovered—would reveal his true identity . . . or rather, *her* identity. For Smith was not a boy at all, but rather a young woman of nineteen years who had stolen on board the *Black Arrow* with only one goal in mind.

To kill the captain.

And now that she'd seen the cutlass, she was more determined than ever to accomplish that goal. Touching it for the first time in almost two years, her throat had closed up in anguished memory.

*He had loved that sword.*

In the distance a bell rang. Only two hours until she would have to become Smith again and appear at Tremayne's door. She curled her lip in distaste. Becoming his cabin boy gave her a chance she'd been hoping for, but spending any time in close quarters with the man turned her stomach.

Still, she would be near him now, day and night. Near enough to take his miserable life when the opportunity presented itself. She'd been tempted while shaving him, but wasn't certain she could complete the task before he could bury that damned dagger in her belly.

No, she would be patient. And when Tremayne had his guard down, perhaps even when he was sleeping—or deep in his vile rum—she would take that cutlass into her hand and slit his traitorous throat.

Crass, perhaps. But she had long abandoned the idea of acting as a proper lady. Since the day her father was killed, the sapphire-embellished sword stolen from his still-warm body, and she'd set out to track down his murderer, only to learn that One-Eyed Jack Tremayne was to blame.

She smiled. Perhaps she'd call him that to his face as he bled to death. Few did and survived, but she would.

Aye.

One day soon, Sarina Talbot would have her revenge.

*Today, as I perused earlier in this record, I realized something I have only as of late began to suspect. My life, such as it is, has become a tedious routine consisting of mundane tasks that no longer hold my interest, if they ever did at all. I trudge to my place of employment every morning, and back home every afternoon, stopping perchance for a pint or a bit to eat. My friends have established themselves and seem content enough, but I remain removed from their happiness, able to observe but not to participate.*

*I find myself waiting, although I have yet to determine for what.*

*- The Journal of
Simon Alistair Mellick
4 March, 1664*

By the time four bells sounded, Sarina was dressed—her breasts re-bound—and was standing at Captain Tremayne's door. She had managed to doze a little, but still couldn't get used to sleeping with the constant noise and activity on board the ship. It was at a frenzied level at that moment; men scurrying here and there readying to get underway. With a deep breath, she rapped on the wooden door while rubbing a knuckle over her gritty eyes.

"Enter!" Tremayne barked. She squared her shoulders before shoving the door open and stepping into the room, nearly giving into a wave of fury as she realized the captain was strapping on her father's cutlass. He had his back to her, so she forced another deep breath, willing her muscles to relax so to not give away her boiling hatred for the man before her.

The captain shot her a glance over his shoulder. "Did you eat?" he asked gruffly.

"No, sir."

Tremayne huffed in annoyance and tossed her a piece of hardtack. "There's ale in the jug," he growled. "Make haste. There is much to do before we set sail."

Sarina hurried over to the table, pouring a mug of ale and breaking the hardtack into it quickly. It softened, absorbing the liquid, and she shoveled it into her mouth with a spoon, trying to ignore the bland taste.

"Are you armed, boy?" Tremayne asked as she wiped her mouth with the back of her hand.

"I've a dirk in my boot," she replied quietly.

"Have you ever used it?"

She shook her head in response, earning another irritated glare. Tremayne crossed to his desk drawer and pulled out a small pistol, handing it to her handle first. "Tuck that into your belt," he ordered as he turned his back to examine his own flintlocks. "You'll not be taking part in the raid, but it's best to be prepared for whatever may happen. I doubt you have the strength to do much damage with a dirk, but any idiot can use a pistol if needed."

Sarina bristled at the insult and her hand trembled. It would be so simple to lift the pistol . . . to point it at the back of his head . . .

Her hand rose of its own accord, and Sarina focused on the spot where a silken scarf revealed the brown hair trailing over his shoulders and down his back. The beads tied into a few long braids clinked lightly as he worked on his guns and Sarina wondered absently why he let his hair grow so long.

It didn't matter. The time had come. In a moment, he would be dead.

"You'll be at my side through the raid," he said absently. "And I expect my orders to be followed explicitly and immediately."

"Aye, sir." The pistol weighed heavily on her outstretched arm as her finger hovered over the trigger. Could she cock it without him hearing? She reached up with her other hand, locking her thumbs over the hammer.

A loud pounding at the door had her dropping her hands to her sides just as Tremayne whirled about. He eyed her curiously, and she wondered if he could see her pounding heart . . . her cold and clammy skin. She lowered her gaze, tucking the pistol securely into her belt as Tremayne turned to the door.

"Enter!" he bellowed.

The first mate, Baines, poked his head into the room. "The men are ready, Cap'n. Shall we weigh anchor?"

The captain grabbed his hat, plopping it onto his head as he neared the door. "Aye," he answered. "Keep the lanterns out. We don't want them to know we're coming. Smith, my spyglass!"

"Aye, sir," Sarina replied, plucking it off his desk and nearly running to keep up with his long strides as he emerged on deck. She dodged between bustling crewmen, noticing that the new moon aided them on their errand by keeping the *Arrow* hidden in the darkness. Her eyes quickly grew accustomed to the lack of light, and she was able to navigate the deck relatively easily, still on Tremayne's heels.

"I'll stay at the wheel with Crawley," he told Baines as he observed the activity of the crew. His head dipped low as he spoke quietly to his first mate. "We don't want the sound to carry. I'll relay my orders through Smith.

"We'll wait in open water. But we'll not move on the *Lady* until it's too late for her to turn tail and run."

Baines turned to the east. "If the sun rises, we'll lose the element of surprise."

"Then we'll make chase," Jonathan replied. "The *Lady* hasn't a chance of outrunning the *Arrow*. I doubt it will come to that, though." He reached out to test some rigging, nodding in approval. "Renard won't want to risk daylight, carrying all that booty on open water. The captain of the *Lady* may be more merchant than seaman, but he's no idiot."

"No," Tremayne mused. "He'll come to us, and he won't realize his mistake until it's too late."

"Is he carrying passengers?" Baines asked.

Tremayne nodded. "I expect so. Remind the men that innocents are not to be harmed."

"Aye, sir."

After that, a stillness overcame the crew as all eyes trained to the west, looking for any sign of the ship rounding the coastline. The soft lapping of the waves, gentle clacking of the rigging, and an occasional low murmur lulled Sarina into relaxation. Her lack of sleep and the current break in activity had her head nodding more than once, and she braced her feet apart, blinking widely to fight the urge to nap. The minutes seemed to tick along with every heartbeat, each man tensed in preparation for the fight ahead. Sarina watched them carefully, trying to maintain the same alertness. Slowly, the stars began to dim as the sky lightened, and the first mate cast a worried eye to the captain.

"Where is she?" he muttered lowly.

"Patience," Tremayne replied.

"You said before dawn."

"Patience," the captain repeated. "Obviously, Renard is more confident, or more stupid, than I anticipated."

"Are you certain he's destined for Santa Marta?" Baines asked nervously.

"He's coming," Tremayne replied, tolerant of his first mate when the same question from anyone else would gain a far less pleasant response. "See? There!" He pointed to the horizon, extending his other hand for his spyglass. Sarina handed it over quickly, and he put it to his eye.

"Aye, there she is," he murmured as the white sails of the *Enchanted Lady* glowed slightly above the dark sea. He turned to his friend with a grin, his blue-green eye twinkling in the early dawn light. "All right, Max. What say we have a bit o' fun?"

The first mate grinned in response and hurried off to relay the order for the *Black Arrow* to get underway. In an instant, the deck was abuzz with activity as the crew weighed anchor and the master rigger, Hutchins—a mountain of a man with a shiny bald head and gold rings piercing both ears—led the hoisting of the sails. As the sun rose, any need for stealth vanished, and instead they'd rely on their appearance as a friendly vessel.

"Raise the French colors," Tremayne ordered. In a moment, the French flag waved overhead, barely visible in the dim moonlight. Captain Mattias Renard would think the *Arrow* carried his own countrymen, at least at first. It was a common tactic among pirates. Not until they were ready to attack would the flag be replaced by Tremayne's standard—a white skull on a black field, the captain's trademark red scarf wrapped around the grisly head.

The captain raised his spyglass again. "That's right. Go about yer business now," he said, his accent thickening somehow as he spoke under his breath. "Nothing to worry about here, ye scurvy dogs." Tremayne smiled as they cut through the sea and the pink light of dawn gave way to daylight.

"Steady, boys," he called out. "Ready the cannons, but hold your fire until we're right on top of them!"

Sarina tensed as the two ships drew nearer to each other. How long would he wait? She glanced at the captain, her skin prickling with nervous energy, but he seemed calm, a small, satisfied smirk on his lips.

"Tell Rafferty to ready the cannons," he told her. She jumped in surprise, not expecting the order that would usually go through Max. The first mate was on the far end of the ship, however, standing readied near the bow. Sarina ran down to the gun deck, seeking out the master gunner.

"The captain said to ready the cannons," she told him breathlessly, trying to ignore the appraising way his gaze dragged over her form. It had been a shock the first time one of the men had looked at her in such a way—not that she'd never been ogled before, but it hadn't crossed her mind that it might happen while she was dressed as a boy. Since coming on board, she'd become used to the lustful glances of some of the crewmen, and Rafferty's were the worst of all. Sarina was usually very careful to avoid the man, certain that he was not used to holding back when it came to his baser desires.

Sarina shuddered at the thought.

"They're always ready," Rafferty replied suggestively, his leering grin made even more distasteful by his rotting teeth. Sarina forced back a grimace, instead looking behind him at the row of cannons. Despite his disgusting nature, Rafferty's boast was true. Each cannon was loaded and manned, only needing to be rolled forward into firing position moments before the assault.

"I'll tell him," she said with a nod, only to be stopped when she turned to go by his sweaty hand on her arm. He tugged her close, his foul breath wafting over her cheek.

"You're a skinny little thing," he murmured in her ear, "but not altogether unpleasing to the eye. And ye'r almost as soft as a wench." His hand trailed down her back and squeezed her backside aggressively. "After the battle, what say you and me have a little private celebration?"

Sarina fought back a rush of bile in her throat and reached slowly for the flintlock in her belt. Rafferty's eyes widened at the sound of the hammer cocking, and he looked down to see the muzzle pressed up against his belly. He released her, stepping back with his hands raised placatingly.

"It was just a kindly offer," he protested, his cocky smile belied by the sweat on his upper lip.

"Consider this my polite refusal," she retorted, backing away as she uncocked the pistol and tucked it back into her belt. "I'll let the captain know you're ready." She hurried up the stairs, pausing just before emerging on deck. She leaned heavily against the wall, her heart hammering in her chest as she tried to catch her breath.

Her encounter with Rafferty had shaken her badly. She knew that if he chose to force his attentions on her, she would not be able to fight him off. Fortunately, the captain was well known for opposing rape in all its forms. It felt strange that she would feel comforted by that—that reliance for her own well-being relied on the very man she aimed to kill.

It was a strange world, indeed.

She shook off her musings and drew a deep breath to steady herself as she hurried back to the captain. "Cannons are readied, sir," she said in a firm voice.

A nod was her only response before Tremayne turned to the quartermaster. "Starboard ten degrees, bring us up on her port side."

"Aye, Cap'n," Crawley responded, turning the wheel slightly.

"Easy," Tremayne murmured. "Easy . . . steady, now. Not too close, we don't want to raise an alarm."

They finally drew near enough to see the crew on board clearly. Sarina picked out the captain easily, and he raised a hand in greeting, still apparently unaware that he was moments from his doom.

Tremayne chuckled, then raised a hand in response as he bellowed. "Raise the colors!"

Sarina watched in awe as everything seemed to happen at once—the French flag was replaced by Tremayne's, its eerie grin flapping in the wind. A loud crack sounded as the cannons locked into position pointing through the gun ports as the captain yelled, "Take aim!"

It happened within seconds, as Captain Renard looked on in confusion, his hand still frozen in the air.

"Fire!" Tremayne bellowed, the order echoed by Baines—then Rafferty—before a cannon blast exploded in the stillness. The warning shot arced over the bow of the *Lady*, the crew scrambling in a panicked frenzy.

The warning went unheeded, though, and Captain Tremayne hadn't really expected Renard to give up without a fight. As his men rushed to load their own cannons, Tremayne bellowed out another order, and the rest of the cannons let loose, this time exploding onto the deck of the ship. Sarina's hands flew to her ears out of reflex, and through the smoke she could just make out the figure of Captain Renard, waving his arms and ordering his men to return fire.

"Bring us alongside her, Crawley!" Tremayne shouted as the *Lady* floundered in the water.

Renard shouted to his crew, then noticed his pilot had been targeted in the latest volley and the wheel was unmanned. He shoved through his frantic men, desperate to get his ship under control.

It was too late.

"Grappling hooks!" The captain's order echoed in the air as the men swung the huge hooks up and away to the deck of the *Lady*. As they caught hold, the men pulled the ropes in unison, muscles straining and voices united in loud grunts and shouts of nearing victory. With the two ships tethered together, the crew of the *Arrow* bounded onto the other ship, swords flashing in the sunlight and pistol fire peppering the air.

The clash of metal and shouts of battle filtered through the smoke as Sarina watched the fight from her position at Tremayne's side. He stood, one foot braced on the gunwale of the *Arrow,* the other on the *Lady,* a flintlock in each hand as he bellowed orders at the men below. He took aim as one of Renard's crewmen raced for the cannons, shooting the man in the leg. He fell to the deck with a cry of pain and Tremayne shot again, this time hitting the rigging on the mizzenmast and releasing the heavy sail onto the heads of three men fighting against his crew.

Tremayne holstered his pistols and drew his cutlass—*her father's cutlass,* Sarina corrected herself—and jumped into the midst of the fray with only a quick, "Stay here, Smith!" grunted over his shoulder. He slashed through the twisting bodies, meeting Baines and turning to fight back to back with his first mate. Sarina couldn't resist getting a little closer, hiding behind a large barrel.

"You call this a bit of fun?" Baines asked wryly, throwing up his own sword to block a heavy blow.

"Oh, come on, Max," Tremayne replied with a slight laugh, spinning to the left to swing at a barrel-chested man brandishing a dagger in each meaty fist. "You can't say you're not enjoying this!"

They fought in a coordinated dance that could only be achieved after dozens of such battles and years of developing trust. Lunging and turning, each defended the other's weak spots, their swords slashing through the air.

Then, as quickly as it started, the fight was over and Renard and his remaining men knelt in defeat on the deck of the *Lady,* their hands bound behind them and heads bowed low. Tremayne's men rounded up a handful of passengers who'd retreated to their quarters when the fighting began, and they stood in a small circle, fear evident on all their faces. The crew of the *Arrow* was scattered about the deck, holding weapons on the prisoners and unable to hide their satisfied grins.

"Baines," the captain said in a firm voice as he paced before the crew. "Divide the men to search the ship. I want the treasure on board before our presence here attracts any interest.

"Smith!" he shouted, and Sarina scrambled out from behind the barrel. "Collect any trinkets the passengers might be hiding away." He turned to glare at the group. "Ye'll not be wanting to keep anything back, if ye value yer lives," he warned, and immediately, they began twisting off rings and pulling out pocket watches. Sarina took a small bag Baines held out to her and made her way to the little group. Holding it out, she fought a sick feeling in her stomach as each valuable was dropped into the bag.

"Please," an older woman begged, as she fingered her gold necklace with tears in her eyes. "It was my mother's." Sarina's heart sank. She never knew her own mother, who'd died when she was born, and the woman's plea put a lump in her throat. She glanced about, looking for the captain, only to find him studying her intently.

Sarina swallowed thickly. He was watching her, seeing if she could handle the responsibility he'd given her. If she failed this test, she'd lose the opportunity to do what she came here to do.

"I'm sorry," she said quietly, not meeting the woman's eyes. Sarina jerked the bag toward her insistently and tried to ignore the woman's quiet sobs as she unclasped the necklace and turned it over. Without another word, Sarina returned to the *Arrow*, putting the bag onto the pile of spoils the quartermaster was already tallying. She went to work with the rest of the crew, quickly transferring the cargo of the *Lady* onto the *Arrow,* all the while keeping an eye out for Crown ships or other buccaneers who might be tempted to steal the treasure for themselves.

Breathing heavily and wiping the sweat from her brow with the back of a hand, Sarina leaned against a large crate for a moment of rest. The men continued to work around her, and she tried not to attract attention as she scanned the crew in search of the captain. He'd disappeared belowdecks of the *Lady* and had yet to emerge.

"Smith!" Crawley barked, making her jump. She turned to him, but he didn't look up from the ledger where he was marking down the day's take. "Get back to work," he ordered. "No rest until we're underway."

Sarina bit back a retort. She was tired of taking orders. Tired of being surrounded by smelly, disgusting men. Tired of being a criminal. She was filled with guilt and anger . . . frustration that this plan of hers seemed to be falling apart around her. Men were trying to touch her. She was stealing necklaces from nice ladies and making them cry. She was carrying a pistol, for heaven's sake!

Then she saw him. Captain Tremayne stepped out onto the deck, smiling at his men, her father's sword swinging at his hip.

*Yes.* There was her purpose.

And Sarina knew she would endure any torment to make him pay for what he'd done. With a deep breath, she crossed to the *Lady* and hefted another box over to Tremayne's ship, hate and fury burning in her gut as she watched the captain celebrate with his men.

A shout drew his attention, and Sarina saw Baines rush over to Tremayne, a small box in his hands. The first mate held it out and the captain's smile grew as he took it and clutched it against his chest. With another quiet word to Baines, the captain hastily climbed over to the *Arrow* and hurried to his cabin without sparing even a glance at anyone else.

"Make haste!" the first mate shouted. "The rest of this to our hold quickly. We make way in fifteen minutes!"

"What of the crew?" Hutchins bellowed back, casting a smirking grin to the men on their knees.

"Leave them bound," Baines replied. "By the time they cut themselves loose, we'll be well on our way."

As the men doubled their efforts, hurrying from one ship to the other, Sarina's eyes strayed to the doorway where the captain had disappeared. He was alone, and everyone was so busy, they'd most likely not notice her absence. She glanced at Crawley, who was hefting a large chest with another man toward the opposite end of the ship.

Could this be her chance? Her fingers drifted to the flintlock at her waist, rubbing the handle slowly. Stepping quickly and staying out of the way as much as possible, she made her way to the captain's quarters. Checking over her shoulder once more to assure she hadn't been noticed, she moved down into the dark passageway, willing her eyes to adjust quickly. She ducked into a doorway, listening closely for voices or footsteps. Hearing none, Sarina picked her way quietly to the captain's door, pressing her ear to it before silently turning the knob.

Through the crack in the door, she could make out the back of Jonathan Tremayne. He was not sitting at his desk, but bent over the front of it, examining something closely . . . so closely, in fact, that he didn't look up when Sarina entered the room, closing the door behind her.

"That you, Smith?" he muttered, still focused on his desk.

Sarina jumped, not realizing he'd noticed her entrance. "Aye, sir," she said out of habit. "How did you know it was me?"

He laughed humorlessly. "Nothing happens on this ship without my knowledge," he replied. "Now, what is it?"

All this time, he had yet to look up at her and Sarina realized that if there were a time for her to accomplish her mission, this was it. Silently, she slipped the flintlock pistol from her belt, holding it up with both hands. She cocked the gun, and at the sound, Tremayne's shoulders stiffened, and he slowly straightened and turned around, his eyes dark and furious.

"What is this?" he hissed.

Sarina fought the tremor in her voice. "I would think that would be obvious."

Tremayne's jaw tightened and Sarina could practically see the waves of anger radiating off his skin. "Are you planning to use that?" he asked, his eyes dipping briefly to the pistol gripped in her white-knuckled hands.

She said nothing.

"Have you ever shot a man while he looked you in the eye, Smith?" he continued in a low voice, taking a slow step toward her. "Locked gazes while you took his life?"

Her hand trembled slightly, but she lifted the gun in determination. "I can kill you."

Tremayne froze.

"And why would you do such a thing?"

Another step. Another jerk of the gun. Another standoff.

"You killed my father."

The only reaction was a slight narrowing of his good eye. "Aye. I'd imagine I've killed a few fathers. You'll need to be more specific."

To Sarina's dismay, a rush of tears pricked at her eyes and she swallowed back the emotion, squaring her shoulders.

"You killed Daniel Talbot."

For the first time, there was a break in Tremayne's cold demeanor, and Sarina thought she saw a glimmer of surprise light his eyes.

*Oh yes*, she thought. *I know the truth, you bastard.*

"Talbot?" he repeated. "Not . . . *Captain* Danny Talbot."

Sarina stiffened. "He resigned his commission before I was born."

Tremayne snorted. "Commission?"

"I've been searching for you for almost two years," she said, ignoring his comment. "Ever since that day you left him bleeding and dying on the floor in his study."

The captain took another small step toward her, and she realized the muzzle of the pistol was now inches from his chest. Her hand tightened on the grip, her finger poised over the trigger.

"I didn't kill your father, boy," he said quietly.

"Liar," she spat.

"It wasn't me."

The determination on his face shook her slightly.

*No. She couldn't be wrong . . . could she?*

But it didn't matter. The brief doubt—the moment of hesitation—was all Captain Tremayne needed. In one fluid motion his hand flew up, knocking the pistol away from her chest as he spun her about and locked his arm around her neck. The pistol clattered across the floor as she struggled against him, but she was no match for his superior strength. He forced her against the desk, the sharp corner of the wooden top bruising her stomach.

"Now," he gritted in her ear, "tell me who you really are, and why I shouldn't kill you right now."

Sarina fought for breath, tears pricking her eyes. She clawed at his forearm, but he ignored her struggles.

"Answer me!" he demanded.

"I ... I can't ..." she rasped. With an exasperated huff, he loosened his hold slightly and Sarina drew in a gasping breath.

"Who are you?" he repeated.

"I told you—"

"You lie!" he interrupted with a shout. "I happen to know that Danny Talbot had no sons. His wife died giving birth to his only daugh ..." Tremayne's voice trailed off, and Sarina felt him stiffen slightly.

"No ..." he murmured, suddenly spinning her about and shoving her back against the desk. His fingers dug into her upper arms and Sarina raised her chin, fighting back the tears. He wrapped one hand around her chin, his eye glittering as it examined her face more closely.

Sarina reached out beside her, her fingers searching the desktop for something ... anything to use as a weapon. Her hand closed around an object, but she dared not look to see what it was.

"It can't be," he said, his eyes dropping from her face to her body as his shock loosened his hold on her ever so slightly.

Seizing the moment, Sarina lifted the heavy paperweight and with all her strength slammed it into Tremayne's temple. His eye widened in surprise as his grip on her tightened painfully. She lifted her hand to strike again, but the captain crumpled to the floor. Sarina stood over him, her heart racing wildly as she tried desperately to breathe.

*Had she done it? Was he dead?*

A moment of euphoria was followed almost immediately by a wave of nausea. She looked down at his slumped form, the paperweight still clutched in her hand. Her dazed gaze drifted to the small statue she held—a bronze casting of a roaring lion standing on its hind legs. A dark smear marred the metal, and as it dripped onto her hand, Sarina realized what it was.

Blood. *His* blood.

With a whimper, Sarina dropped the paperweight, and it hit the wooden floor with a thunk, coming to rest against his shoulder. More blood trickled from his head, winding its way through his tangled hair to seep into the floorboards.

Sarina's hand flew to her mouth as she dropped to her knees.

*What had she done?*

True, Jonathan Tremayne was a murderer. But now . . . now, she was as well.

Suddenly, the door to the cabin burst open and Max Baines rushed in.

"Captain, a Crown ship approaches!" His words ended on a shocked gasp as he took in the scene before him. Sarina jumped to her feet, fear and panic pushing aside the guilt that paralyzed her. She dashed for the door, only to be caught up into the first mate's strong arms. He held her in an iron grip, her toes barely touching the floor.

"Release me!" She kicked at him, but he held her easily. A moan from the floor had both of them stilling their motions.

"He lives," Sarina murmured in relief, quickly followed by a chill of fear.

She would die. Unless she could escape, she would die.

Tremayne groaned again, drawing Baines' attention, and Sarina fought against her instincts and went limp, feigning a swoon. The first mate adjusted his grip, muttering in complaint, and Sarina took the opportunity to sink her teeth into his arm . . . hard.

Baines jerked in surprise, and Sarina whirled about, kicking her knee between his legs with all her strength. With a loud groan, his body closed in on itself, falling to the floor next to the captain.

Sarina knew it was only a matter of time before someone else came looking, so she dashed for the door, pausing only long enough to pluck her father's cutlass off Tremayne's desk. She ran for the stairs, keeping to the shadows, and emerged onto the deck, walking quickly and avoiding eye contact with anyone. The crew ignored her as they hurried about, securing the load and preparing to get underway. She ducked behind a pile of canvas and took a deep breath, trying to think of her next move.

Her eyes darted about the deck, looking for a place to hide.

But she knew there was no place to hide. Once the captain regained consciousness, his crew would tear the ship apart looking for her.

*. . . a Crown ship approaches!*

Baines' words wormed their way into her mind. A Crown ship? She turned to survey the horizon, biting her lip at the sight of the ship bearing down on them, and the long expanse of swirling sea before it.

Could she make it? Sarina was a strong swimmer, but the thought filled her with apprehension. She glanced back at the doorway leading to the captain's quarters.

It was her only hope.

With grim determination, she gripped the cutlass tightly, then drew the belt over her head and one arm and secured the buckle about her body. She climbed up onto the gunwale, relieved to find one of the boarding ropes dangling nearby.

She wouldn't have to jump.

Sarina grabbed onto the rope, wincing at the scrape against her tender skin. Holding herself away from the hull with her legs, she slowly slid down the rope, hand over hand, all the while listening for the alert she knew was coming.

Afraid she was running out of time, Sarina took a deep breath and released the rope, plunging into the angry sea. She pulled against the water, and broke the surface with a sputter and gasp as the waves carried her away, helping her toward the English ship and away from the *Black Arrow*. After a while, she glanced back to find the *Arrow* at full sail, cutting through the water away from her . . . fleeing the Crown ship.

Sarina smiled and began to swim.

Captain Tremayne held the spyglass to his eye, his jaw clenched in anger and determination. Through it he saw young Smith—no . . . young *Talbot*, he corrected—on board the *HMS Intrepid*. His cutlass glinted in the sunlight, and she waved her arms as she spoke to the crewmen on board. After a moment, the commander of the vessel appeared.

Stanton. Commodore Lucius Stanton. Jonathan knew him well.

The *Black Arrow* had easily evaded the *Intrepid,* circling around the island before cutting into a hidden bay. It was a trick that Tremayne had used in the past, and one that had yet to fail him. Changing sails, they'd raised the English colors, but still stayed far enough away from the *Intrepid* as they followed it to avoid identification.

"Captain?" Max approached him, holding out a rag. "You're still bleeding."

"It will pass," he growled, but took the rag anyway, pressing it to his temple. The wench had gotten the better of him, but her actions would not go unpunished.

The first mate followed his gaze to the *Intrepid*. "Are we going after her, then?" Tremayne had revealed Smith's true identity to him.

"Aye."

"Stanton won't like it."

"No, I don't expect he will."

"Perhaps it would be better to leave it alone."

"No," Jonathan snapped, glaring at his friend. "Miss Talbot will answer for her deeds. And I will have my cutlass returned."

"It was her father's," he reminded the captain.

"*Was*," he replied shortly, looking through the spyglass again. "Now, it is mine."

Max decided against the obvious comment that it was actually Commodore Stanton's at the moment. Instead, he asked, "What will you do with her when we get her?"

Jonathan smiled slightly at the thought.

"You wouldn't . . ." Max cleared his throat. "You wouldn't force the girl, would you?" Although she'd all but emasculated him, the first mate still would not wish such a fate on anyone.

"You know better than to ask that," the captain replied distastefully. Still, there were ways for him to get his revenge, short of raping the girl. No, he was not one to harm a female—even one as infuriating as the Talbot chit—but she would pay.

"What will you do?" Max asked.

Jonathan smiled again, watching two of Stanton's men take the girl by the arms to drag her away. He could almost hear her protests and he chuckled slightly. Evidently, the *Intrepid* was not the refuge she'd hoped for.

"Jonathan?" Max asked again. "What will you do?"

The Talbot girl kicked one of the guards in the shin, and this time Jonathan laughed out loud.

"Just have a bit o' fun, Max," he told his first mate. "Just have a good bit o' fun."

*I overheard something today I believe too outlandish to be truth. Still, however, I feel I must investigate. I hesitate to record the conversation here, lest it be discovered without my knowledge and all my plans will be for naught.*

*Perhaps when I learn more. This situation demands I take utmost care.*

*- The Journal of*
*Simon Alistair Mellick*
*28 May, 1664*

"No, you don't understand!" Sarina struggled against the strong hands holding her. "Please, allow me to explain!"

The two guards ignored her pleas, pausing only to strip her father's cutlass from her body before forcing her through a low doorway. She cast one last frantic look over her shoulder, but Commodore Stanton had turned away to address a member of his crew.

Sarina fought a surge of panic and tears. Her wet clothes dripped on the wooden floors as she stumbled down the narrow passageway, and she shivered, her muscles still aching after her long swim. Only desperation had kept her arms reaching, her legs kicking, as she fought against the crashing waves, the Crown ship disappearing then reappearing as she topped every white-tipped crest. She'd thought the *Intrepid* would be her salvation. Instead, she'd been treated like a common criminal.

The commodore had looked down his nose at her distastefully as she heaved and panted, trying to catch her breath.

"Please . . . please . . ." she'd managed to gasp out, before unceremoniously falling to her knees and vomiting on the deck. Wiping the cuff of her shirt across her mouth, Sarina had stood on shaky legs only to face Stanton's icy blue eyes, no longer curious, but hard and cold. It only took a moment for Sarina to determine the reason why. Behind him stood the passengers of the *Enchanted Lady*, including the woman who'd pled to keep her mother's necklace. She pointed a shaking finger at Sarina in accusation, her head held high.

"He's a thief," she said in a firm voice, "one of the pirates who besieged us, the murderous monsters!"

Stanton had spared not a moment ordering that Sarina be thrown in chains.

"The Crown does not tolerate piracy," he'd snarled at her.

"No . . I'm not . . ." Sarina's heart raced, but the words in her defense would not form on her lips. She still could not catch her breath.

"Fear not. You will be treated fairly and will stand trial," Stanton had assured her blandly. "But if found guilty, be assured you will hang."

Sarina's blood froze. "No!"

"Take him," he'd ordered, not sparing her a second thought once he'd turned away.

How had it come to this? She'd been overconfident, Sarina had to admit, racing forward when she should have trod carefully. But when she'd learned the identity of her father's killer, a single focus had taken over her mind—to find and kill Jonathan

Tremayne. And when she had the opportunity to take a position on his ship—to get close enough to accomplish her vengeful goal—she hadn't thought twice.

She should have.

One of the guards released her, stepping forward to unlock a wooden door. It swung open with a creak, and Sarina squinted into its dark interior. A stack of casks and crates stood along the walls of a storeroom of some sort. The guard stepped in and around the corner, only to re-emerge with a pair of shackles dangling from his hands.

"No, please. I must speak to the commodore," Sarina pleaded, desperate to avoid those chains. "I'm not what he thinks I am. Please!"

The guards said nothing as they shackled her hands and shoved her into the room. After locking the shackles to a chain bolted to the floor, the men left, locking the door behind them.

"Please!" she shouted at the door as the darkness enveloped her. "I'm not a criminal! I need to speak to the commodore!" Sarina shuffled toward the door, fear setting in as the weight of the chain pulled at her arms. A small barred window near the top of the door revealed the profile of one of her captors.

"Listen!" she exclaimed, an idea forming. "I can help the commodore. Tell him . . . tell him I have information about One-Eyed Jack Tremayne!" She held her breath, waiting for a response. Surely, Commodore Stanton could not resist such temptation. Tremayne was an enemy to the Crown, a murderer and thief. Capturing such a man would ensure the commodore's advancement, perhaps gaining him a title and lands in acknowledgement of his service.

The guard said nothing, but after a moment she heard him speaking with the other man in a low voice. Sarina sighed, her eyes scanning the small room for a means of escape or a weapon of some sort. Shuffling slowly along the chilled walls, she circled the tiny room as far as her chains would allow, but there was no other opening save a small porthole high upon the wall. She was considering the possibility of opening one of the crates with no tools when a quiet voice called out to her.

"Hello? Is someone there?"

She jumped, despite the low tenor of the man's voice.

"Hello?" he said again, slightly louder.

Sarina turned in the direction of the voice, but could only make out dim shapes and shadows of the cargo before her. She stumbled awkwardly across the small room.

"Where are you?" she asked, her voice a near-whisper to avoid the guards overhearing.

"Here," the voice replied. "In the corner."

Sarina held out her chained hands, fumbling her way through a small opening in the stack of crates. Squinting in the dim light, she could just make out a large black shape in the corner, a man huddled inside a small cell.

"Oh!" she exclaimed. "Are you all right?" She started toward him, stopped short by the chain. "Who are you?" she asked hesitantly. The man was obviously a criminal of some sort, and she dared not venture too near to him.

The man chuckled, almost as if reading her mind. "I will not harm you," he assured her. "Tell me, why would the commodore take a wench into custody? Did you steal the silver whilst your patron slept?"

Sarina stiffened at the intimation that she was a lady of ill repute. "Patron? I'll have you know—" She stopped mid-sentence. "Wait. How did you know I am a lady?"

"I do not believe I called you a *lady*," he replied with a laugh.

"Do not insult me, sir."

"James."

"I beg your pardon."

"My name is James. James Ceron."

Sarina sniffed. "Well, Mister Ceron. I *am* a lady and not of the sort you imply. But since I am attired in the garb of a man, I am curious how you realized this fact."

"I cannot see you."

"What?"

"It is dark. I cannot see you, so I know nothing of your attire," he said, a tinge of annoyance in his tone. "But your voice is obviously that of a female, which leads me back to my original question. Why are you here?"

Sarina sat heavily on a nearby crate and reached up absently to rub at the necklace she always wore under her clothes. It had been a risk to keep it on, but the necklace was a gift from her father and it always brought her comfort.

"It is all a misunderstanding," she said finally.

"It usually is." He laughed. Sarina noticed a slight lilt to the man's voice, a musical accent she'd heard often in the islands.

"The commodore believes me to be a pirate," she said.

"But you are not."

"Of course not!"

"Why does he believe you to be?"

Sarina paused, unsure of how much to tell this stranger. "I was in disguise . . . on a secret mission aboard a pirate's vessel. I needed to act the part, lest I be discovered by the crew."

"A mission for whom?"

"For myself."

"What type of mission?"

"That . . . is private," she replied after a moment. "What of you? What lands you in the commodore's clutches?"

"A similar charge." He adjusted his position and gasped slightly in pain.

"You're injured," she observed, unable to mask her concern.

James laughed humorlessly. "The commodore's methods of persuasion are a bit primitive."

"He beat you?"

"Not him," he corrected. "His men. It matters not, though. Worse awaits me when we make port."

"You'll get a fair trial, certainly?"

James shifted again. "Well, Miss . . ."

"Talbot." Uncertain why, she hurried to add, "Sarina Talbot. But you may . . . my friends call me Rina."

"Are we friends?" She could hear the laughter in his voice.

"I would think our current situation obviates the need for social convention."

"Obviates? Perhaps you are a lady, after all." He choked on a laugh, then groaned in pain.

"Are you all right?"

She could see the shadow of him waving a hand in dismissal. "What were we discussing? Ah, yes, my *fair trial*." He gripped the bars to lower himself to the floor. He sat, his back against the wall, but the cell was not large enough for him to stretch his legs.

"I'd thought you'd know, Miss—*Rina*—fair trials are not for men like me."

"What do you mean?"

"You cannot see me."

Rina blinked, unsure of what that had to do with anything. "I see you. Well, a little at least."

"I am of these islands, Rina," he explained, his voice hard. "I am not English, nor my skin pale enough to warrant a fair trial. I will be fortunate if I am able to enjoy a last meal before I'm sent to the gallows."

Rina was silent, absorbing his words for a moment. Then, she asked, "Are you . . . are you guilty?"

"I stole food for a starving family. If that is indeed a crime, I am guilty."

Rina shivered and pulled her knees up onto the crate, wrapping her shackled arms around them. "That doesn't seem wrong. How can they accuse you?"

"I would think you, of all people, would know not every person accused of a crime is guilty of it."

She started, then felt a small smile lift her lips. "How are you so certain that *I'm* not guilty?"

She saw a flash of white and imagined the man was smiling widely.

"I am an excellent judge of character," he replied.

It was under the cover of darkness that Captain Jonathan Tremayne and his crew made their advancement upon the *HMS Intrepid*, stealing along silently, not a word spoken lest their approach be overheard.

Tremayne nodded at Baines, who in turn whispered a command to a mate at his left. Jonathan winced at the sound of the anchor chain grating against the hull and prayed that the crash of the surf would muffle it.

He glanced at his men, all stripped down to their breeches and shirts, weapons strapped securely around their waists or across their shoulders.

No flintlocks. Only blades.

Without another word, he led the group to the gunwale, grabbing a dangling rope and lowering himself over the side. The others followed closely, and in mere moments, the men were swimming through the black waters toward the looming hulk of the *Intrepid*. Beyond lay the shore, and a few flickering lights indicating that not all in the village slept, even at the late hour.

It wouldn't matter. If the captain's plan was successful, they would be on and off the Crown ship without anyone on land or sea knowing they'd been there.

With a low grunt, he pulled himself up on the *Intrepid's* anchor chain and rested a moment, scanning the hull of the ship for the rope he'd seen through his spyglass earlier in the day. If luck was with them, it would not have been retrieved.

Jonathan smiled. Luck was indeed with them.

Slipping into the water, he floated easily along the bobbing vessel, then kicked his feet to propel himself out of the water so he could grab the rope. It took a few attempts, but he finally gripped it firmly, pulling himself up the outside of the ship, his bare feet slipping slightly against the slimy hull. He paused when he reached the gunwale, and peered over the edge uncertainly. He could make out a couple of slumped figures on the other side of the ship.

*Sleeping.* Jonathan grimaced in disgust. Such a thing would never happen on his ship.

He pulled himself onto the deck and slipped into the shadows, quickly lowering additional rope to his awaiting crew. In a matter of moments they stood next to him, dripping and tense with expectation.

Jonathan nodded at Hutchins and pointed at the two sleeping crewmen. With a mate at his side, the master rigger approached them, and Tremayne knew in a moment they would be bound and gagged and no longer a threat.

"Find the girl," Jonathan whispered to Max, and the two parted, each taking a contingent to search the ship. Slipping his dagger from its sheath, Jonathan approached a doorway, pressing his back flat against the wall and listening intently before peeking around it. Edging into the dark passageway, he waved his crewmen through to the left, while he went to the right. They moved noiselessly in the darkness, and the captain smiled in satisfaction.

He made his way down the hallway, systematically pressing his ear to each door before opening it quietly and peering inside. Just as he was about to turn a corner, he froze at the sound of a low conversation.

Hidden in the shadows, Jonathan edged around the corner to find two of Stanton's men standing guard before a wooden door, their bodies casting flickering shadows in the low light of a lantern.

One of the men leaned forward, using a scrap of twisted linen to capture a bit of fire for his tobacco pipe, and the captain wrinkled his nose at the sweet-smoky scent as the leaves caught the spark.

"Do you think the boy speaks the truth?" the other guard asked. "Should we have told the commodore about Tremayne?"

The captain froze at the sound of his own name.

"Why do you insist on repeating the same question?" the first guard answered, blowing a stream of smoke into the air. "The boy was obviously lying. He knows nothing of One-Eyed Jack that the commodore doesn't know already. He's a powder monkey or a cabin boy with no important knowledge."

He took another pull on his pipe. "Not to mention that the commodore is *entertaining* this evening," he said with a grin. "And I'm sure he would not look kindly on any interruptions."

The other guard laughed. "Yes, did you see the chit he took into his chamber? Comely, but none too bright, I think."

A shuffle behind him drew Tremayne's attention, and he looked back to find his two crewmen, Crawley and Jenkins, coming his way. He held up a finger in warning, and they pressed against the wall, watching for his order.

Tremayne watched the two guards intently, waiting for his opportunity. When they both turned to look through the small window at the top of the door, he nodded to his men, and as one, they swept silently into the small space. Crawley clouted a guard on the back of his head with the hilt of his dagger and Jenkins caught him as he slumped to the floor. Meanwhile, the captain slipped his arm around the neck of the second guard, his own blade pressed to the soft flesh beneath his chin. The man's pipe clattered to the floor, forgotten.

"Be silent now," Tremayne warned in a low voice. "You wouldn't want my hand to slip."

He felt the shift of the man's Adam's apple as he swallowed, and smiled grimly in satisfaction.

"Unlock the door," he ordered, "and make not a sound."

The man fumbled for a ring of keys clipped to his belt, finally inserting one into the lock with a shaking hand. Tremayne reached around into the guard's inside pocket and withdrew a linen handkerchief, wadding it up and stuffing it unceremoniously into the guard's mouth. He shoved the man toward Crawley with a nod.

"Bind them both and be quick about it," he told him. "Make certain they won't be discovered for a while." He twirled his dagger in his hand once as he turned back to the door, and Jenkins took up position at his flank, his own blade drawn.

Tremayne swung the door open and squinted into the dark interior, then stepped inside carefully, scanning the room as Jenkins did the same. A jangling sound caused him to freeze in his tracks, and he looked down to find he'd kicked a chain secured to the floor. His eyes tracked the chain to a gap between two stacks of crates and he glanced at Jenkins, pressing a finger to his lips in warning. Jenkins nodded, and they silently crept along the trail left by the metal links.

A sharp crack rang out, and an equally sharp pain shot through Jonathan's skull, dazing him for a moment before he turned to find the Talbot girl staring at him wide-eyed, holding a plank of wood over her head, apparently ready to hit him again. He staggered, and Jenkins sprang in front of him to block the second blow, grabbing the surprised chit and whirling her about, her back to his chest, and his arms banding around hers in an iron grip. Her makeshift weapon clattered to the floor as she struggled against him, and he quickly shifted, covering her mouth with a palm when she opened her mouth to scream.

Tremayne rubbed at his scalp, glaring at her in the dim light.

"I am at a loss for why you always feel it necessary to bash me on the head," he growled in a low voice.

The girl tried to respond, her voice muffled by Jenkins hand.

"Be still, lass," Jenkins warned. "I'll wager given yer current accommodations ye'll not want to be discovered by the commodore any more than we. I'll release ye if ye vow not to scream . . . or try to kill me captain again."

She considered her options, then nodded once. Jenkins released his grip only after kicking away the plank of wood. She straightened her shirt with her shackled hands then turned a defiant gaze on the captain.

"Tremayne," she said distastefully. "Whatever are you doing here?"

He took a step closer, looming over her tiny frame. She swayed, as if fighting the urge to step back, but held her ground, glaring up at him.

"You did not think you could steal from me and leave me for dead, and I'd not come looking for you, did you?" he asked, his teeth bared and grinding. "Now, where is my cutlass?"

"Your cutlass?" she countered. "I believe you mean *my* cutlass."

He took another step, their bodies almost touching. "Do not press me, wench," he growled. "I've half a mind to leave you chained at the commodore's mercy."

"The commodore will release me," she replied airily. "Once he realizes his mistake."

Tremayne laughed. "The commodore doesn't make mistakes," he said. "A fact you will become vastly aware of once you're facing the hangman's noose."

The girl gulped, the chains binding her wrists clinking as she trembled. Jonathan could see the emotions warring on her face, even in the dim light—fear of Tremayne, combined with a vile hatred, along with a near desperation that he could be correct, that the commodore would not listen to reason.

"Fine," she said finally. "I'll go with you."

"And what makes you think I want you?" he scoffed in reply.

"You cannot leave me here!"

"Oh, I *cannot*?" He shook his head, shooting a mocking glance at Jenkins, who smirked in response. "I believe I can, and I will unless you tell me where my bloody cutlass is!" He struggled to keep his voice low, but the threat was evident, and Sarina shuddered slightly in response.

"The commodore took it," she replied.

"Obviously," Tremayne said with a heavy sigh, "but did you see where he put it?"

She shrugged. "Ask one of my guards, if you haven't killed them, that is," she added with a sneer. "The tall one is the one who took it from me."

Jonathan jerked his head toward the doorway and Jenkins left the room to question the guard, returning a moment later with Crawley. The girl glared at him mulishly in the interim, refusing to break the uncomfortable silence.

"It's in the commodore's quarters," Jenkins said. Tremayne nodded, expecting the answer.

"Take the girl," he said gruffly. "But leave the shackles in place."

"What?" She gaped at him. "But . . . you can't!"

Tremayne ignored her. "I'll go after the cutlass with Max. Get the others off the ship and back to the *Arrow*."

"You must release me!" she demanded.

Tremayne sneered. "You do not give me orders, wench. And if you do not wish to remain on board this vessel, you will silence your tongue!" He turned to Crawley. "Do not let her drown. I have plans for her."

"Drown?" she repeated weakly. "Am I supposed to *swim* with my arms bound?"

"Do not worry," Tremayne replied distractedly. "Crawley is an excellent swimmer and will keep your head above water . . . as long as you do not cause any trouble." He grinned at Crawley, who winked in response.

"You . . . you monster!" the wench exclaimed.

Jonathan shrugged. "Aye." He turned to leave as Crawley flipped through the guard's keys to release Sarina.

"Wait!" she exclaimed. Tremayne turned back in annoyance, and she winced, remembering she was supposed to be quiet.

"What?" he snarled.

"You have to free James."

"Who?"

"James." She pointed toward a dark corner. "The commodore will have him killed if you leave him here."

Tremayne approached the cell, squinting to make out the form of a man slumped on the floor.

"You there," he said, tapping the bars with the tip of his boot.

"He's been beaten," she explained. "He needs help."

Tremayne crouched down and peered through the bars. "Damnation," he breathed. "Is that Jamie Ceron?"

"You know him?" she asked.

He ignored the question, holding out his hand. "Crawley, bring me those keys. And for the love of God, get the wench out of here!"

Crawley tossed him the keys and left with the girl, who thought better of making any further comment. Jenkins approached, leaning against the bars.

"Charlie's son," he said in acknowledgement. "Haven't seen him since he was little more than a boy."

"Aye," Tremayne agreed, unlocking the cell and approaching the man. He touched his shoulder gently. "Ceron," he muttered quietly, then shook him a little harder. "Jamie, wake up. We need to get you out of here."

James blinked, still dazed with sleep. Then he sat up abruptly, his hand flying to his head as a low groan escaped his lips.

"What is it?" he asked. "Who's there?"

"Jonathan Tremayne," the captain replied. "It appears you're in a bit of a tight spot, boy."

James winced. "Tremayne?" Startled, he sat up abruptly, eyes darting around in the darkness. "Where's Sarina? What have you done with her?" he whispered.

47

"Sarina? The Talbot chit? She is safe, on her way to my ship." He tried a few keys before managing to get the cell door unlocked. "You're welcome on board as well."

James stood, swaying slightly on his feet, and Jonathan could feel the uncertainty rippling of him in waves.

"Why are you doing this?" he asked quietly.

The captain sighed. "Your father was a good man," he said. "A friend to me and many others."

James stiffened. "I wouldn't know. I barely knew the man."

"Aye, well . . ." Tremayne's words drifted off. He knew that Old Charlie Ceron had a woman and a child somewhere in the islands. He also knew that the man loved the sea more than anything else. There were no words of defense to be offered. It was the way it was.

"Regardless, I owe him for many things," he said instead, "and it seems you're in need of my help. In fact, we could help each other."

"What do you mean?"

A thump overhead drew their attention, and the captain lowered his voice, hissing quietly, "There's no time for this now. We need to get off this ship, but I must retrieve an item that was stolen from me first. Go with Jenkins." He turned to leave, but James' voice stopped him.

"No."

Jonathan turned to see the man bending through the low cell doorway, then stretching to his full height. He was taller than he'd seemed slumped on the floor of the cell, and broad through the shoulders—almost as big as Hutchins. The dim light from the porthole gleamed off his dark skin, his teeth glinting slightly as he spoke.

"You'll need help," he said finally. "I'll go with you."

"It isn't necessary. You're in no condition—"

"I'm fine," he insisted, rolling his massive shoulders to emphasize the point. "I'll go with you."

Tremayne nodded before sending Jenkins away with a jerk of his head. He handed James his spare dagger as they slipped into the dim hallway, finding no sign of the guards.

Crawley had done his job well.

Wordlessly, they made their way through the shadows, drifting around corners and into doorways like wraiths, all the while listening for the inevitable alarm they both knew would sound eventually.

They emerged upon the dark and silent deck, the ship rocking quietly in the black depths. Crossing to a dim archway leading to what Tremayne knew would be the commodore's personal quarters, he could barely make out the faint splashing of his crew swimming back toward the *Arrow*. He thought he heard a feminine screech of protest and smiled slightly at the sound.

Perhaps the bothersome Miss Talbot might be a little more amenable from now on.

Somehow, he doubted that.

However, having the daughter of Danny Talbot in his possession might prove useful when it came to finding what he was looking for. After all, the cutlass was only part of the puzzle, and who knew how many more pieces Sarina Talbot's father had obtained before he met his death?

Jonathan aimed to find out.

He signaled to James, and the two pressed their backs against the wall on opposite sides of the commodore's door. Jonathan listened carefully, finally leaning over to press his ear to the gleaming wood. Faint snores rumbled from within and he nodded at his companion, slowly turning the doorknob.

The door squeaked lightly as he opened it, and the two men froze in place as the snores stopped, interrupted by a snort and a cough and the ruffling of sheets as a body repositioned itself. Jonathan peered into the dark room to make out two forms in the bunk, one long shapely leg peeking out from under the sheets.

It appeared Stanton had some company this evening.

The snoring began again as the commodore relaxed into a deeper sleep, and James gripped the dagger firmly, his eyes focused on the bed as Jonathan scanned the room. He grinned, spying a metallic glint on top of the desk against the far wall.

Apparently, the commodore had been too intent on his entertainment to appropriately stow away the spoils of the day. As James kept watch, Jonathan quickly retrieved the cutlass, then paused as he spotted a leather pouch next to it. Never one to turn away a bit of profit, he stuffed the pouch into his pocket, relishing the weight of the gold inside.

Tremayne turned back to Jamie Ceron, and the two men made their way to the door, only to be stopped by a soft gasp breaking the silence. They turned in unison toward the bed, where the commodore's bedmate, a pale beauty with a tangle of yellow hair billowing around her head, sat upright, looking shocked, a hand clasped at her throat.

The captain put a finger to his lips, but knew as soon as she drew a deep breath that the motion was fruitless.

"Run," he told James in a low voice, and the two took off down the hallway as an ear-piercing scream echoed off the walls behind them.

"Females," Jonathan muttered in frustration, as around him the ship came to life, the shouts of alert and loud curses mingling with slamming doors and the sounds of booted feet on worn wooden floors.

He swore that if he were caught and hanged because of Sarina Talbot, his ghost would return and haunt her for the rest of her days.

The damned woman would be the death of him. Of that, Captain Tremayne was almost certain.

*Opportunity is a fleeting commodity. One must seize it when it appears, for if one falters for but a moment, it is lost ...*

*- The Journal of*
*Simon Alistair Mellick*
*2 June, 1664*

"Now what?" James asked as they emerged onto the deck seeking escape. The crew had come to life with rousing shouts and barked orders, and a half dozen men scrambled out of the doorway at the far end of the ship, tugging up breeches and checking their flintlocks. Behind him, Captain Tremayne could hear the slam of a door, and the bellowing voice of the commodore.

The captain spared not a moment, realizing that acting quickly in the confusion, before they were spotted, was probably the most prudent action.

Not that he feared a fair fight, but two against a shipload? Even Jonathan was not that arrogant.

He raced to the edge of the deck, James Ceron close on his heels. Eyeing the dangling rope, then the growing number of crewmen stumbling from belowdecks, he realized there was no time to waste.

"We need to jump," he told James, climbing onto the gunwale and strapping the cutlass across his chest. James clambered up next to him and slipped his dagger between his teeth. With a nod, the two men looked back quickly over their shoulders, then took a deep breath and leapt off the ship into the crashing waves. The cold water closed in over them, cutting off the chaos above as they kicked off and swam underwater, both men able-bodied and comfortable in the sea after years spent living on and around it.

They broke the surface a good distance from the *Intrepid*, treading water for a moment to catch their breath, and James pulled the dagger from his teeth. "So," he said, "do you do this a lot?"

Jonathan grinned. "Often enough."

James laughed, biting down on the dagger again as they continued to swim toward the *Arrow*, the commodore's angered shouts carrying over the water. Jonathan glanced back, the moonlight enough for him to make out the form of the man standing at the bow of the ship, his head thrown back as he bellowed one word.

"*Tremayne!*" he shouted, and Jonathan knew this would not be the end of it.

The *Black Arrow's* sails billowed at full mast just as Jonathan and James clambered on board, the former shouting orders that they evade the *Intrepid* at all costs, the latter taking in the surroundings of his father's former home with a somber yet persistent gaze. The instant the captain's boot touched down on the deck, the ship began to move, cutting through the waves with purpose as it picked up speed. The captain eyed the horizon through his spyglass, smiling as the *Intrepid* shrank in the distance, unable to keep pace with the smaller and more streamlined *Arrow*. The ship's black sails would make it nearly invisible to the commodore, while the *Intrepid's* white ones gleamed brightly under the light of the moon.

Tremayne wrung water from his long hair with one hand as he regarded his new guest out of the corner of his eye.

James Ceron's huge form melded with the shadows, but he was far from inconspicuous. Under feigned nonchalance, his intent gaze missed nothing, and he scanned the deck with obvious concern, breathing a sigh of relief only when he saw Sarina coming toward him, apparently unharmed. He frowned, though, when he noticed her wrists still shackled together, her elbow held firmly by the quartermaster.

"Why is she a prisoner?" he asked the captain, who responded with a distracted glance between barking orders at his first mate.

"Because she is a thief and a murderess," he responded through gritted teeth. "Well, *attempted* murderess, at least."

Sarina apparently heard the comment as she neared them, because she quirked a brow. "Give me a chance, and I aim to rectify that situation."

The captain glared at her. "Hence the shackles, wench." His eye narrowed on Crawley as he added, "Why isn't she contained?"

Crawley swallowed nervously. "She insisted on seeing you."

"Oh, she *insisted*? Well, then, by all means," he retorted sarcastically, waving a hand.

Sarina bristled. "I needed to make certain you didn't leave James behind."

Tremayne ignored her, growling at Crawley instead. "She is not a *guest*. She is a *prisoner*. You'd do well to remember that."

Crawley nodded, his eyes dropping to the toes of his boots as his fingers tightened on Sarina's arm.

For her part, Sarina turned all her attention on James, understandably tentative at first—the man was nearly a giant, with thick black hair dripping water from its tangled ends and a curving tattoo sweeping down the left side of his face. She took a small step forward, fingers twisting together at her waist.

James grinned, his teeth flashing in the moonlight, and Sarina smiled in response. "It's good to see you're all right."

He tipped his head in an acknowledging nod. "And you, as well. I thank you for your help."

Jonathan snorted.

James fought a smirk, turning to the captain. "And yours, of course, Captain."

Jonathan simply turned about, bellowing, "Man the capstan! Heave-ho, lads! Stanton is on our stern, but the *Intrepid's* no match for us." He looked through the spyglass again. "Baines!"

The first mate relayed the orders and hurried to the captain's side.

Tremayne lowered his head to his friend. "Keep to open water until we round Arahna Point," he said. "We'll dart into the bay and out the other side before Stanton knows where we've gone."

Baines nodded; it was a ploy they'd used countless times before. "And then?"

"The *Intrepid* will not be able to maintain chase with civilians on board. They'll turn about soon enough to find port," Tremayne replied. "We'll stay hidden for the moment. Send Jenkins to the Point to keep watch."

"Aye, Captain." The first mate hurried off to find Jenkins and prepare him to go ashore at Arahna Point. The *Arrow* would circle around to retrieve him once he'd relayed the signal that the *Intrepid* had moved on.

He looked up to find James and Sarina standing side-by-side at the rail, talking quietly as they watched the burst of activity around them. Crawley had disappeared, apparently finding duties more suited to his liking. Ceron said something in a low voice and Sarina laughed, the light sound carrying over the shouts of the crew.

Tremayne frowned. He couldn't explain the itch of irritation he felt at the sight of the annoying Miss Talbot so carefree, even while bound in chains. She should have been nervous, even fearful, given her situation. Instead, she smiled up at James Ceron as if she hadn't a care in the world.

"Captain!" Max drew his attention, and his wide eyes indicated it hadn't been the first time he'd tried to do so. "We're nearing the Point."

Jonathan nodded. "Hard to port! Drop the mainsail and douse the lanterns! Steady, men . . ." He nodded at Jenkins, who sat with one leg thrown over the gunwale. At the silent order, he lowered himself onto the rope ladder, and in a moment, Tremayne heard the light splash of the man hitting the water.

"Swing the lead," he said quietly as the ship moved in the darkness, the light from the moon barely causing a reflection on the ship itself. A crewman lowered a lead weight off the side of the ship to measure the depth of the water, relaying his measurements every few minutes. The crew worked frantically, dropping the sails as Baines took the wheel, skillfully avoiding the shallow areas of the bay until they came to rest in a small inlet, hidden from the open water.

"What do we do now?" Sarina's quiet voice startled the captain, who was unaware that she had moved to his side. He turned to find her squinting toward the point, just barely able to make out the land above the rippling waves.

"We wait," he said gruffly. "Or I should say *we* wait. *You* will be taken belowdecks until I can deal with you properly."

Sarina opened her mouth to argue, but quickly slammed it closed, her eyes narrowing on him calculatingly.

"Why do you do that?" she asked instead.

"Do what?"

She turned to face him, waving a finger at his mouth, the shackles clinking lightly. "Your speech . . . your accent. It . . . *changes*."

Jonathan frowned. "I do not know what you're talking about."

"See?" she said victoriously. "*I do not know what you're talking about*," she mimicked. "One moment you sound like a regular ruffian—which you are—*Heave ho the jib* and whatnot . . ."

"That doesn't make the least bit of sense," he muttered.

She continued as though she hadn't heard him. "Then the next, you sound almost like . . . a *gentleman* . . . all posh and proper."

The captain huffed. "That's ridiculous."

"I cannot quite put my finger on it . . ."

"Crawley!" Tremayne barked, forgetting for a moment that the ship was in hiding, thanks to Sarina Talbot. The wench was nothing but trouble, and he needed her out of his sight immediately. He glared at the quartermaster as he ran to his side.

"Take Miss Talbot belowdecks and lock her in," he said in a lower voice, holding up a finger when Sarina opened her mouth to interrupt. "One of the empty cabins," he added. "Make sure there is nothing she might find useful as a weapon." He glared at her, then turned in dismissal, ignoring her sounds of protest as Crawley dragged her away.

James Ceron eyed the captain carefully in the darkness. "Surely such a tiny thing is not a significant threat."

Jonathan scoffed, touching at the lump on his head absently. "You'd think not, wouldn't you?"

"You'll not . . ." James cleared his throat, squaring his shoulders. "You'll not harm her, will you? I know I'm in your debt, but I'll not allow—"

"Miss Talbot is my concern," the captain interrupted, rubbing his forehead as the beginnings of a headache pounded at his temples. "But no, I'll not harm her. I'm not a beast, after all, despite popular opinion."

James smiled slightly. "All right, then. What *are* your plans for her?"

The captain turned a scrutinizing gaze on the man. "Why such concern?"

James shrugged. "She was kind to me."

Jonathan huffed, opting for the simplest answer. "The wench stole from me. She tried to *kill* me. I simply mean to make her pay a bit.

"As for you, Jamie Ceron, if you're in need of a ship, I could be in need of your services."

James blinked. "What kind of services?"

"You know these islands better than anyone," he said in a low voice. "I'm in need of a guide."

"Guide to what?"

Tremayne shrugged. "You'll know that when the time is right. But be assured, a handsome reward awaits us, and as a member of my crew, you'd be guaranteed your fair share.

"As for now, you're welcome on board, but I'll need to know your loyalty lies with me, and not the wench."

James considered that for a moment. The promise of treasure was a tempting one. "But you said you'll not harm her?"

Tremayne snarled slightly. "I do not like to repeat myself, Ceron."

James huffed, but held out a hand. "All right, then, Captain. You have a guide."

Tremayne shook his hand, his mouth splitting in a grin. "Welcome to the *Arrow*."

Sarina fumed as she stumbled behind the quartermaster down the dim hallway leading below the deck of the ship.

"Really . . . this isn't necessary . . . " she managed through gritted teeth.

"You heard the captain." He stopped before a door and unlocked it quickly, then pulled her inside, scanning the room to ensure it was empty of all possible weapons. Satisfied, he left the room without another word and locked it behind him.

Giving in to her fury, Rina followed him and pounded on the door with her shackled fists.

"Let me out of here!" she shouted. "Hello?" She kicked the door, wincing at the pain in her foot, and let out a frustrated shriek.

"I really *hate* pirates!" she screamed at the top of her lungs, hoping somehow that the words would carry to the target of her current frustration.

One-Eyed Jack Tremayne. The bastard.

She kicked the door one more time for emphasis, then turned to examine her newest prison. As Tremayne had ordered, the room was empty, save a couple of large casks and a pile of discarded canvases in the corner. She had to admit to a bit of disappointment at the lack of a chair or table . . . something she could dismantle and possibly use to smack One-Eyed Jack on the head.

Again.

Rina sighed. She felt like a failure. She'd set out to kill Tremayne, but the fact was, she knew she couldn't. She wasn't a murderer. The sight of the blood flowing from his head—even now—sent a squeamish twist through her stomach.

No, she couldn't kill him, as much as she'd like to. Sarina hoped her father wouldn't be too disappointed in her lack of mettle.

Her only alternative was to try to make Tremayne pay in another way. Her mind spun with the possibilities. She could gain his trust . . . get close to the man, as much as the thought turned her stomach. And once she'd found the answers she was looking for, she could finally fulfill her mission and avenge her father's death. Perhaps . . . perhaps she could gather evidence against him— enough to turn him over to Commodore Stanton and see Tremayne imprisoned for the rest of his natural life.

Or hanged. Rina shivered at the thought but did not waver in her resolve.

And once she presented herself to the commodore in her own clothes, rather than the rags of a cabin boy, and handed him One-Eyed Jack on a silver platter . . .

Well, Commodore Stanton would have no alternative but to believe her tale and dismiss all charges against her.

Yes. The situation definitely called for a new plan.

An *improved* plan.

Rina was nothing if not adaptable. She would gain Tremayne's trust, and when the time was right, he would pay.

She sighed in dejected frustration when her stomach growled. In the meantime, she was stuck in a windowless room in wet clothes with nothing to eat.

*Perfect.*

She walked over to the pile of canvases—sails, she realized—and picked up an edge between two fingers to peek underneath. Seeing no evidence of vermin or something equally distasteful, she sat down on the pile, pulling a corner over her shoulders as a chill set in.

The sound of a key in the lock startled her, and Rina realized she was lying down and must have drifted off. She had no idea how long she'd been in the room, or what time of day it was. Her clothes were damp but no longer dripping; her stomach more vehement in its protestations, suggesting it had been at least a couple of hours since she'd been locked up. She stood quickly, wincing as the shackles chafed at her tender wrists.

She squinted in the darkness to see the captain's first mate come through the door.

Baines, she remembered. Maxwell Baines.

"Captain wants to see you," he muttered quietly, waving her forward.

Her chin stuck out stubbornly, but she didn't refuse the command, not wishing to spend any more time in the tiny room. Not to mention the fact that if she were to gain the captain's trust, she first needed to gain *access* to the captain.

So, she brushed past Baines airily, blinking as she emerged into the brighter passageway. She could make out light coming from the stairway leading to the deck, and realized the sun was up, the ship rocking slightly, obviously under sail.

"What's happening?" she asked, unable to temper her curiosity.

Baines frowned. "The captain will tell you, if he finds it necessary."

Sarina bit her lip. "You don't like me much, do you?"

Baines chuckled humorlessly. "You lied. Tried to kill my captain. Took a chunk out of my arm, and laid me low, kicking me in the bollocks . . ."

Rina winced.

"So, no," he continued, "I'd say you're not my favorite person."

"Sorry about that."

Baines grunted, then added after a moment, "He didn't do it, you know. Kill your father."

Rina said nothing, not surprised that the first mate would defend his captain. She felt his eyes on her, but after a moment, he turned away and they emerged on the deck, his hand closing around her elbow as he led her across to the captain's quarters.

Rina squinted in the bright sunshine, scanning the horizon but seeing nothing more than endless rippling waves. The sails billowed overhead as the ship clipped along, and she stumbled slightly as the deck rolled.

Baines smirked. "Still need to find your sea legs, it appears."

A smart retort died on her lips as the hair on the back of her neck stood on end—a shiver of awareness that she was being watched. She scanned the deck just before passing through the doorway to the captain's quarters, her eyes finally landing on the blackened, cocky grin of the master gunner. Rafferty's beady eyes passed over her form slowly before coming to rest on her face. He winked, spitting a slimy glob out of the corner of his mouth before wiping the excess from his chin with the back of his hand. Rina shivered.

"What's the matter?" Baines asked, tugging on her arm. She hadn't realized she'd stopped.

Rina tore her gaze from Rafferty, but knew instinctively he hadn't done the same. "Nothing," she replied, her voice cracking slightly. "I'm all right."

The first mate shrugged and dropped her arm as they reached the captain's door. He knocked quickly but didn't wait for a response before opening it, obviously aware that Tremayne was waiting for them. Baines stood back, extending his arm toward the door with a gallant half-bow, and Rina rolled her eyes at the gesture. She stalked into the captain's quarters, her gaze landing on him where he sat sprawled behind his desk, her father's cutlass balanced atop his palms.

He ignored her, running his hand along the cool metal, his eye following the movement. He picked up a cloth and rubbed it on the gleaming blade until it shone. His long fingers wrapped around the hilt, testing the sword's weight as he stood and swept it through the air in a large arc.

Rina jumped. The captain smirked slightly but still did not look at her. Instead, he addressed his first mate.

"Release her."

Baines reached for a set of keys in his pocket and quickly unshackled Rina's wrists, nodding once at the captain before he left the room, the door shutting quietly behind him.

All the while, Tremayne continued to play with the sword—her sword—brandishing it gleefully as Rina looked on in anger.

"Aren't you afraid I'm going to attack you?" she asked.

The captain's gaze finally flicked her way briefly. "Not particularly."

Rina stiffened, annoyed that he would dismiss her so easily. She rubbed at her tender wrists, but quickly crossed her arms over her chest when she saw Tremayne notice the movement.

She didn't want to give him the satisfaction.

Rina waited, a low tap-tapping echoing through the room. The captain turned toward her, his eyebrow arched as his focus dropped to her feet.

Or rather, her foot. Her tapping foot. She froze, a blush rising over her cheeks. The man made her nervous, but the last thing she wanted was for him to know that.

"So," she said haughtily. "Your errand boy said you wished to speak with me."

"Aye."

She huffed at his infuriatingly glib reply. He continued to play with the sword and she planted her fists on her hips. "Well?"

He sheathed the cutlass in a smooth stroke and set it on his desk before propping his hip on the edge. "Well, what?"

Rina fought the urge to throw something at his head. "What did you wish to speak with me about?" she asked through gritted teeth.

He considered her for a moment. "It appears you will be my guest for a while."

"Guest?" She rubbed absently at her wrists again. "You have a strange way of treating guests."

The captain chuckled. "Yes, well. You can hardly fault me for being cautious. You did try to kill me."

Rina shrugged.

"The question is," he continued, "will you be trying again?" He watched her carefully, his blue gaze glittering and unblinking.

Rina sighed. "No," she replied wistfully. "I've come to realize I'm not really the murdering type." She spared him a pointed look, obviously emphasizing that he was—in fact—*exactly* that type.

The captain smirked and walked across the room, throwing open a large chest and sifting through its contents. "I know you don't believe that I didn't kill your father," he said. "But I can prove it to you."

Despite herself, Rina found herself asking, "How?"

He straightened with a mass of fabric in his hand. "Because I know who did." He tossed the cloth her way, and she caught it out of reflex, only absently identifying it as a gown.

"It might be a bit large, but it's better than nothing," Tremayne said. "I can't have you parading about my ship in breeches. It's hardly proper." He grinned wolfishly, and Rina doubted the man was really concerned with propriety.

"Who did it?" she asked quietly.

To his credit, Tremayne did not try to pretend he didn't know what she was asking. "I can take you to him," he said instead. "I'm searching for the man myself. I have my own score to settle." His cheek twitched as he clenched his teeth, and Sarina wondered what the captain had lost to this mysterious individual.

She shook off a brief twinge of empathy and set her chin. "Why would you do that?"

He motioned toward the chest. "There are some other items you might need in here. I had water brought up so you could wash. Not a full bath, mind you, no need for such frivolity, but . . ." He dismissed her with a wave toward the opposite side of the room and returned to his desk, sitting down to huddle over a leather-bound book, Rina apparently forgotten.

She noticed a silk-covered screen set up near the far wall and approached the chest, the idea of clean skin and clothes winning out over curiosity and vengeance, at least for the moment. She tucked the gown under her arm, and dug through the contents until she found some underclothes and stockings, and even a pair of shoes that looked about her size.

"Where did you get all this?" she asked without thinking. When he didn't respond, she glanced at him to find him regarding her with a slight smirk on his face.

Right.

*Pirate.*

"Never mind," she muttered, clutching the bundle of clothes to her chest as she made her way toward the screen and ignored the faint chuckle following her along the way.

*I sometimes question the wisdom of recording my thoughts and discoveries in this book, for I am quickly learning that protecting my secrets is a dangerous and difficult proposition. But as often as I fear my plans being discovered, I also realize that, should something happen to my person, this journal would be the only remaining evidence of my endeavors.*

*It is, in essence, my life*

*- The Journal of*
*Simon Alistair Mellick*
*2 June, 1664*

Rina set her little bundle of clothes on a small bench behind the screen and dipped her hand into the tub of water waiting for her.

*Warm.*

She held back a contented sigh, but allowed a smile to grace her lips since Tremayne couldn't see her.

Peeking through a gap in the screen, she found the captain focused once again on the book on his desk. With only a brief hesitation, she pulled her shirt off and untied the rags binding her breasts, rubbing them slightly in relief. She loosened the leather thong tying up her hair and removed the pendant her father gave her, setting it carefully on a little table.

Dipping her hands in the warm water, Sarina ran it over her arms and neck, and wished the tub were big enough for her to climb in. A sliver of soap sat on a low table, and she sniffed it skeptically, surprised at the light floral scent that greeted her. With another glance through the screen, she undressed completely, washing her body, and then her hair as well as she could in the warm water.

It was heavenly.

Sarina dried off with a rough towel that had been left on the table, squeezing the excess water from her hair with the cloth. A sound from the other side of the room snapped her eyes back to the gap in the screen, only to once again meet the top of Tremayne's head. She watched him for a moment, the towel clutched to her bare chest.

Her eyes narrowed, wondering if he'd noticed the same gap.

She wouldn't put it past him. The bastard.

Stepping closer to the wall and out of range of the infamous gap, Rina dressed quickly and ran her fingers through her damp hair to remove the tangles. She smoothed the skirt of the cream and brown gown, smiling at the feel of the soft fabric, then pulled her pendant over her head and tucked it into the bodice.

It was nice to feel like a woman again, even if the gown was a little too big and gaped slightly around her less than ample bosom. Rina frowned, tugging at the bodice as she emerged from behind the screen. She looked up to find Tremayne's eyes focused on her actions. His attention lingered for a moment, his brow creased in concentration before he returned to his book.

"The water will need to be removed," he said gruffly.

Rina stood silently in confusion for a moment. Well, of course the water would need to be removed. She was at a loss, however, for why the captain would feel the need to voice such an obvious fact.

He glanced up at her again. "You can dump it over the side," he said slowly, as if addressing a small child.

Rina gaped. "You can't be serious! You expect me to haul that tub up to the deck?"

Tremayne stood abruptly and closed the book with a thwack, circling the desk to the still-open chest.

"Everyone on my ship pulls his own weight," he muttered, fumbling through the chest and looking for something. "I am still in need of a cabin boy, and you are familiar with the position."

"You can't seriously expect—"

"Not to mention the fact that it will give me an opportunity to monitor your activities and ensure you stay out of trouble."

"Trouble? The only trouble around here—"

"Unless," he interrupted, raising his gaze to her in challenge, "you'd prefer to spend your days locked up in the hold?"

Rina clenched her jaw, resisting the urge to look away. She fought to remember her mission . . . her new, *improved* mission. She needed to stay close to the captain, and what better way than as his personal errand boy?

Errr . . . girl.

So, Rina swallowed her pride and turned on her heel, her spine straight as she tried not to stomp back over to the water tub. Grabbing one of the handles, she dragged it across the wooden floor, stopping every other step to keep the cooling water from sloshing over the sides. Irritated, she straightened, her hands on her hips as she glared at the now-hated washtub. She would never be able to carry the thing. Glancing around the room, she spied a bucket behind the screen—most likely what was used the fill the tub—and she grabbed it to dip out some of the water before turning toward the door.

Tremayne stood watching her, his lips quirked in amusement.

"Excuse me," she said haughtily, blowing back a strand of hair dangling across her face.

The captain stepped back with a nod, but just as she started to pass him, he held up a hand.

"Take this," he grumbled. Sarina realized he was clutching a handful of cream-colored lace in his beringed fingers. She looked up at him, confused, but he wouldn't meet her eyes. Or rather, his gaze was trained *below* her eyes.

Rina cleared her throat and the captain's eye snapped up. If she expected chagrin at being caught ogling her chest, she was sadly mistaken. The captain simply raised his eyebrow and pressed the lace into her free hand.

"Tuck it into your bodice," he said, turning abruptly to stalk back behind his desk. "That dress is indecent."

"I beg your pardon?"

"I cannot have you parading about my ship with your flesh on display," he grumbled, collapsing into his chair. "My men will be distracted, and I cannot afford to have them so."

Rina flushed, setting down the bucket and quickly tucking the scrap of lace into her neckline. Despite her embarrassment, she noticed the captain's accent had changed again, the vowels rounding, the consonants more crisp. "You're doing it again," she said.

"Doing what?"

"Speaking like a gentleman."

Tremayne's gaze rose from the book on his desk and trailed up Rina's body like a physical caress before settling on her face. She stiffened, silently cursing the blush she could feel creeping up her neck, and tried not to look at the patch, focusing instead on his good eye, a pool of blue-green, dark and dangerous.

"Believe me, Miss Talbot, I am no gentleman."

Rina gaped for a moment, then snapped her mouth shut and picked up the bucket, leaving the room without another word. She took a bit of satisfaction in slamming the door behind her.

Captain Tremayne watched her go, his eye widening slightly at the vehemence with which she shut the door. The girl was stronger than she looked.

He smiled. That was good. She would need to be strong for what he had planned.

He'd almost backed down on his little plan to make the wench pay. When he'd looked up and caught a glimpse of pale, creamy flesh through a gap in the silk screen across the room . . .

Well, for a moment, revenge was the last thing on his mind.

Thankfully, it only took the woman opening her mouth to extinguish any such thoughts. He couldn't afford to be distracted in his mission, even by a soft body.

Jonathan frowned as she re-entered his quarters and swept over to scoop up another bucket of water. It sloshed over the side of the tub, and Jonathan purposely looked down at the journal he was studying before saying crisply, "There are linens in the corner to wipe that up."

He fought a chuckle at her irritated gasp and stomping feet, only daring a glance when he heard the rustle of fabric on the far side of the room. Sarina dropped a cloth onto the spilled water, swishing it around absently with the toe of her slipper. He forced a frown of concentration on his face.

"Once you're finished with the tub, I've some breeches in need of mending." He licked a finger and turned a page, only to be brought out of his nonchalant act by the cold smack of a wet cloth against the side of his head. He blinked in surprise, looking down at the rag now dripping on his desk, then up at a rather satisfied Sarina.

"You just . . . did you just throw a wet rag at me?" he sputtered.

Sarina smirked, picking up her bucket of water. Jonathan shot to his feet, his fingers clutching the damp linen as he waved it at her. "You'd be wise to remember your place, Miss Talbot," he warned, rounding his desk to loom over her.

She dropped the bucket unceremoniously, more water sloshing out onto the gleaming floor, as well as his boots. "My place?" she snapped. "How dare you!"

"How dare *I*?" he spat. "Need I remind you that you are on my ship at my pleasure? And in my quarters for your own protection?"

"I don't need your protection!"

"No?" he snarled mockingly, with a pointed glance directed at her bosom. "You're on a ship of more than a hundred men, Miss Talbot, many of whom have been without female companionship for a good, long while. How long do you think you'd last on your own? Rafferty's already drooling on his shoes each time you walk past. Do you think you'll be able to hold him off if he finds you alone in some isolated corridor one dark night?"

Despite her anger, Sarina blanched at the thought.

Jonathan snatched at the thrill of putting her in her place. "And he's not the only one." He stepped even closer until his breath washed over her face and she cringed back—just a little, but enough so he noticed. "Not all of my men are discerning when it comes to women, Miss Talbot. They'll take what's available, whether or not the lady in question is a willing participant."

"I can handle myself," she said, all indignation and false bravado. "I can wield a dagger . . . shoot a pistol."

"And I can put you in the brig," Jonathan retorted. "I need my men—all of my men—and I'll not risk losing one for your foolish notions of independence!"

"Foolish!"

"Yes, foolish!" Jonathan leaned in further, only belatedly realizing Sarina's breasts brushed his chest with every inhale. He ignored an irrational surge of lust and refused to step away and risk losing his advantage, focusing instead on the task at hand.

"You have two choices, Miss Talbot. You can stay here, do your part, and find out what really happened to your father. Or you can spend the rest of the voyage contained below, and perhaps—" He held up a finger as she opened her mouth to interrupt. "*Perhaps* once my mission is complete I'll leave you on some isolated island to find your way home. If I remember, that is."

He glared at her, and she glared back for a moment, her amber eyes flashing with anger. But Jonathan knew when she drew a deep breath, her chest brushing his again enticingly—not that he noticed—that he'd won.

"What do you expect me to do?" she asked grudgingly, stepping back in defeat.

Jonathan took a step and turned, leaning back against his desk. "What you intended all along, I think," he said. "Fetch my food, keep my cabin tidy, that sort of thing. Whatever needs doing."

Sarina flushed, and Jonathan knew she didn't like that idea very much.

"I'll need to keep an eye on you, of course," he continued, enjoying her discomfort immensely. "So, you'll need to stay close to me at all times."

She looked up at him, eyes flashing. "How close?" Her eyes darted to Jonathan's bed, but she tried to cover up the instinctive movement by crossing her arms over her chest and scowling at him defiantly.

Jonathan smirked. "Rest assured, Miss Talbot, I have no interest in despoiling your person," he said. "You'll sleep on the cot in the corner." Sarina followed his pointing finger to a rather uncomfortable looking pile of blankets resting on a mattress of woven rope.

"However," he continued, "it would be to your best interest to allow the crew to think what they may about our living arrangements." He took a seat at the desk again, and ruffled through some papers. "It would probably be wise to let them believe you're my woman."

"Your . . . your *woman*?" Sarina sputtered indignantly. "Why in the world would I do that?"

He looked up at her with a blank expression. "Because then none of them would dare touch you, of course."

"I can't believe this," Sarina muttered, collapsing into a chair, her face falling into her hands. "What am I doing?"

Despite himself, Jonathan felt a bit of pity for the wench. "You're seeking the truth about who killed your father," he said quietly. "Unless you'd rather give up this nonsense altogether?"

Sarina straightened. "It's not nonsense," she said with a sniff. "And I'm still not convinced *you* weren't responsible."

Jonathan laughed slightly. "Why are you so certain? Surely, I couldn't be the only one with a possible grudge against Danny?"

"My sources point to you."

"Your *sources* are mistaken."

"And you can prove that?" Sarina looked him square in the eye, as if trying to gauge his honesty.

"I can," he said, meeting her gaze. "When I find the man I'm looking for, you will have your proof."

"Why don't you just tell me who it is, and I'll be on my way?"

Jonathan laughed. "Oh, no. I know better than that. The last thing I need is you stepping into the middle of things and ruining my plans."

"You just don't want me to get to him first." She crossed her arms over her chest, causing the front of her gown to dip precariously low. Only the scrap of lace prevented her from falling out of it altogether. Ridiculous, really. She was a woman. She ought to be able to sew it up or something to keep herself decent.

Sarina cleared her throat and arched a brow when he looked up.

"Well, there's very little chance of that," he countered, quickly returning to the topic at hand. "But I definitely don't need you getting in the way. No, I will find him, and when I do, you will get the answers you seek."

"I don't need answers," she said quietly. "I need vengeance."

Jonathan nodded slightly, grim determination giving him clarity and focus. "As do I," he said. "It seems we have allied purposes, Miss Talbot, at least for the moment."

Sarina's eyes narrowed, but she hesitated only briefly. "For the moment," she relented.

"Good, then we're agreed," Jonathan said, turning back to his book. "Now take care of that tub, and see to my supper."

He ignored the indignant huff that preceded Sarina following his orders.

The man was insufferable.

Rina dumped the last of the bathwater over the side of the ship and dropped the empty bucket onto the deck with a thud, wiping her hands on the toweling she'd tied over her skirts.

"Mending his breeches indeed," she muttered, gazing unseeingly out over the vast gray sea, her thoughts a tumultuous blend of fury and confusion. She still didn't believe Tremayne when he proclaimed his innocence. Well, not entirely, at least.

But she'd begun to doubt. And she'd come to understand that doubt caused problems.

If Tremayne was telling the truth—and the *if* was loud and unwieldy—she would never forgive herself for taking vengeance out on him. Not because of *him*, really. The fact was, Tremayne was guilty of a good many crimes, and even if he was innocent of her father's murder, she had no qualms about him having to pay for the others.

But to let the guilty man go unpunished? *That* would be the unforgivable sin.

Rina couldn't let that happen.

So, even if it meant a temporary truce with the scoundrel that was One-Eyed Jack Tremayne—even if it meant serving him as his cabin boy and suffering his impudent orders and insulting innuendo—she would do what was necessary.

"I can do it," she said half to herself as she picked up the bucket and squared her shoulders.

"I've no doubt you can, lass," a nasal voice, thick with mockery drawled behind her.

Rina swung around, the empty bucket dangling from her fingertips as her free hand flew to her chest in surprise. Rafferty stood before her, grinning widely, his eyes not leaving hers as he spat onto the deck. A drip of black spittle hung from his lips. He licked it and chuckled at Rina's look of distaste.

"Mighty prim and proper now, aren't ya?" he said, eyes raking down her form slowly and making Rina's skin crawl. "Put ye in a gown and suddenly ye think yer a lady." He took a step closer, running a finger along the fabric tucked into her bodice. "But I'll not be forgettin' ye running around in breeches, yer assets on display fer all t'see."

She slapped his hand away, but he only leered at her, shaking back a greasy hank of hair. "We both know what's beneath that gown, don't we?" he rasped.

Rina glanced frantically around her, but Rafferty had her cornered between a large crate and a dinghy, out of sight unless someone happened to walk right by them.

"I got a wee taste before, but I do believe I'd like a bit more," he said through his teeth, grabbing her upper arms in a bruising grip.

"Let me go!" Rina shrieked, thrashing about and lifting her knee to kick him. Unfortunately, her long skirts thwarted her attempt, and Rafferty only laughed, sour breath and spittle hitting her face.

"Now, don't be like that," he wheedled, pressing her against the deck rail, his hard body allaying any further attempts at kicking. "Ye can enjoy it, if ye like." He wrapped an arm around her back, pinning one of her arms against her side and gripping the other tightly. Reaching up with his other hand, he took her chin roughly in his fingers. Rina fought his hold, her stomach roiling at the scent of his breath mingled with body odor, and she did the only thing she could think of. Arching backward, she gathered her strength and thrust her head forward with all her might, her forehead meeting Rafferty's nose with a jarring crack.

He released her immediately, an agonized groan escaping his lips as his fingers cradled his now bleeding nose. Ignoring the pain in her forehead, adrenaline forcing back a wave of dizziness, Rina swung the empty bucket at Rafferty's head with both hands, the satisfying thwack and resulting thud as Rafferty hit the deck making her grimace in satisfaction. She stood for a moment, trembling, the bucket rattling in her hands as Rafferty rolled around in pain, blood gushing from his nose as he cursed her rather colorfully. Rina resisted the urge to kick him, half-worried she might trip in the attempt, and instead stepped around him quickly, only to come face to face with Max Baines . . . and Master Rigger Hutchins . . . and James . . . and behind them about a dozen more men watching Rafferty writhe, shock written all over their faces.

Rina sniffed, wondering where they'd all been when Rafferty was manhandling her.

"What did you do?" Baines asked, wide eyes drifting from Rafferty to her.

She lifted her chin stubbornly. "The reprobate would not take *no* for an answer."

"Reprobate?" Baines repeated, shooting a questioning glance at Hutchins, who just shrugged in response.

Rina rolled her eyes. "Regardless, rest assured, he deserved it," she said haughtily, stepping around Rafferty and intending to continue toward the captain's quarters. She stopped short, though, at the rather intense and hungry looks pointed her way from several of the men.

Or rather, pointed toward her bosom.

Her fingers fluttered up nervously, and she realized in the scuffle she had lost the bit of lace tucked into her bodice. She didn't need to look down to know the front of her gown gaped a bit, presenting a clear view of her bosom. She straightened her shoulders, gripping the extra fabric in her tight fist before shoving through the crowd to head belowdecks.

Of course, Captain Tremayne stood leaning against the arched doorway, eyebrows raised in amusement. Rina stalked over to him, stopping only when she realized there was not enough room to squeeze past.

"I told you," he said quietly, picking at his fingernails with the point of his dagger.

"And I told you," she hissed back, "I could handle the situation."

"This time," he retorted, fixing her with a pointed glare. "What happens if Rafferty isn't so careless next time? Or one of the others? Or perhaps more than one at a time?"

Rina gasped, face flushing at the implication. "No!"

"Oh, yes, Miss Talbot," he murmured, leaning in a bit in what Sarina was sure was an attempt to intimidate her.

It was working.

"I told you, my men take what they want," he said simply.

"But," she stammered, "surely you wouldn't let them . . ."

"Of course not, not intentionally, at least," he said quickly. "But I can hardly be everywhere at once, can I? I do have a ship to run, after all." He went back to picking at his fingernails, annoyingly relaxed despite Rina's agitation. She gripped the empty bucket tightly, considering a vague desire to repeat her actions and crack Tremayne against the head with it, as well. She hated the fact that she knew he was right. She'd been lucky enough to catch Rafferty off guard, but it was not a large ship—not large enough, at least—and if he got another opportunity to accost her, she wasn't certain she'd be able to fight him off.

Nervously, she glanced over her shoulder at the crew, all watching in rapt fascination, and some with undisguised lust.

She turned back to Jonathan. "All right. What do I need to do?" she hissed. "Make some sort of announcement?"

Jonathan grinned and slid his dagger back into its sheath. "Oh, I don't believe that will be necessary."

And with no further warning, he lunged forward and captured Rina in his arms. She gasped, clinging to his shoulders as he spun her, bending her slightly backward over his arm, his mouth hovering a hairsbreadth from hers.

"What are you doing?" she snarled through gritted teeth, forcing down a rush of heat she didn't want to consider.

Jonathan winked. "Laying claim," he said, just before he kissed her thoroughly.

*Today, I begin a new life in a New World. It is difficult to leave behind London, the home of my childhood. Yet, the anticipation of what lies ahead compels me.*

*I stand on deck, the salt air bracing, and as I watch England grow smaller in the distance, I feel a strange sense of peace.*

*- The Journal of*
*Simon Alistair Mellick*
*9 July, 1664*

Perhaps he was overdoing it, but Jonathan figured if a man needed to make a point, he may as well make it soundly. And after what he'd just witnessed, he believed the point definitely needed to be made.

He'd emerged onto the deck, automatically searching for Sarina but not spotting her at first. It was only when he heard the loud crash and saw the bastard, Rafferty, collapse onto the deck, clutching at his nose, that he realized what had been going on. The rest of the crew had apparently been unaware as well, all gathering to see what the commotion was about.

Hot anger surged through Jonathan, and with it came an overwhelming urge to rip his master gunner limb from limb. But when Sarina stepped around Rafferty's flailing body, flushed but unharmed and her head held high, his fury was quickly replaced by a resigned appreciation.

Blast, the woman was a pain in the arse, but even he had to admit she was a formidable wench.

So he'd forced a casual air, and proceeded to send an important message to every man on board his ship. It was his duty, after all. As captain, he felt responsible for the safety of each member of his crew.

Still, Jonathan readily conceded that kissing Sarina Talbot wasn't quite as distasteful as he'd imagined it would be.

She was soft—surprisingly so, considering her stiff demeanor—her body forming to his in a rather distracting way. She gasped in outrage when he first touched his lips to hers, her fingers gripping at his shoulders to keep her balance. She struggled slightly, but then . . .

*Then . . .*

Then she softened even further, a quiet sound forming in the back of her throat as Jonathan's hands clutched at the back of her scalp and he tilted his head to deepen the kiss. Her lips parted, breath mingling with his, and Jonathan felt a shot of heat plunge straight to his groin. He snarled under his breath, tongue dipping out to taste her as his arm tightened around her waist.

Suddenly she stiffened, fingers clawing at his shoulders, and she began to struggle in earnest.

Jonathan snapped back into a semblance of control and pulled away, drawing Sarina up to stand on her feet. She swayed a bit, and Jonathan fought back a smirk, holding her shoulders gently until he was certain she wasn't going to swoon.

Instead, her eyes narrowed, and she flounced past him, heading down the hall toward his quarters. Jonathan couldn't resist smacking her backside, grinning back at her unrepentantly as she flushed, glaring viciously at him, only to redden further at the boisterous catcalls coming from the crew.

He turned to Max, keeping his grin in place. "Ten lashes for Rafferty," he said in a low, deadly voice. "Make certain the men witness it, but the wench does not."

The first mate nodded as Jonathan turned back to the crew.

"As you were," he shouted with a wink before turning to follow Sarina into the dim corridor. He winced when he heard a door slam ahead of him, and tried not to laugh when he entered his cabin to find her pacing angrily. She crossed to him, chest heaving in her ill-fitting gown.

Not that Jonathan noticed.

"Well, I think—" he began, but he never got to finish his thought, because Sarina reared back and slapped him across the face. Hard.

"You . . ." she sputtered. "You lecherous rake!"

"Rake?" Jonathan rubbed at his cheek. "You can hardly blame me for trying to protect you."

"That wasn't about protection!" she spat back. "That was you taking liberties!"

"As if you didn't enjoy it."

Sarina gasped and raised her arm to slap him again, but he was quicker this time, catching her wrist before she made contact.

"I believe once can be excused," he said quietly, threat oozing with every syllable. "Female hysteria and all that . . ."

"Hysteria?" She scoffed, struggling to rip her wrist from his grip. "Hardly. More like well-founded outrage. To manhandle me like a common strumpet—"

At that, Jonathan tugged her closer, gritting his teeth in an unpleasant smile. "A common strumpet would know how to kiss," he pointed out, purposely goading her.

"Well . . . I never!"

"Exactly my point."

Sarina swung out with her other hand, but Jonathan caught that as well, his jaw tightening in frustration. "Would you please stop trying to hit me?"

"Would *you* please stop doing things that make me want to?"

Jonathan couldn't hold back a laugh. "Miss Talbot, calm down, please," he said. "If you'd allow me to explain."

Sarina laughed humorlessly. "As if you could." She frowned, but her movements stilled.

"If I release you, do you promise not to slap me again?" He eyed her carefully, only relaxing his grip after her curt nod. He stepped back, holding his hands out, just in case she changed her mind.

She rolled her eyes. "I'm not going to slap you," she said. "Goodness, for a pirate, you're awfully skittish."

"Well, you can hardly blame me," he retorted. "You take every opportunity to brain me."

She snorted. "As if you had one."

"Tut tut, Miss Talbot," he said, rounding his desk to sit in his chair. "Some might think you protest too much."

"And what in the world is *that* supposed to mean?"

He shrugged, tapping a finger on his lips. "Just that there was a moment there when you didn't seem to be protesting at all."

"What?" Sarina gaped, her eyes darting around as she scrabbled for words. "It was . . . my head. I was still dizzy from hitting Rafferty. And . . . you just . . . you took me by surprise. I didn't expect you to be so . . . so . . ."

"Delicious?" he offered smugly.

She glared. "Forward."

"I had to make it believable for the crew."

"And why exactly would you need to use your *tongue* for that? It wasn't as if they could see inside my mouth!"

Jonathan ignored the heat roaring up at the memory of her mouth . . . her tongue . . . the feel of her warm body pressed against his.

"They have seen me with other women before," he replied, absently noting a twitch of her jaw at that comment.

*Interesting.*

"They would have noticed if I held back with you," he added.

Her fight deflated. "Well, you could have warned me," she said begrudgingly. "It would have been nice to have been prepared."

"Oh, come now, Miss Talbot," he said, leaning back in his chair with a grin. "Where would be the fun in that?"

"You're a very irritating man, Captain."

"So I've been told."

"Well," Sarina said loftily, brushing at her skirts as she tried to collect herself. "To avoid such distasteful displays again, I think it best we adopt a few guidelines."

Jonathan smirked. He had to admit he enjoyed battling wits with Sarina Talbot. The woman was infuriating, but definitely not boring.

"I don't abide well with rules, Miss Talbot."

"Undoubtedly," she retorted, brushing back her hair. "Nevertheless, if we are to enact this charade, I am afraid I must insist on a few concessions on your part."

"I abide even less with concessions."

"Would you just listen to me?" she exclaimed, throwing her hands up in frustration. "For heaven's sake, you don't even know what I'm asking!"

He eyed her for a moment, then nodded slightly. "Very well. What are your demands?"

Sarina inhaled deeply. "First of all, I sleep in the bed."

Jonathan snorted. "Now who's being forward?"

"Not with you, you arrogant prat!" she snapped. "*I* sleep in the bed. *You* sleep on the cot."

Jonathan huffed out a laugh. "Not bloody likely!"

"You'd put your comfort before a lady's?" she asked haughtily.

"Always." He leaned forward with a leering smile. "That is, unless she's in the bed *with* me."

Sarina colored, but didn't rise to bait. "Very well. It is your bed, after all. But I'm afraid I must insist on a mattress at least. There is no way I can sleep on those ropes."

Jonathan fought a smile when he realized that Sarina never intended to take his bed, but was using it as a negotiating tactic. "All right," he conceded. "There are some spare ticks in the hold. But you'll haul it up yourself. No bothering my men with menial tasks."

"Yes, well, I suppose menial tasks are my job now, right?" she muttered.

"Exactly." Tremayne leaned his elbows on the desk, fingers tented before his lips. "Anything else?"

"No chamber pots. That is non-negotiable."

Jonathan winced. He could hardly blame her. "Done."

She lifted her chin. "And no sneaking peeks," she said. "When I'm dressing . . . or bathing . . ." He cast a pointed look at her bodice and she hurried to the chest to retrieve another handkerchief.

"And absolutely no more kissing."

Tremayne raised a brow. "No kissing? None at all?"

She tucked the handkerchief into her gown. "You've established our apparent *relationship* with your crew. They're aware I'm staying in your quarters. I wouldn't think it necessary."

He rubbed a finger lightly over his lips, back and forth. "Not necessary, no," he said, voice low, considering. Sarina's gaze drifted to his mouth, where he continued to trace a slow circuit across his lips. "But enjoyable."

She started, eyes snapping up. "Hardly!"

He stood, rounding the desk to stand disturbingly close to her. Sarina took a step back, then forward again, refusing to be intimidated. He loomed over her, eye glittering in the lantern light.

"Are you certain it would be so distasteful, Miss Talbot?" he rasped quietly. "So certain you wouldn't like it?"

"Of course I wouldn't!" she insisted, voice catching. She cleared her throat nervously. "I would never . . ."

"Never?" he pressed, leaning even closer. "No reason to hold back, Miss Talbot. It's not as if your reputation is in danger."

Sarina sputtered, unable to form words.

"You're already sharing quarters with a—how did you put it?—a *lecherous rake*," he prodded, unable to resist. "Why not enjoy yourself?"

He could see her trembling, although whether her discomfort stemmed from his proximity or her own reaction to it, he wasn't sure. She swayed toward him slightly, and his mouth curved in victory.

She spotted it, though, and her gaze hardened as she stepped back and straightened her spine. "Never!" she spat. "This is a business proposition, Captain. A means to an end. That is all. I'll not be welcoming any advances from a man such as you.

"As for my reputation, I am confident it will be restored once this whole troublesome business is over."

"Don't be so sure, Miss Talbot," he retorted, sitting on the edge of his desk. "Some things, once lost, are lost forever."

Sarina lifted her chin. "Regardless, I believe we have an accord?" She held out her hand, and Jonathan ignored the slight tremor in her fingers.

He took her hand, but instead of shaking it, lifted it to his lips, eyeing her over it with a wolfish smile. "You have my word. Should you change your mind, however . . ."

"I won't." She flushed, snatching her hand back and clutching it to her stomach.

Jonathan chuckled humorlessly. Although it was entertaining to goad her, he was beginning to find her distaste rather irritating. And insulting.

"Calm yourself, Miss Talbot," he said, returning to his desk and dismissing her with a wave of his hand. "You have my word. I'm not one to foist my attentions on unwilling females. And, no offense intended, but I prefer my women to be a bit more . . . enthusiastic."

Sarina gasped, but she seemed unsure as to whether she should express disgust at his preferences, or offense at his opinion of her romantic skills. She opted to ignore the comment altogether. "Good. Fine, then," she said, nodding sharply.

"You trust my word, Miss Talbot?" he asked, unable to resist poking her one more time. "I am, after all, but a dishonorable pirate."

"True, but it appears I have no choice, do I?" she said, more comfortable now that the topic had moved away from the captain's bed. "Besides, if you falter, I can always find a bit of wood to knock you back into compliance. I'm sure there's an oar or two on board . . . or how about one of those planks you pirates always have people walking?"

"Miss Talbot, did you just make a jest?"

"Perhaps," she said loftily. "I suppose you'll find out if you challenge me."

And just like that, Jonathan's irritation evaporated. He didn't let her see it, though.

"You know," he said, shuffling some papers on his desk. "You were much more agreeable as Smith."

"Funny," she replied, "you were just as arrogant and irritating."

He flashed an evil smile, continuing as if she hadn't spoken. "In fact, I do believe I'll continue to call you Smith. Remind you of your place and all."

"Not if you expect me to respond."

"Off with you now," he ordered. "I've work to do, and you need to see to my breeches, and then to my supper."

Sarina hesitated for a moment, and Jonathan could practically feel her rage. He braced himself for an attack, but she just said, "Aye, sir," and sat down to mend his breeches.

Rina fumed as she sat in a chair, running a needle and thread through a tear in Tremayne's breeches. Right down the back center seam.

She smirked, wondering who had seen him split the seat of his trousers.

Tremayne whistled to himself as he did whatever he was doing at his desk. She could feel him sneaking glances at her, and knew he was more than likely trying to find additional ways to irritate and annoy her, but she refused to give him the satisfaction. She just sat and mended . . .

. . . and fumed . . .

. . . and plotted.

Mend his breeches? Oh, she would mend his breeches.

Attempting to look as innocent as possible, Sarina clipped the thread, then slid another through the needle. She eyed the trousers carefully, smiling to herself as she placed them back on her lap and surreptitiously began to sew the hem closed on one leg. She hummed as she worked, reaching for a torn shirt when she finished with the trousers. By the time she'd finished with the pile of mending, sleeves were sewn to collars, breeches attached to socks, and one of Tremayne's red scarves dangled from the shoulders of a shirt like a cape.

Sarina nodded in contentment as she folded the last garment and put the stack of clothing into a trunk.

"I believe I'll go and see to your supper, Captain," she said. He grunted acknowledgment but didn't look up as she left the room, trying not to skip along the way.

Rina giggled slightly once the door closed behind her. She knew it was childish, but the man was so arrogant . . . so vile . . .

So . . .

She shook her head, unable to come up with further adjectives that could do Tremayne justice. As she passed through the doorway where he had accosted her, her cheeks heated. Although she now understood why he'd done what he had, she couldn't force down a flush of embarrassment at her reaction.

Because Tremayne had been right. For a moment, she hadn't protested. She'd given in.

Rina had previously been kissed by three men in her life: her father— which didn't really count, she had to admit—a boy named Theodore, who'd helped her up when she'd fallen off her pony when she was five, and Henry Woodward, the young man who'd escorted her to her coming out ball. He'd been shy but determined when he walked with her out into the gardens, gripping her shoulders tightly with a look of resolve on his face before pressing his wet, chapped lips to hers lightly.

It had been nice, actually. Apparently, Henry had not felt the same, however, because he never called on Rina again.

But none of those experiences had prepared her for the assault of Jonathan Tremayne on her senses. There was nothing *nice* about Jonathan Tremayne. He was big and hard and hot—so hot she feared he might sear her skin right through her clothes. And when his lips touched hers, she didn't really notice if they were wet or dry or chapped, because all she could think about was the heat and strange tingling sensation in her stomach, as if she'd spun around in a circle a hundred times and had to hold onto something to keep from falling to the ground.

So she'd held on to him. Shamefully, she'd clung to him, gasping as his tongue brushed her lips. The dizziness all but overwhelmed her at that warm, wet touch, and a surge of panic swept through her at what she might do if he didn't stop.

If it went on any longer, she half-feared she might not want him to.

Thankfully, she'd been able to compose herself enough to pull away, and his smug response had revived her like a bucket of ice cold water dumped on her head. She'd sobered quickly but managed to maintain their charade until they were out of view of the crew.

Oh, she'd enjoyed slapping him. The sting and throb in her palm was immensely satisfying. She would have liked to manage one more, but the man was just too damned fast.

Pity.

But she'd held her own, making her demands in a relatively composed manner. Still, although he'd agreed to her requests, she'd somehow left their conversation feeling he'd won. She could hardly be blamed for using her sewing skills to regain a little control of the situation.

Even if it was a bit childish.

Rina made her way to the galley, her step faltering slightly when she spotted two crewmen talking in the passageway. She stiffened, fists clenching and chin lifting, half-expecting a confrontation—or at least a snicker or two—but the men simply nodded deferentially and stepped out of her way so she could pass.

*Odd.*

She swept by them, following the scent of meat and spices into the cramped and steamy galley. The cook didn't look up from stirring a large kettle inside the brick fire hearth. His muscles bunched, shirtsleeves rolled up as his skin gleamed with sweat, glowing in the firelight. Rina wondered how he could stand the heat. A few portholes and the open doorway were not nearly enough to create a breeze in the stifling room, and she longed for the fresh air on deck. Fortunately, large pipes vented the worst of the smoke out the side of the ship, but a slight haze still colored the air, making her squint. Rina cleared her throat to get his attention.

"Supper's not for another hour, so be off with ye!" he growled, still absorbed in his work. He slammed the hearth's large iron door shut and opened another smaller one to draw a few loaves of bread out of the oven with his bare hands. Before Rina could respond, he turned to drop the bread onto a wooden table and finally glanced up, wiping his sweating face with a rag. Surprise registered on his features, followed by a nervous swallow.

"Beg ye pardon, Miss." He quickly shoved the rag back into his pocket and ran a hand over his greasy black hair. "Ye here for the captain's supper?"

Sarina wiped at the perspiration forming on her upper lip and nodded. He blinked, then began to bustle around the galley, gathering a tray and crockery bowl from an upper shelf. He loaded the tray with two loaves of the bread and a bowl of fragrant stew. All the while, he snuck glances at her, wiping his palms on his trousers intermittently.

*Why was everyone acting so strangely?*

"Are you sure you want to take this, Miss?" he asked finally, wary eyes meeting hers. "It's a bit heavy, and I'm sure I can find a lad to take it to the captain's quarters."

"I'll be fine. Thank you." She lifted the tray, balancing it carefully as she made her way back to the captain's cabin. Despite her focus on not spilling the food, she couldn't help but notice the eyes watching her as she walked carefully across the deck. Conversations stopped; men stepped out of her way. One even hurried to move a cask from her path with an apologetic dip of his head.

Rina set the tray on a barrel in the corridor so she could open the captain's door unhindered. He looked up, startled, when she stepped inside, and she saw him quickly close the chest he'd retrieved from the *Lady* and stash it in a drawer in his desk.

"What is it?" he growled.

Rina rolled her eyes and retrieved the tray from the hallway. "Your supper, Your Worship," she said, placing the food on the table and retrieving the jug of rum from his desk to fill his tankard. With only a brief hesitation, she poured a bit into a smaller mug, adding a hefty dose of water.

Jonathan watched her with a raised eyebrow, circling the desk to sit at the table. "Indulging, Smith?" he asked. "Perhaps you have a bit of pirate in you, after all."

"Don't call me that," she muttered, sipping from the mug. "There's something wrong with the crew."

The captain didn't look up from his meal, dipping bread in the stew and stuffing it into his mouth. "My crew is my concern," he mumbled through his food.

"But they're behaving so strangely."

Tremayne glanced up. "What do you mean?"

Rina shrugged. "Tipping their hats, moving out of my way, saying *excuse me*. They're being . . . *polite*."

Tremayne grinned, shoveling up a spoonful of stew. "Oh, that."

Rina paused, the cup midway to her mouth. "Yes. *That*," she said, wondering at his tone. "Why are they acting like that?"

He just shrugged and continued eating. "It's to be expected, actually. Given your new status as the captain's woman."

She sighed heavily. "Can't we call it something else?"

Jonathan smirked. "Consort? Courtesan? Mistress?"

Rina waved a hand. "Fine. Fine. I suppose *captain's woman* will have to do," she said distastefully. "So now they're afraid of me or something?"

"Not actually *afraid*," he said hesitantly, swirling his spoon slowly in his bowl.

"Well, then what, exactly?"

He wiped his mouth with a linen napkin, glancing at her briefly. Was he nervous? She wasn't sure.

"The crew is aware how you first came to be on this ship, and what happened before you escaped to the *Intrepid*."

Rina winced. "They *all* know I tried to kill you?"

"Few secrets are kept on a ship, Smith." He sat back, crumbling a piece of bread between his fingertips. "They know you tried to kill me, yet I have now—as far as they know—taken you to my bed. They can only assume, therefore, that you must have talents significant enough to outweigh my need for vengeance."

"Talents?" Rina swallowed, feeling a bit nauseous.

Tremayne smiled wryly, holding up a finger. "*Significant* talents."

"In other words," Rina said, mouth dry and face flushing hot, "they think I've seduced you with my incredible skills."

"Indeed."

"But that doesn't explain why they're treating me this way," she prodded, unable to let the conversation go.

The captain chuckled lightly. "It's simple, really. Although I'm known to treat my women well, I rarely keep them for long."

She didn't like where this was going. "And . . .?"

"And," he continued with a wicked grin. "Since you are so incredibly skilled, they're all hoping for the opportunity to explore your charms. Once I'm finished with you."

Rina gasped, her hand flying to her forehead. "Good lord."

"It's rather flattering, if you think about it."

She glared at him, but he only laughed in response.

Rina drained her cup of rum and filled it again.

Forgoing the water this time.

Once Sarina had finished the rest of the stew and bread—Jonathan needed to make sure she brought food for herself from then on—he went back to work, and she left to take the dishes to the galley and relay a few orders to Hutchins.

He watched her leave, listening for her fading footsteps before opening the bottom drawer in his desk and retrieving the chest. He hadn't told Sarina the whole truth. There *were* secrets on his ship. And what he found in the chest was one of them.

With another glance toward the door, he opened the lid and lightly ran his fingers over the contents. A few coins, a jeweled comb, a carved wooden cross about the size of his palm.

But it was the locket he'd been hoping to find, and as he lifted it from the chest, he couldn't keep the victorious smile off his face. The silver oval was tarnished, the chain broken below the clasp, but he knew its shoddy exterior belied its importance. He studied the intricate knot on the front, an inverted triangle wrapped around an emerald the size of his fingernail. Turning the locket over, he picked up a magnifying glass to examine the engraving on the back.

*Ecce sto ad ostium et pulso.*

*Behold, I stand at the door and knock.*

The Apocalypse of St. John, Chapter 3, Verse 20. Another piece of Scripture, and again, Jonathan had no idea what it meant.

With a frown, he returned the necklace to the chest and flipped through the worn journal on his desk. He stopped, running his hand down the faded words, when he saw the familiar sketch along one of the page margins. It was the same locket, a simple rendering, but definitely identifiable. Below the drawing, two hastily scrawled words.

*The Key.*

For the hundredth time, Jonathan read through the rest of the entry on the page, mundane ramblings about daily life in the colonies, shopping at the marketplace, a trip to have a horse re-shod. Nothing to shed any light on the locket or its purpose.

Yet it was important. Evidently, it was *The Key.*

Jonathan sighed, closed the journal, and put both it and the chest back in the drawer. He locked it and dropped the key into a small cup tucked in a corner on the upper shelf behind him.

For the first time in months, he was unsure how to proceed. Rubbing his forehead, he poured himself a bit more rum and swallowed it in one gulp.

There was only one choice, really. He knew it. He just dreaded making it.

The next morning, he'd tell the crew to set sail for South Carolina.

He needed to speak to Charlotte.

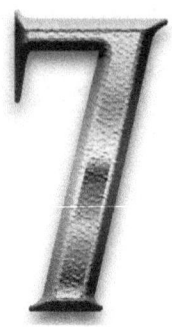

*One would think the gentle rocking of a ship would encourage sleep. I find, to te contrary, it serves only to exacerbate my violent illness. It appears I have not the constitution for sea travel, and I find my only relief is to climb to the deck and recline in the open air.*

*I fear this voyage may never end.*

*- The Journal of*
*Simon Alistair Mellick*
*22 July, 1664*

The dream was always the same. A memory from his past, wrapped in the darkness of his subconscious, lying in wait only to rear its head while he lay coddled in the complacency of sleep.

Although Jonathan *knew* it was a dream—could tell from the surreal way his surroundings blurred at the edges of his vision, melting and swirling like watercolors washed away by the rain—he could not force himself to wake up.

Terror quickened the beat of his heart, the pounding echo in his ears a countermelody to the rattling tick of raindrops on the slickened deck of the *Black Arrow*. Muffled grunts and clanging metal heralded the battle around him as the crew fought to keep the ship. They fought bravely, though many had already fallen, including Old Charlie Ceron—caught by surprise by a blade across his neck as he slept.

Jonathan's fingers clutched at his sword hilt, frozen despite the drip of hot blood down his arm. He held the blade with his left hand, his right clutched at the wound across his ribs, desperately holding together the flayed flesh as he struggled for breath, his back pressed against the wall behind him. The icy rain slashed at his exposed skin as he raised the sword again, unwilling to yield to his opponent.

A chilling laugh cut through the storm. "Why don't you give up, boy? You cannot defeat me. Just give me what I want and perhaps I'll spare your life."

A retort pressed at the back of Jonathan's gritted teeth, but he lacked the strength to force the words out. It took everything he had to hold the sword aloft, to surge forward and strike.

A ring of metal preceded the sharp sting up his arm, and Jonathan's sword clattered to the deck. He staggered, able to fight back the dizziness for only a moment before his legs gave out and he fell to his knees. His opponent grinned, blackened teeth almost invisible in the dark.

"And so it comes to this," he said. "Your great quest for vengeance ends not with a roar, but a pitiful whimper." He stepped forward, sword extended, until Jonathan felt the point prick at his throat. He swallowed, wincing as the blade pierced his skin, but in his exhaustion was unable to do anything but wait for the inevitable.

"You know, *Jack,* it's a pity, really. You put up a far better fight than your father."

A surge of red-hot fury gave Jonathan a burst of strength, and he dove across the deck, fingers scrabbling at the hilt of his sword as a boot landed hard on his back. He screamed in pain . . . again, as the boot shoved him over onto his back, then kicked the sword away.

Jonathan couldn't move. He lay unable to blink against the raindrops, his blood draining and pain numbing his entire body. He could just make out the pair of boots coming to a stop by his head and turned enough to meet his enemy's black gaze.

He would not look away from his death.

"Really, *Jack,* you're only postponing the inevitable." The sword returned to his throat. "Where is the journal?"

Jonathan glared in response. The man shrugged.

"Very well," he said with a sigh. "Make no mistake. I *will* find it, Jonathan. It's only a matter of time, something I have plenty of." He lifted a boot and settled it on Jonathan's chest as he lifted his sword for a final blow. "Unfortunately, you do not."

A flash of lightning lit the blade as it slashed through the air, a sight Jonathan was certain would be his last. He tightened his muscles for the killing blow, but it did no good. The sword sliced through him cleanly across his chest, blood spurting his life force onto the deck, a wickedly grinning face mocking him as he felt his death approach.

With a pained scream, Jonathan awoke in a cold sweat, damp sheets tangled between his legs. He sat up abruptly, his hands flying to his chest as his fingers explored the flesh.

No blood. No wounds. No pain. Nothing but the thick scar running up his ribs, and the other up his cheek, disappearing under his patch. He normally didn't wear it to sleep, but with his new bunkmate, he thought it best.

"Captain?" A soft voice called out, as if she'd heard his thoughts. "Are you all right?"

He started to reply, but the words caught. Clearing his throat, he said, "I'm fine. It's nothing."

"Bad dream?" She sounded closer, and Jonathan panicked slightly at the idea that she might come to him, see him at his weakest.

"I said it's nothing," he spat. Jonathan felt a twinge of regret for snapping at the woman when she'd only expressed concern. He still felt flayed by the dream, exposed in a way he let no one see. Usually, he was alone with his nightmares, able to turn on all the lamps and examine himself closely in the mirror. Only then could he truly believe that it had been nothing but a dream.

He hadn't died. Max had stepped in and diverted the blow, and instead of losing his life, he'd simply lost an eye. Well, even Jonathan had to admit it was a bit more serious than that. His recovery had taken months, and more than once he'd nearly succumbed to fever and infection. By the time he'd returned to the *Arrow,* the worst of his wounds were on their way to healing, but the worst of the scars were not physical.

The nightmares haunted him. Eventually, he learned to control his reactions and harness the pain and fear and hatred into a single-minded focus, a focus that eventually led to him becoming first mate of the *Arrow,* and finally the captain.

A focus that kept him going, even when shadows from the past threatened to cut him off at the knees.

"Fine," Sarina said quietly, and Jonathan could make out the quiet rustle of sheets as she returned to her bed. "I was only attempting to be considerate."

Jonathan settled back, kicking off his blankets and folding his arms behind his head. He knew why the dreams had returned so vividly as of late. He was getting closer to his goal, and his mind—even in sleep—knew he needed to be prepared for what lay ahead.

Or rather *who*.

He rolled onto one side, then the other, unable to get comfortable due to the unyielding hollowness in his stomach. He couldn't understand why he felt so empty. He'd had a fine supper, as well as a few biscuits before bed.

Then it hit him. It wasn't hunger.

It was guilt.

Which was all the more irritating. Why should he feel guilty? He was Jonathan Tremayne, Scourge of the High Seas. He didn't feel guilt or regret. He had a will of iron, a black heart incapable of such emotions.

Yet . . .

He flopped onto his back, throwing an arm over his eyes. With a heavy sigh, he pulled it away, staring unseeingly up into the darkness above him.

He cleared his throat. "Smith?"

No response.

"I . . . uh . . ." He took a deep breath. This should not have been so difficult. "I appreciate your concern," he said finally, waiting for her to laugh, or perhaps chastise him for apologizing without actually saying he was sorry.

Instead, Sarina Talbot surprised him yet again.

"I know nightmares can be frighteningly real," she said. "Would you . . . would you like to tell me about it?"

Jonathan swallowed thickly, overcome with a sudden desire to do just that. He fought back the urge, however. He was not one to rely on anyone, let alone a female.

Still, he managed to force a note of politeness into his voice as he spoke into the darkness. "Not at the moment. But thank you."

"Don't mention it."

Jonathan felt a weight lift, and he couldn't keep a slight smile off his lips. He rolled onto his side, and within a few moments he slipped into a dreamless sleep.

The next morning, Rina stood on deck, the wind whipping her hair loose from the knot at the back of her head. The ocean spread before them, wide and blue and tipped with frothy white. She kept her knees loose under her skirts, absorbing the sway of the ship without much trouble, and gazed out over the horizon, her mind whirling with thoughts as she worried her pendant between her thumb and forefinger.

When she'd come aboard the *Arrow*—on a bit of a whim, she had to admit now—everything had seemed so clear. She had a single goal in mind, to kill Tremayne, and everything she did was with that aim.

But now . . .

Now it had all become so complicated. She still wouldn't mind bringing Tremayne low, but she also had to work with him to make sure she discovered the absolute truth about who killed her father. What that would entail, Rina wasn't quite certain, and until then she found herself in the distasteful position of having to rely on the captain.

To *trust* him.

Her shoulders shifted at the uncomfortable thought, and she looked up, distracted for a moment by a shrieking gull overhead. She envied it a little, its freedom and single-mindedness.

Rina sighed. She still didn't know what she would do when she found out once and for all who was responsible for her father's death. She knew she couldn't kill him, whether it indeed be Tremayne or some other unsavory character. She would most likely need to work within the bounds of the law.

Which meant she would need evidence. Or a confession of guilt. Neither of which she was optimistic she would be able to procure.

Still, Tremayne seemed to want him dead as well. Perhaps the captain would accomplish the deed in her stead. A coward's way out perhaps, but in the end she would get what she wanted.

As for Tremayne? Well, that was yet another unanswered question. If he aided in her quest for vengeance, could she betray him by turning him over to Stanton, even if he was a criminal? Rina shook her head. It was just too much to consider at the moment. She needed to take things one step at a time. It was the only way.

A movement captured her attention, and she spotted the captain emerging from belowdecks to cross to the wheel and address Baines. The two men spoke, heads bent together, then Tremayne glanced her way.

She looked away hurriedly.

She'd been avoiding him since his nightmare, slipping out of his cabin before dawn and hiding out in the galley under the guise of helping the cook, Victor, bake the day's ration of bread. She'd learned from chatter among the crew that they were on their way to South Carolina, although she didn't know why, and had yet to work up the courage to ask Tremayne directly. Their middle-of-the-night conversation felt oddly intimate to Rina, leaving her unsure of what to say in the light of day and feeling a bit awkward about the encounter. It wasn't that she judged him for his moment of weakness. She didn't even see it as that, although she was insightful enough to know that *he* did. Rina had her own bouts with bad dreams after her father's death, and she hadn't been indulging Tremayne when she'd told him she understood.

It wasn't the nightmare, or even the conversation afterward, that left her uncomfortable, exactly.

It was that Jonathan Tremayne finally seemed . . . *human*.

Seeing him as a ruthless barbarian made it much easier to steel herself for what she had to do. But hearing his fearful whimpers as he battled his dream demons reminded her so much of herself. It wasn't pity so much as compassion, really.

But compassion was a dangerous thing. It distracted her. It made her weak.

The ship plunged over a large wave, salty spray washing over Rina's face. She shivered slightly and drew her shawl tighter about her shoulders.

"Sarina?"

She turned at the low voice, and smiled at the tall form of James Ceron. He grinned back at her, white teeth flashing in his dark skin, the details of his facial tattoo more visible in the daylight—a stylized dragon, head curving around his eye and body sweeping sinuously from temple to chin. A dimple in his cheek made the dragon's tail curve in on itself slightly, and lessened the intimidation factor considerably.

"James," she said. "How are you?"

"Well, thank you." He rolled his shoulders slightly. "The sleeping accommodations are much more comfortable on this ship, I have to admit."

She laughed. "Really? And I would have thought a tiny cage would be so cozy."

"You would think so, wouldn't you?" he said, feigning confusion. "Sadly, it is not the case."

His smile faded as he asked cautiously, "And you? Are you well?"

"Oh yes, I'm fine."

"The captain treats you decently?"

Rina flushed when she realized that of course James was under the same impression as the rest of the crew—that she was sharing a bed with the captain.

She leaned toward him, speaking quietly. "Things are not *exactly* as they appear."

"Oh?"

"The captain thought it best, for my own protection, that the crew be under the impression we are . . . romantically entangled."

"For your own protection."

"Yes."

James considered this for a moment, brow knit in concentration. "You know, Rina, you could have asked me for help. I would protect you. You needn't compromise yourself out of fear."

"I'm not compromising myself," she said quickly, glancing around and lowering her voice to ensure their conversation wasn't overheard. "That is the point. The crew believes it, but it isn't true."

"But your reputation . . ."

"My reputation was destroyed the moment I set foot on this ship," she said, resigned to a truth she had only just come to accept. "I can't concern myself with that. I have a higher purpose at hand."

"Ah, yes," James replied. "This mission you spoke of."

"Yes."

"And you must pose as Tremayne's harlot in order to succeed? It is *that* important?" He couldn't keep the bite of distaste out of his voice.

Rina stiffened, looking him in the eyes. "It is," she said. "And I'll thank you not to speak to me in that tone."

James drew a deep breath. "I apologize. I just . . ." He glanced back at where Tremayne stood at the wheel, steering with two fingers. "I don't entirely trust Tremayne."

"Well, that's good. Neither do I," Sarina admitted.

"Then why are you doing this?"

Rina drew a deep breath and turned to look out over the choppy sea. "I was actually standing here considering that very question," she said. "Tremayne says he knows the truth about who murdered my father."

James was silent for a long moment. Rina tilted her head to find him watching her closely.

"That's it?" he asked. "You're out for vengeance?"

"Justice," she corrected.

"Regardless of the word, it is a dangerous proposition, Rina."

"Yes, I'm aware of that."

"And you think Tremayne is going to aid you in this quest?" he asked, shaking his head. "That man is only out for treasure and power. He only thinks of himself."

"He claims his own quarrel with this man."

"Why?"

"He didn't say."

"Well, who is this man?" James asked.

"I don't know. Not yet." Rina looked away.

James ran a hand through his thick black hair, fisting it between his fingers. "You are playing a dangerous game, Sarina, and you don't even know who all the players are."

"I know what I'm doing."

"Do you?"

"James, listen," she said, turning to face him again. "I understand your concern. I do. And I appreciate it. But I am working with Tremayne, at least for the moment. I need to find out the truth about what happened. I *have* to know."

"And then what?"

"Then . . ." She sighed, pulling her shawl tight and hugging herself around the middle. "I'm not sure. I want him to pay, but to be completely honest, I'm not certain how just yet.

"I don't have all the answers," she said. "But I must find out the truth. Right now, that is all that I care about."

They stood, side by side, looking over the water. A fish jumped and a gull swept down just a moment too late to catch a meal.

"I understand . . ." James said finally. "I understand what it's like to lose a father."

Rina felt a wave of compassion. "I'm sorry."

"As am I, for you." He cleared his throat. "I will help you. If I can."

"Thank you, James."

He shrugged. "It is the least I could do for a fellow prison escapee," he joked, and the two shared a quiet laugh.

"I need to get back below," he said finally. "I have duties to attend to. But Rina, if you need me . . . please . . ."

She looked into his imploring eyes. "I'll ask. I promise."

He nodded, then turned to walk away. Rina caught sight of Tremayne across the deck, watching her, his gaze dark and unreadable.

She arched a brow, drew her shawl tighter about her, and returned to perusing the swelling waves.

Jonathan stood at the wheel, steering idly as the wind whipped about him, spray stinging his face. He'd finally dismissed Max to other duties, needing the salt air to clear his head and focus his thoughts.

He hated going to Charlotte for help.

It wasn't that he disliked his sister. Far from it. He loved her deeply and counted her as one of his closest friends, as well.

But Charlotte saw too much and never feared or resisted sharing her opinion. And, Jonathan had to admit, there were times he'd prefer not to hear it. She also worried about him, about his life and his choices, and fussed over him like a mother hen. It was equal parts endearing and irritating, but not something he would ever want his crew to witness.

Except Baines, of course. The man wouldn't stay back on the ship, even if he ordered him to. Max was disgustingly besotted with Jonathan's sister and had been since the day he had first laid eyes on her. When Jonathan had given the order to set sail for Charles Towne, he couldn't miss the stiffening of Max's spine, the slight flush of his cheeks.

It was pathetic, really. Jonathan preferred not to dwell on it though, not particularly enthusiastic about a train of thought that could potentially lead to mental images of his best friend with his sister.

He could hardly be blamed.

Again, his gaze drifted to where Sarina stood at the starboard gunwale, looking over the water. She was alone now, and Jonathan was glad Jamie Ceron had finally returned to his duties. Several times he'd almost stalked over to where the two stood laughing and talking—rather intimately and inappropriately, he might add, given Sarina's status as his woman—to order the man to get back to work. It wasn't that it bothered him, of course, but he would not have his crew viewing him as a cuckold, even if his relationship with Sarina was a fabrication in the first place.

It was the principle of the thing.

He watched her as she stood quietly—the quietest he'd ever seen her, except for sleeping—and wondered what might be going through her mind.

She was insane, thinking she could seek vengeance for her father's death. Jonathan knew who was responsible, and Sarina, as annoying and hardheaded as she was, was no match for him. Still, he couldn't help feeling a bit of satisfaction at the fact that when he exacted his revenge, he would be acting for her as well.

It was the least he could do if Sarina helped him find what he sought.

His mind whirled as he considered the contents of the journal and the items listed which he'd already procured: the cutlass and the locket. But the cup . . . the cup was out there somewhere, and he had no idea where to begin searching for it. The last he'd heard, it was in the custody of Mellick's grandnephew, but the man had died three years earlier, his estate sold off to pay debts and the cup vanishing without a trace.

Which led him to Charlotte.

She'd know he was coming, of course, and she'd know why. She always did. Which made it all the more irritating when she refused to acknowledge it. Charlotte would make Jonathan ask, even though she knew what he was going to ask before he asked it.

He frowned. Sometimes his sister drove him absolutely insane. Jonathan was relatively certain she was aware of that fact and actually reveled in it.

But she kept his secrets, even from his father, and for that, Jonathan had to be grateful.

For Charlotte was the only one who knew, apart from Max, that Jonathan's single-minded goal to seek out the relics wasn't about treasure, at least not entirely.

It was about beating *him*. It was about finding *him*.

For once Jonathan found the man responsible for his nightmares and his wounds, wounds that flowed much more deeply than a few scars, he would make him pay.

The name sizzled through his brain, burning behind his eyes.

*Kane.*

The man had taken everything from him, destroyed his family, destroyed his life. And Jonathan would not rest until he repaid the favor.

He absently noticed as Sarina turned from the water and walked back through the doorway toward his quarters.

She would have her vengeance, too.

But only after she helped him get his.

*I see now why they call it the New World. It is vast, uncharted land, full of mysteries and wonder. Perhaps, once my mission is complete I may explore it further.*

*Until then, I have secured transportation south. I am leery to set foot on a ship again, so will travel by land as far as I am able. Perhaps the warmer seas of the Caribbean will prove more hospitable than the violent Atlantic.*

*I can yet but hope.*

*- The Journal of*
*Simon Alistair Mellick*
*23 October, 1664*

"Damn it, Smith!"

Rina smirked as she scrubbed the captain's laundry, his voice echoing up the passageway to the deck. She rubbed a bit of soap into his breeches and dipped them into the water as she began to hum lightly.

In a moment, Tremayne appeared in the doorway, and Sarina had to bite her lip to keep from laughing. He had a shirt over his head, but one hand was caught in the sleeve where she'd sewn the cuff shut. The other sleeve was completely missing, the armhole sewn closed, so his right hand stuck out the hem of his shirt. His gaze swept the deck until he spotted her, then he stalked over, a murderous scowl on his face.

Rina wrung out the breeches and set them in her basket before drying her hands on her apron and looking up.

"Good morning, Captain," she said cheerfully, getting to her feet.

"Good morning?" he bellowed. "That's all you have to say for yourself?"

She gazed at him blankly. "I'm certain I have no idea what you mean."

"Oh, well I'm certain you most *certainly* do!" He sneered, waving his sleeve at her. "Look what you've done to my shirt!"

She examined the sleeve carefully. "It would appear the sleeve has been sewn shut, sir."

"Oh, really?" he said mockingly, shaking the sleeve at her face. "I hadn't noticed!"

Rina fought to maintain her innocent expression. "That's rather surprising. I would imagine it makes it difficult to wear."

He leaned in, his face inches from hers. "You think this is funny? Do you? Well, we'll see how funny it is when you're chained to the mizzen!"

She frowned. "You can't be serious."

"Try me," Tremayne snarled. "Baines!"

For the first time, Rina noticed the curious glances of the crew gathered nearby. Rafferty, his nose still swollen and bruised, glared at her—a usual occurrence of late—and turned to head belowdecks. The first mate hurried forward.

"Aye, Cap'n?"

"Put this woman in irons!" Tremayne pointed at Rina with his sewed-up sleeve. Baines bit his lip, and for a split-second Sarina thought he might have been amused, but just as quickly, his expression sobered.

"Aye, Cap'n," he said gruffly, taking Rina by the arm and leading her to one of the masts. Another crewman stepped forward with shackles, and Baines pushed her back, stretching her arms behind her and part way around the mast before locking the shackles around her wrists.

"You can't leave me like this!" she shouted.

Baines arched a brow. "'Tis not a good idea to anger the captain."

"No, wait." Tremayne stepped forward, tapping his chin with his free hand. Sarina tried not to notice the expanse of golden skin exposed by the motion. "Bind her to the mast, but free her hands. She still has work to do."

Rina huffed. "As if I'd do anything for you, you barbarian!"

"You'll do as you're told," Tremayne hissed. "Or you'll spend the rest of this voyage tied to this post. Don't test me, wench. You. Will. Lose."

Baines and the other crewman approached with a length of rope. "You should probably sit down," he suggested. Sarina considered refusing for a moment, but then he added, "You're likely to be there for a while. It will be more comfortable."

Rina lifted her chin but slid down the post to sit on the deck. They tied her firmly, the rope looped around her waist and just under her arms, before releasing the shackles.

Tremayne watched with satisfaction, pulling on the ropes to test their strength before nodding at Baines in approval. "Get one of the boys to retrieve my trunk so the wench can get to work." He turned to her, pulling off his shirt and tossing it into her lap. "I expect *all* of my clothes to be mended properly before you're released," he snarled. "*All* of them. And do not toy with me, Smith, or you will pay dearly."

She met his glare with one of her own, trying desperately to avoid looking at his bare chest. Her cheeks flamed with anger and embarrassment, but she knew she'd been bested, at least this time. Her gaze dropped, and she heard Tremayne's victorious chuckle.

He turned on his heel and strode toward the wheel as a young boy dragged Tremayne's trunk over to her and threw open the lid. He handed her a sewing kit and scurried off without a word. Rina picked up the shirt with a frown and began to pull out the stitches on the cuff.

She sighed heavily, annoyed at herself for letting this childish bit of retribution drive her further from her goal. She was supposed to get *closer* to Tremayne, not make him angry. He was just so blasted arrogant it was difficult for her to hold back. Her temper was proving to be her worst enemy.

Rina grimaced, knowing what she had to do. She had to gain Tremayne's trust. Which meant she had to be . . . *nice*. No matter how distasteful the thought, how irritating and frustrating and infuriating the man was, it was the only way. She rolled her shoulders, trying to relax her muscles.

She could do it. She could be nice. How hard could it be?

Rina snipped a thread, glancing up at Tremayne surreptitiously. He stood at the helm, talking with Crawley, his fingers loosely wrapped around the wheel.

She definitely did *not* notice the way his golden skin played over the muscles of his back, or the way his breeches hung on his hips, his sword belt cutting in slightly to the exposed flesh.

She did *not* notice the glint of his teeth as he laughed at something Crawley said.

She did *not* feel her stomach flip or her skin heat as he stretched his arms up and his belt slipped just a *little* lower.

And she most definitely did *not* burst out laughing at the sight of the sock she'd sewn into the back seam of Tremayne's trousers, currently flapping about like the tail of a dog.

Instead she smiled and got back to work, thinking it was completely worth it. Even if she had ended up tied to the mizzen mast.

Jonathan kept a close eye on Sarina as she mended his clothing, or rather, re-mended it. He tried not to show his surprise at the rather impressive pile of garments around her. The wench had obviously been pretty determined in her efforts.

He couldn't keep back a slight smile at the idea. For such a tiny thing, she was a worthy adversary, he had to admit.

As the sun peaked, he quietly ordered that she be brought some water and a bit of hardtack. Despite Sarina's opinion, he was not, in fact, a barbarian. Eventually, he made his way over to her, picking up a shirt and examining it closely before pulling it over his head. He looked down at her, surprised when her eyes dropped and her cheeks flushed pink.

He opened his mouth to comment but for once found he didn't know what to say. Instead, he turned to Max.

"Check her work, and if it's done satisfactorily, cut her loose," he said gruffly.

Max nodded, and—to Jonathan's surprise—Sarina smiled up at him sweetly.

"Thank you," she said.

Jonathan stared at her for a moment, unsure of how to respond. His eye narrowed. "Don't be trying your feminine wiles on me, Smith."

"Wiles?" Sarina said innocently. "I am just trying to make peace, Captain. You were right. I shouldn't have done this to your clothes. It was childish, and I apologize." The ropes loosened and she got to her feet, stretching with a wide smile. "It feels good to be free again. I suppose I should get all of this put away, yes?" Jonathan watched in shock, unable to look away as she gathered the folded clothes, put them in the trunk, and closed it with a satisfied sigh.

She turned to Max. "Mister Baines, do you suppose you could have someone take this back to the captain's quarters for me? It is a bit heavy, and I really should see to the captain's supper."

"Um." Max glanced nervously at Jonathan, who had yet to find his tongue. "Yes . . . yes, of course, Miss. I'll see to it."

"Thank you," she said, brushing her hands over her skirt and flashing Jonathan another bright smile before heading toward the galley. Jonathan and Max watched her go in stunned silence.

"What in the world was that all about?" Max murmured.

"I have no idea," Jonathan replied. "But I don't trust that wench for a second."

"I don't blame you," Max replied. "Have you seen the seat of your trousers?"

Jonathan's hand flew to his backside, and he growled in frustration when he felt the sock dangling behind him. "That woman is evil incarnate."

Max smirked. "You just don't like the fact that she's not afraid of you."

"Well, she should be," he retorted. "I can't decide if she's incredibly brave or incredibly stupid."

"She's not stupid."

"No, I suppose not," Jonathan admitted, turning to head to his quarters.

Max hefted the trunk and walked beside him. "Are you sure it's a good idea? Keeping her on board?"

"You're not going to give me that superstitious nonsense about a woman on a ship being bad luck."

"I'm not the one with a sock sewn to my arse, am I?" At the captain's glare, he forced a sober look. "Superstition or not, a woman on board is a bad idea. The men don't like it."

"What they like or don't like is irrelevant in this case."

"I understand you wish to make her pay—"

"It's not about that." Jonathan glanced about to ensure their privacy before replying, his voice barely a whisper. "She's Danny

Talbot's daughter," he said. "It's possible she has information that could prove useful."

"And you think she'll be sharing that information with you?" Max snorted, shifting the weight of the trunk. "She doesn't exactly seem to like you, let alone trust you."

"Not yet, but she'll come around."

"Oh? What makes you so certain?"

Jonathan grinned, holding his arms wide. "How can she resist?"

Rina gritted her teeth as she approached the captain's quarters, his booming laughter grating on her nerves. She took a deep breath before walking through the open doorway, painting on a smile and balancing his supper tray carefully in her hands. She hummed as she set the tray on the table, arranging the plate and silver and straightening the napkin before pouring a tankard of rum.

"I hope you're hungry!" She looked up to find Tremayne and Baines staring at her suspiciously. Perhaps she'd overdone it. Was it possible to be too nice?

"Is something wrong?" she asked innocently.

The two men exchanged a look and Tremayne approached the table, sat down and took a tentative bite of his meat. Baines sat across from him and poured rum into another mug, drinking it down in two gulps, an amused smile on his face.

"My boots need polishing, Smith," Tremayne said gruffly. "And the bed linens need to be changed and washed."

She glanced mournfully at the pile of linens and blankets on the bed. Washing them would take forever.

"Of course," she said, the words catching slightly.

"You'll need to scrub the floor," he added. "Be sure to move the furniture so you can get it all."

Baines emitted a choked sound, quickly covering it with another swallow of rum.

"Yes, sir."

"Then you can see to my chamber pot."

Rina stiffened. "Your chamber pot?"

Tremayne chewed on a piece of bread. "It needs to be emptied, then scrubbed thoroughly."

"But . . ." She swallowed, trying to keep control of her temper. *Be nice*, she thought. "But, I thought we agreed no chamber pots."

The captain shrugged, washing down a mouthful of food with some rum. "My chamber pot needs cleaning, so I'm renegotiating our agreement."

"You . . . you can't do that!"

*Be nice.*

"No?" he asked. "I believe I just did."

Rina inhaled deeply and let it out slowly. Again. And again.

It wasn't helping.

"Or," Tremayne continued, his tone conversational as he swiveled in his seat, eyeing her intently. "You could tell me exactly what you're up to, Smith."

Rina swallowed, her anger quickly giving way to nervousness. "What do you mean?"

His gaze didn't waver. "I can tolerate many things. But if we are to adhere to this agreement between you and me, one thing I demand is honesty."

"Honesty?" she huffed. "As if you know the meaning of the word!"

"I know it doesn't mean pretending to be some dim-witted female in order to gain my trust."

Rina flushed. Apparently her ruse was not as successful as she'd hoped.

"I may withhold certain information, but I have never lied to you," he added.

"Oh?" she said, hands propped on her hips. "Then tell me what you know of my father."

Tremayne became suddenly interested in his plate, pushing the food around with his fork. Baines swirled a finger around the rim of his tankard, eyes flickering from the captain to Sarina and back again with interest.

"Come now, Captain," Rina wheedled. "Where is all of this newfound honesty? You knew his name. You knew he had a daughter. What I don't understand is how a no-good—" Her words cut off at his irritated glare. "How a *pirate* became acquainted with a law-abiding businessman like my father."

Tremayne considered her challenge for a moment, then glanced at Baines and jerked his head slightly. The first mate rose and left the room without a word, closing the door behind him. The captain gestured toward the now empty chair across from him, and with an irritated huff, Rina sat down.

"Why don't you start by telling *me* what you know of your father," he said. Rina rolled her eyes in annoyance, and he held up a hand. "Just bear with me, please," he said. "It would be simpler for me to fill in the blanks than to tell you things you already know."

She frowned, annoyed at the idea that Tremayne would know any of the blanks in her father's life, but she nodded in acquiescence anyway.

"My father was a good man," she said. "He served in the Royal Navy for most of my life. My mother died when I was born, and his sister, my aunt, cared for me while he was at sea. She died of the influenza when I was fourteen, and he resigned his commission so he could return home to be with me.

"He took up a position in trade and became quite successful. Then, one night a noise awakened me—a gunshot—and I found him in his study . . ." Her words trailed off as she swallowed the lump in her throat.

"I found him," she said roughly, suddenly taken back to that moment, her memories playing out before her. "He lay bleeding on the carpet. There was blood everywhere . . ." She swiped at her cheeks, unsure when she'd begun to cry. "The room had been ransacked, papers everywhere, but all I could see was him. I dropped to my knees, and he looked up at me as I took his head in my lap." She droned on, in a daze as the memories swept over her. "He tried to speak, but his mouth filled with blood.

"In the end, he said only one word," she said, fixing him with a tear-filled stare.

"What did he say?" His jaw flexed, and she knew he already knew.

"Tremayne."

He looked away, his voice a gruff whisper. "And that is why you think I killed him? Because he said my name?"

Rina took a deep breath, gathering herself. "Of course not. I didn't even know who you were, after all. I hired an investigator, who looked into the matter. He was the one who pointed me in your direction.

"But why else, Captain? Why else would he say your name with his dying breath, other than to identify you as his murderer?"

Tremayne gazed unseeingly for a long moment, and Sarina began to wonder if he would reply. Then he turned and looked into her eyes, and she was shocked at the intensity there . . . the resolve.

"Because Danny Talbot never sailed for the Crown," he said. "He was a pirate. And for a few short years, he was my friend."

In the warm waters south of Jamaica, the pirate ship *Abaddon's Curse* stood at full alert, her crew braced for battle with swords and pistols drawn. With a confident swagger, the ship's captain strode across the deck, watching an approaching vessel with wary, yet confident, eyes.

It was not a Crown ship and was smaller than his own, so Captain Kane—known for many years as Kane the Merciless that his proper surname was long forgotten—felt no compulsion to flee. Instead, he readied his crew for the encounter with high hopes there might be some treasure to be had at the end of the day. Why the ship was headed toward them at full sail had him a bit curious, however, and with an unspoken order, he held out a hand to his first mate, Barton. The man placed a spyglass in his palm, and Kane raised it to his eye, the ship coming into focus.

"'Tis the *Enchanted Lady*," he murmured to himself. "What is Renard about?"

"He wouldn't dare attack," Barton replied.

"No." The captain collapsed the spyglass, tucking it into his pocket. As a privateer, Renard had built a considerable reputation in the Caribbean—for both his legal, and not-so-legal endeavors—but no one dared attack the *Abaddon's Curse*. Even the British Navy gave Kane a wide berth unless forced to confront him. "But we best be prepared nonetheless."

Barton nodded, and at his order, the rest of the crew came to attention as the *Lady* drew nearer with every minute. It finally slowed off the port stern and dropped anchor, a white flag flapping wildly in the breeze.

"Sir?" Barton asked quietly.

"Steady," Kane replied. "Let's see what he wants."

After a few moments, he spotted a dinghy making its way toward them with only two men on board, Captain Renard and a crewman pulling the oars. The remainder of the crew stood on board the *Lady*, watching the goings on with interest.

"They are not armed," Kane pointed out, indicating the other ship's crew. He still deferred ordering his crew down from alert. He hadn't become the most-feared pirate on the open sea by letting his guard down easily.

Renard looked up at him as the dinghy approached and held up a hand in greeting, a white flag dangling from his fingertips. Kane granted them permission to board with a curt nod, and his men parted to allow the two men onto the deck, hands still poised on their weapons.

"Captain Kane," Renard said, doffing his hat with a flourish. "You are looking well."

Kane nodded. "What is this about, Renard?"

The *Lady's* captain glanced about nervously. "I was hoping perhaps to speak with you in private. It is a most urgent matter."

Kane eyed him consideringly, then turned to one of his men. "Search him."

"I assure you I am unarmed," Renard insisted, holding his hands up as the crewman patted down his frame. "I come in peace."

Kane snorted. "Peace?"

Renard grinned. "Well, in this case at least."

The crewman stepped back and Kane led Renard, flanked by Barton and his quartermaster, Cromwell, to his quarters. He sprawled in a large leather chair, black eyes regarding Renard piercingly as he perched on a smaller wooden one.

"Now," Kane said, "What is this about?"

Renard's expression sobered and he licked his lips nervously. "I . . . uh . . . understand you have an interest in One-Eyed Jack Tremayne."

Kane maintained a stoic façade. "What do you know of Tremayne?"

"I know he boarded my ship and plundered my cargo," Renard said with a sneer. "Left my crew and passengers bound like animals."

Kane smirked. "Well, that does come along with the territory, doesn't it, Mattias?" he asked. "You are far from innocent in these matters yourself."

Renard shrugged. "Regardless, I believe we could be of assistance to each other."

Kane leaned an elbow on the arm of the chair, running a finger over his lips. "How so?"

"If you are searching for Tremayne, I would like to help."

Kane laughed. "And what makes you think I need your help?"

"Perhaps not," Renard admitted. "But a second ship, a second crew, could prove useful when you finally find him."

"Aye," Kane said thoughtfully. "And what would you be getting out of this arrangement?"

Renard's eyes narrowed. "I simply want to see One-Eyed Jack brought down a peg or two. If you're out to do that, I believe we have the same goal."

Kane stood and paced slowly across the room. Tremayne was a bothersome arse, he had to admit. The fact that he'd retrieved the cutlass still grated on his nerves, and if he'd ransacked the *Lady*, Kane wagered he'd found the pendant as well.

Yes, Tremayne had become a thorn in his side, and one that must be dealt with soon.

Renard was wrong, however, when he said Kane was looking for One-Eyed Jack. Because Kane knew it was only a matter of time before Tremayne came looking for *him*. Still, he had to admit Renard's ship and crew could come in useful when it came to taking down the *Arrow's* captain. Kane knew better than to underestimate the boy. He'd already cheated death once.

He turned, fixing Renard with a penetrating, black stare. "You, your ship, and your crew will be under my command. I will not tolerate any insubordination."

Renard tilted his head in deference. "As you wish. As I said, I only wish to see Tremayne punished, and hopefully retrieve some of my cargo."

"Any booty will be divided by my quartermaster," Kane snapped. "Do not think I am allying myself with you in order to line your pockets, Mattias."

"Of course not," he replied, swallowing thickly. "I only ask that my crew be rewarded for their loyalty as yours will be."

Kane's chin lifted, then he nodded once. "Done."

A slow smile lit Captain Renard's face as he stood and extended his hand. "We have an accord, then?"

Kane took it in a firm grip. "Aye, Captain. We have an accord."

*I had hoped to be nearing the Spanish colonies by now, but a vicious early winter storm has thwarted my attempts. Instead, I find myself snowbound, anxiously awaiting the warmer weather that will allow me to travel.*

*My only consolation is the storm has also delayed my competitors in this venture. I received word today that the expedition's ship was forced to take refuge on a small island off the coast of Spain.*

*So as I must wait, they must also.*

*- The Journal of*
*Simon Alistair Mellick*
*1 November, 1664*

"You're a liar!" Sarina jumped to her feet and slammed her hands on the table. The dishes clattered, a bit of rum sloshing over the rim of Jonathan's tankard. "My father was a good man. He was nothing like . . . like . . ."

"Like me?" Jonathan offered. Sarina's face reddened in fury, and he felt a twinge of compassion. What he had to say couldn't have been easy to hear.

"I told you, Sarina, I'll not lie to you," he said quietly. "But you are the one who asked me about your father. If you want to know the truth, you must listen."

He held her gaze for a moment, and slowly she sank back into her chair. With a trembling hand, she lifted the tankard to her lips, choking slightly as she swallowed. She looked up at Jonathan expectantly.

"I came on board the *Arrow* when I was seventeen years old," he began. "I took a position as cabin boy under Captain George Randall. I did a bit of everything—not unlike you," he said with a slight grin. "Over the next few years, I got to know the ship, the crew, worked a bit with the ship's carpenter, then the Gunner, and eventually worked my way up to mate."

Sarina interrupted. "What does this have to do with my father?"

"Your father," he replied, "was quartermaster of the *Arrow*."

At Sarina's wide-eyed expression, he continued. "He *was* a good man. You were right about that. He spoke often of the wife he lost and the beautiful daughter he had back on the mainland. Kept saying he was just saving his earnings so he could go home to her . . . to you."

Sarina's eyes filled with tears, and her gaze dropped to the table as her fingers fluttered at her throat.

"The captain led us on a raid that promised a vast treasure," he said, his voice a low rumble as he relived the adventure. "We were to board at dawn, thinking to take them by surprise." He paused, taking a gulp of rum. "But they were ready for us. In fact, it was a cunningly laid trap. They were following us from a distance and attacked while we slept.

"I was still young—barely twenty—and had yet to really prove myself in battle. But we all had to fight that night. The air was thick with smoke and screams . . . and the blood. Damn, there was so much blood."

Sarina watched him with rapt attention, but he'd almost forgotten she was there.

"I spotted the captain on the far side of the deck, fighting against two men—sword in one hand, dagger in the other—but it wasn't a fair fight, and it was only a matter of time . . .

"He fell to the deck, and I was the only one nearby. They didn't see me coming. I'd never killed a man before." He paused, gaze lost in the distance, before he cleared his throat.

"I got one, and it was enough of a distraction for the captain to regain his footing and dispatch the other. By the time the fighting ended, we'd lost six men—including our first mate, Old Charlie Ceron, James' father. I myself was severely wounded in the fray." He touched his eye patch lightly.

He met her gaze. "In appreciation for saving his life, Captain Randall named me first mate once I'd recovered. But after that night, Danny was never the same. He'd lost his taste for the sea, I suppose, or perhaps he was just tired of the killing.

"In any event, it was perhaps a year or so later that he got word that his sister had died. He left the ship, said he was going to live a normal life, that he would at least give that to his little girl. I never saw him again."

Sarina wiped the tears from her cheeks, and he could tell her mind swirled with questions.

"And how did you become captain?" she asked after a moment.

Jonathan chuckled humorlessly. "A captain's life is rarely a long one, Smith," he said. "Captain Randall was shot in the leg and died of a fever shortly after your father left. The crew chose me as captain, and I've been serving as such for nigh on six years now."

Sarina stood, slowly pacing across the room as she absorbed all she had heard. Jonathan watched her silently as she came to terms with the fact that her father was not the man she thought he was.

"I can't believe he lied to me," she murmured, half to herself, as she gazed out the porthole on the far side of the room. "All those years, and it was all a lie."

"Not all," Jonathan said. "He did love you, Sarina. He wanted the best for you. He did what he thought he had to do to provide for you. The rest was to protect you."

Sarina snorted. "Protect me? It sounds like he was trying to protect himself."

"Our world is a dangerous one. You, of all people, should understand that now."

"I suppose." She sighed heavily. "It just hurts. I thought I knew him better than anyone."

"You did," Jonathan assured her. "You knew the true Danny Talbot. The man he wanted to be."

Sarina swiped at her cheeks again, squaring her shoulders before returning to sit across from Jonathan and take another sip of rum.

"You seem to be acquiring a taste for that," he said with a grin. "Perhaps we'll make a pirate of you yet."

She smiled, and Jonathan couldn't explain the rush of relief that swept through him at the small gesture.

"So," she said. "If you didn't kill my father, how did you come to possess his cutlass?"

Jonathan raised a brow. "First of all, it's *my* cutlass," he pointed out. She opened her mouth to argue, but he cut her off. "As for how it came into my possession, I liberated it from the man I believe killed your father."

Sufficiently distracted from true ownership of the sword, she asked, "And you still won't tell me who that is?"

Jonathan looked down at his plate with a frown. His instincts warred within him. On the one hand, he hesitated to reveal too much to her, not so much because he feared she would go off on her own. Surely by now she realized that her best chance to find her father's killer lay with him.

No, his concern was more about revealing too much about himself. Aside from Max, and of course, Charlotte, no one knew what drove him. Why he was who he was—why he had become who he'd become.

"I think we've moved beyond secrets, don't you think, Captain?" she added. "If you want me to trust you, perhaps it's time you did the same."

Perhaps just a little. Perhaps he could tell her just a bit, for Danny's sake. And then maybe, just maybe, she would trust him enough to provide some information of her own.

With a deep breath, he looked at her. "His name is Kane," he said. "He's called Kane the Merciless. He is the one who killed your father. The one who took my eye." He touched his patch lightly. "Nearly took my life. And he is the one who will pay."

Sarina held his gaze for a moment before nodding once. "All right then."

Abruptly, Jonathan shoved away from the table. "I'm needed on deck," he said, slipping into his coat and waving at the table. "Be sure and clean this up, Smith, and then see to my boots." He smirked slightly. "No need to concern yourself with the chamber pot."

Sarina's lips twitched. "Aye, Captain."

He hesitated, tempted to say something more, before he turned about and stalked from the room without another word.

She knew there was more to it, of course. Rina was adept enough at reading people to know that Tremayne spoke the truth about Kane—*Kane the Merciless*, of course he would have a name like that—but he still held back from telling her everything.

It was all right. Sarina could be patient.

Or . . .

Her eyes flitted from the closed door to Tremayne's desk and back again.

Perhaps she didn't have to be patient.

She stood and walked to the door, pressing her ear against it and listening intently before sliding the bolt home. She'd have a difficult time explaining why it was locked but didn't dare risk someone walking in on her.

She could always say she was dressing, she supposed.

Rina's heart raced, and she swallowed a lump of guilt as she moved to the desk. True, the captain had shown trust in her by telling her what he had, but she didn't entirely trust *him*, and she didn't like going into something without all of the information possible. Surely that was enough to justify her snooping?

She shook her head irritably. Why was she worrying about, of all things, Tremayne's feelings? He was a bloody pirate, had her working as his servant, and if they were to be allied in this endeavor, she deserved to know what it was all about. Really, *he* should be the one feeling guilty if he was keeping something from her.

And she *knew* he was keeping something from her.

She flipped through the papers on top of the desk, and after finding nothing of import, began to rifle through the drawers. When she came to the bottom one and found it locked, a surge of excitement rushed through her. Rina scanned the room, quickly spotting the dirk she'd kept in her boot lying next to her cot. She retrieved it and worked it gingerly into the lock, wiggling it about.

She'd just about given up hope when she heard a low click, and the drawer slid open. The sight of the chest from the *Enchanted Lady* put a victorious smile on her face, and she lifted it out carefully, along with a thick leather-bound book. With another quick glance at the door, she opened the chest, biting her lip as she examined the items inside: a hair comb, some coins, an emerald necklace, and a carved wooden cross. She held the smooth wood in her hand, examining the engraving running the length of it.

*Latin*, she thought, although she had no idea what it said.

More confused than ever, she placed the items carefully back into the chest and closed it. Why would Tremayne be so possessive of a chest holding only a few trinkets? Although pretty, they really held very little value when compared to the rest of the booty they'd retrieved from the *Lady*. Yet, it had to be important somehow.

Frowning, she turned to the book, running her hand over the worn leather cover. She sat down in Tremayne's chair and opened it to the first page.

*Simon Alistair Mellick*

*15 Kipling Street, Southwark, London*

The address was scratched out, and underneath was added: *Parts Unknown.*

She read a bit and quickly ascertained that it was a journal belonging to a tradesman in London in the mid-1660s. She still did not understand why Tremayne would keep it under lock and key, however. Scanning the pages absently and reading snippets here and there, she'd almost given up on finding anything of use. This Mellick seemed to have been a relatively boring man, his entries bland descriptions of day-to-day life, along with rather sad yearnings for something more. Apparently, he'd come to the Colonies at some point to start a new life.

Sarina almost missed the drawing at first, just catching a brief glimpse as she flipped through the pages. She turned back quickly, mouth dropping open in shock at the rendering of her father's cutlass.

It couldn't be.

At first, Rina feared she was being fanciful, so she sprang to her feet to retrieve the cutlass from the shelf behind Tremayne's desk to compare it to the sketch. Sure enough, it was identical, even to the intricate details on the cupped knuckle guard. Her gaze darted between the drawing and the cutlass, unable to believe what she was seeing. A second sketch depicted the top of the hilt, every facet of the sapphire true to life, and even the engraved words circling the gem proved an accurate rendering. Heart pounding, she quickly read through the entry on the page below the drawing, disappointment warring with confusion when she found no reference to the sword.

She read through it again, just to be sure, but Simon Mellick, whoever he was, simply went on and on about the purchase of some kind of puzzle box to add to a collection that had been handed down from his father. Rina explored the entries on the pages before and after the drawing, but found no mention of it. She glanced nervously at the door, aware that it was only a matter of time before Tremayne became curious about her absence on deck, expecting her to appear at any moment to do his bidding. She flipped through the pages quickly, scanning them as the cutlass lay cool and heavy across her lap.

She'd just about given up when she noticed a loose page near the back of the book. The ragged edge proved it had been torn out at some point, but then tucked back into place. Her eyes widened when the word *sword* all but jumped off the page at her.

*The sword will lead the way.*

Confused, her eyes lifted to the beginning of the entry, the words whispering through her lips as she read.

*Pay heed to the Word*
*'Twill be your true guide*
*Quench thirst with the cup*
*A coin to give sight*
*A key for the door*
*A mind for a map*
*Then cross the bridge, to bridge the gap*
*Seek Aphrodite's kiss, whence light doth play*
*And the sword will lead the way*

Rina read it through three times, but the words were no clearer. Was it some kind of poem? A code? Did it really have anything to do with the cutlass at all? Her gaze dropped to the sword in her lap, and she ran her fingers over the hilt gently, her eyes lighting on the engraving around the sapphire.

*And God said, "Let there be light, and there was light."*

Her father had translated it for her shortly before . . .

Light.

*. . . whence light doth play . . .*

*Let there be light . . .*

It had to be more than a coincidence, didn't it?

With a determination founded in instinct more than knowledge, she shuffled through Tremayne's desk until she found a scrap of paper, then quickly copied the poem and tucked it into her pocket. She replaced the journal and the chest in the bottom desk drawer and set the cutlass back on the shelf, touching it once more reverently before turning to gather the items to polish Tremayne's spare boots.

She knew the captain was keeping things from her, and she couldn't help but think that this Mellick's journal, and the rather obscure entry referring to the sword, had something to do with it. There was a reason the cutlass was important to him, and she believed she'd just gotten the clue as to what it was.

Of course, even having known the captain only a short time, she'd learned there were only three things that truly motivated him—pleasure, vengeance, and treasure—and he generally got the first from the latter two.

*And the sword will lead the way.*

Lead the way to what? Kane? Treasure?

Rina found that either one would give *her* pleasure.

That night, she hid the scrap of paper under her pillow, certain it was the key to something important.

Early the next morning, Rina woke to find Tremayne already up and gone. After dressing quickly, she tucked the poem into her pocket, then stripped his bed, stuffing the soiled linens into the empty washtub. As she made her way on deck, she spotted Tremayne by the wheel, his gaze darting to light on hers. His shoulders relaxed a bit, as if he'd been searching for her.

*Odd.*

She set the washtub down and slipped her hand into her pocket, fingering the scrap of paper lightly. Tremayne may have had his secrets, but Rina felt confident she could discover them in time. If not, she would simply have to convince him to reveal them.

She hazarded one more glance over her shoulder to find Tremayne watching her, brow raised in curiosity. She shrugged and turned back to her laundry.

Tremayne could wonder what *she* was up to for a change. It seemed only fitting.

In the meantime, she would try to untangle the mystery surrounding the sword herself.

She was up to something.

Jonathan watched Sarina scrub his bedsheets, studiously avoiding looking in his direction, and he could tell she was up to no good. She wrung out the last bit of linen, then stood to clip it to a makeshift clothesline strung across a small section of the deck. She caught his gaze and looked away quickly, biting her lip as she dumped the wash water over the side of the ship.

If he were to be completely honest, the woman confounded him. He knew he'd destroyed some of the illusions she'd had about her father when he told her about his past, yet she handled it all with grace and noticeably few tears. She seemed to trust him, at least to a certain extent, but the next moment she refused to meet his gaze, and he knew she was hiding something.

He wondered if it had something to do with Danny.

He hadn't known that Kane had stolen the cutlass from Danny when he in turn had stolen it from him. When Jonathan learned that little fact, a short while later, he'd been surprised. Danny had been adamant about living a *normal life*, and Jonathan doubted he could have been lured back to his former activities, no matter what the temptation. He'd thought Danny above a weakness such as greed.

Apparently, he'd thought wrong.

Of course, during long weeks at sea, the two had often passed the time speculating about the legend of Mellick's Gold, but he'd been under the impression that Danny thought it a myth, a fancy. Unlike Jonathan, who knew it to be real.

And he knew that Kane did as well.

Eyeing Sarina's flush as she dried her hands, he suspected that he was right about her—that perhaps Danny had told her something more about the cutlass than she was letting on. He wondered just how much. Deciding he would try to find out, he followed her as she lugged the washtub back belowdecks, and caught the door to his quarters before she could close it behind her.

She jumped, hand flying to her throat as the tub clattered to the floor. "You startled me!"

"A bit jumpy, are we, Smith?" he asked, stepping by her to sit at his desk. "Why so nervous?"

She sniffed, bending to pick up the tub and put it away. "I'm not nervous. Why are *you* skulking about like a criminal? Oh, wait . . ." She held up a finger. "You *are* a criminal."

Jonathan gave her an impassive look. "Hilarious."

Sarina smirked and began to tidy up a pile of books near the bed. Jonathan watched her for a moment, then turned his attention to the mess of papers on his desk. He scanned one absently and frowned in confusion when he spotted Sarina's dirk half-hidden beneath a manifest. Suspicion bloomed, and he picked up the dirk, tapping the point on the tip of his finger as he waited for her to notice.

Eventually, she glanced at him and her eyes widened before flickering away nervously, throat working as she gulped. She fiddled with an arrangement of chess pieces, dusting them with a cloth and pointedly not looking in his direction again.

"Smith?"

Sarina cleared her throat but didn't turn around, completely focused on dusting the white queen. "Yes?"

"Is there a reason your dirk is on my desk?"

"Is it?" she asked, trading the queen for a rook. "That's odd."

"Hmm . . . indeed." His sharp gaze drifted over the desktop as he toyed with the dirk, scanning the scattered papers idly before opening the top drawer. He glanced down, and his eye narrowed as he spotted the bottom drawer—the bottom drawer that had been decidedly *locked* when he'd last left it.

The drawer that wasn't quite *closed* now.

With his eye on Sarina, he slipped the dirk into the crack at the top of the drawer and pulled it open. He spotted the hunch of her shoulders as the wood scraped along the edges, and he took a deep breath to control his temper.

"It appears you've been busy, Smith," he said, voice deadly quiet. *How much had she seen? How much had she understood?*

"Well . . . you know . . . a lot to do," she replied brightly, picking up a bishop and fumbling with it before dropping it on the floor.

"Smith," he snapped. "Forget about the chess board. What did you hope to accomplish by snooping in my desk?"

He half expected her to deny it; he almost jumped in surprise when she whirled about in fury.

"I wouldn't *have* to snoop if you didn't hide things from me!"

"I beg your pardon?"

"Don't you play innocent!" she exclaimed, waving her dusting cloth, the chess pieces forgotten. "Who is Simon Mellick, and what does he have to do with my father's cutlass?"

"It's *my* cutlass," he muttered in reflex.

Sarina rolled her eyes, fists propped on her hips. "Don't try to distract me. There is more going on here than revenge, and I think I deserve to know what it is!"

Jonathan glared at her. "You *deserve*?" he growled. "You sneak onto my ship, try to *murder* me, steal *my* cutlass . . . then I have to risk the lives of myself *and* my crew to rescue you from Stanton—and you dare to say you *deserve* anything from me?"

Sarina opened her mouth to reply, but he cut her off. "You should count yourself lucky that I don't throw you overboard."

They locked furious gazes for a long moment, both breathing harshly. Then, to Jonathan's surprise, Sarina asked, "Why don't you?"

Jonathan blinked. "Why don't I what?"

She shrugged. "You keep saying you're going to throw me in the brig or leave me on an island . . . or throw me overboard, but you don't. It's almost like . . ." Her eyes narrowed. "You *want* something from me."

"You're out of your—"

"But what is it?" she mused, half to herself. "You already have the cutlass—although I do still plan to remedy that—so what?"

Sarina eyed him carefully, and he fought to meet her gaze. He could see the moment she put it together.

"It's not me, is it?" she said finally. "It's my father. Whatever you're after, you think my father knew something about it. You're keeping me around in the hopes that he told it to me."

Jonathan thought about denying it, contemplated storming out in a rage—possibly even following through on his threat to throw her in chains. Instead, he opted for the more direct route. Perhaps it was time for both of them to place their cards on the table.

"Yes," he said.

A victorious smile crossed Sarina's lips as she folded her arms over her chest. "And what makes you think I would tell you anything?"

Jonathan raised a brow, then reached down to retrieve the chest and journal from the bottom drawer and set them before him.

"There are a few reasons," he said matter-of-factly as he opened the chest, taking out each item and lining them up on his desk. "First, you're curious about all of this. You're practically drooling with anticipation of getting some answers." He flashed her a challenging look as she opened her mouth to speak. "Don't try to deny it."

She didn't.

"Second, you want to know more about your father. The parts he kept hidden from you. The true reason my name was the last word to pass his lips."

"Which was?"

Jonathan leaned back in his chair, eyeing her carefully. "Who is to know for certain? Perhaps because he knew of my own grudge against Kane and sought his own vengeance."

Sarina frowned. "Perhaps," she said noncommittally.

He continued, ticking the numbers off on his fingers. "Third, all of this will play a big part in making Kane pay for everything he's done, and I *know* you're interested in that."

She didn't soften. "Is that all?"

Jonathan smirked. "Well, there is one more thing." He paused for effect and almost burst out laughing as she leaned forward slightly in anticipation. "But I think you already know what it is."

Sarina's lips quirked slightly. "It's treasure, isn't it?"

Jonathan grinned in response. "Aye, Smith. And it's a big one."

More than a thousand nautical miles south-southeast, at His Majesty's Antigua Naval Yard at English Harbour, Commodore Lucius Stanton paced along the dock, a frown on his face. The young informant, who'd come in with the most recent vessel, relayed his message with frantic sincerity.

"And you're certain of this?" Stanton asked, fixing the lad with a glare that emphasized inaccuracy would not be tolerated.

"Yes, sir," the boy said. "Tremayne's bound north toward the Colonies."

Stanton rubbed his chin thoughtfully. By now, the pirate could be as far as Florida if the wind was with him. And the wind always seemed to be with One-Eyed Jack. It was the only explanation the commodore had for the bastard's ability to evade him at every turn.

Stanton flipped the boy a gold coin and turned on his heel to stride toward the *Intrepid*, the crew busily loading up supplies and making minor repairs to the hull. He spotted Lieutenant Cameron peering over the starboard bow.

"Ready the ship!" Stanton yelled. "We sail in an hour."

"An hour, sir?" he replied. "But we've yet to finish repairs."

"They'll have to wait." Stanton crossed the gangplank at a near run, jumping to the deck without missing a step. "I've received word of Tremayne's location."

The lieutenant nodded, knowing the commodore's rather single-minded obsession when it came to the pirate. "I'll send Barley to retrieve the crew. We'll be ready in an hour."

Stanton issued a curt nod in response and turned to bark orders to the men loading supplies. He watched with a satisfied smile as they quickened their efforts. Yes, Tremayne had a head start, but if he was indeed sailing for the Colonies, then Stanton knew where he was going. With any luck, this time he'd finally catch One-Eyed Jack unawares.

The commodore raised his face to the brisk wind, inhaling deeply.

The chase was on.

*The cold is everywhere, seeping through the cracks and crevices and into my very bones. As far as I can see, the world is a blanket of icy white, frigid and crackling ominously.*

*The only thing that keeps me warm is the hope of fulfilling my mission.*

*And Mary, the innkeeper's daughter, a woman so fair she would make the angels weep, I would have won her for my own if she would take me.*

*- The Journal of*
*Simon Alistair Mellick*
*16 November, 1664*

Rina couldn't ignore the thrill of excitement that ran through her at the word.

*Treasure.*

She didn't consider herself overly materialistic or greedy. Really, she'd always had enough to live comfortably, if not extravagantly. That had all changed after her father's death, however. She'd been left with little except for their home in

Boston and a small inheritance from her mother. She'd sold the house to pay for the investigator, and she'd all but exhausted the inheritance in the months of searching for Tremayne.

So, Rina would have been lying if she said the idea of relieving her financial woes wasn't appealing.

Still, it wasn't just that.

"When you say *big*," she asked, taking a tentative step closer, "just how *big* do you mean?"

Tremayne smiled, waving at the chair across from him. "Why don't you sit down, Smith, and I'll tell you." She did as he suggested, too intrigued to argue, and he continued, "Have you not heard of Mellick's Gold?"

"No. No, I don't think so."

He leaned forward on the desk, tapping a finger on the leather-bound journal. "Did you read any of this?"

"A little."

"So you know Mellick was a tradesman in London about ninety years ago, an ordinary man, with a penchant for puzzles."

Rina nodded. "Yes, he mentioned a collection."

The captain leaned back in his chair. "Mellick overheard a conversation that led him to leave England and come to the New World. He detailed rumors of an expedition forming to seek a great treasure of Aztec gold. He set sail immediately."

"Seems a bit impulsive. To leave his home based on rumors."

Tremayne shrugged. "He says in the journal he investigated it thoroughly, although he doesn't go into much more detail. Suffice it to say, he gathered enough information to warrant him joining the hunt, and he apparently left England a month before the expedition."

"Did he find the gold?" Rina asked, mesmerized.

"I believe he did," Tremayne replied. "In autumn of 1665, he alludes to that fact in his journal, but also that he feared it being stolen from him. He became quite paranoid, certain his enemies were close on his heels—including the men from whom he'd originally heard of the treasure. Which leads us back to the puzzles," he said.

"How so?"

"Mellick hid the treasure," he replied. "But he didn't write specifically where. He feared he would be murdered and if the journal fell into the wrong hands, his enemies would take the gold for themselves. He'd met and married a young woman shortly after he arrived in the Colonies, and she was with child. So, to protect his heir, he devised an elaborate puzzle that would have to be solved in order to find the gold."

"The poem," Rina mused. At Tremayne's curious look, she added, "In the back of the journal—*A cup . . . a coin . . . a key . . .*"

"Yes," Jonathan replied. "We've determined the poem points to the relics that need to be gathered in order to solve the puzzle."

"We?"

"Me, your father . . . Kane," he explained. "I've been in a race against Kane to find the items ever since."

"Wait. I don't understand something." Rina said, shaking her head. "If the journal was intended for Mellick's child, how did you get it? And why didn't *he* keep all of these relics?"

"He died before he got a chance," Tremayne replied, waving a hand. "Consumption. His wife as well, a short time later. The child was never born, and with a lack of heirs, all his belongings went to a distant cousin back in London.

"The man was undergoing financial troubles of his own, so he opted to sell all of Mellick's property in the Colonies rather than spare the expense to have it shipped overseas. The relics were scattered to the winds, and it was only by chance that the journal came into my father's possession, and eventually to mine. It, along with the contents of Mellick's library, ended up in a book shop in Charles Towne. My father is a collector, and had also heard the legend of Mellick's Gold. When he found the journal, he knew it would prove invaluable."

He paused, his gaze intent. "Kane thought so, too. When he learned I had the journal, he determined to acquire it. It was he who set the trap for my crew those years ago, he who took my eye and left me for dead. All in a plot to get the journal."

"But he failed."

"Thanks only to Max," he replied. "He managed to wound Kane and get the rest of the crew away safely. He saved my life."

Rina breathed deeply, absorbing all she had heard. "So . . ." she said, swallowing thickly. "Kane killed my father for the cutlass? The sword from the poem?"

"I believe so. He will stop at nothing."

Rina eyed him carefully. "And you? Will you also stop at nothing?"

The captain looked away for a moment, then said in a low voice, "I want the treasure, but despite what you may have heard about me, I am not in the habit of killing innocent people."

He turned to look her in the eyes. "Kane, however, is far from innocent."

Rina nodded, then dropped her gaze at his intensity.

"So you—*we*," she corrected, "have the cutlass. What about the rest?" She noticed Tremayne didn't challenge the *we*.

"This—" He held up the pendant. "I believe to be the *key for the lock.*"

Rina reached for the necklace, turning it in her hand. "It's just a locket." She prised at one edge and it popped open. "There's not even anything inside it. How can it be a key?"

Tremayne flipped through the journal to the page with the drawing of the locket, and showed her where Mellick had identified it as *The Key.*

Rina frowned. "So, you have the key and the cutlass. What about the cup and the coin?" She leaned forward to lay down the locket and pick up one of the coins from the chest. "Is it one of these?"

"I don't think so." The captain took the coin and examined it closely. "These are just ordinary coins. I think we're looking for something special."

"Special how?"

"Good question."

"And the cup?"

With a heavy sigh, Tremayne placed the items back in the chest. "I don't know. It's possible Kane has it. I have no information about it."

Rina was beginning to wonder if there was anything about this so-called treasure that Tremayne *did* know for certain.

"And once you retrieve all of these relics, what then?" she asked.

"It's not simply the relics," he replied. "There is also a map. Kane is in possession of half of it, but the other half is missing. I believe the map will direct us how to use the relics."

Rina blew a strand of hair out of her eyes. "It seems this Mellick was more than careful. Given the intricacy of this puzzle of his, I'd hazard to call him downright paranoid. How are we ever to decipher what this all means?"

Tremayne's mouth curved in a sly smile. "Well, that's part of the challenge, Smith. Nobody ever said treasure hunting was a simple venture. Regardless, that is why we're headed to South Carolina." He hesitated, watching her reaction. "There is a *seer* there who I hope will put us on the right path."

She barked out a laugh. "A seer? Surely you don't put faith in such nonsense!"

He grimaced slightly. "Do not mock what you do not know, Smith. It may sound like nonsense, but it's been proven to me too many times for me to be contemptuous."

"Contemptuous?" Rina stiffened. "I wasn't being contemptuous. Only skeptical."

The captain stood abruptly, leaning forward over his desk. "It matters not. We are going to Charles Towne. Unless, that is, you have a better idea?"

She frowned, but could not come up with an alternative plan. "Fine," she muttered. "But I want to study the journal on the way. Perhaps I'll find a more logical plan of action."

"Very well," he said, placing the journal and chest back in the drawer, then pointedly reached for the key hidden in the cup on the shelf. "I'd prefer you not use the dirk again," he explained. "I'd like to save the lock."

Rina flushed and nodded.

Jonathan straightened after locking the drawer and returning the key to the cup. "Now, Smith, I think it's time you share some information yourself."

Ah ha. She knew he wanted something from her. "What kind of information?"

"As you said," he replied, "I want to know what your father said about any of this. Did he tell you where he got the cutlass?"

Rina exhaled in frustration. "He told me it was a gift from his commanding officer—a lie, of course. I didn't understand why he kept it locked away instead of on display, but it makes perfect sense, now."

Tremayne ran his hands over his face, an aggravated growl low in his throat. "I didn't even know he was looking for it," he muttered. "He seemed to doubt the existence of the treasure as fancy."

"Apparently, I wasn't the only one he lied to," Rina said bitterly.

He stood, his chair sliding back as he began to pace, one hand on the hilt of his dagger. "So, he didn't tell you about Mellick, but perhaps he mentioned the cup or the coin? Or even how to find the missing half of the map?"

She shook her head, "He never said anything—"

"Think! Maybe you know something and you don't even know you know it. Did he keep a journal himself? Or perhaps you have correspondence. He might have been working with someone." He whirled about, a mixture of excitement and hope on his face. "Did he have a lockbox? A place he kept important items?"

"No, nothing—"

"There has to be something!" he snapped. He paused, fingers pinching the bridge of his nose as he tried to stay calm. Rina actually felt a bit guilty. He'd shared so much information with her, and she really had nothing to share in return.

"I'm sorry," she said quietly. "I went through everything thoroughly when I sold our home. There was nothing. No mention of treasure or cups or maps. If my father knew anything, he didn't keep a record of it."

Tremayne sat back down, running his hands over his face in defeat. For a moment, Rina began to worry. If she had nothing to offer, would Tremayne abandon her? Would he finally follow through on his threats now that he had no reason to keep her around?

Then she realized, he couldn't.

Because he'd told her his secrets. And in order to keep *them*, he'd have to keep *her*.

Apparently, the captain had reached the same conclusion, because he fixed her with a piercing gaze. "Baines is the only person outside this room who knows what I've told you," he said, voice tense and warning. "I intend to keep it that way."

"Of course."

"If I learn you've spoken of this to anyone else—"

"You won't."

His stare burned into her, and she leaned toward him. "I promise, Captain. I won't tell a soul. You can trust me."

At that, he blinked and looked away. "I don't trust anyone."

"You trust Baines."

"Yes, well . . . he's earned it."

"I will, too," she said lightly, trying to break the uncomfortable tension. "I'll solve the puzzle and lead you to the treasure."

He smirked, glancing at her sideways. "Just like that?"

She grinned. "Just like that," she said. "You'll find I'm very useful."

Tremayne leered, his gaze drifting over her slowly. "Aye, I'm certain you are."

Rina snorted, rolling her eyes. "Of course, just when I start to actually like you, you find it necessary to revert to being a barbarian."

He wiggled his eyebrows. "You like me?"

"Not anymore." She huffed, crossing her arms over her chest.

Tremayne barked out a laugh. "Oh, Smith, I think you do," he said, standing to round the desk. "You know, if you're ready to renegotiate our arrangement . . ." He glanced pointedly toward the bed.

Rina laughed, too amused to be offended. "No, thank you."

"No?" He raised a brow, stepping toward her. Her stomach flipped.

"No," she said, voice cracking.

Tremayne's smile grew as he leaned over her chair. Rina froze as his cheek brushed hers and his lips grazed her ear, warm breath eliciting an uncontrollable shiver.

"If you change your mind," he whispered, "you know where to find me." She gasped as he stood abruptly and turned to leave the room. His low chuckle echoed down the hallway as he made his way to the deck, and it wasn't until the sound faded that Rina's breath steadied.

She swallowed, her head spinning slightly. Tremayne flustered her, and she was not used to being flustered. She didn't like it, at all.

She was beginning to wonder if perhaps she just might be a little bit out of her depth when it came to Jonathan Tremayne.

Jonathan kept an eye on her for the rest of the voyage and enlisted Max to do the same, but Sarina was true to her word and said nothing about the treasure to anyone else. Not that there was anyone on board she was friendly with anyway.

Except Jamie Ceron, of course. Jonathan frowned at the man as he stood near the bow, arms crossed. He had no doubt that Ceron was an honorable man, but he didn't want anyone to know his business unless it was absolutely necessary. And at the moment, it wasn't necessary.

Max, however, had ears all over the ship, and Jonathan was relatively certain that Sarina had not breathed a word of the treasure to even Ceron. Apparently, the idea of vengeance, along with her own share of the treasure, was enough to keep her quiet.

Jonathan smirked. At least something was.

He reached into his pocket for his spyglass, lifting it to his eye. The coast was barely visible in the distance as the sun sank below the horizon.

South Carolina. Home.

"Baines!" he called, his first mate appearing at his side almost instantly. "We set off at dark. I want to be on shore before the moon rises too high and gives us away."

"Aye, Captain."

He turned to walk with Max toward the bow. "Instruct Crawley to move the ship further out into open waters as soon as we're away. We will rendezvous again tomorrow night after sundown."

"Aye," Max said again. "Captain, there is the matter of Miss Talbot."

"What of her?" he asked, distracted by the crewmen adjusting the mainsail. "Look alive, men!" he shouted. "If ye damage the sail and we're unable to evade the Crown, we'll all be dancin' the hempen jig!"

A chorus of "Aye, Cap'n!" rang out in response, but Max leaned in, catching his eye. "She means to come along."

"What? Who?" Jonathan asked irritably.

"The wench." Max fought to keep from rolling his eyes. "Miss Talbot. She means to go ashore with us."

Jonathan gaped for a moment, then burst out laughing. "You're jesting with me."

"'Tis no joke," Max replied. "She told me she wants to hear from the seer herself." His cheeks flushed slightly at the mention of Charlotte, but Jonathan ignored it.

"Of course she does," he grumbled. "Where is she?"

"In your quarters, I believe."

"Ready the dinghy. I'll only be a moment." Jonathan turned on his heel and stalked belowdecks, bursting into his room without warning. Sarina jumped in surprise, a small bag at her feet. Jonathan noticed the journal peeking out the top.

"And what exactly are you about now, Smith?" He grabbed the bag and rifled through it, finding the chest tucked in the bottom amidst some spare underthings.

"Give me that!" she snapped, a flush stealing up her neck as she ripped the bag from his fingers and dropped it on the chair behind her. "I simply thought you'd like to bring them along. I assumed the seer—"

"Yes, well, it appears you assume quite a bit," Jonathan retorted. "What is this I hear? You actually think you're going ashore?"

Sarina bristled. "Well, of course I am. I want to hear what this seer has to say."

"You'll do no such thing!" he growled. "It's utterly preposterous. You'll stay on board where you belong."

She stared at him blankly. For a moment, Jonathan wondered if she was going to explode, or burst into tears. To his surprise, she did neither.

"Utterly preposterous?" she repeated slowly, mimicking him. "Not very pirate-like, Captain. You're doing it again."

He glared at her. "Doing what, for heaven's sake?"

She shook a finger at him, her eyes narrowing in concentration. "You know what? I believe it happens whenever you're annoyed with me."

"Well, then *it* should happen a lot," he mumbled. "Now, what on earth are you on about?"

"Your accent," she replied, spreading her hands palm up like the words explained everything. "It changes when you're particularly irritated, it seems."

"I have absolutely no idea—" he began, cutting off abruptly and clearing his throat. "Yer daft, wench."

Sarina bit her lip to keep from laughing. "Am I?"

A knock at the door interrupted the rather strange conversation, and Jonathan snapped, "What?" while attempting not to appear relieved. Max poked his head into the room, eyeing them both warily.

"It's time, Captain," he said.

Jonathan nodded. "Aye. Good." When Sarina bent to pick up her bag, he added, "You are *not* accompanying us."

"Oh, yes I *am*."

"No. You're *not*."

Max watched the two of them with amusement.

"Look," Sarina said, dropping her bag on the floor and planting her fists on her hips as she fixed Jonathan with a determined glare. "We can go back and forth like this all night. You can forbid me to come aboard, *Ye'll do what I say, wench* and all that nonsense . . ."

"It isn't nonsense!"

Sarina continued without stopping. "But we both know it won't do a bit of good. If you leave me here, I will find a way to get off this ship. If you tie me up in the hold, I'll escape somehow and steal a dinghy and row myself ashore. I'll *swim* if I have to. You know I will." She leaned forward, and Jonathan wondered if she was standing on her tiptoes to appear a bit taller.

"Let's just skip all this ridiculous arguing and be on our way, shall we?" she said with a beatific smile, picking the bag up again and throwing it over her shoulder. "We're wasting time." And with that, she flounced past both men and headed up to the deck.

Jonathan stood motionless for a moment, trying to determine when exactly he had lost control of the situation. He realized his mouth hung open and shut it with a snap before turning toward the door. He glared fiercely at Max, whose eyes danced with merriment.

"Not a word," Jonathan warned. "Unless *you* would like to be the one tied up in the hold."

"But then who would row the boat?" he asked. At Jonathan's growl, he held up his hands in defense, then offered a small salute. "Not a word. Aye, Cap'n."

Jonathan stormed past him and up to the deck. He spotted Sarina chatting quietly with James and an inexplicable rush of anger swept through him. He stalked over to her and grabbed her arm roughly.

"If you insist on going, I'll not have you delaying us," he said with a scowl.

Sarina smiled and let him drag her away.

Gentle waves rocked the dinghy as the small landing party made its way ashore in the darkness. Rina sat across from the captain and first mate, gripping the wooden bench tightly on either side of her, a bubble of excitement tickling in her stomach. It felt good to be doing *something* other than laundry and cleaning, something to find her father's killer.

Then there was the treasure, of course. And the strange puzzle they'd have to solve in order to find it. Rina couldn't believe how her life had changed. Living with pirates, searching for treasure . . . it was like something out of a bedtime story.

She didn't speak—warned repeatedly by Tremayne that they must be quiet and stealthy to avoid detection—but instead stared silently at the shadows of the two men pulling the oars in a slow, steady rhythm. A glance over her shoulder revealed nothing; the *Black Arrow* already heading farther out to the open sea. Rina turned back to look past Tremayne and Baines, searching for the shoreline.

She couldn't make out anything in the darkness.

Then, just when she thought they'd perhaps turned around and were headed in the wrong direction, she began to discern the lights of a city in the distance. Her eyes scanned the horizon, and she realized they had entered a harbor, surrounded by the dark shadow of land all around them. She could barely make out rows of masts along the edge of the water, dozens of ships docked overnight at the busy trade center.

They rowed to the west of the lights, aiming for a covert landing. Eventually, the boat slid in the muck along the bottom, and Baines and Tremayne pulled the oars up, tucking them into the boat before slipping quietly into the water and tugging the dinghy closer to shore. Their boots squelched in the marshy sludge as Rina watched them, looking up and down the darkened beach, before Tremayne waved her forward. She stood carefully, tucking her bag under her arm, and picked her way over the benches to the front of the boat, peering doubtfully into the black water. Baines held out a hand to help her down, but just as Rina reached for him, bracing herself to wade through the marsh, Tremayne gave an exasperated huff, and swept her up in his arms. She gasped in surprise, clinging to him as he strode through the shallow water. He set her down none-too-gently on the muddy beach before returning to help Max pull the dinghy up the shore and hide it in the trees and underbrush.

The three set off at a fast pace, ducking through the forest, and across mud, then sand. Rina struggled to keep up, finally gathering her skirts into one hand so she could move more freely. They neared a small creek and Tremayne turned back toward her, catching her up in a firm grip and making it across in a half-dozen steps. He stepped back onto dry land, and Rina swore his arms tightened around her slightly before he set her back down—a bit more gently this time.

After a while, they neared the walled city, making their way over one drawbridge, then another.

"Walk calmly, and don't attract attention," Tremayne ordered, pulling back his long hair and tying it tightly with a leather thong, then pulling his hat down low over his face to hide his patch. He reached for Rina's hand and tugged it through his bent elbow.

"What are you doing?" she hissed, trying to pull her arm away.

"Come now, Smith," he said with a chuckle. "Now's not the time to be shy. We'll be far less suspicious as a young couple out for an evening stroll. With a proper chaperone, of course."

Baines snorted. "I assume that would be me."

"Give Max the bag and try to act as if you like me," the captain said, patting at her clenched fists. "And relax, for heaven's sake. People will think I'm a rogue holding you captive against your will!"

Despite herself, Rina giggled, the excitement making her a bit hysterical. "Well, we can't have that, can we?" She handed Max her bag and squared her shoulders. "Let's go, then."

"Are you certain we shouldn't try to go around the city?" Max asked quietly as they drew nearer, the sounds of music and laughter drifting to them.

"No time," the captain replied grimly. "This is the most direct route."

Rina had never been to Charles Towne, and after this visit, she really wouldn't be able to alter that statement. Tremayne kept up a steady pace, but there was no time to dawdle, no time to explore the shops lined up along the street, not that many were open at this time of evening. A commotion broke out before them, a group of raucous men forcibly evicted from a tavern, and Max and Tremayne exchanged a glance before they crossed the street and continued on their way.

Surprisingly, no one paid them much attention, but Rina grew increasingly concerned about the high wall surrounding the city borders, and quietly asked Jonathan how they'd get through it.

"Have a little faith, Smith," he said with a grin.

He glanced over his shoulder before tugging her into the darkness between two houses. They approached the wall, and Jonathan scanned it carefully.

"Over here," Max called from a short distance away. They hurried to meet him at a spot in the wall that was apparently under repair. The fallen bricks had been cleared away and stacked nearby.

"Hurricane," the captain explained. "We're fortunate the treaty talks have been successful, or no doubt this would have been guarded."

"How did you even know it was here?"

He grinned. "Oh, I have eyes and ears everywhere, Smith. Don't you forget that."

Rina couldn't help smiling in return as they made their way through the narrow opening and across the nearly-dry ditch on the other side. With one last look back, they left the sights and sounds of civilization behind them.

"Where exactly are we going?" she asked, noticing she was still holding Tremayne's arm. She pulled away with a jolt, cheeks coloring hotly. He frowned at her, but answered the question.

"Not much farther," he said. "Just past Hampstead Hill near the northern mouth of Town Creek."

She blinked, enlightened not a whit by that. "Of course," she muttered. "Thank you for the information."

He ignored the sarcasm, instead turning to Max. "We'll need to secure horses for the journey back. I don't want the *Arrow* close to shore any longer than absolutely necessary."

"Aye," Max replied. "I'll talk to the stable lad when we arrive."

They turned down a long, winding drive, dust kicking up around them as they walked. Tremayne quickened his pace. "It's just around the bend."

Rina felt a mix of relief and anticipation that they had almost reached their destination. As they rounded the corner, the moon came out from behind a cloud, casting their surroundings in an eerie glow and she noticed the drive was lined by evenly spaced trees, leaves rustling in the slight breeze. Finally, she spotted a sprawling house in the distance, and her breath caught.

It was beautiful. And even in the dim light, she could tell it was enormous.

White columns gleamed in the moonlight, supporting a pediment overhanging the front entry. The two-story home appeared to be made of brick, although it was difficult to tell for certain. Warm light poured from the multitude of windows, and the glow made the house seem almost magical, a fairy tale come to life. She could imagine a deposed duchess living out her days in seclusion there, surrounded only by her prized horses and a fat cat or two.

As they drew nearer, the front door opened, and a young woman stepped out, carrying a lantern. Max's breath caught, and Tremayne muttered something unintelligible under his breath.

"Who is that?" Rina whispered, but no one answered as the woman strode toward them purposefully, stopping just in front of their little group. She wore a simple cream-colored gown and was a few inches taller than Sarina, but slimmer, lithe, her body almost vibrating with energy as she bounced on her toes. Her long black hair was caught back from her face, the ends blowing wildly in the breeze. Large, dark eyes dominated her delicate features and darted from one person to the next, absorbing every detail. As the woman's gaze focused on Rina, she tilted her head slightly, studying her. Rina fought the urge to squirm under the scrutiny. It felt like the woman could see straight through her; all of her secrets laid bare.

The woman giggled as though she knew Rina's thoughts. Then, with a soft cry, she turned away and threw herself against the captain, wrapping the arm not holding the lantern around his neck.

Tremayne chuckled slightly and hugged her to him, his large hands spanning her back easily.

Rina watched the exchange with wide eyes, a strange and hot feeling curdling in her stomach. The woman pulled back, looking up at Tremayne with a slight grin.

"You're late," she said with a wink. She pulled away, lashes dipping slightly as she nodded to Max. "Mister Baines."

He nodded back. "Miss Eaton."

Then, a most curious thing. She turned to Rina with a friendly smile. "And you must be Sarina," she said. "I've been looking forward to meeting you."

Rina searched for a response, finally opting for a stammered, "Thank you?" that sounded more like a question. She cleared her throat, trying to regain her balance. She determined that this must be the seer the captain spoke about, and apparently the two were well-acquainted.

She couldn't explain why that thought made her just a little bit nauseous.

The woman laughed lightly, her head again tilting to the side. "Since Jonathan's time at sea has apparently robbed him of civilized manners, I suppose I should introduce myself," she said, casting him a reproachful glance. "I'm Charlotte Eaton." At that, the captain snorted, and Charlotte rolled her eyes.

"Fine," she muttered. "Charlotte Eaton *Tremayne*."

It took Rina a moment to fully grasp what she'd said. "I'm sorry. Did you say Tremayne?" she asked, turning to Jonathan, mouth gaping in shock. "This is . . . is this your *wife?*"

Charlotte burst out laughing, and even Max snorted a bit. The captain looked scandalized, clearing his throat as he lifted a hand to rub the back of his neck. Rina could swear that even in the lamp light she could make out a slight flush of color on his cheeks.

"God, no. Not my wife," he said, not meeting Rina's eyes. "Smith, meet my sister."

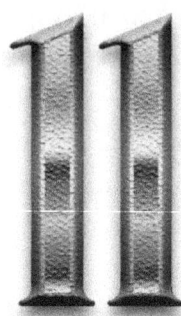

*Christmas is but a few days away, yet I have already received a most precious gift.*

*My Mary has consented to become my wife.*

*- The Journal of
Simon Alistair Mellick
22 December, 1664*

"Your sister?" Rina's disbelieving gaze moved from Tremayne to Charlotte and back again.

"Well," Charlotte said, "half-sister to put a finer point on it, but it's no matter." She waved a hand to change the subject, then hooked her arm through Rina's, drawing her toward the house. "You must be tired after your journey . . . and hungry, I'll wager. I had Cook prepare a light supper, then perhaps a nice hot bath before retiring, yes?"

"Errr . . ." Rina's head spun, still trying to grasp the fact that One-Eyed Jack had a sister. And a rather charming one, at that. "A bath would be lovely, thank you."

"Of course," Charlotte replied. "I'm certain my brother hasn't provided you with the basic necessities on that ship of his. How can you abide it?" Without giving Rina a chance to respond, she continued, "Oh well, you're here now, and we'll make sure you're treated properly."

Tremayne cleared his throat. "She has not been mistreated."

"No?" Charlotte glanced back at him. "Cleaning your quarters? Polishing your boots? Really, Jonathan, is that how you treat a lady?" She turned back to Rina. "I don't blame you for sewing his sleeves shut."

Rina gaped, uncertain how to respond. "How did you know about that?"

Baines stepped up to her other side and leaned in conspiratorially. "Don't worry, you'll get used to it," he said. Charlotte granted him a sunny smile, and Max's cheeks heated. He rushed ahead to open the door, holding it gallantly.

"Thank you, Mister Baines," Charlotte said with a genteel nod as they walked into the home.

Rina blinked in the brighter interior light, a row of sconces casting the vast entryway in a warm glow. A curving staircase swept up to her left, culminating in a railed balcony spanning the wall above and in front of her. Beneath it, a hallway led to the back of the house, but Charlotte led her to a pair of double doors to the right. A uniformed servant stepped forward to push both doors open, then moved to the side with a deferential bow.

"Thank you, Job," she said as they passed him. "Now, Rina— you don't mind if I call you Rina, do you?" Rina nodded, but Charlotte continued without waiting for a response. "I thought we'd sit in here rather than the dining room. Much more homey, don't you think?"

Homey wasn't exactly the word that crossed Rina's mind. The room positively gleamed, from the dark, polished wood floors to the intricately carved furniture, to the sparkling chandelier hanging from the center of the ceiling, candlelight reflecting off dozens of crystals dripping from its ornate arms. As Job pulled the doors quietly closed, Charlotte led her toward a pair of velvet settees facing each other on a thick Persian rug. Rina sat down stiffly, worried she was going to soil the furniture.

Captain Tremayne, however, seemed to have no such qualms, sprawling on the settee across from her, his legs splayed wide. Baines opted to stand next to the fireplace—and next to Charlotte, she noticed—with his hands loosely clasped behind his back.

Rina cleared her throat. "You have a lovely home. Do you live here alone?"

Charlotte laughed. "Jonathan really told you nothing, did he?" She shook her head, shooting her brother another exasperated glance.

He rubbed his forehead. "Well, to be fair, I really haven't had the opportunity—"

"Of course you did," Charlotte said, waving a hand in dismissal and turning back to Rina. "This is our *father's* home."

A door slammed somewhere in the house, and Tremayne stood up and moved to stand next to Baines as footsteps approached.

"I assumed he'd be with Grace," he said, Adam's apple bobbing as he swallowed, shoulders stiff.

"Of course not. He wanted to see you." Charlotte turned back to Rina, wincing apologetically. "I told him you'd be here at sundown, but he's always late."

Rina still felt lost in the conversation of half-sentences and obscure innuendo. "Who?"

"Charlotte," Tremayne interrupted in a low voice, glancing toward the doorway as the footsteps grew louder. "Perhaps you should show Miss Talbot to her room?" Rina could swear he looked nervous. Almost . . . *afraid.*

"Oh, Jonathan." Charlotte laughed. "It's too late now."

And with that, the double-doors opened admitting a tall, distinguished-looking man in a navy coat and breeches. His thick dark hair was gray at the temples and caught back in a queue, the pristine cravat at his neck and heavily embroidered waistcoat speaking of wealth and taste. Sea-blue-green eyes—the same as Tremayne's—scanned the room before coming to rest on the captain.

The older man smiled, moving forward to extend a hand. "Jonathan. It's good to see you."

Tremayne cleared his throat, taking the man's hand in a firm grip. "Father. You're looking well." Rina realized his accent had changed again. In fact, he'd been speaking differently ever since Charlotte had appeared.

Charlotte. His sister. And now his father. Rina wondered who would come through the door next.

Tremayne's father shook Max's hand, greeting him politely, then turned to Rina.

"And this must be the famous Miss Talbot I've heard so much about."

Charlotte smiled. "Sarina, Father. She's practically family, after all."

Tremayne groaned and muttered something under his breath.

"Ah, Sarina," he said, stepping toward her and reaching for her hand. She placed her fingers in his, and he bowed slightly. "It is a pleasure. I am Sebastian Tremayne."

Rina swallowed nervously. "The pleasure is mine, sir."

"I trust you had a pleasant journey?" he asked, as he sat down across from Rina and Charlotte. He smiled kindly, but Rina couldn't help but notice a tension around his eyes, a sadness she couldn't quite place.

"Pleasant?" she repeated, remembering the dinghy, the scrabbling through the woods, the walk through the center of town, trying not to attract attention. "It was uneventful, sir."

"Yes, well." He cast a significant glance at his son. "Considering the company you keep, I suppose that is a good thing, no?"

Rina was still out of her depth. Apparently, Tremayne didn't hide his lifestyle from his family. Of course, with a sister like

Charlotte, she imagined it would be difficult to hide anything. Still, she had no idea how to respond. Fortunately, the double doors opened again at that moment, and Job entered.

"Excuse me, my lord," he said gravely. "Shall I bring in the refreshments?"

Rina's eyes widened.

*My lord?*

"Yes, Job," the elder Tremayne replied. "That would be lovely."

Rina turned her shocked gaze on the captain.

*My lord?*

He cleared his throat, looking down at the floor.

"I think you've stunned poor Sarina, Father," Charlotte said with a knowing grin as Tremayne fidgeted, hands first in his pockets, then clenched tightly against his thighs.

"It appears Jonathan has neglected to tell her much about the family," she said.

"Charlotte . . ." the captain grumbled.

"Oh, there's little point trying to hide it now, don't you think?" she replied turning to Rina, who continued to watch the interaction with confusion.

Although certain things were finally beginning to make sense.

"My father didn't introduce himself quite completely," Charlotte explained. "Sarina Talbot, please meet our father, Sebastian Tremayne, Viscount Coffey."

Tremayne's father snorted, waving a hand. "Titles are ridiculous in this place, don't you think?" he asked. "It's a long way from England."

"A viscount?" Rina all but squeaked.

Charlotte patted her hand, leaning in to whisper, "His great-grandfather on his mother's side was an earl."

"An *earl*?" Rina choked.

"Yes, but his grandfather was a second son, so he'll likely not inherit that title," Charlotte said, brightening as Job rolled in a cart carrying a pot of tea and several covered dishes. "Ah, some refreshment. I hope you're hungry."

Rina stared at Jonathan, who continued to stare at the floor. She heard Baines snort slightly, and when she glanced at him, he winked.

"If you'll excuse me," Tremayne said abruptly, striding toward the door. "I need some air." He left without a backward glance. Charlotte patted Rina's hand again.

"Go on, then," she said resignedly. "I'll try to keep the tea hot while you both settle this matter. Mister Baines?" She handed Max a cup of tea as Rina stood and excused herself quietly.

She found Tremayne on the front porch, leaning against a column and regarding the stars with a resigned air.

"So," she said after a moment, "you really are a gentleman."

He snorted. "Well, I suppose that depends on your definition of the term."

She moved to a low bench, settling down behind him. His broad back blocked the moonlight, creating a glowing aura around his form.

"I don't understand. Why keep it a secret? That is, I assume your men don't know."

"Only Max."

"But . . . why?"

Tremayne exhaled heavily, pushing away from the column to pace across the porch. "I never misled them intentionally," he said. "When I came on board the *Arrow*, nobody asked where I came from. They all assumed I was like them—a man in need of work, searching for his fortune. Later, they feared me too much to question my background."

"Wouldn't they know the name?" she asked.

"Did you?" Jonathan challenged, turning to face her. "My father lives a quiet life here. He doesn't flaunt his title, and very few people in Charles Towne even know of it. Job is the only one determined to adhere to such societal niceties."

"It's hardly something to be ashamed of."

"I'm not ashamed," he replied, rolling his shoulders and rubbing the tension out of the back of his neck. "Not precisely. It's only that my men have certain *expectations*. They need a strong, ruthless captain, not a coddled dandy.

"And the fact of the matter is, I've left this life behind," he added quietly. "My life now is the *Arrow* and its crew."

Rina watched him turn to lean against the column again. This time facing her. "But you seem close to your family," she said. "Isn't it difficult being away from them?"

He stiffened, looking away abruptly. "Yes, well that is neither here nor there. There is no point regretting what must be."

"But—"

"We should get back inside," he said gruffly. "Charlotte will be wondering what happened to us."

"Cap—*Jonathan*—"

"Sarina," he interrupted, moving toward the entrance. "I do not wish to discuss this further, please. My past life is irrelevant. I only answered your questions because I have said I will not lie to you.

"I trust I can rely upon you to be discreet?" he asked, hand on the door knob.

"Of course," she agreed without hesitation. "This is your business. No one else's."

He swallowed, then nodded. "Thank you."

He started to open the door, and Rina called out, "Jonathan?"

He paused.

"I think they would understand," she said. "Your crew, I mean. I think you could tell them the truth."

Jonathan said nothing for a long moment, then he murmured, "Perhaps." He held the door open, extending a palm. "After you, Smith."

The sun had barely peeked over the horizon when Charlotte made her way up the stairs to the room of their current houseguest. She paused briefly in the filtered sunlight by Max's door, laying a hand on the warm wood with a faint smile on her face.

Perhaps she would be able to spend a little time with him today before he swept out of her life again for who knew how long.

She could but hope. Charlotte's visions regarding Max were often hazy and uncertain. She could only assume it was because her own emotions were so strong in the matter.

Hope was a powerful thing. Sometimes it could overshadow fate and make it difficult for her to discern what *would* be from what *could* be . . . and what she *wished* to be.

With a sigh, she moved on. There was no use worrying about it. Over the years, Charlotte had learned patience above all things.

She neared Rina's door with a smile. Now, Rina was a different story altogether. Charlotte had seen her—sharp and vivid—years before she knew anything about her or the connection she would have with her brother.

At the thought of Jonathan, Charlotte released a light chuckle. Seeing the two of them together had been both amusing and intriguing. It was obvious there was an attraction there—Charlotte had foreseen that there would be—but they both seemed to be either denying it or fighting it for some unknown reason.

After the two returned to the sitting room the evening before, they'd both been pensive and distracted. Jonathan had eaten little, pressing Charlotte for information. She'd denied him, not to be cruel, but because she knew in order to get the answers he sought, she would have to be fully prepared. There were things to be gathered, rituals to be performed.

It could not be rushed.

Jonathan finally relented when she promised a reading at midday. He'd relaxed after that, laughing and smiling, and for a while, it seemed almost like the old days, the days before . . .

Charlotte sighed again and knocked lightly at the door. At Sarina's quiet invitation, she pushed it open, poking her head through.

"Good morning," Charlotte said quietly. "I'm sorry it's so early, but I thought you might like an early-morning walk."

Rina sat up in bed, brushing her hair back from her face. "Actually, that would be nice," she said. "I have so many questions racing around in my head. I can't sleep anymore anyway."

Charlotte laughed as she walked into the room. "I thought you might," she said. "That's why I'm here."

"Really?" Her eyes lit up with interest.

Charlotte sat down on the edge of the bed. "There are things you should know that my brother does not talk about easily. I thought it might be easier if I shared them with you."

"What kinds of things?"

"Not here," Charlotte said, standing up and crossing the room to a large chest of drawers. "Let's get outside and enjoy this morning air, and I'll tell you all about our family and what has led us to these rather unique circumstances." She turned around, offering Rina fresh clothing. "These are my mother's. I think you two are of a similar stature, so they should fit adequately. The servants will bring up some water for you, then I'll meet you outside?"

"All right," she said, taking the clothes. "Thank you, Charlotte."

She smiled softly. "I haven't done anything yet," she said. "But given what I've seen of you and my brother, I have a feeling I should be thanking you."

Charlotte winked and left the room, Rina staring after her in confusion.

Rina washed and dressed quickly, eager to learn what Charlotte had to tell her. The green gown fit her better than the one she'd been wearing, and as she pinned her hair up into a loose bun and slipped on her shoes, she wondered a bit about Charlotte's mother, and Jonathan's, and, well . . . just about everything about the Tremayne family.

She padded quietly down the stairs, the house still silent in the early morning hours, save for an occasional clink or clatter from the kitchen, where she assumed breakfast preparations were underway. Charlotte waited for her on the front porch, and once again linked their arms to lead her away from the house. Rina chewed on her lip, her heart racing as she eyed the woman out of the corner of her eye.

"Go ahead and ask," Charlotte said, a smile tugging at her lips.

Rina flushed and looked away. "I don't mean to pry."

"Pry. I have nothing to hide."

Rina swallowed, then asked tentatively, "Is it true. That you're a seer?"

Charlotte tilted her head in acknowledgement, but said nothing.

"You know the future?"

She let out a quiet laugh. "Nothing quite so simple," she said. "My grandmother used to say the sight is like standing at a crossroads of a dozen paths. You may see what's down the way of one, perhaps, but someone might choose to take another."

"Your grandmother? Was she—"

"Like me?" Charlotte nodded. "Yes, she had the sight. I never met her in person, but she wrote to me a few times. The gift skipped over my mother, so it helped to have someone who understood."

The air was cool but comfortable, a slight dew sparkling on the grass as they made their way past a row of small, brick buildings. A dark-skinned woman emerged from one, shaking a rug furiously, before raising a hand in greeting as she spotted them. Charlotte waved back.

"Does your family own many slaves?" Rina asked. In the daylight, she could see the property was much larger than she'd thought—with acres of fields stretching out behind the house. She could only guess at how many people it would take to maintain such a place.

"Oh, no," Charlotte said, shaking her head. "Father is an abolitionist. The fields are farmed by hired hands, as well as a few sharecroppers."

Rina felt a sense of relief at that. "Your father seems like a good man."

"He is. He tries to do what is right." Her face clouded slightly. "Unfortunately, that is not always clear."

"What do you mean?"

They approached the river and Charlotte led her to a fallen log. "Let's sit here for a bit," she said. "And I'll start at the beginning."

Rina settled next to her, looking over the rushing water. The sunlight glinted off the ripples, sparkling like so many diamonds, as Charlotte began her story.

"Father grew up like many of his class, in a life of privilege. Summers at the country estate, the Season in London, that kind of thing," she said. "Of course, there were certain expectations that came along with being heir to Viscount Coffey, one of which was a suitable marriage. As daughter of a marquess of considerable wealth, Elisabeth Jacobs was a logical choice."

"The captain's mother," Rina mused.

Charlotte nodded and continued. "Theirs was not a love match, but one of respect and resignation, I suppose one could say. They got on well enough, and although there was no great passion, their life seemed happy. Jonathan was born, and for a short time they were content. Unfortunately, as is often the case with such a marriage of convenience, respect began to erode, turning instead to regret.

"Then, my mother came along."

"Grace," Rina said, remembering the name Jonathan had mentioned the night before.

"Yes. She became the Tremaynes' housekeeper, and—to hear her tell it—the attraction was instantaneous. Father was away conducting business when Elisabeth hired her, but when he returned . . . well, my mother says it was something akin to being struck by lightning.

"They fought it for many months, but all the while, Father and Elisabeth grew further apart. At first, the arguments escalated, then eventually, they began to ignore each other instead. They say anger can kill a marriage, but believe me, Sarina, apathy is a far more dangerous weapon.

"Elisabeth took a lover, and eventually, my father turned to my mother." She looked out over the water, her face soft. "Perhaps it was wrong, but who can lay blame, really? When both were so unhappy . . . so lonely? I don't know. Perhaps I only try to make excuses because if not for their indiscretion, I would not exist."

Rina didn't know how to respond to that, so she said nothing.

"When my mother told Father she was expecting, he was thrilled." She glanced at Rina. "I know it seems strange, but he really was. He loved her so, and for them to share a child . . . Well, it was the one thing he could give her, even though he couldn't give her his name.

"The scandal was disastrous, of course. Lord Tremayne was furious that his son would throw his life away on a common strumpet—his words," she added with a wince. "Elisabeth was humiliated. It wasn't the fact that my father had an affair, you understand, or even that he'd fathered a bastard. It was that it all became so very public.

"Elisabeth demanded they leave London, and both her parents and Father's agreed. In fact, Lord Tremayne threatened to disinherit him if he did not take care of the situation satisfactorily. They decided to come to the Colonies.

"My father insisted that my mother come along. She was heavy with child, and he refused to leave her behind. Elisabeth begged him to reconsider, threatened to leave him, but he would not be swayed. So they all boarded a ship and ended up here. I was born shortly after we arrived.

"Elisabeth, however, said she could not bear the humiliation of sharing a house with her husband's mistress. So, my mother took a small house on the edge of the property. Father cared for her—continues to care for her—and claimed me for his own, giving me his name, although I still feel awkward using it, to be perfectly honest. It seems a betrayal to my mother, since she does not have the same privilege.

"Lord Tremayne died a few years ago, the title passing to Father. His mother wrote and tried to persuade him to return to London, but he has a life here now. And he won't leave my mother."

"What happened to Elisabeth?"

Charlotte's face fell. "She was killed."

"She was murdered," a low voice corrected.

Rina turned to see Jonathan standing a few feet behind them, looking past them at the river. He'd changed his clothes as well, now dressed in a fine dark suit with a brocade waistcoat. His long hair was caught neatly back in a queue, his normally scruffy face clean-shaven and his trademark red scarf replaced with a simple black hat.

Charlotte patted her arm gently. "I think Jonathan can tell you the rest," she said, standing and rounding the log to head back in the direction they'd come. She paused next to Jonathan and reached out to squeeze his hand before continuing on her way. After a moment, he walked toward Rina and braced his foot on the log, leaning his elbows on his knee. They remained in silence for a while; the only sounds the rushing river and the occasional call of a bird overhead.

"It was Kane," he said finally, eyes dropping to the log as he worked the heel of his shoe against the bark. Bits broke off, falling to the sand below. "He came to the house searching for the journal. My father was away . . . with Grace. My mother knew nothing of the journal, not that it mattered. I'm not certain exactly what happened. She was alone in the house—" His voice broke, and Rina reached out instinctively to touch his hand. He stiffened and stepped over the log to walk to the water's edge.

"It was a blow to the head of some kind," he continued, his back to Sarina and voice so low she had to strain to hear him. "Perhaps it was an accident. Perhaps not. In any regard, it doesn't matter. Kane killed my mother.

"My father was never the same. Theirs was a loveless marriage, but he had vowed to protect my mother. He could never forgive himself that he wasn't there to fulfill that vow. He punishes himself for that failure every day. It is why he denies himself happiness with the woman he loves, even all these years later.

"As for me, I chose to go after the man who killed my mother. It's the reason I left home and boarded the *Arrow*."

He turned his head to look at her, his expression fierce. "Now you know it all, Sarina. This is not just about my eye, or any treasure. It is not some kind of game. Not to me," he said. "You are not the only one seeking vengeance. It appears we have more in common than you imagined.

"Kane destroyed my family," he said through gritted teeth. "I will not stop until *he* is destroyed."

Rina held his gaze, then stood and walked toward him. He watched her steadily as she looked up at him, then lifted a tentative hand to touch his cheek. He flinched but did not protest as she traced the scar beneath his eye patch, her hand finally coming to rest over his heart.

"I'm sorry," she said quietly.

"I don't seek your pity."

"It is not pity," she countered, willing him to believe her. "I *understand*."

He looked away. "My father doesn't."

"He knows what you're doing then?"

Jonathan sighed. "He suspects, but after so many arguments, he's decided it's best that we not discuss it. In any regard, he thinks I should give this all up and come home."

"That's not his choice."

Jonathan turned back to her. "No, it's not."

"It all makes sense now," she said. "When I told you why I wanted to find the man who killed my father, you never tried to discourage me. You never told me it was a foolish notion, or that I was doomed to fail. Many people did, you know."

His lips quirked. "Well, I may not have *said* it . . ."

She smirked. "Now, don't ruin the moment."

He laughed.

"The point is," she said, leaning forward slightly, determined he hear her. "I understand better than anyone your motives, the depth of your need to bring Kane to justice. For that is what it is, Jonathan. Justice. For you. For your family. And for me and mine.

"You say you want Kane destroyed. Well, so do I. I will help you in any way I can. I hope you believe that."

Jonathan held her gaze for a long moment, then swallowed thickly, his hand moving to clasp hers where it still lay over his heart.

"Thank you," he said, his thumb stroking her skin gently. Rina's face heated and she stepped back, hand falling to her side.

"We should probably get back," she said.

Jonathan nodded, clearing his throat. "Yes . . . yes, of course." They started down the path toward the house. "Charlotte has promised a reading at midday, so after breakfast, I thought perhaps a bit of sword training."

"Training? For who?"

"For you, of course."

"Me?" Sarina came to a halt. "You're joking."

Jonathan grinned. "You're a pirate now, Smith. You need to know how to use a sword."

Rina chewed her lip, oddly intrigued by the idea. "You really think you could teach me?"

"Well, enough to keep you alive, at least," he replied. "But it won't be a gentlemanly type of swordplay. I hope that doesn't offend your delicate sensibilities."

She snorted. "I don't have delicate sensibilities."

"I'm beginning to see that."

They turned to continue toward the house. "What do you mean? About gentlemanly swordplay?" she asked. "Are you saying you're going to teach me to fight dirty?"

Jonathan laughed, the sound ringing clear through the air.

"We're pirates, Smith," he said with a wide smile. "Of course we fight dirty."

*The New Year brings with it unwelcome news. I have received word that the expedition has left port and is sailing for the mainland.*

*Time is running out, I fear. I can no longer wait for the ice to melt. I journey south before week's end.*

*I can only pray that God will see me safely delivered to warmer climes.*

*- The Journal of*
*Simon Alistair Mellick*
*2 January, 1665*

"It's these skirts! How am I supposed to be able to lunge or parry or *move* in these ridiculous skirts?" Sarina threw her sword to the ground in frustration. Jonathan fought to keep a straight face, but he feared he was failing miserably.

"For heaven's sake, Jonathan, don't you dare laugh at me!"

"I don't know why you insist on complaining about things you can do nothing about, Smith," he said instead, holding his own cutlass aloft and waving her forward with his other hand. "Now, let's try again."

She fisted her hands on her hips, glaring at him for a moment in the dim light filtering through the windows of the barn behind his father's home. She bit her lip, then bent over at the waist to pick up the hem of her dress. Jonathan watched in surprise as she gathered the skirts between her legs and tucked them into her waistband. He tried not to stare at the lower half of her legs exposed by the action, but he could hardly be blamed for his inability to do so.

"What . . . what are you doing?" he asked in a choked voice.

"I'm up here," she replied dryly, waiting patiently for him to raise his gaze to her eyes. "I need more freedom of movement," she explained. "I trust this isn't too much for *your* delicate sensibilities?" She smirked, mimicking his earlier words, and picked up her sword.

"*Now*, let's try again," she said.

"Very well." Jonathan straightened, focusing on the goal at hand. "Remember, you must try to deflect the blow so you don't receive the full impact. Your size and agility are your strengths."

"I know." She nodded impatiently. "Slip. Slide. Spin. Smack."

"Precisely. Ready?"

Sarina held her sword with both hands in front of her, eyes focused in grim determination. "Ready."

Jonathan moved in—slower than usual, but not so slow it wouldn't be a challenge for her. He swung the cutlass in a wide arc from right to left, pleased when Sarina stepped back and to the side to evade the worst of the assault.

"Slip," she murmured under her breath.

She swung her sword along an intersecting arc, not trying to block his, but instead using her sword to change the angle of his blow. The two weapons rang out, metal gliding against metal as Jonathan's cutlass dipped to her side.

"Slide."

In a fluid motion, Sarina twirled around, her sword flashing. "Spin."

Then the flat of her sword tapped against his temple. "Smack."

Another spin, and the hilt touched his nose. "Smack."

And Sarina grabbed his shoulders, her knee coming up to nudge him between the legs.

"Smack," she said, smiling proudly as she looked up at him.

Jonathan grinned back. "Well done." It took a moment for him to recognize the strange warmth that filled him at her glowing expression.

Pride.

And something . . . *else.*

Her fingers flexed on his shoulders, her smile falling as a flush of pink climbed her cheeks. Jonathan realized she had yet to move, her knee still lodged between his legs, her body pressed up against him tantalizingly. Without realizing it, his own hands had drifted to her waist, and he swallowed thickly as they slid around to hold her closer. Both swords clattered to the floor, forgotten.

"Jonathan?" Her hesitant whisper seemed a mixture of confusion and wonder. Her eyes widened as he leaned down, so close her breath teased his tongue as his lips parted.

It was too much temptation, really. There was no way he could resist.

He closed the distance between them, taking her mouth without another moment of hesitation, and a shocked sound escaped her, the vibration sending a surge of heat through Jonathan's body. He pressed against her, one hand sliding up to hold her head in place. His fingers weaved through her hair, a few pins falling to the ground as it came loose in his grip, silken tresses falling over his wrist in a delicious tangle.

Sarina softened in his arms, fitting into the curve of his embrace with a quiet sigh. Teasing her mouth open, he dipped his tongue between her lips, shocked when she sucked it lightly, her fingers clutching his neck as if to hold him in place.

Like he was going anywhere.

He tightened his grip, lifting her so her toes barely brushed the ground, and turned his attention to her neck, burying his nose in her concentrated scent. He kissed the soft skin below her ear, his tongue darting out to taste her, eliciting a delicious shiver. Her head fell back as he slipped his tongue under the chain she always wore, following its trail down to where it disappeared beneath her bodice. She gasped as he teasingly licked into the cleft between her breasts, then nipped his way back up to the hollow of her throat.

"Jonathan . . ." A moan. A plea. A promise.

"Jonathan?" He stiffened at the more distant sound of a voice calling his name. A voice other than Sarina's.

He stepped back abruptly, loosening his grip on Sarina, but not releasing her. She swayed slightly, eyes wide and dazed.

"What . . ." she asked, steadying herself on his arms.

"Someone's coming."

She blinked twice, then seemed to grasp what he'd said. She started, hand flying to her throat . . . her disheveled hair. She swept it back, twisting it quickly as she searched the floor for her missing pins.

"Jonathan?" the voice called out again, closer now. At any moment, the barn door would fly open. Jonathan retrieved his coat and slipped it on quickly, buttoning it in an effort to hide the very obvious evidence of what they'd been doing. He adjusted himself, wincing slightly, and bent to pick up the swords.

"Mbbffmmm," Sarina mumbled through the pins in her mouth. At his confused glance, she removed the pins, sticking them quickly into her newly-formed bun, then straightening her skirts. "Who is it?" she whispered, taking her sword from him.

"Grace," he hissed back, raising the cutlass. "Come on, now. As you were."

Sarina raised her sword, swinging it with both hands and taking Jonathan a little by surprise when it clanged against his with more force than he expected. He stepped back, bracing himself, just as the barn door swung open and Grace Eaton stuck her head through the door.

"There you are!" she exclaimed, squinting as she entered the dim interior. "I'm sorry I wasn't here to greet you. Ellen Waltham went into labor and the midwife was dealing with another birth." She crossed to Jonathan, popping up on her toes to kiss his cheek.

"Is she all right?" Jonathan asked, smiling down at the woman he'd come to think of as family. Despite their rather unique relationship, Jonathan had always been close to Grace. It was odd, he supposed, but he had never felt anger toward either Grace or his father about their relationship. Perhaps he'd never seen the point.

Grace smiled. "She's fine. She had a strong baby boy." She turned to Sarina with a smile and slight nod. "You must be Sarina. I'm Grace Eaton, Charlotte's mother."

Sarina glanced at Jonathan nervously before smiling in return. "It's a pleasure to meet you, Miss Eaton."

"Please, call me Grace. No need to stand on ceremony." She looked between them, an unreadable glint in her eye. "Charlotte sent me to find you," she explained. "She says she's ready."

"Ah, good," Jonathan said brusquely, sheathing his sword and reaching for Sarina's to do the same. "Where is she?"

"In her hut. She's been preparing all morning."

Jonathan nodded, turning to Sarina. "We should go."

She didn't meet his eyes. "Would you mind?" She lifted her hands, and Jonathan noticed they trembled slightly. "Could I have a moment to clean up? I won't take long."

Jonathan pretended not to notice Grace studying him closely. "Of course. Go ahead, and I'll put your sword away. Meet us in front of the house." He and Grace followed Sarina out of the barn. Sarina turned to head to the pump behind the house as they continued toward the front porch.

"She's a beautiful girl," Grace said quietly.

Jonathan hummed noncommittally, studying the hilt of Sarina's sword.

"You two seem to have become quite close."

He snorted. "It will be fortunate if we don't kill each other before this is over."

"Oh, I don't think there's much danger of that," Grace said, amusement coloring her tone.

At that, he looked up, meeting her kind gaze before looking away.

"You like her," she said.

"Don't be ridiculous. She's the most stubborn, infuriating—"

"You *like* her." Grace's smile was smug. "It's nothing to be ashamed of."

He sighed and rubbed the back of his neck. He could almost feel the imprint of Sarina's fingers there, holding him close.

"Perhaps. A bit," he admitted. "Not that it matters."

"Of course it matters!"

Jonathan laughed humorlessly. "Why?" he asked. "Nothing can come of it."

"Why ever not?" Grace asked, searching his face.

Jonathan said nothing for a long moment, then replied, his voice a quiet rumble, "I've nothing to offer her."

"Now who's being ridiculous?" Grace linked her arm through his, drawing him near. "My daughter isn't the only one who sees things, Jonathan. It's obvious Sarina feels something for you, as well."

"Well, she shouldn't." He grunted. "What kind of a life could I give her? Always on the run . . . living day to day?"

"It doesn't have to be that way," Grace prodded, her voice quiet, tentative. "You could come home."

He laughed humorlessly. "It's too late for that," he said. "I'm a wanted man, Grace. It's dangerous for me to be here now, even for this brief time. It's dangerous for all of us."

They reached the house, and Jonathan tucked Sarina's sword just inside the front door before rejoining Grace, sitting on a bench next to her as they waited for Sarina.

Grace looked over the grassy area in front of the house. "You know, Jonathan," she said, "Charlotte is always telling me that the future is not set. Every decision we make alters our path and takes us in a new direction. It's why she sees some things clearly, and others are muddled and vague."

"Yes, she's said the same to me."

Grace smiled, patting his hand gently. "I find that comforting. To think that we make our own destiny. That there is always hope for the future."

Jonathan leaned forward, balancing his arms on his knees, gaze focused on his hands loosely clasped before him.

"Things change," Grace said fervently, reaching out to touch his cheek and draw his gaze. "Don't give up hope."

And as he looked into Grace's earnest face, he could almost believe it was true.

Rina's hands trembled as she dipped them into the water trough and splashed water on her cheeks to cool the burning there. She could still feel Jonathan's hands on her, his lips . . . his tongue. The way heat shot through her body like a bolt of lightning.

The shameful way she threw herself at him, begging for more.

Pressing a damp hand against the back of her neck, she drew in a heavy breath. What was she thinking?

The fact was, she hadn't been thinking at all. When he touched her, all rational thought dissolved away, leaving behind only touch and taste and scent . . .

And instinct. The instinct to draw him closer, press against him completely . . . if she could, to climb inside him and wrap herself in his warmth.

Thank heavens Grace had come along, or Sarina had no doubt she would have stopped at nothing to have him. Like a common strumpet, she would have thrown herself at him, begging—or even demanding—that he give her what she wanted.

And Rina could no longer deny that she wanted. She *wanted* . . . desperately.

But such a liaison could only end in disaster, and lord knows her life was disaster enough already. No, giving in to these cravings would only lead to pain. Jonathan Tremayne admitted himself that he never kept a woman for long. There was no doubt he would break her heart.

Rina straightened and patted her hair into place, regaining her poise with every deep breath. She needed to be more careful; keep her guard up around Jonathan. And for goodness sake, she needed to avoid getting close enough to touch the man.

Yes, she could do this. She just needed to stay in control of the situation.

Focus on her mission. Finding Kane. Finding the treasure.

Working with Jonathan to avenge her father's death, and then getting back to her own life—although she had no idea what exactly that would entail at that moment.

She did know, however, that she no longer planned to try to turn Jonathan over to the Crown. Rina wasn't precisely sure when she'd decided that, but she knew it now without a doubt. Jonathan Tremayne may have broken the law, but she knew in her heart he was a decent man—driven to his actions by pain that few could understand.

Sarina understood.

No, there would be no gathering evidence, no seeking Commodore Stanton when all of this was over. Instead, she and Jonathan would go their separate ways amicably.

She didn't want to consider why that thought left an empty feeling in her stomach.

Rolling her shoulders, Rina walked around the side of the house to find Jonathan and Grace sitting on a bench on the front porch. The woman resembled Charlotte—or vice versa, Rina supposed—a bit slighter in stature, but with the same dark hair. Her eyes, though, were deep blue, where Charlotte's were brown. And she was calmer, quieter than her vivacious daughter, though no less friendly, as she demonstrated by smiling when she spotted Rina approaching. Jonathan stood in turn, tall and handsome in his refined suit of clothes, and Rina looked away quickly, fighting to control the flush on her cheeks.

"Ready?" Jonathan asked, his attention drawn by the sound of approaching hoof beats. They looked up as Lord Tremayne rode up on a black stallion, hair disheveled and breath a bit heavy from exertion.

"Good day," he said, climbing down from the saddle and handing the reins to a young boy. He smoothed a hand over his hair. "Lovely day, isn't it? I apologize for missing you at breakfast. I had business to attend to in town." He turned to Jonathan. "Max asked me to tell you he would be along shortly." Jonathan nodded as his father smiled at Sarina. "I trust you slept well?"

"Yes, thank you. I was quite comfortable."

"Good. That's good," he replied, a bit distracted. Sarina understood why when his gaze drifted to Grace, still sitting on the porch bench.

"Miss Eaton. I hope you are well this morning."

Grace smiled. "Very well. Thank you."

Rina watched as they stared at each other for a long moment, feeling a bit like an intruder. Then Lord Tremayne started slightly and turned to Jonathan. "You're off to see Charlotte, then?"

Jonathan nodded.

"And then I suppose you'll be leaving us."

"At sundown."

Jonathan's father took a deep, resigned breath. "Well, then. We'll need to have Cook prepare a special supper before you depart." He turned back to Grace, his face softening and the ever-present sadness in his eyes vanishing as he gazed at her. "Perhaps you could help me create a suitable menu, Miss Eaton?"

"It would be my pleasure," she replied, cheeks coloring lightly.

He started toward her, then held out a hand. "Would you like to take a turn about the property first?" he asked quietly. "As I said, it is a lovely day. It would be a shame to waste it."

Grace smiled prettily and laid her hand in his. He gently drew it into the crook of his elbow and led her off the porch without a glance back.

Rina watched them walk away. "Are they always like that?" she asked Jonathan.

"Aye," Jonathan replied. "Like there is no one else in the world."

"I don't understand," she began. "They're so in love. It's obvious they belong together. It seems such a waste." Realizing her words might offend, she turned to Jonathan wide-eyed. "Not that it's any of my business. I'm sorry. This must be a sensitive subject for you."

Jonathan continued to watch his father and Grace as they neared the tree line. "Not really. You would expect so, but you would be wrong," he said quietly. "We should go." He started off the porch, and Rina fell into step next to him. She'd thought the subject dropped until he spoke again.

"I knew from a very young age that my parents didn't love each other," he said. "They both loved me. I was fortunate in that regard. And they respected each other, I suppose you could say. But the truth is, theirs was a marriage based on money and power, not love.

"But what my father and Grace have . . ." His voice trailed off as he thought for a moment. "Well, that is something that is rare and pure. I would never be one to deny it." He flashed a grin at her. "Did Charlotte tell you about the first time we met?"

Rina shook her head. They neared a path through the woods, and Jonathan held a branch out of her way. The air was cooler there, damp and mossy, and she drew her shawl closer around her shoulders as she followed behind him.

"I was ten years old at the time," he said. "Charlotte was about four, and I came upon her playing on the beach. She was a tiny thing with wild hair sticking out every which way. I was a bit full of myself at the time—" Sarina snorted, and he glanced back at her wryly. "I demanded to know who she was and why she was playing on *my* beach. She looked up at me with these huge eyes— much too big for her face—and said she was Charlotte Eaton Tremayne, and it was *her* beach because her father told her so.

"I was outraged, naturally," he continued. "I called her a liar and went home to tell my mother. But when I mentioned the girl's name, my mother broke. She said I was making it up and there was no such girl, and I should never speak of her again.

"I insisted I was telling the truth, but she would hear none of it." He paused, turning back to her. "It was the only time my mother ever beat me."

Rina gaped at him, lost for words as he turned to continue down the path. "Afterward, my father found me hiding in the barn. He dried my tears and told me Charlotte was my sister. That as her elder brother, it was my duty to protect her. I was to never mention her to anyone else—especially my mother—but I was to care for her above all others. He said he counted on me to take the responsibility seriously.

"I asked about her mother, and he told me it was Grace. She continued to work in our house, you know, although my mother would no longer allow her to live under the same roof. I learned later how she tormented Grace. She was unbelievably cruel . . ."

He shook his head. "My father didn't say much about Grace, but even at that young age, I could see the love in his eyes. It was something I'd never seen there for my mother." He paused, leaning his hand on a tree and looking up toward the sky.

"People are rarely either good or evil," he said. "It's easy to judge my father and Grace for what they did, to judge my mother for the times she was cruel, but there were just as many times she was kind, doting on me as only a mother can. The strain of everything took its toll on her, I suppose. Like anyone, she was imperfect. But she was still my mother, and I loved her.

"As for my father and Grace, who can say they wouldn't do the same for love? Charlotte and I have both encouraged them to get married, but my father won't hear of it. He is consumed by guilt over my mother's murder, and insists on punishing himself by keeping away from Grace."

He glanced at Rina. "But, as you could see, sometimes he cannot resist."

She nodded sadly. "What about Grace? How can she live like that?"

He sighed. "Grace lives in faith that things will change," he said. "She waits patiently for him to exorcise his demons, convinced that someday they will be together."

"You're not certain that will happen."

Jonathan shrugged but said nothing. He continued on the path and Rina noticed the trees had become thicker, the sunlight barely penetrating the canopy overhead as they weaved between the gnarled trunks. They came to a small clearing, and in the center stood a little stone hut with a thatched roof and smoke trickling from a crooked chimney. To Rina's surprise, the air smelled almost sweet.

Jonathan came to a stop and reached for her arm. She flinched at his touch, and he pulled back quickly.

"I'm sorry—"

"No, it's fine. I was just—"

"My fault—"

"No, it's mine—"

"Smith!" he snapped, pinching the bridge of his nose in frustration. "Let's just forget it, shall we?" At her flushed nod, he added, "I only wanted to warn you that Charlotte may seem a bit . . . odd when you see her."

Sarina cocked her head. "What do you mean odd?"

Jonathan glanced toward the hut, lowering his voice, slightly. "With Grace working for our family much of the time, Charlotte grew up with the people who worked for my father, most of them natives from the islands, or even as far away as Africa."

Rina nodded in understanding, and he continued. "Many of them were practitioners of strange religions, and Charlotte came to study under a local priestess from Hispaniola who taught her rituals to help her sharpen her natural-born sight."

"What kind of rituals?" she asked, her voice taking on a hushed tone. "Do you mean magic? Dark arts?" She had heard tales of such things but dismissed them as fancy. Now, in the thick quiet of the forest with the strange, sweet smell around her, an inadvertent shiver raced down her spine at the idea.

"They call it Vodou," he replied. "I don't understand much of it. Spirits and sacrifices. There was a time when I thought it all a bunch of rubbish, but it does seem to help Charlotte. I no longer find it that easy to dismiss. I wanted you to be prepared," he said. He leaned in with a teasing wink. "There's still time to run back home, Smith."

Rina's eyes narrowed. "I believe I can deal with it."

Jonathan shrugged. "Very well. Just be certain you don't swoon, would you? It's getting too bloody hot to carry you back."

"Can we go in now?" she asked in irritation, ignoring the tingle she felt at the thought of Jonathan carrying her. She headed toward the hut and lifted her fist to knock at the rough wooden door, Jonathan at her heels.

"Enter," a voice called.

Rina lifted the latch and shoved the door open, stepping into the cool, dim interior. The sweet smell was thicker inside, and as

Jonathan closed the door behind them, she had a strange sense of being trapped . . . locked in another world. Candles flickered all around the room—on tables, benches, shelves set into the walls at varying heights, casting everything in a warm glow. Charlotte watched them carefully from where she stood behind a table, dressed in a rich gold gown, the sleeves flaring wide from elbow to wrist. She wore no wig. Instead, her hair hung in waves about her shoulders, dark and thick. But it was her face that gave Sarina pause. Thickly powdered and so pale she resembled a corpse, Charlotte had outlined her dark eyes with a thick line of kohl. The effect was disturbing, and once again, Rina shivered.

Jonathan nudged her forward, and she stepped toward the table in a daze, noticing for the first time the items lined up before Charlotte. Mellick's journal and the chest from the *Lady* sat next to a plate of some kind of roasted meat, a cluster of dried flowers, a glass of water, a cloth bag, and yet another grouping of candles. Charlotte lifted her arms, the sleeves of her gown falling back to reveal her slender forearms, and Sarina could have sworn a light wind swirled around the room.

A low murmur reached Rina's ears, and she realized Charlotte was chanting something quietly; exotic words in a foreign tongue. Charlotte began to sway, her head tilting back as she chanted, the words growing louder . . . faster . . . with every rhythmic repetition. Suddenly, with a sharp cry, her head snapped up and she clapped her hands loudly once, the candles flaring in unison before settling once again to a low flicker.

"The Lwa—the spirits—are pleased," Charlotte said in a low voice, one hand drifting over the table in front of her. "I have offered gifts on your behalf, and they are prepared to hear your request." She turned to address Jonathan.

"Jonathan Tremayne, what do you seek?"

Jonathan stepped forward, clearing his throat. "I seek the cup . . . and Kane the Merciless."

"Ah, yes, the cup," Charlotte replied, opening the journal to a page marked with a black ribbon. Rina could make out the sketch of a cup she'd seen when exploring the book herself—a crude rendering, as if drawn in haste, unlike the sketch of the cutlass. Charlotte ran her fingers over the picture lightly, then picked up the cloth bag and pulled the drawstring open. She shook the bag, eliciting a rattling sound, then upturned it, pouring its contents over the open pages of the journal. Charlotte looked down, poking through the mixture of seashells, rocks, and small whitewashed bones, her brow creased in concentration.

"South," Charlotte said, her words a quiet drone. "You must go south to Savannah. You'll find the cup behind a blue door." She didn't blink, barely breathed. "As for Kane, your paths will cross soon. Sooner than you expect. But first—" She glanced up at Jonathan, eyes wide. "First, the king's man will come for you."

"King's man?" Jonathan repeated. "Do you mean Stanton?"

Charlotte poked through the items on the journal again. "Yes. He is coming, Jonathan. You must go."

"What of the coin?" he asked. "The map?"

Charlotte's eyes glazed over for a moment before focusing on Jonathan once again. "The map is coming to you. It's in the box as you suspect, and you'll receive word soon where to find it."

"What box—" Sarina began. Jonathan held up a finger to silence her.

"As for the coin . . ." Charlotte continued, her brow creased in concentration. "It's shrouded in darkness. It's somewhere familiar, but I cannot see it clearly."

She shook her head as if to clear it. "You need to go, Jonathan. Before Stanton arrives."

"The ship won't return until nightfall," he said, leaning forward as if he could read Charlotte's stones and bones himself. "Is there enough time?"

Charlotte frowned. "I don't know. It's unclear. It will be very close, Jonathan. You will need to hurry."

Jonathan nodded and reached for Rina's elbow. "We should get ready. I want to be on the beach at sunset."

They turned to leave, and Charlotte called out. "Jonathan?"

He looked back at her, waiting.

"There's more," she said, eyes now staring straight ahead, unseeing.

Or perhaps, Rina thought, *seeing*.

"I see . . . a betrayal," Charlotte said. "Someone will betray you, Jonathan."

He stiffened. "Who?"

"I don't know. But it's someone close to you. Someone you trust." She blinked, her black eyes regaining focus. "Be careful, Jonathan." She gathered up the journal and the chest and handed them back to him, her hand lingering on his arm for a moment to punctuate the warning.

With a grim nod, he turned and opened the door. Rina looked back to see Charlotte watching them closely as all the candles in the room flared high for a moment, then sputtered out, leaving the room in darkness. Charlotte's eyes gleamed, reflecting the light from the open door, and Rina turned away to follow Jonathan outside, her hands clutched together to keep them from trembling.

*With each step I closer to my goal. Now in the warmer southern waters, I find memories of the horrible winter fading, replaced by hope for what is to come.*

*Yet hope, as always, is tempered with caution.*

*- The Journal of*
  *Simon Alistair Mellick*
  *15 January, 1665*

Charlotte's words haunted Jonathan as he and Sarina walked back toward the house. Stanton was closing in. Someone was going to betray him. He glanced at Sarina beside him, not wanting to believe what he suspected.

*Would she be the one?*

Sarina caught him looking at her. "What is it?"

"Nothing."

Sarina sighed, her exhale loud in the quiet forest. "You think it's me."

"Think what's you?"

"Don't play innocent, Jonathan. It really doesn't suit you." Sarina stopped and reached for his arm, pulling her hand back quickly when he flinched. She flushed and looked away abruptly, and he felt a twinge at the idea that he might have actually hurt her feelings.

"You think it's me who will betray you." She hurried to continue, not giving him a chance to respond. "Not that I blame you. You hardly know me, and I haven't done much to gain your trust since we met." She started forward again, not looking back to see if he followed. "But it isn't me, just so you know, and I'm willing to wait until you believe that. I won't even ask about the box Charlotte mentioned, just to prove to you I'm not gathering information to go out on my own."

Jonathan watched her walk away, a leaden feeling twisting in his gut when he realized he really *didn't* suspect her. He couldn't explain it, but he knew—for some strange reason—that he could trust her.

"Smith, wait," he said, raising his voice to call out louder when she didn't stop. "Sarina!"

She paused and he hurried to catch up with her. She brushed at her eyes before turning to look up at him, and he realized she was hiding tears.

"Are you crying?"

She scoffed. "Of course not. It's just . . ." She waved a hand around. "The dust."

Jonathan laughed. "I should have known you could never betray anyone," he said with a smirk. "You're a dreadful liar, Smith." She huffed and turned away, but he grabbed her arm to still her movements.

"I'm sorry," he said quietly.

She blinked in surprise and opened her mouth to respond, but no sounds emerged.

Jonathan laughed again. "Speechless, Smith? If I'd known all it took was an apology to get a little peace and quiet, I would have done it sooner."

Sarina tried to feign irritation, but the quirk of her lips gave her away. "You really are a bastard." Somehow, the words came out rather fond.

Jonathan grinned, shaking a finger playfully. "Now, Smith, you've met my father. You know that's not true."

Sarina shook her head in exasperation. "It's more a comment on your personality than your parentage."

Jonathan's hand flew to his chest, his face grave. "You wound me."

"Somehow, I feel your ego will survive."

They turned together to head out of the forest as Jonathan snorted. "Oh, Smith. What would I do without your charming conversation?"

"Well, if Charlotte is right, it won't be long until we find the treasure—and Kane—and this is all over. You won't have to wait long to find out." She said the words with a teasing lilt, but for some reason, they left Jonathan feeling rather empty. She glanced at him curiously, obviously noticing the falter in his step, and he forced a smile.

"Speaking of Charlotte," he said, "the box she spoke of is a puzzle box once owned by Mellick. I believe the other half of the map is in it and have several people searching for it on my behalf."

"People you can trust?"

Jonathan shrugged. "For a price. They don't know of the map, just the box, and the promise of a handsome reward should be enough."

Sarina bit her lip in consideration. "Well, you must be right if Charlotte says you are."

"Does that mean you've become a believer then?" He watched her carefully.

Sarina shrugged. "I've no reason to doubt Charlotte," she explained. "And I've no better idea than to follow her instructions."

Max was waiting for them when they returned to the house, pacing back and forth across the front porch. He looked up as Sarina and Jonathan approached and walked over to meet them. Like Jonathan, he had opted for a sophisticated suit given their temporary surroundings—dark gray with an emerald waistcoat— his dark hair smoothly clubbed and gleaming in the sunlight.

He nodded in greeting to Sarina, then turned to Jonathan. "Did you get your answers?"

"Some," he replied. "As well as more questions. But that is not unusual when dealing with Charlotte."

Max laughed, nodding his head as he ran his hand over his hair. "Yes, well, at least you had *some* success."

"Did you learn anything in town?" Jonathan asked, as they turned to head toward the house. Max was excellent at ferreting out information, and Jonathan had sent him to see what he could learn about Kane's whereabouts. It was difficult to track him while they were on the ship, and he'd hoped that perhaps on the mainland there might be some rumor of where he could be found.

"Nothing," Max said with a heavy sigh. "No news of Kane . . . or Stanton, for that matter. The good news is the Crown seems to be focusing its search for the *Arrow* near Hispaniola at this point."

"Not Stanton," Jonathan corrected. "Charlotte says he's already on his way."

Max frowned. "How soon?"

"She didn't know, but we sail for Savannah at sundown."

"Savannah?" Max frowned slightly. "For what purpose?"

"Charlotte says that's where we're to find the cup. *Behind a blue door*."

"A blue door? Well, that should be simple. How many doors can there be in Savannah?" Max laughed as they neared the house. He held the front door open for Sarina with a slight bow. "Did you ask Charlotte any questions of your own?"

Sarina looked genuinely surprised. "No. I hadn't thought of it, to be honest."

"It doesn't matter. She'll know the questions already, as well as the answers," he said with a fond grin. "Of course, she won't share them unless you ask."

"She says it's rude," Jonathan added as he led them into the sitting room and sprawled on the settee. "I think she just enjoys tormenting people."

Sarina sat across from Jonathan and watched Max as he assumed his usual position at the fireplace. "Have *you* ever asked her anything?" she asked.

Max flushed slightly, eyes drifting to look out the window in the direction of Charlotte's hut. "Aye. Once or twice."

"Did what she say come true?"

Max looked back at her, a soft smile on his face. "Not yet."

A flash of movement at the window drew his gaze back as Charlotte emerged from the woods. His smile grew, eyes focused on her form as he said, "If you'll both excuse me. I have some matters to attend to before we leave."

He nodded at Sarina once before striding from the room. Jonathan stood, taking his position by the fireplace, and after a moment, spotted Max approaching Charlotte out the window. She'd tied her long hair loosely at the nape of her neck, and her face was scrubbed clean from the powder and kohl. She looked so young, he mused. The two turned and walked away together, faces beaming.

"They're in love," Sarina said quietly.

"Aye."

"For how long?"

Jonathan sighed. "Forever, it seems."

"They have so little time together. It must be difficult." She stood and walked to the window, leaning her face against the cool glass and watching them stroll along the edge of the woods. "So much sadness here," she mused. "Your father separated from Grace. You separated from your family. Max and Charlotte."

Jonathan cleared his throat but said nothing. Sarina turned to look at him, her eyes sorrowful, and a rush of warmth filled him. Part of him longed to cast aside his doubts and cross the room and gather her in his arms. She leaned toward him slightly, and for a moment, he wondered if she might have been thinking the same thing.

Thinking about what had been interrupted in the barn.

But just as quickly, the moment passed, and Sarina shook her head slightly, returning to the settee.

"Do you think . . ." she began hesitantly, "when all this is over, you'll come back here?"

Jonathan stiffened, running his fingers lightly along the fireplace mantle. "There is no place for me here now. My life, such as it is, is on the *Arrow*."

"Ah," she said, "yes, of course." Did he detect a note of disappointment in her voice?

For some reason, Jonathan felt a need to explain himself. "It would be dangerous for me to remain here. I am, as you are well aware, a criminal." When he turned to look at her, he found her watching him, face impassive. He swallowed, fighting the urge to squirm under her direct examination.

"But how long can you live like this?" she asked, her voice barely a whisper.

Jonathan held her gaze for a moment before turning to look back out the window.

"As long as I must," he said.

There were times in Max's life when he felt as if the weight of the world were on his shoulders, when the responsibilities he had—the promises he'd made—became a dark cloud enveloping him, almost cutting off his very breath.

But when he emerged from the Tremayne home and saw Charlotte standing across the lawn in the bright sunshine, all that weight melted away. She spotted him, her face blossoming into a smile, and he couldn't help but return it. Her golden gown glowed in the sun, skirts billowing about her legs in the light breeze. She brushed back a few loose strands of hair from her face, and he quickened his pace, eager to get to her.

Every moment was precious.

"Nice suit," she teased as he drew closer.

Max laughed, unable to hold it in. "Well, you know. When in Rome and all that . . ."

Charlotte grinned as he took her hand, rubbing his thumb over it in gentle circles. "One would hardly know you're a dread pirate."

"Don't let the gentlemanly exterior fool you," he said, leaning in with a wink. "I'm still quite the dastardly fiend inside, where it counts."

He tucked her hand into his elbow, leading her on a quiet stroll across the property. They nodded at the few people they saw—most out working in the fields after a short luncheon break—and enjoyed a companionable silence. Max relished these times together, however few and far between. He had treasured them since the first time he'd laid eyes on Charlotte so many years ago, when Jonathan was wounded so badly and had to return home to recover. It was when Max had first learned the truth of Jonathan's parentage, and he'd been the only one Jonathan trusted enough to take him home.

Charlotte had been but a girl of fourteen then and had swept into the room wild-eyed and frantic, only calming once she held Jonathan's hand in her own. She never left his side during the first days when the doctor doubted he would survive, and even when it appeared he'd turned a corner, she was never away from him for long.

Then, she'd approached Max one morning as he stood looking out over the creek, lost in thought. She'd eyed him carefully, hands on her hips, then said simply, "Give me your hand."

Max was barely eighteen himself, but when his fingers touched hers, he knew there would be no other for him . . . knew it even before she looked down to trace a line on his palm, then meet his gaze with a soft smile.

"I've been waiting for you for quite a while," she said. Max had the strangest urge to apologize, but before he could, she added, "and I fear I will have to wait a while longer."

"What do you mean?"

Max could feel each of her fingers as if they burned into his skin, her eyes dark and intent as she stared into his.

"I must ask for your vow, Maxwell Baines."

Max knew he would promise her anything, but still he asked, "What vow?"

Charlotte's eyes glazed over for a moment before she focused on him again. "You must protect Jonathan," she said. "You must stand by his side at all costs."

Max had been confused at the request. He and Jonathan had been friends since he'd first set foot on the *Arrow*, and they'd formed an alliance in those early days. They looked out for each other. Indeed, their friendship had been what had saved Jonathan from Kane's sword. Max knew Jonathan would do the same for him if the situation were reversed.

"Of course," he said quickly.

"You don't understand, Max," Charlotte had added, her voice taking on an urgent tone. "I am asking you to put Jonathan before yourself—his needs before your own. It will require great sacrifice on your part, perhaps even your own life.

"I cannot see it clearly, but your destinies are intertwined," she continued. "But for all to be as it should be, you must not leave his side, no matter how much you may long to." The last words were spoken wistfully, a sparkle of tears appearing in her eyes. "No matter how much we *both* may long for it."

"I don't understand . . ." Max's words had drifted off as he looked into her eyes. In that moment, he knew he would give her whatever she asked. "All right," he said. "I promise."

And Charlotte had smiled sadly before releasing his hand. "It will be all right," she said. "We just have to be patient."

Max hadn't known then what exactly she meant, but when Jonathan became captain and named him first mate, he began to understand. When late one night, over a jug of rum, Jonathan had revealed his plan to kill Kane—to find the treasure—it became even clearer.

And each time he'd returned to Charles Towne, only to leave Charlotte behind when every fiber of his being fought against it, he truly comprehended what his vow entailed.

And still, he kept it. Because he'd promised her, and he never faltered in his duty.

He turned to look at her briefly, even years later awed as he always was by the curve of her cheek, the soft radiance of her skin. She caught his eye, blushing slightly.

"So, Jonathan said we're headed to Savannah," he said after a while. "To a blue door."

Charlotte tipped her head in acknowledgment.

"Was there anything more?" he asked.

Charlotte smiled at him. "You have what you need."

Max nodded, trusting her as he always did, and they turned down the trail leading to the creek. "We haven't had much time to talk," he said. "How have you been?"

"Fine," she replied. "You know how it is here. Nothing changes, really. Time moves, but rather slowly, it seems."

Max raised a tentative hand to stroke her fingers. "I wish . . ."

Charlotte shook her head, leaning into him slightly. "If wishes were pennies I'd be the wealthiest woman in South Carolina," she said. "We both have our destinies to fulfill. Our time will come."

"Are you certain?" he asked, looking into her dark eyes. "Is it wrong for me to keep you waiting like this? I often feel like the most selfish man alive—"

"There is not a selfish bone in your body."

"I should release you. Free you to find a husband, have children."

Charlotte stopped short, eyes flashing as she turned to face him. "You sound like my father."

Max walked away a few steps, his back to her. "Perhaps he is right. He only wants the best for you."

"*I* choose what's best for me," Charlotte said, crossing to look him in the eye. "I choose you."

"And what do I have to offer you?" he asked. "No home. No name. No fortune of note . . ."

"Max, you know I want none of those things" she said, lifting her hands to cup his face. "But perhaps it is you who has regrets?" Her smile fell, her eyes searching his. "Do you wish your freedom?"

His hands covered hers. "Never," he said. "There is no other for me, Charlotte, not in this life. And although I may regret I have but a few stolen moments with you, it is no hardship for me to stand at Jonathan's side. You know he is like a brother to me.

"And I will wait forever for you, if that is what must be."

Charlotte smiled. "Then you must trust me. This will all turn out for the best." She glanced over her shoulder briefly, then popped up on her toes to kiss his lips lightly. Max wished she would linger, but she stepped back with a smile.

"Besides," she said. "I may be an old maid, but I'm not *that* old. Barely one-and-twenty. There is still time for a husband." She ran her hands down his arms to take both of his, a mischievous smile on her face. "And a family."

Her grin was infectious, and Max found himself matching it. "You're sure you still want me, then?"

"No one else will do."

At that, Max raised a brow, looking around quickly before pulling her down the path into the forest. He led her deeper into the trees, then drew her into his arms.

"In that case, perhaps I need to give you something to remember me by," he said, dipping his head to nuzzle her neck.

Charlotte giggled. "Just what did you have in mind?"

"Just a few things I've learned from Jonathan about claiming a lady."

Charlotte grimaced. "Please, do not mention my brother at a time like this."

Max chuckled. "Point taken." He pulled her closer and wrapped his arms around her tiny waist. Charlotte's fingers trailed up his arms before linking behind his neck, and he leaned down to kiss her once . . . twice . . . before sighing deeply and taking her mouth more possessively. As always, in Charlotte's arms he felt right—like coming home after a long voyage.

She was his home, after all. No matter where he traveled, she was what steered his life. His true north in the midst of a vast ocean.

When they finally broke apart, both gasping for breath, he held her close, whispering promises of love and hope and a future.

And she whispered them right back.

Waiting for sunset was torturous.

To Rina, it seemed the sun would never sink below the horizon. She stood with Jonathan and Max in the underbrush where they'd hidden the dinghy, eyes scanning the beach for any signs of life. Jonathan's father had provided horses for the journey, accompanying them nearly all the way before taking their mounts back home, bidding them all goodbye with a firm nod, and a "God be with you." They'd made it the rest of the way on foot, Rina's heart racing the whole way.

She thought she might expire on the spot when a pair of soldiers on horseback approached, hoof beats muffled in the mud. She gasped when they passed close by their hiding spot, and Jonathan took her hand, squeezing it tightly in warning. She clung to him, barely daring to breathe until the men rode out of sight down the beach.

"It's all right," Jonathan murmured, his lips close to her ear. His breath tickled her skin, and she shivered, eyes fluttering closed briefly. She realized she still gripped his hand and released it abruptly, stepping away and nearly stumbling out of the brush.

Jonathan reached for her, his large hands closing on her hips to steady her.

"Easy," he said, voice low, his eye glittering in the dwindling sunlight. "Don't swoon on me now, Smith."

Rina's skin felt hot, her mouth parched, and she licked her lips to moisten them. His gaze dipped, following the motion, his own mouth curving into a smirk. He met her startled eyes, his fingers tightening on her waist, and Rina's breath caught, dizziness sweeping through her.

So much for her plan not to get close to him. Actually, at that moment, she really couldn't recall her reasoning behind that decision. It seemed a bit silly, when being close to him felt so, so good.

A throat cleared. "Sun's going down," Max said with a pointed look as he tossed away the branches camouflaging the dinghy. "Perhaps you two could continue this discussion later?"

Jonathan pulled away, focus lingering for a moment before he turned to help Max drag the dinghy down to the water. Rina scanned the beach, following behind them and taking Max's hand when he offered it to help her into the boat. He froze, turning his head in surprise, and she followed his gaze to see Charlotte standing on the shore a short distance away. Max helped Rina into the boat and turned to Jonathan.

"I'll be but a moment," he said quietly.

Jonathan nodded, and Rina settled on the bench, watching Max approach Charlotte. The two spoke in quiet tones for a moment, their voices lost amidst the crashing waves. Then, Charlotte reached up to her nape and pulled the ribbon from her hair to tie it around Max's wrist. He lifted his hand, touching her face in almost reverence, and Rina looked away, embarrassed at witnessing such an intimate moment. She caught sight of Jonathan standing on the other side of the dinghy, gaze focused resolutely out over the water. He caught her eye briefly and cleared his throat.

"The winds are with us," he said. "Should be a short trip to Savannah."

"That's good." She examined his profile, the strong line of his jaw . . . his throat, now fully on display since he'd traded his fine suit and cravat for his usual open-necked shirt, breeches and boots. He swallowed, and in the dwindling light, she could just make out the movement of his Adam's apple as it bobbed. He turned toward her again, and she flushed, embarrassed to be caught ogling.

She needed to get better at this.

He was silent, so she snuck a look at him, only to find him regarding her carefully. He licked his lips. "Smith . . . I . . ."

Max, of course, chose that moment to step up to the dinghy and throw in a large cloth bag with a thud. "From Charlotte," he said to Rina. "She said it's something you'll find useful in the coming days." He leaned down to push the dinghy off the shore, glancing up at Jonathan, who still had yet to move.

"Jonathan? Are you ready?"

Jonathan cleared his throat and set to aiding him in the task. They stepped into the water, giving the front of the boat a shove before getting in and settling at the oars. Sarina looked over her shoulder to find Charlotte still standing on the beach, the wind whipping at her skirts and her hair flying wildly around her head.

Sarina lifted a hand to wave, and Charlotte returned the gesture before fading away in the darkness.

Rina turned back around as they made their way slowly out of the harbor and into open water, silence thick around them. Jonathan refused to meet her eyes, his own gaze fixed at some point over her shoulder. Max's melancholy was a tangible thing, and Rina's heart broke a little when she spotted the yellow ribbon peeking out from the edge of his shirt sleeve. The quiet dip of the oars set an easy rhythm, and before long they'd left the shoreline behind, surrounded only by dark water as far as they could see.

When the hulking shadow of a ship appeared before them, Rina let out a sigh of relief. Jonathan looked over his shoulder, then nudged Max to gain his attention. The two stopped rowing abruptly and exchanged a concerned glance.

"What's wrong?" she asked. Jonathan pressed a finger to his lips, leaning forward to whisper in her ear, his words sending a chill down her spine.

"That's not the *Arrow*."

Rina sat back, mouth dropping open in horror as she looked up at the ship before them. Men rushed about the deck, carrying lanterns and shouting orders as it headed toward the harbor. She gasped when she finally recognized it as the *Intrepid*, Commodore Stanton's ship.

Charlotte was right.

Max tapped Jonathan's arm, pointing off to the left, and Rina squinted, barely able to discern the shape of another ship in the distance. Jonathan nodded and the two began to row again, tension in every stroke of the oars. All three of them kept their eyes fixed on the *Intrepid* as they pulled farther away, waiting for someone to shout—to notice them and spring into action. But apparently the lanterns on Stanton's ship were enough to diminish their view of the waters surrounding them, because Sarina heard no alert—no sign that the Crown ship had spotted either the dinghy or the *Arrow*.

Still, she didn't draw a steady breath until they'd reached Jonathan's ship and her feet stepped firmly on the deck.

With quiet efficiency, the crew set sail away from Charles Towne and Commodore Stanton as quickly as possible. They had to head north and east to avoid him, circling around to approach Savannah once they were certain he was no longer a threat. Jonathan dismissed Max with a nod and turned to discuss their course with Crawley. After a short chat with James, Rina took the opportunity to escape belowdecks. She started toward the captain's quarters, but decided she really needed some time alone with her thoughts . . . time to absorb all she'd learned about Jonathan and his family. Time to think about what was obviously growing between them and what exactly she should do about it.

Instead she headed toward the hold, seeking out the small storage room where she'd slept while masquerading as Smith. Out of habit, she quickly scanned the hallway, although there was no reason anyone would question her activities now, before shoving the door open and slipping into the room. To her surprise, it wasn't dark inside, but lit by the soft glow of a lantern sitting on an upturned crate. Max looked up from where he sat on the other side of the crate, a jug of rum in his hands.

"Are you lost?" he asked, lifting the jug to his lips and taking a deep swallow.

"No. I . . ." She started to turn back to the door. "I'm sorry. I didn't mean to intrude."

"Not at all," he said. "I suppose I wouldn't mind some company, if you don't mind me getting roaring drunk." He took another gulp from the jug and wiped his mouth with the back of his hand as he eyed her carefully. "In fact, you look like you could use a nip yourself."

Rina hesitated, then realized that perhaps that was exactly what she needed. Not to dwell and think and obsess about everything, but to forget about it—if only for a few hours. She stepped back inside and closed the door behind her before crossing the room. Max reached over to push another crate toward her and she perched on it, trying not to stare at the ribbon tied around his wrist. He noticed her interest, however, and set the jug on the table as he fingered it lightly.

"She wanted me to have something to remember her by," he murmured, his words already beginning to slur. "As if I could ever forget."

"I'm sorry."

"No need," he said, reaching for the jug and taking another drink before offering it to Rina with a raised brow. She took it from him, tipping it to her lips and taking a tentative sip. The rum burned going down, but she'd grown somewhat accustomed to it as of late, and she took another swallow before handing it back to Max.

They sat in silence for a while, the only sound the glug of rum as they passed the jug back and forth. Rina's body filled with languid warmth, her mind growing soft and muzzy.

Finally, Max spoke.

"You want to talk about it?"

Her thoughts immediately flew to Jonathan, and she frowned. "Not really. You?"

"Not really." He tipped his crate back, rocking on one end. He took another drink, swishing the rum around in his mouth before swallowing. When he looked at her, Rina noticed his eyes seemed a bit glazed. Of course, it was getting more difficult to tell, since there seemed to be two of him.

"It's just that I made a vow," he said, leaning forward and missing his knee with his elbow a couple times before making contact and bracing himself. "She made me promise, you see. And because of that promise, I can't be with her."

"What kind of promise?"

He waved a hand in the air. "To watch over Jonathan, of course. To protect him. As if he needs protecting!"

Rina swayed a little in her seat, gripping it slightly as she tried to focus. "Charlotte made you promise?"

Max laughed. "Who else?"

"And now you have to stay with Jonathan and you can't be with her?"

Max snapped his fingers. "Aye."

"But . . . that's so . . ." Rina searched for the word, but it seemed to elude her. "It's so . . . so . . ." She hiccupped. ". . . *sad*."

"Aye." Max sighed.

"Because you *love* her," she said mournfully, suddenly overcome with emotion. She reached for Max's arm, almost falling off her crate in the attempt. "You *love* her," she repeated, a bit louder.

"Aye."

She stood, knees wobbling for a moment before crossing to the porthole. "So now, she's out there . . . and you're stuck on this stupid ship!" Rina kicked the wall, then again for good measure.

"S'not stupid," he slurred.

"It is!" She kicked it again.

Max belched.

"That's disgusting," Rina said, nose wrinkling.

"Beg yer pardon, Your Majesty."

She waved a hand in dismissal, swiping up the jug to take another swig. "You shouldn't give up on Charlotte," she said, losing her balance and sitting down heavily on her crate. "You can't let all of this nonsense get in the way of true love."

"You're one to talk," he snapped back, taking the jug from her.

"What is that supposed to mean?"

"I mean you and Jonathan, of course," he said, stifling another belch. "The touching and looking and breathing . . . it's ridic . . . ridic . . ." Max shook his head. "Ridiculous!" he exclaimed with a satisfied smile.

Rina blinked. "Breathing?"

"You know . . ." He pressed his hand to his chest, feigning a gasp. "All the gasping and breath-catching and panting—"

"I never panted!"

"I was talking about Jonathan."

At that, Rina's face heated. Max wagged a finger at her accusingly. "You like him."

"I do not!"

"You do!"

Rina gave a resigned sigh. "It doesn't matter." She leaned forward onto the crate they were using as a table. It was surprisingly comfortable. "The thing is, he's a pirate," she confided.

Max snorted. "I'm aware of that."

She laid her head down on the crate, forehead resting on the wood slats as she mumbled, "His life is the sea and all that rubbish. There's no place for someone like me."

Max was silent for a long moment, and when Rina rolled her head on the makeshift table to look at him, she half expected to find him asleep. Instead, he regarded her with heavy-lidded eyes.

"You shouldn't give up on him," he said, mirroring her words from earlier.

"To what end?" she asked, weight heavy in her heart. "After this is all over, we'll go our separate ways."

"A lot of things can happen before this is all over."

"I suppose," she conceded. "But nothing that will change the outcome."

Max smiled. "You can't know that. Charlotte always says the best thing about the future is it can always be changed."

She straightened, head swimming. "Do you really believe that?" She had a fleeting thought that she might regret it in the morning, but reached for the jug anyway.

Max took another gulp before handing it to her. "I'm not sure," he admitted, "but Charlotte does. And she should know."

Rina nodded and took another drink as they lapsed into silence, each lost in their own thoughts—a silence only broken by the slosh of rum and the gentle sounds of the sea as they cut a path to their next destination.

*The expedition has landed in Boston, and is joureying south.
Each day I draw nearer to my goal. Yet fear of them, and of
the dread pirates in this area, forces me to take care when I'd
much rather act quickly.*

*Once I find what I seek, I know I must also find a way to
protect it.*

*- The Journal of
Simon Alistair Mellick
2 February, 1665*

Jonathan scanned the horizon through his spyglass but could make
out nothing in the darkness. No sign of a pursuing ship, and they
were so far out into the open sea that there was no sign of the
shoreline, either. Only his compass and the stars above assured him
of their course. He slapped the glass closed and stowed it in his
coat pocket.

"I'm to my quarters," he told Crawley as he surrendered the
wheel. "We sail through the night. Wake me when we draw close
to Savannah."

"Aye, Cap'n."

"And if there is any sign that bastard, Stanton, is about—"

Crawley nodded. "I'll send word immediately."

"Good." Jonathan cast a glance across the deck, wondering where Sarina had disappeared to. "Good," he repeated distractedly as he turned to head for his quarters, a strange kind of excitement brewing in his chest. His mind had been occupied since they'd returned to the ship, focused on their destination and evading Stanton. But now that the danger seemed past, he had a sudden urge to see Sarina again, memories of their encounter in the barn flashing through his memory, searing his skin.

He wasn't certain, to be honest, exactly what would happen once they were alone together again. He knew what he wanted— what his body craved—but he also knew what his mind reasoned in more rational moments.

It seemed mind and body were at crossed purposes when it came to Sarina Talbot.

Still, he had to rest, didn't he? And to do so meant returning to his quarters. The fact that his steps quickened as he neared the doorway leading below had more to do with the call of his bed than the fact that Sarina would be there also, lying on her cot just across the room.

Soft and warm, pliant in sleep.

Jonathan swallowed, shaking his head to clear it. He was a grown man, for heaven's sake, not a besotted school boy. His life was laid out before him. A life on the sea—most likely a short one—centered on vengeance and treasure and pleasure . . .

*Pleasure.*

A flash of memory assaulted him—Sarina in his arms, clinging to his neck as her mouth opened below his. The warm wetness of her tongue, the soft curves surrendering tantalizingly to his fingertips, the quiet whimpers . . .

Jonathan stopped abruptly outside his door, fighting an urge to slam his fist into the wood. He needed to gain control of himself. Sarina Talbot, despite recent evidence to the contrary, was a lady—a lady destined to return to polite society, a place where he could never again set foot. Once she'd seen justice for her father's murder, she would take her part of the treasure and make a life for herself . . . get married . . . have a family.

Another man would feel her pleasures one day, a man more deserving. A man able to give Sarina what he could not. The thought left a sour taste in Jonathan's mouth, but he knew it was the only way.

After all, Jonathan knew the realities of the world. There were ladies. There were servants. And there were whores.

And he knew which were destined for him.

With a deep breath to solidify his resolve, Jonathan squared his shoulders and entered the room.

He needn't have been so worried, however, because when he looked over to Sarina's cot, he found the blankets neatly tucked and undisturbed. His gaze swept the room.

"Smith?"

But there was no response. With a frown, he made his way to his desk to light a lantern, but the illumination still did not reveal her presence.

*Where was she?*

Jonathan took the lantern to the door, sticking his head out and quickly scanning the hallway.

"Smith?"

When greeted only with the silence belowdecks and the faint sounds from above, Jonathan's thoughts first flew to Rafferty. It would be just like the wench to go flitting about the ship in the middle of the night with no thought to her safety, and—despite his recent punishment—Rafferty would no doubt take advantage. The bastard was never one to think of the consequences of his actions, and a few moments of pleasure would far outweigh any lingering pain from the lash, or Sarina's bucket, for that matter.

Not to mention, Jonathan was certain Rafferty felt he had a score to settle with Sarina. His pride had taken a beating, and

Jonathan had noticed the hateful looks cast her way, had perhaps dismissed them when he should have taken action. With a grimace of determination, he strode purposefully across the deck, ignoring Crawley's questioning glance, and went below to the gun deck. He held the lantern aloft, peering around the cannons and piles of balls and shot and weaving between the swinging hammocks filled with snoring crewmen. He paused outside the door of the small room where the master gunner bunked, glancing back before lifting his fist to knock.

He stopped, hand raised midair, at the distinctive sounds coming from within. Holding his breath, Jonathan pressed his ear to the door, shock turning to red-hot fury at the masculine moans of uninhibited pleasure drifting through the wood. Without another thought, he burst through the door, clutching the lantern in his white-knuckled fist.

"Unhand her!" he exclaimed, eye wild as he reached for his sword.

He needn't have bothered.

Rafferty gaped up at him from where he lay on his narrow bunk, sheets and blankets shoved down around his legs. He stared at the captain, frozen in shock, his face pale in the lantern light, the bruises under his eyes and around his swollen nose dark against his skin. Jonathan's brow furrowed in confusion after a moment when he realized his master gunner was alone in bed. He spun around quickly, searching for Sarina, but the room was decidedly empty. Turning back to Rafferty, who still had yet to move, his gaze traveled down the man's form, widening in shocked awareness where his right hand disappeared beneath the thin blanket.

Jonathan quickly looked back at Rafferty's face. The gunner seemed to gain back his faculties, because he sat up quickly and reached down to pull the blankets up a bit higher before clearing his throat.

"Is there a problem, Cap'n?" he asked. "Are we under attack?" He reached over the edge of his bed for his trousers, ready to report to his station.

Jonathan shook his head, turning away from the man's gaze. "No . . . no . . . I thought I heard . . ." he stammered, unable to form a coherent sentence.

Rafferty stiffened slightly. "S'no rule against a man I' his pleasure on his own time, is there?"

"Of course not." Jonathan backed toward the door. "Just . . . be sure ye get enough sleep," he blustered, covering his embarrassment with a gruff order. "I'll not have ye falling asleep at yer post!"

Rafferty eyed him carefully before reclining back on the bed. "Aye, Captain."

Jonathan nodded, turning toward the door. "Carry on," he muttered before walking out and closing the door tightly behind him. He leaned back, pounding his head lightly against it.

"Sir?" Rafferty called from inside.

"Nothing," Jonathan replied, turning to walk away before he embarrassed himself any further.

He shook it off, thoughts quickly returning to the task at hand. Holding the lantern aloft, he picked his way back through the gun deck, pausing when he spotted the large frame of Jamie Ceron, arms and legs dangling out of his hammock as he snored lightly. He approached him, reaching out to nudge his shoulder.

"Ceron," he hissed. Then louder, "James!"

James startled awake, nearly falling out of the hammock as he tried to get to his feet. He gave up, half-sitting instead.

"Captain? What is it?" he asked, rubbing the sleep out of his eyes.

"Have you seen Sarina?"

"Sarina?" he repeated. "No, not since you came back from the mainland." James' thoughts evidently followed Jonathan's, because he straightened, alert at once. "Rafferty."

"No," Jonathan assured him. "I just checked. Rafferty is alone."

"Oh, well, that's good then." James relaxed slightly but made to get out of the hammock. "I'll help you search for her."

"No." Jonathan held up a hand. "No need. Most likely she went for a walk about the ship and is back in my quarters already."

"Are you sure?" James asked, but he was already yawning.

"Sleep. I'll come back if I need you."

James nodded and closed his eyes as Jonathan left, turning down the hall leading to the hold. Perhaps Sarina was snooping about—that would be so like her—and lost track of time. He poked his head in several of the storage rooms as he made his way methodically down the passageway, peering around the stacks of crates and barrels. He half thought he might come upon Max as well. The man rarely drank, but it was not unusual, after a visit to Charles Towne, for his first mate to end up in a dark corner with a jug of rum or two. Jonathan overlooked it for the most part because Max always showed up at his post the next morning, ready to work, bleary eyes and an unshaven jaw the only indication of the previous night's indulgences.

Not that Jonathan would begrudge his friend a night of drowning his sorrows in any regard. He had more than earned it.

Jonathan rounded the corner and paused, tilting his head at the muffled sound of voices behind the door in front of him. He couldn't make out what they were saying, but after a moment, raucous laughter broke out, and he could identify one of the voices as decidedly female.

*Sarina.*

Jonathan breathed in a rush of relief, quickly followed by gritting his teeth in frustration and annoyance. Here he was, worried about Sarina's safety, waking his crewmen up at all hours in his concern, and she'd been down here laughing without a concern in the world with—

*Who was she with?*

She laughed again, light and bubbly, a lower-toned chuckle accompanying the sound. Jonathan could stand it no longer. He burst through the door, ready to brain whichever of his men had the audacity to approach his woman . . . to laugh with her . . . to—

He came to an abrupt stop at the scene before him. Sarina perched on an upturned crate across from Max, who had apparently abandoned his own crate to sprawl on the floor, back propped against the wall. A small lantern sat on another crate between them, a jug of rum balanced precariously on the edge and a second, empty jug on the floor at Sarina's feet. The laughter cut off when he entered the room, and they both stared up at him with mirroring expressions—mouths slightly open and wide eyes blinking slowly.

"What is going on here?"

"Jonathan!" Sarina sprang to her feet. "I mean . . . Captain . . . I mean . . . Captain Jonathan!" She started toward him, stumbling slightly over the empty rum jug. She stared at it as if mildly offended for a moment before continuing on.

"Smith? Are you drunk?" He looked at Max accusingly, but the first mate simply shrugged, taking up the jug for another gulp.

"I'm not drunk!" she exclaimed, swaying before him slightly, then hiccupping. She pressed her fingers to her lips. "I beg your pardon," she said, glancing back at Max before bursting into giggles. Max started to laugh as well, sliding even further down the wall, and Jonathan fought the urge to throw them both overboard.

"Baines! She's loaded to the gunwales! How could you let her get like this?"

"Hey!" Sarina narrowed her eyes, poking him in the chest. "Don't get mad at Max!" She poked him again. "He's a good"— poke—"man." Poke. "Even if he is a pirate."

"Ho, me hearty!" Max called from the floor, raising the jug in salute. At Jonathan's glare, he added, "Not my fault, Cap'n. The wench has a taste for rum." He belched loudly, and Sarina giggled again.

"I beg your pardon," Max slurred.

"I do like it," Sarina whispered loudly, leaning toward Jonathan with a conspiratorial wink. "It makes me feel . . . *warm*." She swayed on her feet and reached out to steady herself, her palm landing on Jonathan's chest. He hissed at the touch, taken by surprise at the heat of her hand seeping through his shirt. She looked up at him, eyes glassy, and licked her lips, her gaze dropping to his mouth before slowly rising to meet his. Jonathan's breath caught in his throat, mesmerized by the invitation in her eyes, and for a moment he considered accepting it.

Then she hiccupped again and began to giggle, and Jonathan abandoned all romantic thoughts with her in such a state.

"Come on, then, Smith," he said with a resigned laugh. "Let's get you to bed, yes?"

"To bed, *yes!*" She exclaimed with a leering grin, turning to wave to Max. "Good night, Max. I'm going to bed with Jonathan!" She laughed again, reaching for Jonathan's arm as he opened the door.

He shook his head at her with an amused half smile. "Make sure to put out the lantern," he told Max. "I'll not have you burning down my ship."

"Aye, Cap'n," Max slurred, leaning forward to blow out the lantern before curling up on the floor and tugging his discarded coat over his shoulders as a makeshift blanket. He was already half asleep by the time Jonathan closed the door behind them.

Sarina stumbled, clinging to his arm, and he disentangled himself from her grip, shifting to hold her around the waist. She leaned heavily against him, her scent mingling with the rum on her breath in a surprisingly pleasant way. Jonathan led her through the passageway, bending down to whisper as they neared the gun deck.

"Be quiet, now," he murmured, his lips brushing her ear. "The men need their rest."

Sarina shivered in response, but said nothing as they made their way through the crowded area, then up to the main deck and out into the fresh air. She leaned back, nearly falling over.

"Look at all the stars!" she exclaimed, stumbling and sliding out of his grip and collapsing to the deck in a heap, her skirts billowing about her. She blinked in surprise, then burst out laughing. Jonathan heard another choked chuckle from across the deck, where Crawley was watching them in amusement.

"Everything all right, Cap'n?" he asked wryly.

"As you were," Jonathan muttered, bending down to sweep Sarina into his arms. She half-shrieked, arms linking around his neck as he adjusted his grip.

"What are you doing?" she asked, her tone a mixture of indignation and confusion. "I'm quite capable of walking, you know."

"Apparently not," Jonathan retorted as he continued toward his quarters, the lantern dangling from his fingers at her side. "Bloody hell, Smith. You really can't hold your spirits, can you?"

"I can hold them just fine, thank you," she grumbled. "Although, if you think about it, that's rather ridiculous, isn't it?" She hiccupped. "How can you hold spirits? They'd slip right through your fingers." She wiggled her fingers to emphasize her point. "Unless you have a cup . . ." Her words trailed off as Jonathan pulled her closer, guarding her head as they ducked through the doorway leading belowdecks. Jonathan felt her nose pressed against his neck, and she inhaled deeply.

He loosened his grip, eyeing her warily. "Did you just *smell* me, Smith?"

"You smell nice," she murmured, eyes blinking sleepily. "Like soap and leather and . . . *man*." Her head lolled back, and he thought she might have added *delicious*, but he couldn't be sure.

With a little fumbling, he made it into his quarters, depositing Sarina on his bed as carefully as he could. When he straightened to move away, she reached for him with a whimper.

"Don't go," she mumbled.

Jonathan couldn't help a fond smile as he brushed her hair back from her flushed face. "I'll sleep on the cot tonight."

"No."

"No?"

Sarina looked up at him briefly before her eyes fluttered closed again. "I might have a bad dream. You might have a bad dream. You should stay with me . . . just in case."

Jonathan hesitated, unsure how to proceed. He didn't want to take advantage of Sarina in her current state, but at the same time, that cot looked extremely uncomfortable. He eyed it warily, shifting on his feet in indecision.

"Now you're a gentleman?" Sarina asked wryly.

Jonathan snorted. "I'm no—" he began. "Fine then. Shove over," he muttered, sitting on the edge of the bed to pull off his boots. He stripped down to his shirt and breeches and slipped into bed, pulling the blankets up over the both of them. "Don't say I didn't try to protect your virtue," he said, glancing down at Sarina curled up beside him. She only snored lightly in response, already asleep.

Jonathan exhaled heavily. "Smith, you'll be the death of me, I fear," he murmured, reaching out to run a finger down her cheek. She sighed, leaning into the touch slightly, and he pulled away, watching her sleep for a moment. Unable to resist, he sat up and leaned down to press a chaste kiss on the side of her mouth.

"Good night, Smith. Sweet dreams."

Her lips curved a little in response, and Jonathan chuckled under his breath as he reached over to turn out the lantern and settle into much-needed sleep.

Off the coast of South Carolina, Commodore Lucius Stanton sat at his desk in his quarters, brooding and sullen. He didn't even bother to light a lantern, his mood so foul the darkness seemed a welcome respite, surrounding him in a sightless cloud so he needn't lay eyes on those who'd failed him so completely.

Lieutenant Cameron entered, carrying his own lantern, and the commodore squinted at the unwelcome glare. Cameron quickly slipped the lantern behind his back to shield him from the light.

"Any word?" Stanton grunted.

"Nothing useful, sir," Cameron replied. "The first mate, Baines, was spotted in town asking questions, but no one made mention of Tremayne."

"Of course they didn't," Stanton spat, standing up so quickly his chair toppled over. "But where Baines is, Tremayne is. Everyone knows that."

Cameron had no idea how to respond, so he said nothing.

"What of the witch?" he asked. Stanton knew that Tremayne consulted with his half-sister, a fortune-teller of some regard in the area. He prided himself on the knowledge of the pirate's family and kept the information close and protected. *He* was the one who would bring Tremayne in, not some up-and-comer looking to steal his promotion from under his nose. No, he—and a few of his most trusted crew members—were the only ones who knew of Tremayne's connection to South Carolina, and Stanton aimed to keep it that way.

"She claimed not to have seen Tremayne for nearly a year."

"Of course she did," he snapped. "Did you press her?"

Stanton could hear Cameron swallow thickly, his next words measured. "Her father is a viscount, sir."

"I'm aware her father is a viscount, Lieutenant!" The commodore was *distinctly* aware of that fact. Dishonored by scandal and living in near isolation, Lord Tremayne still held the title and the wealth, which meant Stanton could not enact more aggressive means of persuasion. "I assume Lord Tremayne was equally unhelpful?"

"He assured me that he had washed his hands of his son," Cameron replied, "and that if he encountered him, he would be sure to surrender him to the Crown."

Stanton laughed humorlessly. "Noble citizen," he muttered. "Tremayne was here, and we missed him—probably by hours, maybe even minutes. How did that bastard get by us?"

Cameron cleared his throat. "We can dispatch more men in the morning," he offered. "Canvass the town. Question people more thoroughly."

Stanton waved a hand, righting his chair and taking a seat. "It's no use. Tremayne is sneaky. He'd have left no sign of where he's headed." He lit a lantern, finally, examining the map stretched across his desk. "Nothing to do now but head south. You know he's after Kane, and I've word he's been spotted near Hispaniola."

"Aye, Commodore."

"Tell the men to keep an eye out for Tremayne. Hell, for *any* ships along the way."

"Aye, sir."

"Dismissed."

Cameron tipped his head in acknowledgement and left to follow the commodore's orders. Stanton examined the map before him, running a finger along the edges of the land masses, then swirling it through the blue of the sea.

"Where are you, One-Eyed Jack?" he murmured to himself. "What are you up to?"

He stared at the map long into the night, finally falling asleep with his head cradled in his arms and his commitment to catch the elusive pirate burning in his chest.

A grinding roar that threatened to split Sarina's head in two woke her from a deep sleep. She struggled to force her eyelids open, but they seemed weighed down, the very motion sending a rush of pain through the sockets. She groaned, then immediately regretted the action as another wave of pain shot through her aching head.

*What was wrong with her? Was she dying?*

*And what was that bloody racket?*

She tried to stretch but found herself unable to, something warm and hard pressed up against her side, her hand resting on a solid—

*Good lord.*

Slowly, she took stock of her surroundings, realizing she was not in her usual cot, but in Jonathan's large, and she had to admit, particularly comfortable bed.

And she was not alone.

Laying next to her and snoring loudly—the noise that had so inconveniently awakened her. Why was it so bloody *loud?*—lay Jonathan, sprawled on his back, his arm across his face.

But that wasn't the worst of it.

Sarina was draped half on top of him, dressed only in her shift, which was currently gathered up around her thighs. Her leg was thrown over his, curled around his calf, her hand up underneath his shirt and resting on his warm muscled chest.

*What had she done?*

The night before was a muddled blur of rum and laughter . . . dizzy images of Max . . . and Jonathan. Yes, Jonathan had been there.

She rolled her eyes, then fought back another groan at the resulting agony spearing through her head. Of course Jonathan was there; otherwise, why would she currently be in bed with him?

She was in bed with Jonathan.

*Bloody hell.*

Rina steeled herself against the pain, moving slowly and quietly so as not to wake him. She tried to pull her arm away, but Jonathan stirred, his hand flying up to still her movement.

She froze, holding her breath as she watched him. Maybe he would go back to sleep.

His good eye drifted open.

No such luck.

He turned to her, blinking in sleepy surprise for a moment, then his lips curled into his trademark smirk.

"Good morning, Smith," he said, voice raspy and sending an inexplicable rush of heat through Rina's body. Her breath hitched, and he noticed, his hot gaze dipping to her parted lips. He rolled over, up onto his elbow, and reached toward her, cupping his hand around the back of her neck.

"I could get used to this," he murmured, leaning toward her. He was going to kiss her. Rina's heart pounded. Her head pounded. Her stomach . . .

Her stomach . . .

"Oh God," she muttered, swallowing thickly as the nausea hit her. Her hand flew to her mouth. "I think I'm going to—"

Jonathan grimaced. "Chamber pot's on the floor," he said, just before Rina dragged herself across the bed, head hanging over the edge as she retched pitifully.

"Well, Smith," Jonathan said, lying back with his hands tucked behind his head as she vomited what felt like her entire being into that chamber pot. "I have to say you certainly know how to ruin the moment."

Rina groaned and wished—quite fervently—that she might curl up into a ball and die.

*After weeks of following false information and trails leading nowhere, I finally feel I am making progress.*

*Mary has questions, but I fear giving her the answers. 'Tis only for her protection, although she fails to see the logic of my actions. Still, I know once I find what I seek, she will forgive me. And I can truly be the husband she deserves.*

*- The Journal of*
*Simon Alistair Mellick*
*14 March, 1665*

"What happened?" Rina asked once the contents of her stomach had been fully eliminated. She glared down at the chamber pot, swallowing another rush of nausea as she rolled over onto her back with an agonized moan. "I think I might be dying."

Jonathan chuckled. "The perils of overindulgence, Smith," he said—a mite too gleefully, she thought.

"Do you have to speak so loudly?" she muttered, her head throbbing. "And can you stop breathing, please? It's giving me a headache."

"Stop breathing?" he repeated. "'Fraid not." The bed dipped, and Jonathan got up, shuffling around the room before coming back to sit next to her. She groaned at the movement, but then startled as Jonathan laid a cool, damp cloth on her forehead. It felt so good on her clammy skin, she couldn't keep in a relieved sigh.

"Here," he said quietly. "Drink this."

Rina peered up through half-opened eyes to see him holding a cup of water. Slowly and carefully, she propped herself up on an elbow to take the proffered drink. Once it touched her tongue, she gulped it eagerly.

"Easy," Jonathan warned. "Unless you want that to end up in the chamber pot as well."

She grimaced, sitting up fully to sip at the cup as she handed the cloth back to him. "Thank you."

"Think nothing of it," he replied, gaze intent.

Rina squirmed under his scrutiny, focusing her attention on the cup and its delicious contents. Unfortunately, as often happens, it soon emptied, leaving her with nothing to distract her.

Jonathan reached for it. "Better?" he asked as he set it on the side table, discreetly shoving the chamber pot away with his foot.

She nodded, avoiding his gaze and picking at the blankets absently.

"So," she said, swallowing nervously. "You didn't answer my question."

"Question?"

"About what happened last night," she explained. "How I, uh, ended up . . ." She waved at the bed, then realized the sheets were down around her hips and quickly pulled them up to her chin.

Jonathan snorted. "It's a little late for modesty, isn't it, Smith?"

Sarina flushed. "I didn't, uh, we didn't . . ." she stammered. "Did we?"

Jonathan leaned forward on his arm grinning wickedly. "You don't remember?"

"Umm . . . not really," she said, voice cracking.

"Well, Smith, I must admit, I'm hurt," Jonathan murmured, reaching out to trace a finger over the top of her hand where it peeked out of the blankets. "After all we shared together—"

"We shared?" Her eyes widened. "What exactly did we share?"

"Everything." He wiggled his eyebrows and Rina gulped, her stomach flipping, but not from nausea this time.

"Surely you wouldn't . . ." She gaped at him, horrified. "I was hardly in the condition to . . ."

Jonathan laughed, wincing when Rina pressed her hands to her head. "Sorry," he said, lowering his voice. "Don't worry, Smith. Your virtue is intact."

"It is?" She sighed in relief. "I mean. It *is*. Of course it is. I wasn't worried."

"Of course you weren't." Jonathan smirked. "Not that you didn't try to force my hand."

"I did not!"

"You did." Jonathan shook his head ruefully. "Quite shameless, really. Don't you recall telling me I smelled *delicious*?"

Rina's hands flew up to cover her flaming cheeks. Because she did remember something of the sort.

"And then you begged me to share your bed."

"Oh no," Sarina moaned into her hands.

". . . and then stripping your clothes off in the middle of the night—"

She gaped at him. "I didn't!"

"Oh, but Smith . . ." He eyed her shift, then glanced pointedly to the pile of clothing—her dress—hanging haphazardly off the back of the chair, as if it had been flung there in haste. "You most certainly did."

Rina groaned, flopping down on the bed and pulling the covers over her head. Perhaps she could just live there, hidden under the pillows and blankets, and no one would ever know her shame.

Jonathan laughed, pulling at the blankets. "Come now, Smith. No need to be shy with me. Not after all we've been through."

"I want to die," she grumbled into the sheets.

"No need," he said, finally granting her a reprieve. "Nothing happened."

She peered up at him sideways, her face still smashed into the mattress. "Nothing?"

He shrugged. "Nothing important," he said. "Just a bit of friendliness inspired by too much rum. You're hardly the first to succumb."

"Friendliness?"

"Crawley once offered his fortune to a comely wench in exchange for a dance, you know. And Hutchins would be wed to half the whores in Tortuga if anyone took him seriously."

"How did I end up in my shift?" she asked nervously.

Jonathan chuckled. "You did strip your gown off in the middle of the night," he said. "After threatening to brain me for being *so bloody hot*."

Rina flushed, but couldn't keep from laughing herself. "I'm sorry," she said. "I'll never touch rum again. I was right to think it was evil."

"Oh, don't abstain on my account, Smith," Jonathan said with a leering grin. "I rather enjoyed you with fewer inhibitions."

She raised an eyebrow, the effect a bit diminished since her head was still half-under the pillow. "Don't get your hopes up," she muttered. "My inhibitions are in fine form once again, and I don't plan on losing them any time soon."

Jonathan shook his head with a sad frown. "Pity."

She sat up to throw the pillow at him. Unfortunately, Jonathan was a bit faster on his feet and evaded the attack, grabbing his jacket and boots as he headed for the door.

"We should be near Savannah," he told her as he reached for the knob. "If you plan to accompany us ashore, I suggest you and your inhibitions get dressed." He grimaced, his gaze dipping to the floor. "And I know I promised no chamber pots, but I think in this case, it's your responsibility."

Rina couldn't even find it in herself to argue. She dragged herself to her feet as Jonathan left the room, splashed her face with cool water and scrubbed her grimy teeth. Surprisingly, once she'd emptied her stomach and cleaned up a bit, she felt quite a bit better. Her pounding headache had eased to a low throb—hardly pleasant, but definitely tolerable. She began to get dressed, then her gaze fell on the bag Charlotte had sent for her. She still hadn't had time to examine its contents, but decided she probably should, since Charlotte obviously thought it was important.

Sarina opened the bag and peered inside, a slow smile lighting her face.

She'd never doubt Charlotte again.

Jonathan was still grinning when he emerged on deck, the early-morning sun making him pause to become accustomed to the light before he continued toward Crawley, stopping along the way to speak with a few crewmen and check on their work. As expected, Max was already chatting with the quartermaster, his voice cracked and raspy, eyes red and bleary, but his attention focused on the task at hand. He turned toward Jonathan as he approached.

"Dinghy's ready, Cap'n," he said.

Jonathan nodded in acknowledgment. "Tell Hutchins and Ceron to accompany us," he said. "Jenkins as well. We need more eyes to find what we're looking for as quickly as possible."

He turned to Crawley. "I know you've not slept—"

"Don't need sleep, Cap'n," Crawley said quickly. "Bit of coffee and I'll be right as rain."

"Good man," Jonathan replied. "Keep a weather eye out for Stanton," he warned. "Keep moving and watch for my signal."

"Aye, Cap'n."

"And don't forget—" The rest of his command was lost when he saw Max's glance over his shoulder and resulting smirk.

"I take it Rina will be going with us again," he said.

"Sometimes it's easier to succumb to the wench's whims than to fight them," Jonathan said gruffly.

"Wench?" Max said wryly. "You sure about that?"

"What are you talking ab—" Jonathan spun around to see what Max was looking at, the question dying on his lips.

Rina had traded her green gown from the night before for a simple white shirt, open at the collar, and dark breeches tucked into knee-high black boots. Her hair was pulled back in a tight queue and topped by a black tricorn. A dark blue coat with brass buttons hung open on her slight frame—though it fit perfectly, as if made for her, the flared hem swinging about her knees. A sword swung at her hip, and as she strode toward him, she gripped the hilt, her chin lifted in challenge.

"What are you . . ." Jonathan gaped at her. "Why are you . . ."

"Aren't they wonderful?" Sarina asked, spinning around so the skirt of the coat flared out. "Charlotte gave them to me. And they actually *fit*!"

"You can't. It's not . . ." Jonathan still couldn't seem to form his thoughts into words. His eyes drifted from her knees, to her thighs—God help him, her *thighs*—continuing up without conscious thought to her bosom, which was definitely *not* bound as it had been when she was in disguise.

He swallowed, fighting down a surge of irrational lust. "You are *not* leaving this ship dressed like that," he said finally, his voice deadly serious. He tore his gaze away to glare at the scattered crewmen looking their way with interest. "In fact, you're not *staying* on this *ship* dressed like that either," he hissed. "Go and change immediately!"

"Whatever for?" she asked in confusion. "It's much more comfortable, easier to clamber about after you. And if I need to fight . . ." She drew her sword and lunged forward with a sharp thrust. "Much better than skirts."

Jonathan grabbed her arm, dragging her out of view behind a stack of crates. "It's indecent," he hissed, glancing down once again, then away just as quickly when he noticed the dark hollow between her breasts. "And button your shirt, for heaven's sake!"

Sarina ripped her arm away and sheathed her sword. With a frown, she fastened one more button on her shirt. "There. Satisfied?"

Jonathan glared. "Go. Change. Now."

Sarina glared right back, fists on her hips. "No."

Jonathan growled, turning to pace away a few steps and back again. He could feel hairs on his head graying with every moment, seconds of life dribbling away with every beat of his furious heart. At this rate, he'd keel over of old age before he reached thirty.

"Why must you fight me on everything?" he asked through gritted teeth.

"Not everything," Sarina replied. "Just when you're being impossible." She paused for a moment, pondering. "You're just impossible more often than most."

For some reason, the comment hit Jonathan as funny. He blinked at her, fighting the urge to laugh, but lost the battle. His shoulders shook as he tried to hold back, anger and frustration finally giving way to helpless surrender as he burst out laughing.

Sarina eyed him warily. "You're really quite mad, aren't you?"

Of course, that only made him laugh harder, tears springing forth as he clutched his stomach.

She huffed in frustration. "What on earth is so funny?"

Jonathan struggled for breath, wiping the tears from his cheeks. "Oh, Smith," he said through the remaining chuckles. "Why do I even *try* to tell you what to do?"

Sarina shrugged. "I've no idea."

A strand of hair had sprung free of her queue, and without thinking, he reached out to tuck it behind her ear. Sarina flushed when his fingers lingered on her cheek briefly before he pulled away.

"Captain?" Max's voice cut through the moment. Jonathan straightened, stepping back from Sarina.

"What is it?"

"The men are ready."

Jonathan nodded. "Good. Fine. That's . . . good, then."

Max tipped his hat with a significant glance at Sarina before turning away.

"We should go," Jonathan said finally. "Unless you've changed your mind about the gown?"

Sarina sighed in exasperation. "Don't you see this is much more practical?" she asked, indicating her garb with a sweep of her hands.

Jonathan knew he'd lost the battle. "Could you at least fasten your coat?" he asked. "So your . . ." He waved a hand toward her breasts, her legs. ". . . assets aren't quite so fully on display. It's distracting," he said gruffly.

Sarina smirked. "You find me distracting, Captain?"

Jonathan leaned in, determined to regain his footing. He leered at her, raising an eyebrow. "Immensely," he said, the words a low rumble. Sarina reddened and looked away with a slight gasp, and he knew he'd at least scored a point. She stepped back and buttoned her coat with trembling fingers.

"I don't know how I'm supposed to get to my sword now," she grumbled.

Unable to resist prodding her further, Jonathan moved toward her and reached under the lowest coat button for her belt. Sarina's eyes flashed up toward him as she froze.

"What are you doing?" she whispered breathlessly.

Jonathan held her gaze, slowly unbuckling the belt, his fingers brushing over her waist. He could feel her warm skin through the thin material of her shirt, her quick, shallow breaths vibrating under his hands. It would be easy to slip his arms around her and draw her close. He could smell her already, the fresh scent of soap wafting off her skin. He could duck beneath that ridiculous hat, press his lips to the soft skin behind her ear.

Taste her one more time.

The splash of a dinghy hitting the water brought him back to his senses, and instead of indulging his fantasies, he pulled back, the belt and sword dangling in his hand. Sarina swallowed thickly, looking up at him—lovely and pink-cheeked, eyes glassy and wide—and for a moment, he considered forgetting all of it. Kane, the treasure, his vengeance.

For a moment, he considered sweeping her up into his arms and carrying her back to his quarters, not to emerge for hours . . . or days.

Perhaps weeks.

But instead, he reached around her waist and re-buckled the belt over the long coat, adjusting the sword so it hung properly at her hip.

"There," he said gruffly.

"What?" Sarina licked her lips, still a bit dazed.

Jonathan looked away, rubbing the back of his neck. "You can reach your sword now."

"Oh." Sarina looked down, touching the buckle absently. "Oh! Yes. Yes, of course. Thank you." She fidgeted, patting her hair, making sure it was tucked securely behind her ears. "Well, then, we should probably go, right?"

"Right."

She looked up at him hesitantly, biting her lip, then drew a deep breath and turned on her heel without another word.

"I can't believe you stole horses," Sarina hissed at Jonathan as they made their way cross-country toward Savannah. The ship had dropped the dinghy closer to shore, near a hidden alcove to the north, and made a quick retreat to deeper waters. They'd rowed inland along the Savannah River but put to shore well before reaching the town. To Sarina's surprise, they'd found the horses tethered to a few trees only a short distance away. Jonathan had somehow sent word to a contact in Savannah, who provided the mounts.

Or rather, *liberated* them for Jonathan's use.

"Not stolen," Jonathan corrected with a grin, looking at her over his shoulder. "Just borrowed for a bit."

Rina didn't respond, focusing instead on staying astride her rather skittish horse. She'd been surprised that Hutchins, Jenkins, and James accompanied them in the dinghy—filling it to its capacity, much to her rather nervous observation—but grateful that Rafferty did not come along. The master gunner had leered at her when he saw her attire, eyes raking down her form and back up again, leaving a chilling shudder in their wake. He finally spat onto the deck, holding her gaze for a disturbing moment before turning to return to his post. The man both disgusted and unnerved her. She'd hoped the encounter with the bucket had cooled his interest, but instead she feared he might be just biding his time.

"Just relax," James said, riding up beside her. "The horse can sense if you're nervous."

"Well, then she should be sensing a lot," Rina muttered as the white mare sidestepped a bit before continuing onward. She leaned forward over the horse's neck. "You should be a bit more supportive as the only other female in this lot," she said. "Where is the bond of sisterhood, I ask you?" The mare shook its mane, whinnying loudly, and James burst out laughing, earning a glare from Jonathan.

"Quiet!" he ordered, although he had been just as loud a moment earlier. "We need not attract unnecessary attention."

Rina rolled her eyes at James, who shrugged in response, but they kept quiet for the rest of the journey. It wasn't long before Jonathan held up a hand and the little group stopped right outside the town. They tied the horses to some scraggly trees and continued on foot. Rina couldn't keep herself from stealing a few glances at Jonathan along the way, still a bit muzzy and confused after what had happened—or nearly happened—on the ship. When Jonathan had touched her, she'd lost all rational thought, once again caught up in the feeling—the hot, achy feeling—that he seemed to pull out of her whenever he got near. She had no doubt that if they had been somewhere a bit more private, there would have been a repeat of the incident in the barn. Or perhaps even worse—or better, depending on how you looked at it—at any rate, something *more*.

Rina sighed at the thought. Her self-control was sadly lacking.

She couldn't understand how he could make her so furious, so frustrated one minute, and the next—with one hot look or one lingering touch—she was putty in his hands.

It was rather irritating. And confusing.

"We should split up," Jonathan said as they neared the town square. "Jenkins, you go with Hutchins and start at the northwest corner of town, working your way along the river. Ceron—"

"I'll take Rina," James offered.

Jonathan's eye flashed. "Sarina is with me," he said sharply. "You and Baines start at the southwest corner. Miss Talbot and I will begin here. Building by building, tything by tything, ward by ward, men. No stone left unturned. We're looking for a blue door.

We'll meet in St. Lucius Square once every inch of this bloody town has been searched. Understood?"

A low chorus of "Yes, sir," met his order before the men turned to go their separate ways.

Searching the town turned out to be a rather simple proposition. Savannah was laid out in an organized grid pattern, with rows of buildings arranged around several open squares. It took less than an hour for Jonathan and Sarina to walk through their allotted portion of the town, examining every door they came across. The search, however, was fruitless, and they made their way to St. Lucius Square, hopeful that the others had found what they were looking for.

Their disheartened expressions quickly ended that hope.

"I don't understand," Jonathan muttered as they gathered on the side of the road to avoid the carts and foot traffic moving along. "It has to be here." He fixed each of his men with a rigid look. "You're certain you didn't miss anything?"

"We looked everywhere," Max replied, and the others nodded in agreement. "There was no home, or shop, or even a bloody stable with a blue door." He frowned, leaning in to add quietly, "Maybe she was wrong."

"She's never wrong."

"There's always a first time."

Jonathan tugged at his hair, conversing in low tones with Max, and Rina took the opportunity to look around the crowded square and let her mind wander. A few children played in front of what appeared to be a school, tossing rocks in some sort of competition. A couple large men stacked sacks of grain in front of the general store, pausing to wipe sweat from their foreheads every few minutes. A young couple walked along the opposite side of the road, the woman blushing prettily at something the man had said.

A shout drew Rina's attention, and she turned to see that one of the children—a young boy—had run out into the middle of the road, a cart loaded with barrels headed straight for him. She stared in horror as the driver finally noticed the boy and quickly pulled up on the reins, his eyes wide and frantic. The boy stood frozen in terror as the horses bore down on him, tossing their heads in protest as the driver wrestled with the reins.

Rina opened her mouth to scream. Then, in a flash of movement, the boy was thrown to the side of the road, and it took a moment for her to realize that Jonathan had done the throwing. He lay in the dusty grass, his body taking the brunt of the impact, the boy lying on his chest, his mouth open in shock.

It was too late for the cart, though. The horses reared, panicked whinnies filling the air as the driver fought to get them under control. Instead they fought back, breaking free of the cart with a mighty jolt. The driver jumped off, rolling across the dirt road, and the cart careened down the road, weaving erratically before falling over onto its side. Barrels bounced out in every direction, a few breaking open and releasing a flood of indigo dye onto the street.

When it was all over, Rina finally drew a breath and raced across the street to check on Jonathan and the little boy. The driver got to his feet, weaving his way in the same direction.

"Jonathan? Are you all right?" she asked, falling to her knees next to him. She helped the little boy up, brushing off his knees. "Are you hurt?" she asked him.

The boy shook his head, but his eyes filled with tears.

"Albert?" A woman pushed her way into the small group gathered around them. "Albert, oh my heavens, are you all right?" She gathered the child up in her arms, and Rina realized she was the boy's mother.

The boy sobbed, holding her tightly around the neck as she got to her feet. She kissed his damp cheek, examining his arms and legs. Finding no lasting damage, she turned to Jonathan, who'd finally managed to stand up as well.

"Thank you," she said, "Mister . . ."

Jonathan cleared his throat. "Carlson," he said.

"Mister Carlson," she repeated. "I can't thank you enough."

Jonathan shrugged, cheeks pink with embarrassment. "It was nothing. Anyone would have done the same." Waving off any further thanks, he added, "Perhaps you should get the boy to the doctor? Make certain there's no unseen injury?"

The woman nodded, thanking him again before hurrying off down the street. The crowd broke up, many reassembling by the overturned cart to help the driver right it. Jonathan swept the dust off his clothes as Max retrieved his hat.

"Well, that was exciting," Max said wryly. "So much for not attracting attention."

Jonathan beat his hat against his leg to remove the dust before replacing it on his head. "Couldn't be helped," he said. "Now, back to the problem at hand."

"We could start again," James suggested. "Perhaps we missed something."

"Or question some of the townsfolk," Hutchins offered. "Maybe the door is *inside* a building."

Jonathan held up a finger. "Good thought," he said. "But how to go about it without raising suspicion?" He began to pace, lost in thought.

Rina sighed, watching the men re-loading the cart as they stepped around puddles of dye to retrieve the unbroken barrels. She looked across the street, spotting the remains of one of the crushed barrels on the front porch of a little shop, a flood of indigo dye down the steps finally slowing to a trickle.

She gasped.

"Jonathan," she murmured.

"There's no other way," Jonathan said, as if he hadn't heard her. "We'll divide up and talk to people. Try to be subtle," he ordered.

"Jonathan?" Rina repeated, a little louder.

"Perhaps start at the general store," he continued. "Or the church."

"Church?" Hutchins snorted. "Do you wish to be hit by lightning?"

Rina took a deep breath. "Jonathan!" she shouted.

Jonathan turned toward her in irritation. "Good lord, Smith, no need to shriek like a madwoman. What is it?"

She glared but was too excited to properly chastise him. Instead, she pointed across the street. "Look!"

As one, the men turned to see what she was pointing at: a small shop with the remains of one—no, *two*—barrels scattered about the front porch, indigo dye splattered everywhere, the blue liquid streaking the entire façade.

Including the door.

They stood and stared, until Max let out a soft chuckle.

"Bloody hell," Jonathan murmured, and they started across the street.

*I dare not describe in excessive detail my latest discovery, at least not until I deem whether or not it proves trustworthy. If my enemies were to liberate this record from my possession, I would not wish my errant words to lead them to what I intend to claim for myself.*

*I do believe, however, that I draw closer to discovering the treasure's final resting place with every passing day.*

*- The Journal of*
*Simon Alistair Mellick*
*30 March, 1665*

They converged on the shop porch, gingerly stepping through the spreading dye. Max gallantly pulled a handkerchief from his coat pocket, wiping off the doorknob and opening it with a flourish. A bell sounded overhead, and with a glance at Sarina, Jonathan gripped his sword hilt and stepped through first, the others following close behind.

"Hello?" he called, blinking in the dim interior. "Is anyone there?"

Silence greeted them as they spread out, moving between the tables and shelves. Jonathan scanned a collection of snuff boxes, picking one up and toying with the latch.

"Odd to leave a shop unattended," Jenkins said, his voice loud in the hushed room.

"Look around," Jonathan ordered. "We know what it looks like, but not its size, so if you see a cup of any kind—a tankard, a chalice . . . a bloody sherry glass, let me know."

They made their way quietly through the shop, closely examining the displays, flipping through stacks of books, even searching stacks of clothing, just to make sure they didn't miss anything. It only took a few minutes—the shop was not overly large—until they gathered near the counter at the back, all empty-handed.

Max eyed a curtained doorway behind the counter. "Perhaps back there?"

Jonathan was about to agree when the bell over the door rang again, and a boisterous voice called out, "Deepest apologies, gentlemen. Quite a mishap involving a cart of indigo dye." The man kept rambling, rubbing at his fingers with a handkerchief, his hands stained blue. "I fear I will never remove it," he muttered. "My wife will be quite displeased, quite displeased." He looked up, taking in their little group.

"Horace Abernathy," he said, "and how may I be of assistance today?"

Jonathan took in the man from the top of his shiny head—quite obvious since it barely reached Jonathan's shoulder—to the round belly bursting forth from a crimson waistcoat. The man removed a pair of spectacles from his pocket and wiped them with a clean edge of his handkerchief before placing them on his nose. He peered at them through the glasses, blinking owlishly at Jonathan. Then he gasped, glancing about nervously.

"Are you One-Eyed—" At Jonathan's low growl, Abernathy's words cut off. He tugged at his collar. "Are you C-Captain Tremayne?" he asked instead, his words barely a whisper.

Jonathan crossed his arms over his chest, a menacing glare burning into the man.

"Perhaps."

The shopkeeper rushed to the front door and quickly locked it before pulling the shades down over the front window.

"What are you on about?" Jonathan asked, losing patience.

"Mayhap he's a bit daft?" Hutchins offered through the side of his mouth. "Had an aunt like that once. Believed she was the Queen of England."

Jonathan shrugged but watched the man carefully as he returned to them, stepping behind the counter to open a drawer.

"He said you'd be coming," he told Jonathan, mopping his face with his handkerchief and leaving a streak of blue on his upper lip.

"Who?"

"Said his name was Kane." The man all but shuddered when he said the name. "Rather intimidating chap."

The group of pirates groaned, watching the captain for his reaction. His anger was apparent in his dark gaze, the clench of his jaw. He reached across the counter and grabbed the shopkeeper's lapel. "What did he want?" he asked through his teeth, slow and deadly.

Abernathy gulped. "He was after a cup. I don't know why. 'Twasn't anything of significant value—"

"What of the cup?" Jonathan shook him slightly when he took too long to answer.

"He took it," Abernathy replied, eyes wide with fear. "Paid me handsomely and asked me to give you a message when you arrived."

"Jonathan," Sarina said quietly, reaching for his arm.

Jonathan tore his gaze from the shopkeeper and focused on her.

"It isn't his fault," she said.

He stared at her for a long moment, then with a heavy sigh, Jonathan uncurled his fingers, releasing the man. The cup was gone. Kane had it. But Sarina was right. His anger should not be aimed at an innocent man.

Abernathy smoothed his coat, then his nonexistent hair. "He asked me to give you a message," he said again.

Jonathan nodded, rubbing the tense muscles at the back of his neck. "What message?"

The man fumbled through the open drawer for a moment, and Jonathan felt his patience slipping away yet again.

"It's in here somewhere," he muttered, pulling out a pile of papers. "I didn't really expect you to come. Didn't know when you might, if you did—"

"Bloody hell, man!" Max exclaimed. "Just find the blasted message, will you?"

The man's hands trembled, but he held up a square of parchment victoriously. "Here it is!" He handed it to Jonathan with a wide grin, his hand remaining extended as Jonathan took the note from him. Jonathan eyed the man's palm distastefully, and Abernathy's fingers twitched as he began to pull it back. But the captain nodded at Max, who pulled a coin from his pocket and tossed it to the shopkeeper.

"Thank you for your assistance," Jonathan said before turning on his heel to head for the door, not missing Abernathy's fallen expression. Obviously, he had either hoped for a greater reward or at least to find out what the message contained. Jonathan examined the parchment. It was still sealed, a blob of wax imprinted with the K of Kane's signet ring yet intact over the edge of the paper. Fortunate thing, that. Jonathan would have hated to have to kill the shopkeeper for being nosy.

He ran his finger over the seal, an inadvertent shiver rippling through him at the touch. It wasn't the first time he'd seen the symbol, pressed into blood-red wax, that instance forever imprinted on his memory. A similar note, lying next to his mother's bloodied form. His father's fingers trembling as he broke the seal, reading the one-line missive with a blank expression. The parchment fluttering to the floor, only to be retrieved by a grief-stricken Jonathan once his father walked aimlessly out of the room.

*Innocents are harmed when I am kept from what I desire.*

His father had answered Jonathan's questions with single words, uttered in shock, colored with pain and numbness.

*Yes.*

*No.*

*Kane.*

*Kane.*

*Kane.*

The name forever emblazoned on his heart, giving him purpose . . . giving him meaning. He'd taken the journal then, interceding when his father threatened to throw it into the fire, vowing his vengeance as Sebastian's shoulders slumped in defeat and shame.

He had eventually burned the note, however, unable to look at it without seeing his mother's broken body in his mind.

Kane had left other notes along the way, always taunting, goading . . . daring him to stop or to continue in his quest.

When Kane had retrieved half of the map: *It seems you are falling behind in this little game, Jack. Perhaps it is time you retire to more leisurely pursuits?*

When Jonathan lay recovering from the wounds he'd inflicted: *I bide my time until we meet again.*

When Jonathan stole the cutlass: *Well played, Tremayne. But this is far from over.*

His fingers gripped the latest message as the crew emerged into the sunshine, walking toward the edge of town and—

hopefully—their hidden horses. Jonathan kept his stride quick and purposeful, anxious to get back to the ship now that their search had proven fruitless. They mounted the horses in silence, setting off toward the shoreline at a gallop. Once they reached the place where the dinghy was hidden, they released the horses with a shout and a slap to the rump, and the men dragged the little boat to the water.

Jonathan stood off by himself, staring down yet again at that blood-red seal.

Sarina approached him tentatively. "Aren't you going to read it?"

"I already know what it says."

"How?"

"Because they're always the same," he spat. "That bastard is always a step ahead of me, and he likes to drive home that fact." He handed the parchment to Sarina. "See for yourself."

Sarina reached for the paper and slid her finger under the edge to break the seal.

"*The cup is mine. Yet again, I prove victorious,*" she read. "*You may bear the title of Captain, Jack, but you are no pirate. Why not surrender to failure before your crew is destroyed by your ill-fated attempts at revenge?*"

She looked up at him. "Mighty full of himself, isn't he?"

Jonathan snorted, taken by surprise at her comment and how—somehow—it alleviated his frustration and anger. He glanced down to find her watching him closely, eyes twinkling. Reaching for the message, he crumpled it up and shoved it in his coat pocket.

"Aye, Smith. That he is," he replied with a smirk. "I'd say it's about time we put that bastard in his place, though, don't you?"

Sarina gripped her sword, her face turning grave and determined. "Aye, Captain," she said. "It's about time."

The landing party made its way back to the ship without incident, but Crawley sought out Jonathan as soon as they stepped on the deck.

"Cap'n, we've received a message," he said urgently, "from Tortuga."

Jonathan's jaw tensed. "Baines!" he shouted. When the first mate looked at him, he gestured toward his quarters meaningfully, and the three set off together, Rina trailing behind, trying to go unnoticed lest she be excluded from the conversation.

"How long ago?" Jonathan asked.

"Not long," Crawley replied. "It was relayed from our contact in Savannah."

"I hope you thanked him for the horses," Jonathan said wryly.

Crawley nodded as the little group made its way into the captain's quarters. Jonathan lifted an eyebrow at Rina but made no effort to keep her out of the room, simply closing the door behind her and taking a seat behind his desk.

"We've word from Pearl," he told Max.

"Who's Pearl?" Rina asked.

Max turned to her. "A friend in Tortuga."

"Tortuga?"

Jonathan leaned back in his chair. "It's a haven for businessmen of our sort," he said with a slight grin. "Pearl often provides..." He searched for the right word. "*Entertainment*, when we're in port."

Rina tilted her head, searching for the hidden meaning. "What type of entertainment?"

Jonathan crossed his arms over his chest, biting the corner of his lip. "Various types."

She opened her mouth to pursue the point, but Jonathan waved a hand in dismissal. "At any rate, she also supplies information that sometimes proves useful."

"How did you get a message from so far away?" she asked.

Jonathan sighed in frustration, obviously wanting to get on with business, so Max interjected.

"We've contacts all through the islands, and up the coast of the mainland," he explained. "Using lanterns at night, or mirrors reflecting sunlight during the day, they can pass along simple messages. Sometimes it's a warning to avoid a certain area—if Crown ships have been spotted, for example. Or, in this case, I predict, that we need to *go* somewhere."

"Indeed," Jonathan murmured, turning to Crawley expectantly.

"Five flashes, then three," he said. Sarina turned to Jonathan for a translation.

"Pearl's signal," he explained.

"Yes," Crawley replied. "Then two . . . four . . . two."

"Come."

"Then, one I didn't recognize," Crawley continued with a frown. "Six . . . three . . . three."

Jonathan stiffened. "Are you certain?"

"Yes. The message repeated several times." Crawley shifted uncomfortably. "What does it mean?"

The captain sat thoughtfully for a moment, elbow braced on the arm of his chair, finger on his lips.

"It means we're setting sail for Tortuga," he said finally. "See to it, then your bed, Crawley. Baines will be up shortly to take the wheel."

"Aye, Cap'n," the quartermaster replied, leaving the room to fulfill his duties. Jonathan sat back in his chair, a satisfied smile on his lips.

"What was that all about?" Max asked. "What does six, three, three mean?"

"It means Pearl has word of the box."

"The box?" Rina interrupted. "You mean the box with the map? The one Charlotte mentioned?"

"Aye."

"But how did she get it?" She crossed the room, pacing excitedly. "Where did she find it? Did she see the map?"

Max laughed. "It's a rather simple form of communication, Rina," he said. "Not one for detailed information."

She collapsed into a chair. "How frustrating!"

"Well, we'll get the answers soon enough," Jonathan said, right as an urgent knocking sounded at the door. "Enter!"

Crawley poked his head in. "Cap'n, you're needed on deck. A Crown ship approaches."

Jonathan was on his feet before he finished talking, pushing past him through the door. "Stanton?"

"Can't tell for certain, but could be."

Rina followed behind him as Jonathan emerged on deck, pulling his spyglass from his pocket. "Full sail!" he barked, Max quickly relaying the order. The men sped to obey, and once again she was awed by the coordinated effort to get the ship underway.

Jonathan squinted, peering through the glass at the approaching ship, still a speck in the distance. "It's Stanton all right," he said.

"How can you tell?" she asked, raising a hand to block the sunlight.

Snapping the spyglass shut, he stalked to the wheel. "I can tell.

"Move it, men, Stanton's on our stern!" he bellowed as they hoisted sails, the wind filling them to bursting. "Avast! Ready the cannons! He'll not catch us easily, but if he does, we'll be ready for him!"

Max watched the men with a critical eye. "The *Arrow* is faster than the *Intrepid*," he said. "Stanton won't catch us."

Jonathan frowned, his fingers tight on the wheel. "No, but he'll follow us all the way to Tortuga."

"We can't let that happen."

"No."

Rina watched the interchange silently. When neither spoke again, she asked, "So what's to be done, then?"

They exchanged a significant look. "There's only one thing," Max began.

"No," Jonathan said gruffly. "We'll let him follow, then evade him in the Bahamas. He won't be able to maneuver as quickly as us once we reach the islands."

Max glanced in the direction of the approaching ship warily. "A diversion would ensure our escape."

"What kind of diversion?" Rina asked.

"No," Jonathan said stubbornly. "I'll not throw one of my men to the wolves."

"Jenkins is strong and fast."

At that, the man in question appeared, as if out of nowhere. "I can do it, Cap'n," he offered.

"I didn't ask," Jonathan muttered.

"No, sir. I believe I volunteered."

"Ready yourself," Max said hastily. "We won't be able to stop to drop the dinghy—"

"Belay that!" Jonathan bellowed.

Jenkins straightened. "Cap'n, I can give you the time you need to get to Tortuga, and Stanton will be none the wiser." At Jonathan's skeptical look, he added with a smug grin, "The commodore won't catch me. He won't even come close."

Jonathan studied him for a moment, then nodded grimly, slipping out of his coat and hat. "Take Thomas and Allegheny. They're strong rowers and quick on their feet. If there's trouble, relay a message to Tortuga."

"Aye, Captain." He put on the coat, then the hat, tugging it low over his eyes.

"We'll return for you."

"Or we'll find our way to you." Jenkins grinned. "I'm quite resourceful, ye know."

Jonathan nodded, clapping the man on the shoulder. "I'm well aware. Just be careful. Don't let Stanton get his bloody hooks into you."

"Not a chance, Cap'n." With that, he hurried off to find the other men.

"Ready the dinghy abaft!" Jonathan shouted, and a group of crewmen raced to pull the little boat over the side, repositioning it toward the stern of the ship. They began to lower it over the side by a pair of ropes tied at its bow and stern. When Jenkins reappeared with two large crewmen Rina assumed were Thomas and Allegheny, Jonathan nodded once, then shouted. "Heave to! Mind the yard arm!"

Sarina watched in awe as he spun the wheel, men ducking nimbly as the sails swung wildly across the deck. The ship slowed as they headed into the wind, and with a shout, the men lowered the dinghy to the water, keeping hold of the ropes to keep it from floating away. Jenkins and the other two men climbed over the gunwale, clambering down the rope ladder and into the dinghy. With a shout, the men released the ropes, and the dinghy bobbed away in the *Arrow's* wake. With another shout, Jonathan spun the wheel again, and the ship sped up, heading south yet again.

It all took less than a minute.

"That was . . ." Rina looked up at Jonathan, wide-eyed.

"Impressive?" he offered, with a rather self-satisfied smile.

She snorted. "I was going to say insane," she said. "Did you just launch a dinghy full of men off a moving ship?"

Jonathan shrugged, his hand resting lightly on the wheel. "No time to stop."

She glanced back at Jenkins sitting in the bow of the dinghy, Thomas and Allegheny rowing side by side. In Jonathan's coat and hat, he could easily be mistaken for the captain.

"You think Stanton will follow them?" she asked doubtfully.

"He won't run the risk that it could be me," he replied. "He's doubtlessly aware that I've been spending some time on the mainland, and if he suspects I've left the ship, he won't be able to resist the chance to catch me. By the time he realizes the truth, we'll be well into the islands."

"Will Jenkins be all right?"

"Aye," Jonathan replied, but tension showed in the clench of his jaw, and she knew he was worried. "None of us are inexperienced when it comes to evading the law."

Rina wasn't sure if he was trying to convince her or himself. "Well, he is a pirate, after all," she said loftily. "You are a slippery lot."

He smirked at her. "Aye. That we are."

She turned to face the wind, her hair blowing loose around her face. "There's something I don't understand," she said after a while. "Why did Charlotte send us to Savannah if we had no chance of finding the cup?"

Jonathan glanced over his shoulder, keeping an eye on Stanton as he piloted the ship. "We had a chance," he said. "Charlotte can only see the future based on the path we are on at that particular moment. It's possible Kane hadn't decided to go to Savannah yet, or perhaps something happened to speed Stanton's arrival in South Carolina. Any one thing could have changed the path we were on, making us miss our opportunity to beat Kane to the cup."

Sarina considered that, her mind whirling at the possibilities—the infinite consequences of every action. "It's rather complicated, isn't it?"

He laughed. "I suppose you could say that."

They stood in companionable silence, the ship rocking beneath their feet. Rina was highly aware of Jonathan beside her, his masculine form braced against the wind, his long hair the only part of him giving it quarter. He was quite a sight, she had to admit—a figure from a story book. Not a hero, exactly, but not quite a villain either.

"So, tell me about this Pearl," she said after a while, fighting to keep from appearing too curious.

"Pearl?" Jonathan grinned at her, his eye twinkling merrily. "Oh, Smith. You're going to love her."

On board his ship, docked in the waters off Nassau, Kane the Merciless gulped down a tankard of rum, holding it out to be refilled with an absent wave of his hand. His cabin boy rushed forward to pour the rum carefully, then Kane set the tankard on the table before him, dismissing the boy with a jerk of his head. Finally alone, he stood and moved to the locked chest against the wall. He unlocked it with the key he kept on a chain around his neck and drew out a cloth-wrapped item before returning to his chair.

He smiled with satisfaction as he unwrapped his latest acquisition, the cup he'd found in the shop in Savannah. It was a bit smaller than his tankard and simple hammered metal—not even silver, to his surprise—the intricate carving circling the rim the only thing to set it apart as unique.

*Pones coram me mensam ex adverso hostium meorum inpinguasti oleo caput meum calix meus inebrians*

Kane ran his finger over the words, murmuring them quietly to himself. He was not an educated man, but knew enough Latin to recognize the verse, a childhood of *spare the rod, spoil the child* serving to beat a few pieces of Scripture into his memory.

*"Thou preparest a table before me in the presence of mine enemies: thou anointest my head with oil; my cup runneth over."* The Book of Psalms, Chapter twenty-three, verse five.

It had been fortune, combined with invaluable information he'd paid heartily for, that led to procuring the relic. The *Abaddon's Curse* had chased a Spanish vessel up the coast of

Florida, finally boarding it just south of Georgia to relieve it of its rather considerable booty when he received word that Tremayne was heading to Savannah. Seeking out the cup proved a bit more of a challenge, but some well-placed coin yet again proved fruitful, and he'd obtained the cup at far less of a cost than he'd anticipated.

And managed to leave Georgia long before Tremayne arrived.

Kane laughed to himself. He wished he could have seen One-Eyed Jack's expression when he realized he'd been bested yet again. Setting the cup down, he trailed a finger over the half of the map he'd nearly memorized after spending so much time studying it. Unfortunately, it revealed nothing new about the location of the treasure. Without the missing half, it was all but useless. There was no way to discern the location of the land masses, or even determine which sea filled much of the page.

The same could be said for the little he knew of the journal. He'd had only a page from it for a short time before Tremayne managed to retrieve it and return it to its place within the journal's leather bindings. Kane had already committed the verse to memory, though, and it was enough, combined with the information he'd later obtained, to determine what he needed in order to find the gold.

Kane sighed, rubbing his chin in consternation. He had no doubt he could retrieve the cutlass from Tremayne when the time came, but there was really no point until the missing half of the map had been found. He had men searching—as he knew Tremayne did as well—but to no avail. As for the coin, well, he didn't have it, but at least One-Eyed Jack didn't either.

Begrudgingly, Kane had to give the boy credit. He had not expected him to last as long as he had. Driven by his mother's death, Tremayne had proven single-minded in his quest for vengeance. Surprisingly so, actually.

Yes, he'd learned not to underestimate the young captain. The boy had become a force to be reckoned with. A rather annoying force, at that.

A knock at the door brought him out of his musings, and he realized he had no idea how long he'd been sitting there brooding. "What?" he barked.

His first mate, Barton, stepped in. "We've word on Tremayne," he said. "He's set sail for Tortuga."

Kane straightened. "Tortuga?" He tapped a finger against his lips. "Interesting. I wonder why."

Barton leaned against the door jamb. "Perhaps some recreation?"

"Perhaps," Kane agreed. "Or perhaps One-Eyed Jack has procured some useful information after all." Regardless, he had nothing else to go on at the moment, so finding out what Tremayne was up to held some appeal.

He stood and headed for the door. "Weigh anchor," he said. "We're for Tortuga."

Barton grinned. "Are we going to take the *Arrow*?" he asked, pleased at the thought. Kane knew his men relished the idea of taking the ship—the only one that rivaled their own in reputation, and he had to admit, in reality.

"No, we're not to engage the *Arrow*. Not yet at least," Kane said as they headed toward the deck. "Stealth is the key in this instance. I mean to find out what Tremayne's about. It's possible he has information about the coin or the map."

"You want me to follow him?"

Kane nodded. "Aye," he said, patting the man on the shoulder. "Once we spot him, you'll take a few men and see what he's up to. And if he *is* in Tortuga solely for entertainment, perhaps it will be an opportunity to retrieve my cutlass."

Barton smiled in response as they emerged on the deck and set about to raise the sails. Kane inhaled the fresh salt air, feeling a change in the wind.

Aye, things were finally going his way.

*I believe I know where to look, or at least, where to begin to look.
I've discovered an ancient record scrawled on a cave wall that
speaks of the treasure I seek.*

*Interpreting the writings proves difficult, however. And I
dare not ask for assistance, lest others discover my intentions.*

*- The Journal of
Simon Alistair Mellick
7 May, 1665*

Commodore Stanton took the bait.

Rina stood alone at the stern of the *Arrow* as it cut through the
waves at top speed. The wind whipped about, fortunate for them
because it aided their attempt to escape. She could barely make out
the *Intrepid* in the distance, the dinghy having disappeared from
her sight long before. She'd held her breath as Stanton closed in
with frightening purpose, only releasing it when it turned to follow
the path of the little boat.

The blast of cannon fire, however, had terrified her.

"Don't worry," Jonathan had said, appearing at her side. "Jenkins is doubtless already on shore. Stanton is simply sending a message."

"He speaks loudly," she muttered.

"Aye, that he does." Jonathan grinned. "But although the Crown wants me captured, dead or alive, Stanton would prefer the latter and to avoid the former."

"Why?"

Jonathan smirked as he glanced at her, the wind whipping a thick strand of his long hair across his face. "So he can gloat, of course."

She shook her head. "Men are an odd lot."

"I could say the same about women."

He returned to the wheel, and once she could see nothing in their wake but endless blue, Rina wandered idly around the deck, watching the men perform their duties. It felt odd not to be working herself, but Jonathan had yet to order her to wash his drawers or mend his stockings. She'd decided to take the reprieve while it was allowed and put aside her worries about Jenkins and his companions, turning her attention instead to Charlotte's words. She'd had little time since the reading to really consider what she'd said, but now that they were on route to Tortuga, there was little else to do until they arrived.

She took a deep breath, unsurprised to find herself once again standing next to Jonathan at the wheel. It seemed she was unable to stay away from him for any length of time, even if she put her mind to the task. She was drawn to him by some unseen force—a force that both frustrated and mystified her. She wasn't certain what it was about him that attracted her so. Certainly, he was a handsome fellow, tall and broad, with fine-tuned muscles and golden skin that all but glowed in the sunlight. Rina hid a blush at the memory of seeing him without his shirt that day she had to fix the mending, his strong back flexing under a slight sheen of sweat.

She swallowed hard, pressing cool fingers to her cheeks and glancing at him to be certain he hadn't noticed her discomfort. She frowned slightly as she continued her perusal, carefully avoiding a direct stare. His hair was unfashionable, overly long and unkempt, save a few strands twisted in braids and tied with beads and bits of this and that . . . his scars and eye patch relieving what would otherwise be a face too beautiful to be real. In fact, they not so much detracted from his looks as added a dangerous edge to them—an edge that Sarina could admit, if only to herself, she found somewhat intriguing.

All right. Perhaps *somewhat* was understating it a bit.

And then there was his good eye. The power behind that deep blue-green gaze all but undid her when he turned its focus on her. She had no doubt that had that force doubled with *two* eyes, she would do little but melt into a puddle at his feet at every opportunity.

"What's got you thinking so hard, Smith?" Jonathan asked, leaning idly against a post, fingers of one hand barely resting on the wheel.

"Oh, errr . . ." She tucked a wayward strand of hair behind her ear, fighting to maintain her composure. "Nothing, really. Just . . . Charlotte." She tried not to smile too widely at her brilliant deception. "I was running over her predictions in my mind, trying to make sense of it all."

Jonathan nodded. "Aye. Me, as well. It can be a difficult thing to know the *what*, but not necessarily the *who, why,* or *how.*"

"You're thinking about the traitor."

He frowned. "To know it's coming, but no idea from which direction, or how to prevent it . . ."

"Do you wish you *didn't* know?"

Jonathan shook his head. "No, of course not. 'Tis always better to be prepared."

Rina took a deep breath, glancing about the deck idly. Crawley stood talking with Hutchins, smacking him on the back with a grin before heading belowdecks, she assumed to get some sleep. Max and two other men were hauling a torn sail across the deck, rolled up and braced on their shoulders. A couple boys, on their hands and knees, applied grease to some rigging, their hands black with the slick mixture.

"Do you think it's one of them?" she mused, half to herself.

"Hmm?"

"Your betrayer," she said. "Could it be one of your crew?"

"I hate to think so, but I suppose it is possible."

"Charlotte said it was someone close to you. Someone you trust."

"Aye."

"That's a very short list."

Jonathan raised a brow. "Aye." When he didn't say anything more, Rina turned to look at him. He stared unseeingly forward, deep in thought.

"What is it?" she asked. He blinked, as if he'd forgotten she was there for a moment.

"Nothing, really," he said quietly. "It's just that, with Charlotte, it's difficult to get the true meaning of what she says sometimes. She says it's someone I trust—and immediately we think of the people I *truly* trust—my family, Max . . ."

Rina waited, a brow arched expectantly.

Jonathan laughed. "Yes, even you, Smith. God help me."

She smiled, waving a hand. "And . . ."

"Well, I was just thinking, there are varying levels of trust, aren't there?"

"How do you mean?"

The wind shifted, and Jonathan adjusted his stance, spinning the wheel slightly, brow creased as he put his thoughts to words. "I trust Hutchins to ensure the sails are properly repaired, Rafferty to keep the cannons clean and in working order. I trust Victor to have the bread baked daily." He pointed to the two grease-spattered boys that were now laughing and throwing globs of the slime at each other. "Hell, I even trust those boys to keep the deck and the head scrubbed."

Rina sighed, absorbing his words. "So, really, it could be anybody, then."

"Aye. I'm afraid so." She felt his gaze on her, and he hesitated briefly before slowly adding, "And then there's Ceron."

She stiffened. "What about him?"

"Well, he is the newest to my crew—apart from you, that is. And, as you said, it could be anybody. I can't afford to let him escape suspicion."

Rina frowned. She wanted to argue the point, but Jonathan was right. He had to consider everyone a possible threat. Still, she felt a need to defend her friend.

"You know, it wouldn't make much sense," she said with a shrug. "He was imprisoned with me on the *Intrepid* and you rescued him. You were the one who approached him about staying on board, weren't you?"

He considered that with a nod.

"So, why betray you?" she asked. "What could he possibly have to gain?"

"Perhaps it has something to do with his father," Jonathan suggested. "A father who was a pirate, whose life at sea took him away from his family. A life that eventually led to his death."

"But that wasn't your fault," she pointed out. "He knows it was Kane. Wouldn't that be motivation enough to fight with you rather than against you?"

Jonathan was silent for a long moment. "I've not told him we're after Kane."

"Why ever not?" she asked, surprised. "It would seem a wise course of action."

"Few know the true nature of our journey, other than to seek out booty," he replied. "Those with knowledge would not speak without my direction."

"Perhaps it's time you told him," Rina said, trying to keep the irritation out of her voice. Apparently, she did not do a very good job of it, because Jonathan tilted his head, studying her.

"Why do you come to his defense so vehemently?" he asked, his jaw tight, although whether from suspicion or some other emotion, she wasn't certain.

She shrugged. "He's my friend."

"Perhaps you need different friends," he grunted.

"Perhaps you need to seek out the truth before you point the finger of blame at what could very well be an innocent man!"

They stared at each other for an angry moment, and Rina waited for him to explode, to pound his fist, pace the deck, and rant in that oh-so-irritating way of his. Instead, his lips quirked.

"Perhaps you're right," he said simply, and turned back to place both hands on the wheel.

Jonathan checked his compass as the sun slipped to touch the horizon, despite the fact that he'd navigated this course a hundred times before. The *Arrow* eased between a small chain of islands to port—if they could even be called that, since they were actually just reefs that barely broke the surface of the waves—and a larger island to the starboard side.

*Isla de Cotorras.*

Isle of the Parrots.

He spotted Boccen Bay just ahead, its waters deep enough for the *Arrow*, and surrounded nearly on all sides by thick trees. Between the reefs and the hidden port, they would be safe from view through the night, at least. Moving into the bay would prove a tight fit, but Jonathan knew his men were up for the challenge.

"Ready about!" he called as they drew nearer to the bay, the order echoed across the deck as they always were. "Windward ho!

Bring a spring upon her cable, men!" With satisfaction, he watched his men jump to action, two manning the capstan, their arms whirling at blurring speeds, as others helped to drop the sails at just the right moment. Smoothly, they maneuvered into the narrow channel deep enough to admit them, with barely a bump or a scrape to mark their way.

Jonathan ordered the anchor dropped, then relinquished the wheel once they'd come to a bobbing stop in the middle of the bay. He spotted Sarina standing at the bow and made his way over to her. The setting sun cast her hair in a myriad of colors from brown to gold, and as she turned to smile at him, her eyes—the color of fine whisky—sparkled in the most beguiling way, stealing his breath.

Jonathan's steps faltered.

"Are you all right?" she asked, her smile replaced by concern.

He waved a hand dismissively, moving to stand next to her but unable to meet her gaze. "Fine. Just a bit of grease on the deck." When Sarina turned to look for it, he hurried on. "We'll stay here for the night."

She blinked, grease smudge forgotten. "Really? I thought we were going to Tortuga."

"We can't make it there before sunset. We don't dare make way on open water with Stanton on our tail, but these islands are far too treacherous to sail after dark."

She nodded. "It's not far, though."

"No. We should be there by midday, if not sooner." Sarina sighed and looked out over the beach, and Jonathan took advantage of the moment to steal another glance at her. It was a dangerous thing, he knew, because looking was quickly becoming not enough.

Not nearly enough.

The times he'd touched her—tasted her—burned in his gut, and like a drowning man needed air, he found he needed more. All his arguments against it paled in his single-minded desire to reach out and—

"How did you come to know this Pearl?" Sarina asked.

"What?" Jonathan stammered, still caught up in his thoughts.

She turned to him, head tilted in confusion. "Are you sure you're all right?"

He cleared his throat. "Fine. Pearl you say?"

"Yes. I wondered how you met her."

Well, that was a complicated question, wasn't it? Jonathan didn't know why he should feel guilty about the fact that he came to know Pearl over a jug of rum and a rather eager whore named Flora. Or that their relationship had been built by Jonathan's frequent patronage—and that of his crew, of course—seeking drink and the other more exotic entertainments she offered in her establishment.

He shouldn't feel guilty about it. He was a man, damn it. And a man had needs. He had a right to quench his thirst—or his lust—whenever necessary, didn't he? It only made sense.

Yet, he had a feeling that the lovely Miss Talbot might not agree. She was, after all, a lady.

So instead, he said vaguely, "She owns a local business, and we've had occasion to do business with her."

"You said that, but what kind of bus—"

"By the way." Jonathan acted like he hadn't heard her. "I have a surprise for you."

She started, and Jonathan fought down a victorious smirk.

"Surprise?" she asked. "What kind of surprise?"

"Well, if I told you that it wouldn't be a surprise," he replied with mock exasperation. "I swear, Smith, for an intelligent woman, sometimes you say the most inane things."

She rolled her eyes. "Oh stop and tell me about this surprise."

Jonathan arched a brow. "Did you just stomp your foot at me?"

"Jonathan!"

"All right. All right." He laughed, holding up his hands in defeat. "It's in my quarters."

Sarina's eyes narrowed dubiously, and Jonathan laughed again.

"So suspicious. It's appalling, really," he said, shaking his head. "Relax, Smith. I'll be staying here." He spoke slowly, pointing at the deck, then to Sarina. "You can go to my quarters—*alone*—and see your surprise."

"Oh, all right then," she said, flustered and blushing. Jonathan found he quite enjoyed Sarina flustered and blushing. She turned on her heel but only made it a few steps before turning back, her face flaming. "Thank you for the surprise," she said, fidgeting with her fingers. "Whatever it is." And with that, she hurried belowdecks.

Jonathan chuckled, then turned toward a shout at the stern. He could spot Hutchins and a few others stripped down to their drawers and plunging off the side of the ship. Max approached, a wide smile on his face.

"You going in?" he asked.

The captain grinned and pulled off his shirt. "Aye," he said, kicking aside his boots and unbuckling his belt. "I do believe I will."

As she made her way down the cool passageway belowdecks, Rina feared she might die of embarrassment. When Jonathan had said he had a surprise for her in his quarters, her mind had flown to all sorts of inappropriate ideas of what he might have had in mind. She thought she'd managed to hide her true thoughts, but she feared Jonathan had seen right through her.

And he'd laughed.

*Of course* he'd laughed.

The idea that he might want from her what she was beginning to want from him? Well, it was ridiculous. A few stolen kisses were hardly an indication of further intent. He was a man, after all, and responding to a willing female was ingrained in their very bones.

And she'd been more than willing.

She stopped outside the door to the captain's quarters, taking a deep breath and trying to shake off the rest of her mortification. Jonathan had told her she was a terrible liar, and she knew it was true. Her every emotion showed on her face. The only reason she succeeded in living aboard the *Arrow* as a boy for as long as she had was her ability to be unnoticeable ... invisible. Nobody looked too closely at her, so she hadn't had to rely on her deceptive abilities, or lack thereof. She feared it was only a matter of time before Jonathan became aware of her increasing attraction to him.

Well, he was apparently already painfully aware of it, but she doubted he realized the *extent* of it. Because Rina was quickly coming to realize that what she felt for him had grown beyond mere attraction, or even admiration, into something she was leery to put a name to. She sighed, leaning forward to bump her forehead lightly on the door.

What was she doing?

Giving her heart to someone like Jonathan was like asking to have it crushed. She had nothing to offer him, and he had nothing he could give her in return. They were a match doomed to fail, and her only hope was to resist him. There was no alternative.

But *could* she?

The question answered itself when she walked into the captain's quarters and spotted the bathtub in the middle of the floor, full of steaming, scented water. Not the usual tub for a brief wash with a damp cloth, either. No, this was a full-sized copper tub, polished to a sheen, a small table beside it holding soap and drying linens.

"How . . ." she said to herself as she closed the door and crossed to the tub, trailing her fingers through the water. She smiled in delight, wondering when Jonathan had arranged for this special treat. Not willing to let a second of it go to waste, she undressed quickly and sank into the hot water with an indulgent sigh. She lathered up twice and washed her hair, dunking under the water to rinse, then lay back to enjoy a relaxing soak until the water chilled.

Jonathan was quickly breaking down her defenses. It was a thought that echoed through her mind as she dressed—choosing the green gown over her shirt and breeches this time—then emerged on deck a short time later to the sounds of laughter and shouting. She held a lantern aloft as she surveyed the deck of the ship in the darkness, the newly risen moon casting a grayish tinge on her surroundings. She followed the sounds to the stern of the ship, finally leaning over the side to see what in the world was going on. She could just make out the bobbing figures in the water below, the crew members splashing in the gentle waves of the bay.

"Peeping, Sarina?" She jumped as James appeared next to her. He laughed. "Sorry. I didn't mean to startle you."

She smiled at him, noticing his hair was wet, dripping onto his shirt. "It looks like you've been enjoying the sea as well."

He shrugged, leaning against the railing next to her. "It seems rare to have a moment for such things on this ship. I figured if everyone else was taking advantage of it, I should as well." He reached out, lifting a damp strand of her hair with a questioning look.

"Jonathan gave me a bath," she said dreamily. At James' wide-eyed gaze, she realized what she'd said. "I mean, he *left* me a bath. He *had* someone leave me a bath. Which I had. Alone. By myself." James snorted and she smacked him in the arm. "You knew what I meant."

"Aye," he said, still laughing softly. "I ran into the boys filling the tub earlier."

They turned to watch the men swimming below, and as the moon broke over the trees, Rina could see Jonathan's head bobbing among the others, his teeth glinting with a wide smile. She wasn't certain, but his head tilted up, almost as if he was looking back at her.

"You're getting on then?" James asked.

"I'm sorry, what?" She tore her eyes away from Jonathan's form to look at him.

"You and the captain," he clarified. "You seem to be getting on all right?"

"Oh, yes. Fine, I suppose," she said, Jonathan's suspicions about James coming to mind suddenly. "And you? How are you getting on with him?"

James blinked in surprise at the question. "All right," he replied. "He's a man of few words, but fair overall, I think."

Rina nodded in satisfaction. He hardly sounded as if he had a grudge against the captain. "And you're happy on board?"

He pursed his lips thoughtfully. "Aye. Never thought I'd find a place on a pirate vessel, what with one taking my father and all, but Tremayne's assured me I've a chance for vengeance."

"Vengeance." She turned to him, surprised. "So he finally told you about Kane?"

"You know of him?"

She nodded, and James drew a deep breath. "I barely knew my father," he said. "I'm sure it seems strange to you that I would want to avenge his death. It's not for him, though, as much as for my mother. When he died . . ." He looked out over the water, eyes glistening in the moonlight.

"Well, it almost killed her," he said. "If Tremayne will give me a chance to repay Kane for that, well, I suppose I'll stay with him. At least for a while."

"And then?"

"Then? I don't really know," he admitted. "I don't see a life on the water. Perhaps it's a bit I, but I think someday I'd like a home. Maybe even a family."

She reached out to touch his arm comfortingly. "Why is that I?"

James' eyes fixed on her fingers. "I'm like these men. Wanted by the law for crimes against the Crown. It's hard to see a future beyond that."

Rina's heart sank at the words. For James. For Jonathan. For Max and Charlotte. For herself. So many people with their hopes bound by fate like an ever-tightening coil of rope. She sighed, squeezing his arm gently.

"Don't give up hope," she encouraged him. "It's only a matter of—"

"Smith?" Jonathan's voice interrupted her consoling speech, and Rina jumped in surprise, whirling around to face him. Her mouth dropped open and she found herself unable to form words.

Or even thoughts, for that matter.

Jonathan stood before her, soaking wet and all but naked. She couldn't control her gaze as it followed a rivulet of water dripping from his hair down his sculpted chest and along the angry scar running down his ribcage . . . to the thin cotton drawers that covered him from hip to knee. Or perhaps *covered* was over-stating it a bit. The wet fabric was nearly transparent where it clung to him along his hipbone, his thick thigh, the crease where he—

Her eyes snapped up. At his smirk, they dropped back down to the deck. And Jonathan's bare toes. His ankles, his knees . . . and back up—

Good lord, she had to get a hold of herself. She spun around to focus on James. Yes, James was safe.

"So, yes. Right," she stammered, trying to remember what they were talking about.

James watched her warily. "It's only a matter of . . ." he reminded her.

"Time!" she shouted gleefully. "Yes. Only a matter of time. That's right."

"Bloody hell, Smith, what's wrong with you?" Jonathan asked. Sarina hazarded a glance his way, relieved he had his back turned and was apparently fastening his breeches. He pulled a shirt over his head and turned back to face her. "I never took you for such a shrinking violet."

She bristled. "I'm no shrinking violet. But it's hardly proper for a man to go about half-dressed."

"Since when have I ever been concerned with propriety?" He all but leered at her, and Rina's face flamed. His gaze hardened as he turned to James.

"Ceron? Don't you have duties to attend to?"

James ran a hand through his wet hair. "All finished, Captain. About to turn in for the night." When he made no move to do so, Rina eyed him curiously, then Jonathan. The two men stared at each other, seeming to communicate through dark gazes but what, exactly, she couldn't determine.

After a long moment, Jonathan's face tightened almost imperceptibly, then relaxed as he looked at her. "I'm to my quarters, then. Smith, would you care to join me for some dinner? I hear Victor has a pot of salmagundi on the hob. I choose not to ask what he puts in it, but it's usually quite satisfying." He scooped up his boots and coat as Sarina continued to stare at him in confusion.

"Smith?"

She started. "Yes," she said. "That sounds fine. I'll be along in a minute." He nodded, then sent another significant look in James' direction before heading toward his quarters, calling for a cabin boy to see to his food. Rina tried not to stare at the bottoms of his bare feet as he made his way across the deck, unsure why she found it so difficult to look away.

She cleared her throat. "What was that all about?" she asked James.

He laughed. "I should think it was obvious." At her blank look, he rolled his eyes. "He's making certain that I know my place."

"Your place?"

"When it comes to you."

Rina had to think about that for a moment and when she ordained his meaning, she flushed. "Oh, well. He has to keep up appearances, you see. He doesn't know that you know the truth about our relationship, such as it is."

"Mmm hmm. And that truth would be?"

"You know." She waved a hand dismissively. "That it's only a ruse. For my protection."

James said nothing for a long while, and once she could no longer stand the silence, she peeked at him sideways to find him fighting a smile.

"What?" she asked irritably.

"You don't really believe that, do you?"

"It's the truth." She stared stubbornly forward over the railing, eyes fixed on a tree in the distance. "There's nothing more to it than that."

"Who are you trying to convince?" James asked quietly. She glared at him, and he held his hands up in front of him.

"I mean no offense," he said. "But I see the way you look at him, Sarina. And that's no ruse."

She thought about denying it, but instead leaned forward on the railing, her head in her hands. "Is it that obvious?"

"Not to everyone. But then again, not everyone has seen your reaction to the captain in his drawers." He laughed and Rina groaned, covering her face in embarrassment.

James sobered. "It must be difficult to live this deception for the crew and yet another for him." At her silent response, he turned to lean sideways on the railing, eyeing her with concern. "I consider you a friend, Rina."

"And I, you," she replied quietly.

"Good," he said. "And as your friend, I feel I must ask if you're all right."

She turned to take in his black, somber gaze, and sighed. "I don't know," she said. "It's foolish, isn't it? To have such feelings for a man like him?"

"Foolish? Perhaps," he said, as they turned once again to look out over the railing, side by side. "Love is often foolish."

She choked slightly. "I said nothing of love."

"You didn't have to."

James' words haunted her as she made her way back to Jonathan's quarters. She'd acknowledged her attraction to the captain. Even the fact that she'd grown to like him.

But love? Now that was a dangerous proposition. A terrifying proposition, to be perfectly honest.

Rina took a deep breath, rubbing at the slight ache between her eyes. There was no denying it. She was getting into trouble when it came to Jonathan Tremayne, and efforts to guard herself against him seemed to prove fruitless time and time again. He kept taking her by surprise with a smile or a wink, disarming her when she most needed to protect her heart. She was quickly coming to suspect that she had no weapon against him, no way to avoid what now seemed unavoidable.

It was a suspicion that leaned more toward a feeling when she walked into his quarters to find him pouring rum into a tankard, the table set for two with bowls of steaming salmagundi as well as a plate of fresh bread.

And that feeling became more of a belief when he looked up at her, his handsome face cast in stark shadows by the lantern light as he pulled out a chair for her to sit.

But it was when he reclined across from her, long legs extended and crossed at the ankles —and winked cheekily as she noticed his feet were still bare—that the belief became a full-fledged conviction.

Yes, that was pretty much when Sarina Talbot realized she was done for.

*The expedition is on my heels, and I must divert its attention.
Leading them astray proves times consuming, but essential.
My efforts bear fruit, however. They have turned to
Hispaniola, as I intended. On the morrow, I depart for the
treasure's true location.*

*It will be mine.*

*- The Journal of
Simon Alistair Mellick
14 September, 1665*

Jonathan lifted the tankard to his lips, watching Sarina across the table. She stirred her bowl of stew but had yet to take a bite, apparently lost in thought. She refused to meet his gaze. Refused, really, to look his way at all. In fact, every time her eyes hazarded a peek in his direction, she flushed and looked away as if she'd done something wrong, her spoon stirring a bit more violently.

"Something bothering you, Smith?" He took a sip of rum and set his tankard down, idly running his finger around the rim. "You seem troubled."

She watched his finger's slow circuit, blinking slowly. He paused, lifting his finger to his lips and rubbing them gently. She followed the movement, then her eyes widened and dropped back down to her salmagundi.

Jonathan smiled. It appeared the lovely Miss Talbot was not unaffected by him, after all. He'd begun to wonder after her reaction to him on deck. At first, he thought her simply embarrassed—and he had to admit he reveled in that a little bit. It wasn't easy to unsettle her, but for some reason, he found it extraordinarily satisfying. He shifted, uncrossing then re-crossing his ankles. Sarina watched him surreptitiously—or at least he imagined she thought it surreptitious. Her nervous swallow betrayed her, however.

Jonathan decided to have a bit of fun, schooling his expression into one of haughty irritation.

"Blast it, Smith! Are you drunk again?"

Sarina jumped. "What? No. Of course not."

"Well, then what in the world is wrong with you?" He broke off a piece of bread, dunking it into his stew and popping it into his mouth. He purposefully licked at an errant drop at the corner of his lips, fighting a smile at her gaping reaction. He dipped his finger into the stew and lifted it to his mouth, sucking it loudly as he raised an eyebrow in challenge.

Sarina's eyes narrowed as she finally caught on to his game. "Stop that."

He forced an innocent look. "Stop what?"

"You know what."

"I've no idea what you're talking about." At that, he grinned and took another bite of his stew, washing it down with a sip of rum. "So, tell me, Smith," he said, finally granting her a reprieve. "What do you plan to do with your share of the treasure?"

She was silent for a moment, considering. "I'm not certain, actually," she replied, sitting back in her chair. "I suppose I could go back to Boston, although there really isn't anything there for me now."

Jonathan tilted his head. "No boring suitors anxiously awaiting your return?"

Sarina's eyes flashed. "And why would my suitors be boring?"

Jonathan shrugged. "Most suitors are, aren't they? Any worth considering, that is." He stood, swirling the rum in his tankard. "A man of good breeding, steady income, reliable, and trustworthy."

"You make those sound like bad things."

"Not bad, no," he replied, glancing over his shoulder as he slowly paced across the room. "Just seems a bit tame for a wench such as yourself." Jonathan didn't know what made him say that, but he realized it was true. Sarina was unlike any female he'd ever encountered before—beautiful, of course, but also smart, stubborn and brave as any man. She needed someone wise enough to listen to her counsel, but strong enough to stand up to her lest she walk all over him.

Someone who wouldn't try to mold her into a prim and proper lady; someone who wouldn't extinguish the fire burning inside her. Someone who would not only accept her, but treasure and love her for all that she was.

No, an ordinary man would not do for Sarina. She needed someone who . . .

Someone like . . .

Jonathan shook his head, unable—or perhaps unwilling—to finish the thought. A thought he knew was not only dangerous, but absurd. Still, a strand fought its way through, not so much a conscious thought as an idea.

Almost a *longing*.

But as quickly as it reared its head, he fought it down as an impossibility. Jonathan Tremayne did not long for unattainable things.

Or people.

He turned around, hoping Sarina hadn't noticed his preoccupation. She seemed lost in her own thoughts, however, belatedly asking, "And you? What will you do with the gold?"

Jonathan leaned against the wall, clearing his throat. "It will go to my family. I've no use for it, after all." He shrugged, staring into his mug for a moment before draining it.

"I think your family would rather have you," she said quietly.

He glanced sharply at her. "I've already told you that is impossible." He crossed back to the table to fill his tankard again. "But the least I can do is to give Charlotte what she wants."

"What Charlotte wants," she repeated, shaking her head when he offered more rum. "You mean Max."

"Aye." He sat down, throwing an arm over the back of the chair as he stretched out. "With my share of the gold—along with Max's—they can find a life together, somewhere the Crown can't touch them. I owe them both at least that much."

He felt Sarina's eyes studying him. "You know about the vow, then," she said.

Jonathan nodded. Max hadn't meant to tell him, but he let it slip after one of his late-night rum indulgences. "I've tried to dissuade him," he said. "Tried to convince him to leave the *Arrow* now, but he won't hear of it. The bastard is too damned honorable for his own good. Says he can't break his promise.

"But once this is over and Kane's dead? He will finally be released from his blasted vow, and can have the happiness he deserves, far away from all of this." He waved a hand absently and frowned at his tankard before setting it down heavily on the table.

After a long moment, Sarina asked, "And what of *your* happiness?"

Jonathan looked up, shocked by the tenderness in her eyes. He swallowed thickly but couldn't look away.

And he didn't have an answer.

Rina's heart broke at Jonathan's bleak expression. In that moment, she realized that he truly saw no future for himself beyond the *Arrow*—that he believed he would captain the ship until the day he died.

And that he believed that day was most likely not far off.

Before she even realized what she'd done, she found herself extending her hand and laying it over his. He startled in surprise, glancing down before hesitantly turning his own palm over, long fingers wrapping around to squeeze hers gently.

"Perhaps things can change," she said quietly.

"How?" The word was harsh. Sad. Hopeful.

In that moment, a string of longing passed between them, joining them together with a tight knot she doubted could be untied—and she could almost feel that he yearned for her as she did for him.

"I don't know." She held his gaze, but he didn't look away. In the distance, Rina could hear the plaintive tones of a fiddle player tuning his strings.

"Who's that?" she asked as the notes formed into a lively melody, quickly accented by a flute and the rumbling beat of a bodhran.

Jonathan tipped his head, a slow smile lighting his face. "The men like to play when there's an opportunity. Sadly, there's not been much opportunity of late." He stood, not releasing her hand. "Tell me, Smith, do ye dance?" He thickened his accent to lighten the mood, and Rina couldn't help smiling in return.

"Aye, Cap'n," she shot back, mimicking him as she stood up and let him pull her around the table. "That does sound like a good bit o' fun."

He laughed. "Are ye mocking me, wench?"

"Usually."

Her eyes twinkled, and Jonathan twirled her under his arm before catching her around the waist. She squeaked out a laugh, and he started to lead her around the small room, dodging the table and chairs as the music played merrily. Rina tried to keep up, her heartbeat quickening as much from his proximity as the dancing. The pensive Jonathan from a few moments ago had vanished, replaced by the rakish charmer she knew could be devastating to any woman within reach.

And she was definitely within reach.

He twirled her and dipped her over his arm with a cheeky grin. Rina's fingers tightened around his, her other hand gripping his shoulder tightly as her stomach dropped. She gasped, and his gaze flickered to her lips, his smile falling. Slowly, he lifted her to her feet, his arm firm and strong about her waist.

"The music stopped," she whispered. He licked his lips—opened his mouth to speak—but then the flute started up again, a slower song this time, the tune filling out as the fiddle and drum joined in. Jonathan held her pressed up against him, watching her intently as they began to sway to the music. Then, a masculine voice began to sing the haunting melody, the words floating toward them through the ship.

*My boat's by the tower, and my bark's on the bay*
*And both must be gone at the dark of the day*
*The moon's in her shroud, and to light thee afar*
*On the deck of the daring's a lovelighted star*

Rina's eyes fluttered closed as Jonathan pulled her closer, tipping his head slightly until his cheek brushed her temple. She could feel his breath on her hair, the heat of his body tingling along her skin, even through her clothes. He began to hum, low and rumbling, along with the song.

*So forgive me my rough mood unaccustomed to sue*

271

*I woo not, perhaps, as your landlubbers do*
*My voice is attuned to the sound of the gun*
*That startles the deep when the combat's begun*

"Smith, I . . ." Jonathan pulled back a little, and she opened her eyes to look at him, but he seemed to forget what he was going to say. Holding her gaze, he released her hand, fingertips slipping tantalizingly down her arm, across her shoulder, until they came to rest cupping her neck, his thumb rubbing gentle circles against her skin. She stared at him, mesmerized, any pretense at dancing lost as he muttered a low curse and lowered his lips to hers.

*So wake, lady wake, I am waiting for thee*
*Oh, this night or never my bride thou shalt be*

Any thoughts of why this was a bad idea—a terrible idea, bound to result only in a broken heart—flew out of Sarina's mind, scattering like dust in the wind. All she could think about was *more*. More kissing. More touching. More of this.

More of him.

She clung to Jonathan, trying to regain her balance, but the dizziness refused to dissipate. When his tongue traced along her lips, it seemed natural to part them, to breathe him in and taste him, heat and wet and rum deluging her senses. Her fingers found their way under his thick mass of hair, beads clicking lightly as she scratched at his scalp. He groaned in response, pulling her closer, crushing her to him as he devoured her mouth, the words from the song wrapping around them like a caress.

*So wake, lady wake, I am waiting for thee*
*Oh, this night or never my bride thou shalt be*

"Bloody hell, what am I doing?" Jonathan murmured against her mouth, lips trailing to tease lightly at her neck. "What are you doing to me?"

Rina tried to respond, but no words would come—only a slight whimper as he tugged at the shoulder of her gown, pulling it down and licking over the revealed skin.

"Yes," she whispered.

*Yes.* What else had she, really? No future. Despite Jonathan's talk of suitors, she knew there would be none, not after the life she'd lived in the past few weeks. Why not take this now? Why not take whatever Jonathan could give her?

Tomorrow would worry about itself.

"Jonathan . . ." She choked on the word, breath hitching in her throat with every touch of his lips. His fingers scorched her flesh, burning a trail to her very center. Her head fell back as he nosed at her skin, licking into the hollow of her throat.

"Aye," he grunted, low and raspy, as he pulled her even tighter against his hardness. His mouth pressed open, hot and damp against her skin. It was all happening so quickly . . . so fierce and all-consuming. She clung to him, lightheaded and dizzy, only able to gasp out his name.

He pulled back, and she was finally able to draw a deep breath.

"I don't understand what is happening," she whispered.

He lowered his head, touching his forehead to her cheek. "Neither do I, Smith."

They stood there for a long moment, wrapped in each other, the only sound their harsh breaths and the ripple of the waves—the music long since silenced. Rina half expected Jonathan to pull away, to raise the wall between them once again, but instead, he lifted his fingers to stroke her cheek before kissing her softly.

"I think it's time for bed," he said, reaching up to pull the pins from her hair. She watched him as he loosened the tresses, stringing them between his fingers and gently rubbing her scalp.

Finally, he stepped back and sat on the bed, bending down to scratch absently at his ankle. Rina clutched at the bodice of her gown, confused and overwhelmed at everything that had just happened. After a moment, she started toward her cot.

"Where are you going?" he asked, dropping his breeches.

She looked away quickly. "I was just—" She motioned toward the cot.

Jonathan chuckled. "Bit late for that, don't you think?" He reached out and grabbed her by the wrist to pull her toward him. With a smirk, he spun her around and unfastened her gown, then untied her corset with deft fingers. He shoved it and the gown to the floor before dropping to his knees and removing her shoes and stockings. Rina stood stunned, lifting arms and feet when instructed until she stood before him in only her shift. He pulled his shirt over his head and threw back the blankets, sitting on the bed and glancing back at her expectantly. When she hesitated, he rolled his eye and reached out to take her hand, tugging her between his knees and planting a kiss on her stomach.

"I'm tired, Smith," he murmured against her. "Let's go to sleep."

Unable to resist, Rina lifted her hands, running them over his head before kissing it gently.

"All right," she said.

They crawled between the sheets and Rina rolled onto her side, facing away from him, her heart hammering with nervous uncertainty.

What had she done? What was she *doing*?

With an impatient huff, Jonathan wrapped an arm around her waist, pulling her flush against his chest. He pressed his lips to the back of her neck, and she gasped, shivering slightly.

"You think too much," he said quietly. "Just go to sleep."

Sarina closed her eyes and Jonathan took her hand, his fingers lacing with hers against her chest. His steady breath and the heat of his body lulled her into relaxation, and she found herself melting into him, his heartbeat matching hers—or perhaps hers conforming to his.

A lone flute began to play on deck, the gentle melody fading away as she drifted off to sleep.

Jonathan awoke before the sun, Sarina's soft warmth along his chest bringing a smile to his face. It was odd to feel so satisfied when all they'd shared was a kiss. Well, a bit more than *just* a kiss, he had to admit. Touching Sarina, tasting her skin and feeling her pulse beneath his lips—it had been heady, hypnotizing. He wasn't certain why he stopped it when he did. He had a feeling Sarina would have let him continue, would have encouraged it, actually.

He'd nearly given in.

But wisdom won out over baser desires in the end, although he couldn't put her out of his bed. He counted it as his reward for showing such restraint—to indulge in one night of soft, warm limbs and sweet scents.

Still, the intimacy of waking with her in his bed touched something deep inside—something he couldn't quite name, and wasn't sure he wanted to.

Not yet, at least.

Sarina mumbled in her sleep, and Jonathan lifted his head, propping it on his bent arm as he watched her. The blankets were bunched around her waist, one slender leg peeking over the edge. The strap of her shift had fallen off one shoulder, the pale flesh calling to him tantalizingly.

He leaned down, unable to resist pressing a kiss there . . . and there . . . lips nibbling along the tender skin. His tongue flicked out, teasing her, and Sarina gasped, her eyes flying open.

"What are you doing?"

He smiled. "Good morning." He leaned down to kiss her, a quick touch of lips, a slick of tongue, his hand drifting to her throat. When he started to pull back, she turned toward him, lifting a hand to the back of his neck to keep him in place.

Jonathan laughed against her mouth. "Needy wench." Then he stifled her indignant retort with another kiss.

The first light of dawn filtered through the porthole, and Jonathan pulled away reluctantly. "We'll need to set sail for Tortuga soon," he murmured, kissing her once more. "I'll not be wanting to start something I'm not able to finish satisfactorily."

Sarina blushed. "Of course not." She started to get out of bed, but Jonathan held her in place.

"Not just yet, Smith," he said, kissing along her neck. "We have a few minutes."

"A few minutes?" she repeated, gasping as he bit her earlobe. "But what if someone comes by?"

"So what?"

"They'll—*Oh!*—catch us."

Jonathan considered that. On the one hand, he had no problem—obviously—with the men knowing Sarina was his. On the other hand . . .

He looked at her, splayed across the bed, all flushed skin and heaving breasts. No, no one else should see her like that.

Ever.

"Perhaps you're right," he said, shifting away from her.

"What?" Her eyes were glazed, lips full and bruised from his kisses. Jonathan felt a surge of satisfaction at the sight but pulled the sheets up over her chest.

"We should get dressed."

"But—" Sarina sat up, the strap of her shift descending further, revealing an expanse of creamy skin. "It's barely sunrise."

Jonathan swallowed thickly, reaching out to touch her without realizing it. His fingers traced the curve of her shoulder, stroked the dip of her collarbone, curled around the chain she wore around her neck.

"Damn it, Smith, what you do to me," he muttered, pulling the chain and leaning in to kiss her. She sank into the kiss, and he smiled against her lips. "But I'll not have my men privy to all your many charms, you tempting wench."

Sarina frowned at him, but her cheeks pinkened, and Jonathan thought she might have been secretly pleased. He toyed with the chain.

"Why do you always wear this?" he asked, lying on his side and again resting on his elbow.

She shrugged, pulling up the strap of her shift. It fell down again, and Jonathan grinned victoriously.

"My father gave it to me," she said. "He said it was a good luck charm."

"Good luck?" Jonathan pulled the chain out from beneath her shift, examining the silver charm hanging from it. It was a flat disk, worn and misshapen around the edges—about the size of a button on his best coat—with a small hole punched in the top for the chain, another larger one just off center.

"He used to tell me stories about it, and how it came to have the hole," Sarina explained, sitting up and tucking her knees under her. "Once it stopped the ball from a pistol fired by a revolutionary against a Russian prince. Another time he told me it was an arrow—destined for a fair maiden but caught in the charm when her true love threw himself in its path." She smiled at the memory, and Jonathan couldn't help smiling back.

"No tales of pirates?" he asked with a wink.

"Of course," she grinned, taking the charm and tapping it against her lips thoughtfully. "The dastardly pirate—" She smirked at him. "—kept it close at all times, because peeking through the hole gave him unbelievable power."

Jonathan watched her lips as she rubbed the charm over them, hypnotized. "What kind of power?"

"To see other worlds—worlds of adventure and treasure."

"What good to see them, if you couldn't reach them?"

Sarina laughed. "Who says he couldn't reach them?" She released the charm and it fell against her chest, spinning slightly and catching the growing daylight.

Jonathan froze, then sat up abruptly, reaching out to take the charm in his fingers.

"What's wrong?" Sarina asked.

He studied the silver disk. One side was worn almost flat, the carving barely detectable at first, and not discernible at all.

Jonathan flipped it over, his heart beginning to thump in his chest. The design on the other side was a bit more evident, enough visible around the hole for him to recognize the familiar image of a shield.

"Jonathan? What is it?"

He looked up at her. "Do you know what this is?" Why hadn't he considered it? Why hadn't he thought of it before?

"It's just a trinket," she replied. "Only of sentimental value, nothing more."

Jonathan shook his head. "You don't understand," he said, excitement building in his chest. "This is a Spanish *reale*."

She frowned. "A *reale*?"

"I can't believe you had it the whole time," he muttered. "I can't believe you didn't *tell* me."

"Tell you what, Jonathan?" she asked, and the confusion in her expression put to rest any suspicion that she'd known what she had in her possession.

"This!" he said, lifting the chain until the charm dangled before her eyes. "It's not a charm, Smith. It's a coin! A Spanish coin!"

Sarina gaped at him as understanding set in. "But . . . but it can't be. You said the coin would be something special. This is . . . it's *nothing*."

"It's not nothing," he retorted. "Ponder it, Smith. Your father—who found the cutlass—just happened to also pass on a coin to you. It can't be a coincidence."

She took the coin in her hand, looking at it with new eyes. "He told me never to take it off," she murmured. "To keep it close to my heart and it would always keep me safe."

"A perfect hiding place. No one would ever suspect."

"More lies," Sarina muttered. "More secrets." She pulled the chain over her head, holding it out to Jonathan as she fought off tears. "You might as well take it. Put it in the chest with the rest."

"Sarina, your father—"

"My father was a liar," she said flatly.

"Your father," Jonathan continued, reaching out to take the coin, "was a good man. And I believe if he was after the treasure, it was for you. He loved you, Sarina. I know that. *You* know that."

She closed her eyes, forcing tears down her cheeks as her shoulders fell. "I don't know what I know anymore."

"Yes, you do."

She looked up at him with shining eyes. He reached over and placed the chain back over her head, settling the charm gently against her chest.

"Whatever reason he gave you this, it is something that was important to both of you," he said. "You should keep it."

"But what about the treasure?"

"We'll address that when the time comes." He leaned in to kiss her, then smiled. "Now, we're for Tortuga, Smith. I suggest you get dressed if you expect to go ashore."

Sarina sniffed, smiling slightly. "Aye, Captain."

"That's more like it," he said with a wink, turning to get out of bed. "And for God's sake, don't wear those dreadful breeches."

"I wouldn't dream of it." Sarina smirked and he knew she was going to wear the breeches.

Jonathan sighed in resignation. "Well, at least button your bloody coat."

He opened the door and shouted for his breakfast, the sounds of the ship coming to life bursting through the open door. He turned back to see Sarina studying the coin, a tender smile on her face. Then, with a heavy breath, she tucked it into her shift and wiped away her tears, heading behind the screen to get dressed.

Jonathan didn't know exactly what would happen once they did find the treasure—and Kane—but he did know one thing.

Leaving Sarina Talbot would be the most difficult thing he'd ever have to do.

In fact, he was beginning to wonder if it was even possible.

*At long last, I have found it.*

*- The Journal of*
*Simon Alistair Mellick*
*19 September, 1665*

The sun was high in the sky when the *Black Arrow* made port in Tortuga, the men completing their tasks in double time in the hopes of making the most of their time ashore. The ship was relatively secure—tucked in a hidden cove around the point from the town proper—so all but a few were allowed to indulge in the entertainments the island had to offer. Jonathan had assigned a couple of men to keep watch at the entry to the cove, and a few cabin boys were left behind on the ship with a cask of ale and instructions to fetch help if anything went amiss.

Jonathan would have preferred to procure whatever information Pearl had obtained and leave soon after. He knew, however, that these brief moments of respite were what kept his men going through weeks on the run—or worse yet, fighting for their very lives. So he'd granted them a few hours of drink and debauchery while he visited Pearl, along with a stern warning that each man would be expected to do his duty when he returned to the ship, so they'd best not indulge too heavily.

He wasn't too worried. If there was one thing he knew about his men, it was that they could handle their rum.

With an impatient sigh, he leaned against a palm tree, waiting for the others to join him, his eye warily watching James Ceron. The man stood talking with one of the younger crewmen, a native like James, and the younger man listened raptly to whatever Ceron was saying. James gestured wildly as he spoke, then stopped, staring at the crewman expectantly. After a moment, the younger man burst out laughing, and Ceron smacked him on the back with a smile before turning to walk toward Jonathan.

Jonathan bit the inside of his cheek. Sarina was convinced that James was trustworthy, but Jonathan still had his doubts. He knew his decision to take the native along on this mission raised some eyebrows, particularly on the part of Max, but Jonathan firmly believed in keeping his friends close and his enemies closer.

He wasn't quite certain which Jamie Ceron was just yet.

"Where are the others?" James asked as he drew nearer.

Jonathan nodded toward the water where Hutchins was splashing through the shallow water, carrying Sarina in his arms while Max trailed behind. The cove was ideal for their purposes, a deep channel edged by shallow water enabling them to disembark without use of a dinghy, and they'd used it many times before. Jonathan fought back a rush of jealousy at the sight of his master rigger with his hands on his—on Sarina. He knew Hutchins was simply trying to keep the woman's boots dry, and he would have done the job himself if he hadn't had to see to the early scouting party. Hutchins set her down on the sand with a grin, steadying her with a hand on her elbow as she regained her footing. She was wearing the blasted breeches—of course—and gripped her sword hilt with a wide smile, straightening her hat before starting across the sand toward Jonathan.

"I'm surprised you let her out of your sight," James mused.

Jonathan growled in response. James chuckled.

"Sorry, we took so long, I needed to—" Sarina came to an abrupt stop, her eyes widening slightly.

"What's wrong?" Jonathan asked.

"What are you wearing?" she blurted, clapping a hand to her mouth as if she could force the words back.

He looked down at his clothes in confusion. Jenkins had his coat and hat, but other than that, Jonathan was dressed in his usual shirt, breeches and boots, his cutlass and flintlocks strapped about his hips. "What are you talking about?"

Max, insightful as always, pulled Hutchins along the path, motioning for James to join them. "We'll be waiting over here," he said in response to Jonathan's confused look. The captain turned back to Sarina, frowning at her open collar.

"Would you please button your shirt?" he muttered. When she made to do so with trembling fingers, not meeting his gaze, he crossed his arms over his chest. "Now, what are you on about, Smith?"

"It's nothing," she muttered, face aflame. "It's just . . . your . . ." She waved a hand toward his legs.

"My what?"

"Your breeches," she hissed, looking for all the world like she'd rather be somewhere else—anywhere else. "You weren't wearing those earlier."

Jonathan wondered if perhaps Sarina had hit her head on the trip from the ship.

"No," he said carefully. "I caught them on a nail and ripped a hole in them, so I had to change. You can feel free to mend them whenever you've a mind to."

"Don't you have any others?" she asked, almost desperately.

"Aye, but I chose these," he replied, confusion quickly turning to irritation. "Now what on earth is wrong with my breeches?" He looked down, examining them closely. "Are they torn?" He turned around and Sarina let out a choked sound. When he turned back to her, she seemed even redder, if that were possible, her mouth parted on a gasp.

"It's just . . . they're so *tight,"* she said, swallowing thickly. "And *leather.* That can't be comfortable." She tore her eyes away.

It took Jonathan a moment, but he was nothing if not insightful, and with the dawning of realization, he leaned his shoulder against the tree with a satisfied smirk.

"Actually, they're quite comfortable," he said archly. He might have also purposely hitched his hip outward just a little bit more than usual.

Perhaps.

Sarina's eyes widened again. She turned her attention to another tree, apparently finding its bark extraordinarily interesting. She cleared her throat.

"Shouldn't we be going?"

"In a moment." He turned so his back was against the tree, hips thrust outward invitingly. "Smith?"

"Hmm?" She tracked the pattern in the bark with a fingertip, before she turned abruptly to look out over the water. "Lovely weather, isn't it?"

Jonathan laughed. "The weather? Are you serious?"

"Well, it is lovely," she stammered, waving at the sky. "So clear and blue. And the sea is so . . . clear. And blue." She swallowed, shifting uncomfortably on her feet.

"Smith." Jonathan twisted again, not missing the quick dart of her eyes at the movement. "Do you have a problem with my breeches?"

"Problem? No, of course not. Whyever would I have a problem?" She studiously avoided looking his direction.

Jonathan pushed off the tree and moved toward her. He saw her start slightly and step away, then her jaw tightened and she stepped back.

Brave girl.

He moved to her side, a little behind her, so her left leg was bracketed by both of his. She glanced down when his leather-clad thigh brushed hers, and gulped.

"What are you doing?" Her voice cracked.

He leaned in, unable to resist, his lips brushing against her ear. He felt her shudder as he murmured, "You like them."

She inhaled sharply. "I don't."

"Oh, I think you do." He reached out to grab her wrist, all teasing forgotten with the wave of heat coming off her body. She gave no resistance as he pulled her hand toward his leg, laying her open palm over his thigh. Sarina gasped, her fingers clenching involuntarily in the soft leather, molding to his muscular flesh.

Jonathan hissed, pressing his open mouth to her neck. At the sound of a throat clearing, he stifled a groan and stepped back reluctantly. Sarina's hand drifted from his thigh and fell against her side. He turned to see Max watching him with an amused expression.

"Captain, I hate to interrupt, but we really should be going."

Jonathan took a deep breath, realizing that now his breeches really *were* a little uncomfortable. "Yes. Of course. Right. Be right there." Max nodded, turning to walk away, and Jonathan adjusted himself, under the guise of adjusting his sword belt. "Shall we, Smith?"

She glared at him. "That wasn't very nice."

"I'm rarely nice."

She gave him a measured look for a long moment, then lifted her chin in challenge. "You know?" she said sweetly. "It is a bit warm, isn't it? I don't think I need this coat." She removed her sword belt, then unbuttoned the coat, folding it carefully and draping it over a low log. The slight sea breeze fitted the thin fabric of her shirt to her body, making it cling along her breasts, her tiny waist. With another glare at Jonathan she pointedly unbuttoned the top two buttons of her shirt, then propped her fists on her hips. "There. That's much better."

Jonathan gritted his teeth, ignoring the surge of lust shooting through him. "What do you think you're doing?"

"What?" She mimicked his guileless expression.

"Put your coat back on."

"I think you like it," she taunted, throwing back her shoulders.

Jonathan ripped the coat from the log, thrusting it at her. "Smith, if you don't put this coat on, you are not coming along." They glared at each other stubbornly for a moment, before Jonathan sighed heavily, looking into her eyes. "It's imperative that you escape unwanted attention," he said earnestly. "Believe me, if you go into town like that, Stanton will be the least of our problems."

Sarina studied him carefully, then rolled her eyes and grabbed the coat. "Doesn't seem fair," she muttered.

Jonathan hid his relief under a smug grin. "Life usually isn't." She buckled her sword belt with a mulish frown, and Jonathan couldn't resist adding, "Look on the bright side. You can enjoy my breeches all you like."

"Arse," she muttered.

"Such language!" He laughed, then on impulse wrapped an arm around her waist, drawing her close and planting a hard kiss on her mouth. He pulled away and took her hand to lead her toward the others, only releasing her when they started down the path toward town.

Every now and then he'd glance back to find Sarina's eyes fixed on his leather-clad backside. But instead of blushing when he caught her, she'd stick out her tongue and mutter to herself.

Jonathan decided perhaps he should get another pair of leather breeches.

Rina couldn't take her eyes off those blasted breeches. No matter how much she tried to focus on the trees or the sand before her feet or even the conversation James was trying to have with her, her gaze kept returning to Jonathan's firm backside, clad in soft, supple leather.

She might have even caught herself trying to reach out and touch it once or twice.

Jonathan knew, too, which was embarrassing, but did little to stop her apparently uncontrollable libido. He'd smirk at her and she'd want to be angry, but then she'd have a flash of the night before, that indescribable pleasure he'd brought her, and all she could do was force a glare until he turned back around.

Then she'd stare at his backside again.

Sarina feared she was becoming quite the insatiable trollop.

Fortunately, they arrived in town, enabling her to firmly push back any further considerations of Jonathan, his breeches, or his rather talented thighs. They gathered at the edge of the main road, and Jonathan fixed them all with a firm look.

"We all know the plan," he said. "Ceron, you and Sarina keep watch outside while Hutchins, Baines, and I go in to speak to Pearl. I doubt Stanton will find his way here anytime soon, but the bastard has fooled me before."

James nodded grimly. "Aye, Captain."

With that, Jonathan, Max, and Sam made their way to the entrance of the *Red Pearl*. James sauntered over to a shop across the street and leaned casually against the corner porch railing. Rina took a spot under a tree just outside the tavern, one that provided a view through the wide front window.

If she was going to be kept out of the action, she was going to make certain she could at least see it.

It only took a moment before she spotted Jonathan and the others sitting down at a table, a serving wench placing jugs of ale before them. She smiled at Jonathan, before sitting in his lap, and Sarina stiffened. He whispered something in the girl's ear and she giggled, wrapping her arms around Jonathan's neck with a familiar air.

Was this the elusive Pearl? Rina pulled her hat low over her eyes to hide her appraising stare. The girl was petite, larger than Sarina, but still small enough to fit comfortably in Jonathan's lap. She wore an ill-fitting, garish blue gown, hanging loose off one shoulder to reveal her pale skin. Blonde hair was piled on her head, a few strands clinging to her face from the heat, and her eyes were dark—outlined with kohl, no doubt—her cheeks rouged and lips red with stain.

Sarina bit her own lip, pale and pink, jealousy burning in her gut.

After a moment, Jonathan whispered in the wench's ear again and she nodded, standing up. Jonathan smacked her backside and the group laughed as the girl slapped his arm playfully, then proceeded through a dark hallway at the back of the room.

Rina shifted against the tree, sparing one look across the street at James before turning back to the window. A few minutes later, the wench came back into the main room with another woman— tall and beautiful with bright red hair curling wildly around her shoulders. The redhead smiled at the group of men, embracing each of them before settling down in the empty chair at the table. She and Jonathan spoke—apparently in hushed tones, since they all leaned in to listen. After a moment, she stood up, turning to Sam Hutchins and beckoning with a finger and a wink. The master rigger grinned and stood immediately, taking her hand as she led him up the stairs in the back of the room. Jonathan and Max, meanwhile, sat back, exchanging a frustrated shrug before signaling the serving wench for another mug of ale.

"Sarina?" James' quiet voice startled her, and she jumped, stifling a shriek.

"What?" she hissed.

James raised an eyebrow. "For someone who's supposed to be keeping watch, you don't seem to be watching much. Out here, at least." He gave a pointed glance toward the window, where the serving wench was leaning on the table next to Max, offering a view of her ample bosom.

Rina glared at James. "Did you need something?"

All joking aside, he nodded. "I think I saw someone suspicious down the street a bit," he said. "I'm not certain, but I thought I'd go look into it. I wanted to make sure you'll be all right here by yourself."

"Suspicious?" She felt a chill down her spine. "Who?"

"I don't know. I thought I saw someone watching the tavern, but I also might be imagining things. I'd rather poke around a bit before interrupting the captain." He looked toward the window, where Jonathan was laughing at something the wench said. "He's obviously quite busy."

Rina snorted. "Obviously." She straightened. "Do you want me to come with you?"

"No, it's better if you stay here and keep an eye on things. I shouldn't be long."

"All right then. Be careful."

James nodded before melting into the shadows of the buildings and making his way down the street. Rina scanned the area but saw nothing out of place—just a lot of drunken men walking, some singing gleefully off-key. A group sat crouched on the ground in an alley a short distance away throwing dice and cheering loudly. She sighed and looked back toward the window. She had a sneaking suspicion that Jonathan's decision to have her stay outside had little to do with keeping watch and more to do with keeping her out of the way.

The wench was in Jonathan's lap again, laughing at something Max had said. Rina gritted her teeth, eyes narrowing consideringly when she spotted a shadowed alcove near the open front door serving as a storage area for a few stacked crates.

If she was there, she could still keep watch *and* see and hear what was going on inside the tavern. It seemed a logical choice, much better than standing outside near a tree where she'd be of little use should something happen.

The wench wrapped a long strand of Jonathan's hair around her finger. He winked. Sarina fumed.

Yes. It would be a much better position. Logistically speaking.

With a quick glance over her shoulder, she made her way to the alcove, slipping easily behind the boxes. From her position, no one could see her unless they were looking, but she could easily see the street, as well as Jonathan's table inside the tavern. She could hear the laughter, the teasing comments, and for a moment she felt sick to her stomach when she thought about what had happened the night before.

What was she thinking? Obviously, their encounter meant little to the pirate. Things like that probably happened to him all the time—women throwing themselves at him, debasing themselves for him. She'd been ridiculous to think it could be of any importance to such a man.

She watched him sprawled in the chair, the blonde wench comfortably seated in his lap, and felt like such a fool.

A movement near the street caught Rina's attention, and she stiffened at the sight of a group of men walking toward the tavern. The leader wore a red coat with brass buttons, a sword buckled about his hips and—of all things—a parrot sitting on his shoulder. He turned to one of his companions, and Rina caught the word *Tremayne*, eliciting a flash of panic in her chest. She ducked further into the shadows, wondering what to do.

"Are ye certain he's inside?" the leader asked, the parrot echoing "inside" with a loud squawk.

"Aye, sir."

The leader grinned. "Excellent. The reward on his head will be well worth my trouble. Is he alone?"

"Dunno. Jest heard the *Arrow* made port and Tremayne came straight here."

"No matter. We'll slip inside and see what's what, yes?" The parrot squawked "Yes!" and the men went into the tavern.

Rina came out from her hiding place, quickly scanning the area in search of James. She could go find him, but by then, who knew what the man with the parrot could do? She fisted her sword, wishing she could signal Jonathan, but he had yet to spot her. Instead, she hurried around the side of the tavern, exhaling with relief when she spotted another entrance. She slipped quietly into the main room and took a seat in a quiet corner. She watched the man with the parrot circle the room, his men moving in the opposite direction. After scanning the faces, he nodded at his men and bellowed, "I'm looking for One-Eyed Jack!"

The room fell silent, the parrot's echo of "One-Eyed Jack! One-Eyed Jack!" resounding in the quiet. She saw Jonathan's fist tighten around his tankard as the wench quickly got up from his lap and hurried up the stairs. He exchanged a look with Max, and the parrot man smirked, approaching Jonathan from the front while his companions circled around behind, casually leaning against the wall. The man stood, legs splayed with his back to Rina, and her eyes darted about, coming to rest on the jug of rum on a shelf beside her. Quietly, she seized the half-empty jug, bringing it to rest on the table before her.

"You One-Eyed Jack?" the man demanded.

"I'd watch yerself, man," Max warned.

He laughed. "Watch myself? I'd say yer captain here ought to watch himself. There's quite a bounty on 'is 'ead, you know? And I, fer one, aim to claim it."

A flurry of things happened all at once.

The parrot squawked.

The man in the red coat reached for his sword.

Jonathan reached for his.

And Rina emerged from the shadows, swinging the rum jug at the man's head with all of her strength. He fell to a knee, the parrot alighting on a nearby table. The blow didn't incapacitate him,

291

however. Instead, he turned angry eyes on Sarina, rising up to his full height and raising his sword with a furious growl.

"Bloody hell," she murmured, reaching for her own sword.

"Bloody hell!" the parrot squawked.

The man's sword flashed toward her, and for a moment she thought it was all over. But with a mighty yell, Jonathan barreled toward them, boots clunking on the wooden tables until he flew toward the man, knocking him aside at the last moment. They landed on the floor in a tangle of limbs before Jonathan deftly leapt to his feet. He glanced at Sarina.

"I thought you were waiting outside."

She swallowed nervously, the near-blow making her more than a little dizzy. "I thought you might need my help."

The parrot man surged to his feet, swinging his sword at Jonathan, who deflected it easily. "Well, I appreciate the gesture, Smith. But next time, use a pistol."

Sarina heard a shout, and the man's companions came toward them, one intercepted by Max, the other dodging around them, lunging toward Jonathan. Sarina drew her sword.

"Behind you!" she shouted, swinging at the man and slicing his upper arm. Surprised, he turned on her with a bellow.

And that was when all hell broke loose.

Jonathan whirled about just in time to see Sarina strike the man on his flank across the upper arm. Blood oozed from the wound, and he turned on Sarina with an angry shout.

"Damn it," Jonathan muttered, shoving his attacker back with a well-placed kick to the stomach. The man stumbled over a chair and fell to the floor, and Jonathan whirled about to help Sarina.

She clutched her sword with both hands, brow creased in concentration as she tried to remember what he'd taught her. She moved quickly, dodging and deflecting the man's quick blows. Fortunately, he was no expert swordsman, and Jonathan felt a surge of pride that she was holding her own. Sarina spun around and slashed at the man's leg, and he howled in pain when she hit home.

The tavern had erupted in chaos, fists flying and swords flashing in the light from the windows. Sarina clambered up onto a table, gripping the beam above her head with one hand as she kicked at her opponent's face with all her might. With a mighty crack, the man's head jerked back, blood spurting from his surely-broken nose. He clutched at it with his free hand, advancing on her with his sword held high. Jonathan stepped in and, with a few precise thrusts, disarmed the man and knocked him out with an elbow to his broken nose.

"I had him," Sarina said, lifting her sword to deflect the blow from another drunken fighter.

"You're welcome," Jonathan replied with a cocky grin, lifting Sarina down from the table. Parrot man had regained his footing and came toward them with a determined expression. Around them, the fight had no rhyme or reason—aside from Max fighting off one of the parrot man's accomplices, everyone was drunk and punching whoever came into range.

This was not what Jonathan had planned when he'd entered the *Red Pearl*. Pearl had told him a man named Hayward would bring the box to the tavern, but she had no idea when, exactly, he might show up. She'd shrugged apologetically and offered the comforts of her establishment while they waited.

Including Flora, of course. The wench wasn't picky about her company, but she always preferred Jonathan when he was in town. He'd flirted with her out of habit, more than anything, and an attempt to remain inconspicuous. Inconspicuous, however, now seemed a bit out of reach.

"If anyone gets blood on my new coat, I will not be happy," Sarina muttered, picking up her discarded jug of rum to smash it into a man's face.

"Seawater's good for blood stains," Jonathan replied, his sword clanging mightily. Sarina handed him the jug—it still hadn't broken, and she would later wonder at the sturdy nature of rum jugs—and he swung it at the man with the broken nose, who was crawling to his feet. He crumpled to the floor once again.

An ear-shattering crack filled the air and everybody froze, turning as one toward the stairway at the back of the room. Pearl stood on the landing in all her glory, fiery hair flowing wild about her head and a lace dressing gown hugging her every curve as she lowered a smoking flintlock, a second held in her other hand.

"That will be quite enough!" she shouted. Hutchins stood behind her, his shirt untucked and rumpled. Jonathan knew he was aching to join the fight, but Pearl would have none of it. Abruptly, she raised the gun, and Jonathan followed its aim to see the man with the red coat and his companions inching their way toward the door. Pearl cocked the gun and they froze at the sound.

"I take it you're the ones responsible for this nonsense?" she asked.

When they didn't respond, one of the drunken fighters spat on the floor. "He's after the bounty on One-Eyed—" At Jonathan's glare, he corrected, "Err . . . on Captain Tremayne."

The parrot fluttered his wings and squawked, "One-Eyed Jack! One-Eyed Jack!"

"Indeed?" Pearl hissed, eyes narrowing on the backs of the men by the door. "Turn around and face me," she ordered.

The men did as instructed, hands held high.

"My place is a safe haven to all," she said, flintlock never wavering. "But it no longer is for you. Come around here again, and I'll fill you full of shot, is that clear?"

The men nodded, the one in the red coat mumbling, "Yes'm."

"I'll be speaking to my friends, as well. Others with business concerns on the island," she warned. "And they won't take kindly to greedy bastards such as yourselves bringing trouble to Tortuga. I suggest you set sail and don't return to the island for a good, long time."

She paused, then rolled her eyes in irritation. "Go on now!" she shouted. "Be gone!"

The men scrambled out the door, their colleague with the broken nose staggering out after them.

"You!" Pearl shouted, pointing at a couple of large men by the door. "Clean this mess up, and be quick about it." She descended the rest of the stairs, making her way to Jonathan.

"You all right?" she asked, taking Sam's hand and wrapping it around her waist as he moved next to her.

"Fine," Jonathan replied, sheathing his sword. "Sorry for bringing you this trouble."

Pearl waved a hand in dismissal. "All in a day's work." She turned penetrating green eyes on Sarina. "And who might this be?"

"Pearl McKinnon, Sarina Talbot. She's a guest on board for a while."

"A guest?" Pearl lifted a perfectly shaped eyebrow. "I wasn't aware the *Arrow* was a passenger vessel."

"I'm not a passenger," Sarina replied, sliding her sword back into its sheath, and wiping her hands on her breeches. "Not really, anyway."

"Sarina's part of the crew," Max interjected, smiling when Sarina shot him a surprised look.

"Really?" Pearl's appraising gaze raked over Sarina, taking in her masculine clothes. Sarina shifted uncomfortably but raised her chin, looking the woman directly in the eyes.

"That's right," she said, squaring her shoulders in challenge.

Pearl studied her for a moment, then a slow, wide smile split her face. "Well, you certainly know how to use a sword," she said admiringly. "Do you think you could teach me that?"

Sarina let out a breath, smiling back. "You seem to do all right with a pair of flintlocks."

Pearl laughed. "All part of the job," she said, reaching out to tuck her arm through Sarina's elbow. "Come on, now. Let's sit down and you can tell me all about life on a pirate ship."

"Pearl," Sam whined, glancing longingly toward the stairs.

"Oh, drat." She glanced at Sam, then shrugged apologetically at Sarina. "Duty calls."

"Hey!" he shouted, reaching out when she darted out of his reach.

"I'll be back, Sarina, and we'll have a good, long chat," Pearl called as she raced up the stairs, Sam hot on her heels. "Until then, a round of ale on the house!"

Cheers rang out at the announcement, and Jonathan turned to Sarina with a questioning grin.

"You were right," Sarina said, smiling back. "I like her."

"No surprise," Jonathan retorted. "You're both stubborn wenches."

Sarina took a deep breath, eyes scanning the disorder in the room and coming to rest on a puddle of blood on the floor. She blinked, her face growing pale—a little green, actually—and she swayed slightly on her feet.

"Smith? You all right?"

Sarina looked up at Jonathan, blinking quickly. "I've never . . . I just . . . the blood . . ." She began to gasp for air.

"Smith?" He reached for her as she lifted her hand, staring at the splatter of red across the palm.

"I think I'm going to—"

If Sarina had remained conscious, she might have been impressed by Jonathan's rather colorful curses as he hurried to catch her before she hit the floor.

*I live in constant fear that what I have claimed will be taken from me. And now I have learned that it is not only my fortune that is at risk, but that of my unborn child.*

*My dear Mary says he will come with the spring. His future is of the utmost import. For my heir, I must find a way to protect the treasure.*

*- The Journal of
Simon Alistair Mellick
2 October, 1665*

Rina sipped her ale, more embarrassed than dizzy once she'd recovered from her swoon, and Jonathan finally left off teasing her to relay what Pearl had told them.

"This man bringing the box—Hayward. Can he be trusted?" she asked.

"Pearl said she paid him well. For enough coin, anyone is trustworthy."

"I don't know about that," Rina said doubtfully. "This whole thing makes me nervous."

"Me, too," Max muttered.

"Well, we don't have much choice at this point." Jonathan sat back, swirling the ale in his tankard before taking a long drink. "Hayward says he has the box, so all we can do is wait." He studied his mug for a moment, then turned to Rina. "Where is Ceron, anyway? How did you get in here without dragging him with you?"

She flushed, embarrassed that she'd completely forgotten about James in the melee. "He thought he saw someone suspicious down the road. He went to check it out, but he should have been back by now."

Jonathan stiffened, and Max stood immediately and hurried out the front door. He returned a few minutes later, looking much relieved.

"He's out front," he said. "Everything is fine."

"Oh, good," Rina said with a heavy exhale. "I can't believe I forgot—"

At that moment, the blonde serving wench propped her hip on the table, leaning forward on her arm as her breasts all but fell out of her gown. "You boys need another round?" she asked with a suggestive wink. "Or maybe a bit o' entertainment upstairs?"

Rina ground her teeth in irritation. "No, thank you," she muttered.

The girl turned to Sarina, eyes widening in surprise. "You're no boy."

"Brilliant one, aren't you?"

Jonathan raised a brow, but Rina reddened and looked away.

"Thank ye, Flora, but no more ale at the moment," he said to the girl, pouring on the accent. "We've business t'discuss and need t'keep our wits about us."

Flora pouted, toying with Jonathan's hair again. "Oh, that's no fun, Jack. You used to be much more fun."

Rina fought the urge to gouge her eyes out.

Jonathan, however, was much more diplomatic. He nodded toward a man watching the exchange from across the room.

"There," he said. "That lad looks more than willing to sample yer charms."

Flora followed his gaze, then patted her hair, shooting the man a smile. "Aye," she murmured. "And he looks like he has a bit o' coin as well." Without another word, she stood up from the table and sauntered over to the man, slipping into his lap with a laugh.

"Rather fickle, don't you think?" Rina muttered.

Jonathan laughed. "Flora's all right," he said. "The girl has to make a living." He leaned across the table, running a finger along Rina's flushed cheek. "Why, Smith, I do believe you're jealous."

"I am not!" She took a gulp of ale and wiped her mouth with the back of her hand. When Jonathan fixed her with a smug stare, she added, "I simply think you should keep your mind on business, that's all. There's no time for dalliances."

Jonathan raised an eyebrow. "You didn't seem to mind last night."

Rina gasped in outrage, and Max stood up abruptly, his chair scraping across the floor.

"Right then," he said, not looking directly at either of them. "I'll just . . ." He waved a hand toward the back of the room. "Outhouse," he muttered, turning on his heel.

"How dare you!" Sarina hissed. "Perhaps for you that was a mere dalliance, but for me—" She blinked, embarrassed at what she'd almost revealed. The last thing she needed was for Jonathan to realize how much it had meant to her.

Jonathan took a deep breath, his gaze softening.

*Too late.*

"I apologize," he said quietly. "I didn't mean to belittle—"

"It's nothing."

"It wasn't . . ." Jonathan fixed her with an intent look. "Nothing."

"Jonathan—"

"Smith!" Jonathan shook his head, as if trying to find the right words. "Sarina," he corrected. "I owe you an apology for last night. I never should have taken advantage—"

"You can't be serious," she snapped. "You're going to take the blame for last night? Like I am some weak-minded female who couldn't help herself?"

"I'm trying to be chivalrous!" Jonathan replied, affronted.

Rina snorted. "You're being ridiculous!" When Jonathan stared at her, stunned, she added, "I knew what I was doing last night, Jonathan. For you to try and take the blame . . . Well, it's insulting, that's what it is."

"It is?"

"It is."

"Oh." Jonathan swallowed, still looking a bit unsure. "Well, then. I apologize for that, I suppose."

"Apology accepted." Rina took another sip of her ale.

Jonathan still appeared to be trying to figure out what had just happened. After a moment, he said quietly, "Flora is a friend. Nothing more."

Rina shrugged. "It's none of my business."

He hesitated briefly before reaching across the table to brush a fleeting touch across the back of her hand. "I wanted you to know."

She met his gaze, trying to read his intent. She was lost when it came to Jonathan, in a constant state of confusion and want. And right when she thought she had figured out where she stood, he would do something like this, knocking her off balance yet again.

"Thank you," she said.

Jonathan opened his mouth to say something more, but a loud squawk and a flutter of red feathers interrupted. The parrot that had apparently been hiding in the rafters landed on Jonathan's shoulder with a loud, "Bloody hell!"

Rina's mouth dropped open. "That man forgot his parrot!"

"Apparently so," Jonathan said distastefully, waving a hand toward the bird. "Go on now!" he hissed. The parrot flapped his wings a bit but ignored him.

"I think it likes you." Rina grinned, more than a little amused by Jonathan's discomfort.

"Well, I don't like him," he muttered. "Can you get it off me?"

"What? Are you afraid of a little bird?"

"I simply don't want to hurt it." He tried again, unsuccessfully, to shoo it away.

"Well, I think we should keep it." Rina snagged a half-eaten roll from an abandoned plate and offered it to the parrot. It blinked at her curiously for a moment, then bent to peck at the bread.

"We're not keeping it."

"Why not? Every pirate ship needs a parrot."

"Where on earth did you get such a ridiculous notion?"

Rina shrugged. "Everybody knows that." She smiled at the parrot. "What's your name, pretty bird?"

The parrot squawked. "Pretty bird! Pretty bird!"

Jonathan glared. "It doesn't need a name. It's not a pet, and we're not keeping it." He shook his shoulder to dislodge the bird, but it just looked at him with steady black eyes. "Bloody hell," he muttered.

"New friend, Jonathan?" Pearl appeared at the table, fully dressed this time in a yellow cotton gown, her flaming hair artfully arranged on her head. She motioned to Sam, who dragged another table over, then took a seat next to Sarina. "Sorry to keep you waiting," she said, tipping her head toward Jonathan. "You know how these boys are." She winked and Rina flushed.

"I don't . . . I mean . . . we're not . . ."

Pearl looked from her to Jonathan and back again. "No? But I thought for certain—" She waved a hand. "Never mind. So, tell me, Jonathan, when did you become such a bird enthusiast?"

"I'm not," he said grumpily, slouching forward on the table. "Damned thing won't go away."

"Go away!" the parrot echoed.

"Exactly!" Jonathan shouted. The bird whistled and set to preening its feathers.

Max returned and sat down next to Sam, smiling when Flora came by with another round of ale. His eyes widened slightly at the sight of the parrot, and he shot a questioning glance at Rina.

"I'm thinking of calling him Blackbeard," she said.

"Absolutely not!" Jonathan snapped.

"Hmm." Max rubbed his chin. "How about Captain Kidd?"

"Oh, I like that," Pearl said.

"We're not naming the bird after a bloody pirate!" Jonathan rubbed his hands over his face, and the bird squawked, "Bloody pirate!"

"Anne Bonny?" Sam offered. At everyone's curious looks, he added, "It might be a girl, and she's the only female pirate I know of."

"There are female pirates?" Rina asked, eyes wide.

"Aye," Jonathan muttered. "One or two."

She considered that for a long moment, looking into her mug thoughtfully.

The name debate continued until the front door of the tavern opened, and a boyish-faced man clutching a burlap sack walked in.

Pearl stiffened. "That's Hayward," she said, effectively cutting off all parrot talk for the moment. He spotted her and nodded slightly, making his way across the room.

She stood as the boy approached, instructing her girls not to disturb them before leading the group down the hallway, past the kitchen to a storage room at the back. The boy glanced over his shoulder before following them into the room, hovering inside the doorway.

"This 'im?" he asked, jerking his head toward Jonathan.

Pearl nodded. "Do you have the box?"

Hayward checked over his shoulder again before reaching into the bag and pulling out a small wooden box. He placed it on a barrel, both hands resting on the top as his fingers tapped nervously.

"If it's all the same to ye," he said. "I'll take my coin and be going."

"If it's all the same to *you*," Jonathan replied, "I'll be seeing the box before you see any coin."

Hayward hesitated only a moment before he sighed heavily, shoving a hand through his messy hair and sliding the box toward him. Jonathan picked it up and examined it carefully. It was smaller than he'd expected—about the length and breadth of his hand and as thick as it was wide—and expertly carved out of several different types of wood. The pieces fit together tightly, smooth and polished in an intricate mosaic, with no apparent lid— no hinges or latches of any kind.

"How do you open it?" Jonathan asked.

Hayward shrugged and leaned against the wall. "Dunno. Fellow I got it from said it was some kind of puzzle box, but he didn't know how to open it either."

"And what fellow was that?"

Hayward's gaze hardened. "Didn't get to be the man who can get things by tellin' everyone *how* I get those things." He glanced at Pearl. "Can I go now?"

She and Jonathan exchanged a significant look, and Jonathan reached into his pocket to withdraw a pouch of coins and tossed it to Hayward. The boy shook it once, listening to the tinkle with a satisfied smile before tucking it into his coat pocket and leaving the room with a curt nod.

Jonathan studied the box a bit longer, tapping it thoughtfully, before passing it around to the others.

"I suggest a rock," Sam suggested. "Just smash the damned thing."

Rina rolled her eyes. "Let me see it," she said. With a shrug, he handed her the box, and she slid her fingers over the polished surface.

"I've seen a box like this before," she murmured, half to herself, as she prodded the box in various places. "It's just a matter of finding the right spot—" She pressed a rectangular section and it slid out easily. "Ha!" she shouted as the others gathered close, eager to get a peek. She pried at another piece that flipped up, revealing a rectangular section that pivoted on an axis, locking into place with a quiet snick. After that, it was a matter of sliding sections out, then back again—until the box split in two in Sarina's hands, revealing a shallow drawer in the bottom.

Rina grinned. "I did it!"

"Well done, Smith," Jonathan said, patting her on the shoulder and reaching into the drawer to pull out a folded-up piece of paper.

"Is that it?" Max asked, as Jonathan carefully unfolded it.

"Aye," Jonathan breathed. He looked up, waving them back. "Let me put it on the barrel."

They gathered around as he smoothed the creases on the map, frowning at the torn edge.

"It doesn't say much," Max noted, running a finger along the edge of a land mass. "This could be any place."

"An island, obviously," Sam added, "but which one?"

Jonathan grunted noncommittally. "This area looks familiar," he replied, pointing to another spot. "I'm not certain, though."

"Jonathan, do you see that? At the bottom?" Rina pointed to a small drawing some distance off the coast of whatever island they were looking at. "Is that what I think it is?"

Jonathan picked up the map to scrutinize the sketch more closely. It wasn't complete—part was torn off with the other half of the map—but there was enough for him to recognize the shape of a misshapen disk with two holes, one large, one smaller. Along the edge of the disk, some numbers: *43, 14, 6.*

"Bloody hell," Jonathan murmured.

"What is it?" Pearl asked.

"The coin."

"What coin?"

"It doesn't matter," Jonathan hastily folded the map. "We need to get back to the ship. I think—"

A low laugh cut Jonathan off mid-sentence, and as one, the group turned toward the doorway leading to the tavern. A dark-haired man dressed all in black leaned against the jamb, a satisfied smirk on his face.

"Barton," Jonathan hissed, sliding the map into his pocket. "Kane still has you doing his dirty work, I see." He reached for his sword.

"Ah ah ah." Barton waved a finger back and forth tauntingly and nodded toward the back door. It swung open, and James came through, flanked by two more men, a pistol pointed at his head. Blood dripped from a cut on his cheek, and he winced as they shoved him into the room.

"I'm sorry," he said, spitting blood onto the floor. "Didn't see them coming until it was too late."

Barton pushed away from the door and stepped toward them. "Yes, your friend here has good instincts. Thought he was onto us for a while there. Unfortunately, he was no match for my men." At Jonathan's glare, he added, "I have more outside, in case you should get an itch to fight your way out of this."

"How did you find us?" Jonathan asked.

"You can't expect me to give away all our secrets, can you?"

"Where is Kane?"

Barton leered. "Oh, he'll find you when the time is right, *Jack*. I think you're beginning to realize that he's always one step ahead of you." He pulled out a pistol and pointed it at Rina's chest. "Sorry about this, miss. It's nothing personal." He turned back to Jonathan. "I'll be having that map, now." With a cheerful smile, he added, "And I'd thank you all to have a seat. You're going to be here for a while."

Rina twisted her wrists, trying to no avail to loosen the ropes tight around them. The scarf tied across her mouth chafed at her skin, and as she looked to her left, she could see Jonathan dealing with the same situation.

Barton had bound and gagged them all, then made them sit back-to-back in a circle and tied all of their wrists together. He'd smacked the map against his palm and slipped it in his pocket with a grin.

"You're lucky Kane said not to touch you . . . yet," he'd said, leaning over the captain. "Until we meet again, *Jack*." With that, he and his men had left the room, securing both doors and leaving Jonathan fuming.

They were all angry, but Rina had never seen Jonathan so furious. And that was saying a lot.

The room was quiet except for the shuffling of clothing as they fought to free themselves, and the occasional grunt muffled by the gags. She was surprised that he'd only tied them up and left, half expecting him to kill them all.

More games, she supposed. She was beginning to understand that Kane really liked his games.

The bastard.

The door to the main room opened, and they turned as one, all shouting through their gags.

"Miss Pearl? I know you said not to interrupt, but there's a man—" Flora stopped in the doorway, eyes wide. "Good lord!"

Pearl grunted something, eyes flashing, and Flora hurried into the room and removed her gag.

"Cut us loose," Pearl ordered. "Hurry."

Flora grabbed the dagger from Max's belt and sliced through the ropes. Within minutes, they were free, rubbing their wrists as they vowed revenge. Jonathan stalked through the tavern, the others following close behind.

"I'm sorry, Jonathan," Pearl said, lingering in the doorway.

"It's not your fault. Thank you for your aid."

She nodded, and Sam pulled her into a quick but passionate kiss before whispering a goodbye. She stood on the porch, watching as they hurried back toward the ship.

Jonathan turned to Sam. "You and Ceron go through the town. Get all the men back to the ship. Now."

He nodded grimly and the two men rushed down the street.

"What are we going to do?" Rina asked as they headed toward the path to the cove. "Go after the map?"

"No. Kane's already well under way, I'm sure."

"What then?"

"I remember now why that section of the map looked familiar," he said, shoving aside some brush as they all but ran down the path. "I know where he's heading."

"You do?" Max asked. Jonathan nodded curtly.

Rina's stomach flipped with a combination of anxiety and excitement. "Are we going to stop him?"

Jonathan's lips quirked. "No, we're not going to stop him," he said. "But we are going to beat him."

As they emerged from the trees, a squawk and a flurry of red feathers burst from the branches overhead, and the parrot landed heavily on Jonathan's shoulder.

"Bloody hell!" he shouted, swatting at the bird.

It flapped, hovering above his head for a moment before coming to rest on his other shoulder and screeching, "Bloody hell! Bloody hell!"

Despite their current situation, Rina laughed. "You're a bad influence on that bird," she said. Jonathan glared at her and turned to stalk toward the ship.

The parrot squawked, "Pretty bird!"

"How about Barbarossa?" Max offered as they hurried after Jonathan. "I think that's an excellent name for a parrot."

"We're not naming the bloody parrot!"

The bird repeated, "Barbarossa! Barbarossa!" for the next half an hour as they set sail after Kane.

The crew took that as an approval.

Commodore Lucius Stanton was not a happy man. He stood at the bow of the *Intrepid*, glaring unseeingly at the crashing waves, the wind forcing him to hold his hat in his fist, strands of blond hair escaping his queue to flutter about his face. He blew them aside with annoyance.

Blasted Tremayne had outsmarted him yet again.

He'd followed the dinghy, of course, and had been close enough when it landed to see the face of the man wearing the captain's hat and coat through his spyglass.

Close enough to see the man had two good eyes.

"Damn him," the commodore muttered, recalling the cocky salute the man had offered before disappearing into the undergrowth. Stanton had no doubt he would have been long gone by the time he could get ashore and make chase.

Not that he cared to. No, the man was a lackey, nothing more. Tremayne was the prize.

"Sir?" Lieutenant Cameron stepped tentatively to his side, hat in hand.

"Any word?" Stanton asked gruffly.

Cameron cleared his throat. "Not of Tremayne, no, sir. Sorry. But we have received a report that the *Abaddon's Curse* has left Hispaniola, apparently bound for Tortuga."

Stanton grunted, shrugging his shoulders. "Hardly news, Cameron. It's a pirate port." Tortuga was an aggravation to the Crown. Although he knew pirates frequented the island, it was nearly impossible to catch them there. He suspected the locals aided in their escape, somehow able to spot Crown ships approaching in time to alert the criminals. They also were notoriously close-lipped, pleading ignorance when questioned, or simply disappearing into the woodwork until Stanton or his contemporaries left the island.

He'd come to accept that it was a safe haven for Tremayne and his kind, and generally not worth the effort.

"That's not all, sir," Cameron added, pulling the commodore from his thoughts. "The *Enchanted Lady* is apparently sailing with them."

Stanton turned to him in surprise. "Renard? Are you certain?"

"They were seen in close company." No one would sail close to the *Curse* unless they were allied somehow. It was only asking to be boarded.

"Why would he sail with Kane?" Stanton mused. He hadn't spoken with the *Lady's* captain since he'd rescued him after Tremayne's attack, but had been under the impression that Renard was trying to establish a legitimate trade.

Perhaps he was wrong.

Abruptly, Stanton turned to pace across the deck, Cameron at his heels. "So Kane and Renard are both heading to Tortuga. Together for some reason." There was no love lost for Tremayne when it came to Mattias Renard. And it was common knowledge that Tremayne and Kane had a longtime feud. Could the two have joined forces?

"Tremayne was sailing south as well," he muttered, half to himself. Could the captain of the *Arrow* have the same destination in mind? And if so, why? He supposed it could all be coincidence. They all frequented the same waters but generally tried to avoid each other unless . . .

Unless they were planning an assault.

But, Stanton wondered, who was doing the planning? Kane? Tremayne?

"Sir?" Cameron shifted on his feet, watching his commanding officer warily. "Do you have orders?"

Stanton rubbed at his chin thoughtfully. If Kane and Tremayne were bound to finally battle each other, it could work in his favor.

He'd long ago tired of the heat and crudeness of the islands, longing to return to the civility of England. He'd clung to the idea of capturing Tremayne to ensure a promotion—perhaps a command in Port Royal or Antigua, or even on the mainland, away from ships and hardtack and bloody goddamned pirates.

But to remove them *both* at one fell swoop? Such a thing had never before seemed possible. If Kane were to remove Tremayne—or vice versa—and Stanton was nearby, ready with chains for the survivors?

Well, it could mean far more than a promotion. It could mean everything—gold, lands, perhaps even a title.

And leaving these bloody islands to return to London a hero.

"Sir?" Cameron repeated. Stanton smiled, visions of luxury dancing in his head.

"Set sail for Tortuga immediately," he said. "But lower the Crown colors, and inform the men to don civilian garb. Stealth is the key, Cameron. I don't want them to see us coming."

"Aye, sir."

"Double the watch. I want everyone on the lookout for those three ships. I want to know what is happening, but I can't emphasize enough that I do *not* want to be noticed."

Cameron saluted and turned on his heel to follow his orders. Stanton headed for his quarters to change out of his uniform and into the drab clothes of an ordinary man.

An ordinary man he had no intention of ever being again.

No, Commodore Stanton would have to be very careful in this little game, but if he was right, once Kane and Tremayne had destroyed each other, he would be the one to reap the rewards.

*Lord Lucius Stanton.*

He smiled.

Yes, he definitely liked the sound of that.

*After much desperate searching, I have found the place to secure my treasure. It is in need, however, of measures beyond the natural defenses of the area.*

*I have devised a complex plan that will require the best tradesmen the area has to offer. It will be an expensive undertaking to be sure. But fortunately for me, money is no longer an insurmountable obstacle.*

*- The Journal of
Simon Alistair Mellick
17 November, 1665*

"No, that's not right," Rina insisted, pointing to the squiggly black line Jonathan had drawn on the sheet of parchment. "This part curved down—or south—if this is north, that is."

Jonathan frowned, then dipped the quill in ink and scratched out the line he'd just drawn, following her instructions. "Like this?"

She hummed, watching him continue to sketch a replica of the half of the map Barton had stolen. Sam, Max, and James completed the circle crowded around the captain's desk, all scrutinizing the work with a critical eye.

"Don't forget the coin," she said once he sat back, the main part of the map complete. He nodded, sketching it in the same location and adding the mysterious numbers along the edge.

"How do you know it's a coin?" James asked.

Rina reached for her necklace, ready to explain. "Because—"

"We don't," Jonathan said flatly, flashing a quick warning look her way. "Looked a bit like a coin, but it could be anything, really."

Rina took the hint, her hand returning to her side without another word. Jonathan studied the map for a moment, then looked up at James carefully.

"You know these waters well," he said. "What do you make of this?" He punched his finger at a small group of circles toward the edge of the map.

James' eyes narrowed on the drawing. "I'm not certain."

"No?" Jonathan produced another sheet of parchment, lining it up with the edge of the map. Quickly, he added another few larger shapes. "How about now?"

James stared at it blankly for a moment and inhaled sharply. "*The Dogs*."

"Aye," Jonathan agreed, once again pointing at the small group of islands. "I thought I recognized the configuration. If these are *The Dogs,* then this . . ." His finger trailed to the coast of a larger island to the east.

"*Virgin Gorda.*"

"Aye."

Rina watched the interaction with interest. "Are you saying you know what these are? I mean, you know *where* these are?"

Jonathan nodded and turned to Max. "Set sail for *Virgin Gorda*, but keep a weather eye open for Kane. I don't want him to know we're coming."

The first mate nodded and left the room, followed quickly by Sam and James. Jonathan bent over the map again to study the drawing of the coin. Rina took a seat across the desk from him and opened her mouth to speak, but he beat her to it.

"I don't want anyone else to know about the coin," he said. "Not yet. Not until it's absolutely necessary." He leaned back in his chair and rested his chin in his palm. "Somebody led Kane to us at the *Red Pearl,* and I fear it would have to be somebody on this ship. The coin is our only advantage over Kane right now. He doesn't know we have it, and I aim to keep it that way."

"Surely you don't suspect Max?"

"No. Of course not. But I still think it wise to keep the coin between us for now."

Rina wasn't sure if she should feel flattered by Jonathan's trust or wonder if he was trying to test her in some way. If Kane *did* learn of the coin, after all, the circle of blame would be exceedingly small. In other words, on her.

Jonathan seemed to read her mind. "I don't suspect you either, Smith."

"Of course not. No reason to, after all."

"Just thought you should know." His lips quirked a bit. "Come here."

"I am here."

"No," Jonathan said, pushing his chair back and gesturing to his lap. "Come *here.*"

Rina's eyes narrowed. "I don't think so."

"Why not?"

"Your lap has been a bit busy lately. I wouldn't wish to overtax it."

Jonathan's brows rose. "I told you. Flora is only a friend."

"A friend who sits on your lap," Rina snapped, feeling a bit like a nagging fishwife, but unable to help herself. Jonathan, for his part, seemed to find her state rather amusing, something that only served to irritate her more.

"It's not funny," she muttered.

"Smith . . ."

"Don't call me that!"

"Sarina," he began again. "You're too far away for this conversation. Come here. *Please.*"

With an exasperated huff, Rina got to her feet and circled the desk. She refused to sit on his lap, however, and simply leaned back against the desk next to Jonathan, eyes focused on the floor. He reached out and took her hand in both of his.

"Look at me."

Slowly, stubbornly, she raised her gaze, her chin jutting out slightly. Jonathan smiled.

"It's not funny," she grumbled again.

"It is," he protested. "It's exceedingly funny that you could think Flora could be any kind of rival for my affections."

"You *seemed* pretty affectionate."

"Habit, nothing else," he replied. "Shoving her off my lap would have been out of character and drawn undue attention."

Rina almost smiled at the picture of Jonathan doing just that, but the urge passed quickly.

"Did you . . . have you . . ." She reddened and tried to pull her hand free, but Jonathan held it fast.

"What?" he asked, searching her face. "You mean me? With Flora?"

"Never mind," she said abruptly. "I don't think I want to know."

"There's nothing to know," he said. "Nothing recently, at least." When she blushed and looked away, he rubbed his thumb against her wrist gently. "I am an imperfect man, Sarina. I have a past."

"I know that."

"But I haven't been with Flora in that way in years," he added. "With *anyone* in months . . . long before I met you."

"It's none of my business."

"It *is*," he said, and when he tugged on her arm this time, she allowed him to pull her into his lap. "I've never . . . been with a lady before. This is new to me."

She met his gaze, finally, with a small smile lifting her lips. "It's new to me as well."

He reached up to touch her cheek. "I can't offer you much, but I can promise to be true for as long as this lasts."

It was less than she wanted, but more than she expected. Sarina had no illusions of fairy tale endings and happily ever afters with Jonathan Tremayne. Still, a part of her mourned that this would be a short-lived tryst, and one day just a magical memory she would relive on lonely evenings.

No, there would be no other for her. Of that she was certain. Who else could inflame and antagonize her so? Who else could stimulate such passion and exhilarating pleasure? She could fight it, of course, and try to retain some semblance of decorum and innocence. But why save herself for a husband she would never have, nor want? Rina had to admit that entertaining the thought was useless, if not utterly absurd.

Because she didn't want to fight it. Jonathan made her feel alive, her blood pumping hot and heavy through her veins like it never had before. Whether arguing with him about his stubborn views or blushing over his teasing or melting under his hot gaze and lingering touch, Rina couldn't resist how he made her feel. Perhaps it was selfish. Perhaps it was stupid. But she doubted she could stop even if she wanted to.

She would take what he offered, for as long as he offered it, and when it was over? She would hold the memory close to her heart.

He watched her intently, trying to read her thoughts through her expression, so she offered him a teasing smile. "All right then, Captain. But that means no more wenches on your lap—or anywhere else on your person for that matter." She leaned down saucily, her lips brushing the corner of his mouth. "I don't like to share." She felt his lips twitch under hers.

"Aye, sir," he murmured.

"Sir?" Her lips swept across his swiftly to the other corner. "Surely you can do better than that."

"Mmm . . ." He captured her mouth with a teasing nibble and caught her gasp in a searing kiss. "Better?" he asked.

Her heart pounded as she tried to catch enough breath to speak. "Much."

Jonathan grinned and was about to kiss her again when Rina pressed a hand against his chest, stilling him. Her eyes took on an unfocused glaze, and she blinked hard a few times.

"What is it?" he asked.

"Just . . . wait . . ." Something nagged at the edge of her thoughts, and she turned on his lap to reach for the map. "I was just thinking about these numbers."

Jonathan's lips brushed against the nape of her neck. "Really? I must be losing my touch."

Rina ignored him, tracing a finger over the numbers: *43, 14, 6.*

"All of the other relics are engraved with a Scripture passage," she said. "The cutlass has the Genesis verse. The locket's passage is from Revelation. From the sketches, we know the cup is engraved with a verse from the Psalms."

Jonathan straightened, abandoning seduction for the moment. "But not the coin."

She smiled. "Not the coin."

"Unless . . ." Jonathan's gaze drifted to the numbers on the map. "We need a Bible." He shifted, and Rina quickly got up from his lap. He crossed the room to the large chest and opened it, digging through and tossing contents here and there.

"You actually have a Bible in there?" she asked wryly.

"I am a man of many interests, Smith," he muttered in response, holding up a worn volume with a victorious smile. He placed it on the desk, and they huddled over it.

"It can't be page numbers," Rina thought out loud. "It must be book, chapter, verse?" She looked up at Jonathan questioningly, and he nodded in response.

"The forty-third book is . . ." Jonathan flipped through the Bible, counting under his breath. "The Gospel of St. John."

"Go to chapter fourteen, verse six," Rina said, gripping his arm in excitement.

"I'm trying, Smith. Calm yourself." He turned to the page, reading it in silence.

Rina rolled her eyes and read it out loud. "*Jesus saith unto him, I am the way, the truth and the life. No one cometh unto the Father, but by Me.*" She read it again and frowned. "So, what on earth does that mean?"

Jonathan shoved the Bible away. "I've absolutely no idea. I swear if Mellick wasn't dead already, I'd have him hung from the yard arm!"

Rina snorted. "Well, I might fight you for that honor, but I've no doubt it means something. We just have to figure out what." She was convinced they'd correctly interpreted the numbers and felt no little pride at the fact. "We're getting close, Jonathan. I can feel it."

Despite his frustration, Jonathan smiled. "Aye, Smith. I do believe you're right."

"Come about! Steady as she goes!" As the crew rushed to obey his orders, Jonathan peered at the island through his spyglass, the shape of the *Abaddon's Curse* easily recognizable near the shore of Virgin Gorda, even from the distance. The *Arrow* stuck close to the coastline, and Jonathan hoped his evasive maneuvers were sufficient. Kane, after all, would not expect him, and was most likely focused on the task at hand. In short, following the instructions on the map.

With practiced precision, the crew of the *Arrow* brought the ship around the far side of Virgin Gorda, rounding Moskito Island and dropping anchor in Saddle Bay, a peninsula separating them from where the *Curse* was anchored. Once the ship was secure, Jonathan called the crew to him, a grim look on his face.

"Today, we retrieve what is ours," he said, meeting the intent gaze of the crewmen surrounding him. "Today, we finally confront that bastard Kane and show him what the crew of the *Arrow* is made of."

Knowing better than to let out a cheer, the men only nodded, making grumbling noises of assent. Sarina stood off to the side, watching with a slight smile on her face. With a loud squawk, the parrot, Barbarossa, descended from the mizzen mast and landed on Jonathan's shoulder with a flutter of wings. Jonathan ignored the bird.

"Our goal is the map," he said. "Stealth is the key. Keep to the shadows and wait for my orders." The men nodded and Jonathan grinned. "To the sea!" he commanded, and with a muffled shout, the men rushed to the rope ladder, climbing down into the water with quick precision.

Sarina appeared at his side, offering a bit of cracker to Barbarossa. "He seems to be growing on you," she said.

Jonathan's gaze narrowed. "I don't suppose I can convince you to stay on the ship?" When she smiled in response, he sighed. "I thought not. Well, at least stay close, all right?"

"Of course," she said loftily. "Don't worry, Jonathan. I'll guard your flank."

He smirked as they made their way to the rope ladder. "You have an unhealthy obsession with my flank."

"It is a nice flank."

Jonathan laughed as they climbed over the gunwale and down the rope ladder to the water. The parrot abandoned him, taking to the air as he swam to shore alongside Sarina and his men.

They crossed the peninsula in silence, the only sound the soft crunch and swish of sand under their wet boots. Jonathan could spot Max and Hutchins to his right, keeping the men quiet and on task. Ceron stuck close to his side, with Rafferty and Crawley to his left. At the sound of voices, they took cover in the underbrush, Jonathan and Sarina ducking behind a cluster of trees. His jaw tightened when he spotted Kane talking with Barton, and he felt Sarina touch his elbow gently. He turned to see her watching him, eyes wide, and he nodded to reassure her he knew what he was doing.

He *hoped* he knew what he was doing.

His heart pounded as he assessed Kane's forces—five, no, six men in addition to the captain and Barton. He spotted a few more standing guard on the far side of the clearing, obviously expecting any infiltrators to come from the bay where the *Curse* was anchored.

Jonathan smiled. This was going to be easier than he thought. He nodded at Max and saw his first mate take a group of men around to the other side of the clearing. Crawley did the same in the opposite direction. They had Kane's boarding party outnumbered more than two to one and in moments would have them surrounded. Finally, he'd gotten a leg up on the bastard.

He counted silently to himself as he slid his sword from its sheath, allowing his men time to get into position, before jerking his head for Sarina to stay behind him. She rolled her eyes—of course—and he fixed her with a steely glare until she relented with a single nod. She moved closer, brushing against his back as she peered around his arm to watch the goings-on in the clearing.

"Ready?" he whispered. He felt her nod against his shoulder and glanced down to see her gripping a dagger in one hand, ready to draw her sword with the other. He took a deep breath to shout the order to attack.

With a squawk and a flurry of feathers, Barbarossa descended from the treetops into the clearing, screaming "Bloody pirate! Bloody pirate!" over and over again. He dove at Kane, knocking his hat from his head, then swooped away onto a high branch.

"One-Eyed Jack! One-Eyed Jack!" the parrot squawked, flapping its wings. As one, Kane's men drew their swords, eyes darting toward the tree line.

Jonathan growled, moving quickly out from behind the tree as his men did the same. "Damned bird," he muttered. "So much for the advantage of surprise."

It didn't matter much, actually. The crew of the *Arrow* emerged from the trees with swords drawn, and it only took a moment for Kane to see the futility of fighting. With a curt nod, he and his men dropped their weapons. Kane grinned, though, crossing his arms over his chest as Barton stood beside him.

"Well, well, well, Jack," he drawled. "Nice of you to join us."

Jonathan's jaw tightened, and he motioned with his sword. "Give me the map. And the cup while you're at it."

"So rude!" Kane grinned at Barton, who smirked in return. "Just because we're pirates, *Jack*, doesn't mean we can't act as civilized individuals. It's been so long. How are you? How's the family?"

"The map. And the cup." Jonathan's men took a step forward, and Kane held up his hands defensively.

"No need to get pushy," he said. "Just trying to make polite conversation. The map, you say?"

"And the cup while you're at it."

At this, Barbarossa descended from the trees and landed on Jonathan's shoulder with a loud, "The cup! The cup!"

Jonathan ignored him, his icy glare focused only on Kane.

The captain of the *Curse*, however, seemed unconcerned. "Well, Jack, I don't think that will be possible. You see, the cup and map are mine. And soon, the cutlass will be as well."

Jonathan snorted. "And how do you plan to accomplish that? In case you haven't noticed, my men have you surrounded."

"Oh, I think you have that wrong." Kane's smile fell, his shoulders squared, and his black eyes took on a flinty quality. "You see, Jack, it's you who are surrounded."

And with that, a group of men appeared, stepping out of the trees with their weapons drawn. Jonathan felt the press of a flintlock into his back and jerked suddenly.

"Now, now, no sudden movements," a heavily accented voice whispered into his ear. "Wouldn't want to shoot you accidentally, after all. Much more fun to do it on purpose."

Jonathan let out a defeated breath. He recognized that voice.

"Renard," he muttered.

"One and the same." The pistol poked harshly into his back. "Drop your weapon."

He thought about refusing—thought about trying to fight—but when one of Mattias' crewmen stepped forward with an arm around Sarina's throat and a pistol at her temple, all the fight went out of him. They were outnumbered again. Kane had won.

So he dropped his sword, and at Mattias' direction, pulled the dagger from his belt and allowed it to fall to the sand, as well. His men followed suit, then were herded into a cluster surrounded by Renard's men as Kane's retrieved their weapons.

"Captain Renard has proven to be a valuable ally," Kane said, standing in front of Jonathan with his sword swinging lightly from his fingertips. "Looks like you've made some enemies along the way, Jack. Fortunately, it's been to my advantage."

"And mine," Mattias added, spitting at Jonathan's feet. "It appears your luck has run out, Tremayne."

The journey back to the *Arrow* was considerably more tense and less quiet. Kane's men laughed loudly, pleased with their success, and the crew of the *Lady* seemed equally thrilled. Jonathan had no doubt that Kane had promised a significant reward for his capture, let alone that of his ship, and he felt sick thinking of the treasure in his hold which was sure to be liberated quickly—not to mention the cutlass and the locket.

And the *Arrow itself.* He gritted his teeth at the idea of Kane captaining his ship.

Renard had left a half-dozen dinghies on the shore, and his and Kane's men rowed back to the ship—taking Sarina with them—while Jonathan's crew swam, flintlocks pointed at them the whole way. Through the blur of water on his face, Jonathan could see Sarina sitting grim-faced between the grinning Frenchman and Kane—the bastard—and he considered trying to upend the dinghy, just to see what might happen.

He didn't, of course. Even if he survived, he had no doubt that Kane wouldn't hesitate to kill any of his men—or Sarina—for such a transgression. At the moment, Jonathan's goals were simple. First, stay alive. Second, keep the crew alive. Third, escape. Fourth, stay alive.

They treaded water off the stern while some of Kane's men boarded the *Arrow* first, then climbed the ropes and fell to their knees on the deck while they waited for the rest of the enemy to board. In the end, Jonathan's men were locked in the hold, but he and Sarina accompanied Kane, Barton, Renard, and a couple of other crewmen to Jonathan's quarters.

"It's only fitting," Kane said with a leering grin at Sarina, "since you both have played such a part in bringing me the cutlass."

Sarina reddened, and Jonathan could feel the rage radiating off her.

"You'll pay for this," she spat. "And for what you did to my father."

Kane laughed. "Perhaps," he admitted. "But you won't live to see it." He rubbed his chin, glancing at Jonathan.

"I fear I've tired of our little games, Jack. Once I've gotten what I've come for, you and your little wench here will be taking a trip to the Locker."

"The Locker?" Sarina stumbled slightly, and one of Kane's men grabbed her elbow, jerking her along.

"Davy Jones' Locker," Jonathan explained. "He plans to kill us."

Rina knew what the Locker was, of course, after living all this time on a pirate vessel. She just couldn't believe it had actually come to this, and she fought not to look as terrified as she felt, although she feared she was failing miserably. She eyed the man walking next to her—tall and thick with a scruff of black whiskers and arms bulging with muscle—and knew escape was not an option, at least not at the moment.

Things didn't look good. The crew was locked in the hold, stripped of weapons and under guard. Even though not all of Kane's and Mattias' men had come on board, they were the only ones armed, so they clearly had the advantage. Still, if there was one thing Rina had learned during her time on the *Arrow*—one thing that Jonathan had taught her—it was to always be on the lookout for an opportunity. They just had to be patient and stay alive, and when the chance presented itself, they would find a way to escape.

After killing Kane, of course. Rina found she craved the idea, even though she still doubted she could do the deed herself. The man was pure evil and deserved to die, and she was certain no one would mourn his passing. In fact, she was relatively certain many would celebrate.

So she bit her tongue and kept her eyes open as Kane entered Jonathan's quarters, Renard and Barton following behind him closely. The other two crewmen stood outside the door, weapons at the ready, and she shared a look with Jonathan before they entered as well, the door closing quietly behind them.

"Have a seat," Kane said, setting a large oilskin bag on Jonathan's desk and indicating the two chairs in front of it with a wave of his hand. Once they were seated, Barton standing behind them with his flintlock at the ready, Kane turned to retrieve the cutlass from the shelf behind the desk. He smiled and drew it from the sheath to admire the gleaming blade.

"Well, it's been a bit of trouble, but well worth the effort in the end," he said, whipping the sword through the air and making Rina jump. He grinned at her and sheathed the cutlass. "This makes the second time I've had to steal it, but at least it will be the last."

"You bastard," she snapped. "You could have just taken it. Why did you have to kill him?"

Kane raised a brow. "Well now, lass, I'm afraid that was your father's fault. I intended to leave him alive, but he just wouldn't let things go."

Rina's eyes filled with hot tears of fury, and she blinked them back desperately.

Kane didn't seem to notice. "He did seem rather partial to you, though, if that's any consolation."

"Don't you talk about him!" She felt a squeeze and looked down in surprise to find Jonathan holding her hand. She took a deep breath, trying to rein in her anger. It wouldn't do any of them any good, and she needed to think clearly.

"Enough of this," Kane said, setting the sword on the desk. "Tie them up and help me look for the chest."

Without another word, Barton went to the door and returned with a length of rope from one of the guards. He directed Sarina and Jonathan to sit on the floor and quickly tied their wrists and ankles together, slicing through the rope with deadly precision. He manhandled Sarina around—ignoring Jonathan's warning growl—until they were back to back, then tied their bound wrists together.

Meanwhile, Kane and Renard went through Jonathan's trunk, tossing items aside and pocketing anything of value. Renard smashed the table, smiling gleefully at Jonathan as he did it, and upended the chessboard, purposely taking a few of the pieces. Barton pulled out the desk drawers, methodically dumping the contents on the floor.

"It's not here," Mattias said once they'd reached the bottom of the trunk, just as Barton reached the locked drawer.

"Ah," Kane said, eyes flashing as he noticed Jonathan's jaw twitch. He crossed to the desk, pulling a dagger from his belt to pry open the lock. "Let's just see what we have here, shall we?" With a low click, the drawer opened, and Kane laughed, pulling out the chest and Mellick's journal.

"That's it," Renard confirmed. "That's the one he took from my ship."

Kane seemed a bit irritated, as though he hardly needed the confirmation, but said nothing and opened the chest. It only took a few minutes with the journal to confirm the locket was the key.

"Now," he said, gathering up the coins in the chest. "Which of these is the coin?" He held his open palm out to Jonathan, who only glared at him in response. "No matter," he said with a shrug. "I'll take them all. Now that I have everything I need, the treasure will be mine in short order." He gathered the items, sliding them carefully into the oilskin bag, along with the cutlass, the sheathed blade sticking out a few inches once he pulled the drawstring closed.

"Time to go ashore," he said to Barton.

"What of them?"

Kane waved a hand dismissively. "Leave them here. Guards at the door."

There was no mistaking the disappointment on Barton's face. "But I thought—"

Kane stepped closer to Jonathan, looming over him silently until he looked up. "I want them alive when I find the gold," he said, voice low and dangerous. "You'll see me win, *Jack*, and then you'll die." With that, he turned to leave the room, Barton and Renard following closely behind him. Rina heard him relay quiet orders to the men outside, then the disappearing footsteps as they headed toward the deck. She shifted, pulling against the ropes.

"There's no point," Jonathan said quietly. "They're tight. If we can get to the other side of the desk, maybe I can find something . . ."

"Jonathan—"

"They took all the weapons out of the trunk . . ."

"Jonathan—"

"Perhaps I can break a piece of pottery without raising an alarm . . ."

"Jonathan!" Sarina hissed, yanking against his bound wrists.

"What?"

"Lie down." With that, she threw her weight to the side. Jonathan, surprised at the movement, fell with her with a slight *oof.*

"What are you doing?" he asked as she wiggled around, arching backward slightly.

"I can't quite get it. Your fingers are longer. Can you reach my boot?"

She heard Jonathan laugh under his breath. "Bloody hell, Smith. You have your dirk, don't you?"

"Of course. It's always best to be prepared."

Jonathan stretched out his fingers, speaking through gritted teeth. "Almost . . . just a little bit more . . ."

Rina shifted, her muscles straining as she stretched her ankles toward Jonathan's questing fingers. She held her breath as she felt him fumble with the top of her boot, only exhaling when she felt the slide of the dirk pulling free of the leather.

Within minutes, he had them cut loose and they stood, smiling at each other.

"Now what?" she whispered.

"We need weapons."

They scoured the wreckage of the room in silence for a moment, then came together again near the door. Jonathan held a large chunk of the broken table. Sarina clutched a half-empty rum jug.

Jonathan grinned. "That seems to be your weapon of choice lately."

Rina hefted the jug. "They're surprisingly durable."

Jonathan reached out with his free hand to grasp her around the waist and pull her in for a hard kiss. "Ready, Smith?"

She nodded, a bit breathless, and they took positions on either side of the door. On Jonathan's signal, they both began to yell at the top of their lungs. It only took a moment before the door flew open, and Kane's two guards stormed into the room, coming to an abrupt stop at the sight of the ropes lying discarded on the floor.

It was the last thing they saw for a while.

The last thing they *heard* was the loud crack of wood hitting bone and the smash of a rum jug against a hard skull.

*Progress is quicker than I expected, yet slower than I'd hoped.
Soon, I will be able to begin relocating the treasure to the new
more secure location. However, with every day, I dread I fear I
must do to protect it.*

*Gold can purchase secrets, and I have been very careful that
only a select few men know all of mine. But those few are a
risk, and one that I must eventually deal with.*

*- The Journal of
Simon Alistair Mellick
12 January, 1666*

Jonathan had an idea.

He and Sarina quickly tied up the unconscious guards, stuffing
a couple of scarves into their mouths to keep them quiet. They
relieved them of their weapons, and Jonathan tossed a pistol and
sword to Sarina, strapping the other sword around his hips and
tucking three more flintlocks into the belt. Sarina headed for the
door, but Jonathan stopped to dig through the mess from the trunk.

"What are you doing?" she asked.

He held up a large oilskin bag triumphantly. "Looks a bit like his, doesn't it?"

"Well, yes . . ."

Jonathan tossed a few items in the bag—a leather-bound book, a small box, some discarded clothing. He wrapped an empty tankard in a cloth and slipped it inside as well, before drawing it closed and throwing it over his shoulder. He turned to Sarina, who was watching him with a slight smirk.

"What about the cutlass?" she asked, obviously catching on to his plan.

Jonathan grinned. "Let's get the men first, then we'll deal with the cutlass."

They made their way down the dim hallway, weapons poised at the ready, but came across surprisingly few of Kane's men. Besides the two left behind to guard them, they found four on deck—dispatched easily with a few well-placed punches and a slam to the foremast—and two more wandering the passageway leading to the hold. The men had liberated a couple jugs of rum along the way and swayed on their feet when they came face to face with Jonathan and Sarina.

Jonathan punched one in the nose while Sarina kneed the other between the legs before Jonathan knocked him out, as well. They had both crumpled to the floor, the jugs rolling away and leaving a crooked trail of rum behind.

"See?" Sarina said as they stepped over the unconscious men. She picked up a jug to tuck under her arm. "Durable."

They made their way silently toward the hold, sliding close to the walls and peeking around corners. The sound of low voices brought them to a halt, and Jonathan carefully set the oilskin bag down before drawing his sword and signaling for Sarina to do the same.

She lifted the rum jug with raised eyebrows. Jonathan fought down a laugh and nodded instead. He edged around the corner, just enough to catch a glimpse of the two men guarding the hold. They both sat on upturned crates, passing a jug between them. Jonathan frowned. Kane's men obviously had no discipline whatsoever.

They were absorbed in a discussion of the merits of blondes versus brunettes and didn't hear when Jonathan and Sarina tiptoed closer. They sprang to their feet, reaching for their swords, as Jonathan held his sword to the throat of one right as Sarina bashed the other in the head with a rum jug.

"I think you enjoy that a bit too much," he said wryly as the second guard collapsed to the floor.

"It is rather satisfying," she replied, poking the man with the toe of her boot. "And there's much less blood."

Jonathan swapped his sword for a dagger, pressing it to the guard's neck as he unlocked the door to the hold. Kicking it open with his foot, Jonathan quietly called out to his men.

"All right ye lazy swabs, enough lying about. Time t' retake the ship and find the treasure, if ye' can be bothered!"

His men shouted in response, and he turned the guard over to Hutchins.

"Where are our weapons?" Jonathan asked, towering over him menacingly as Hutchins tightened a beefy arm around his neck. When the guard hesitated, he added, "Think carefully, man. Would ye rather deal with me, or Kane once he learned ye let us escape?"

His men were armed within ten minutes.

Once again, the crew of the *Black Arrow* picked their way through the trees on the peninsula of Virgin Gorda, however this time they were under no illusions that Kane worked alone. Jonathan hoped to accomplish his goal without notice, if possible, but nevertheless the entire crew made the journey in the event the manpower proved necessary.

Well, not the entire crew, actually. A few had apparently escaped the ambush, including Rafferty and Ceron, and had yet to turn up.

As they neared the clearing, the men moved in practiced synchronicity, circling the area without making a sound. The parrot, thank the heavens, had been secured back on the ship, ensuring there wouldn't be a repeat of the last attempt. Jonathan stepped forward, moving quickly from tree to tree as he searched for Kane.

He spotted him near a large rock, huddling over the journal with Barton. The oilskin bag sat near the base of a tree a few feet away, the sheath of the cutlass glinting in the sunshine.

Jonathan heard a soft gasp over his left shoulder and turned to see that Sarina had noticed the bag as well. He pressed a finger to his lips, and she smiled encouragingly.

With a steadying breath, Jonathan slid through the shadows under the trees, gaze darting from the bag back to Kane and Barton. The rest of his men were absent. Evidently, Kane wanted to keep the journal to himself and had sent them back to the ship, or at least to the beach. He signaled to Max to keep his eyes open. He'd been overconfident before and didn't want to make the same mistake again.

"*A coin to give sight*?" Kane said, slapping a hand against the open book as Jonathan froze in his tracks. "What the bloody hell does that mean?" Barton, apparently, had no answer. They returned to the journal, Kane flipping pages rapidly, and Jonathan quickened his pace as well, soon finding himself an arm's breadth from Kane's oilskin bag.

"I don't understand the man's damned obsession with the Bible!" Kane shouted, slamming the journal shut and turning on his heel. Jonathan retreated abruptly, back against the tree as he forced himself to take quiet, shallow breaths. Sarina was crouched behind a low bush, her wide amber eyes flickering from him to Kane and back again. Jonathan could hear him mumbling and finally held his breath altogether. Kane was mere feet away. Too hasty a movement, and he was sure to see Jonathan. A shift of the wind and he could probably *smell* him. Jonathan closed his eye, counting his own heartbeats.

*One . . . two . . .*

Kane picked up the bag and rummaged in it for a moment before pulling out the chest from the *Lady*. "Damned puzzles. Why can't the man just have a map with a bloody X on it like a normal person?"

*. . . three . . . four . . .*

He opened the chest and took out the handful of coins before dropping it back into the open bag.

*. . . five . . . six . . .*

Finally, he turned and stalked back over to Barton, allowing Jonathan to draw a shaky breath. Sarina watched him closely. He raised a questioning brow at her, and she nodded, indicating that Kane had his back turned. He turned to peer around the edge of the tree, gaze darting to the open bag and back to the two men.

"Renard will be back soon," Barton said. "You can't keep him distracted for long. He wants part of this treasure, too."

Kane snorted as he examined the coins in his hand. "The man's a lapdog. He's proven his usefulness with Tremayne, but I no longer need him."

Jonathan dropped to his knees, then to his belly. He shifted as his sword hilt dug into his stomach, sliding the sheath silently to his side.

"How do you plan to deal with him?" Barton asked. "He won't go quietly."

"He'll get his fair share of Tremayne's booty, then I'll make it clear our alliance is over."

Jonathan eyed Kane's oilskin bag as he carefully slid forward in the sand. He reached out with the other bag, gaze darting to Kane nervously, then set it down next to Kane's. Truly, they did look similar. He untied the drawstring a bit and adjusted the sword sheath poking out from the top. It was a good thing Kane hadn't put the cutlass in the bag hilt up or he would never be fooled by the substitute. Finding another sword with a sapphire in the hilt would have proven quite a challenge.

"Enough about Renard," Kane said, turning back to the journal. "Help me figure out this damned riddle."

With a steady hand, Jonathan reached for Kane's bag, sliding it slowly . . . carefully . . . toward him. The sound of oilskin against the soft sand seemed to blare in Jonathan's ears, although logic told him there was no way Kane could hear it from where he was. A bead of sweat formed on his forehead, dripping down his nose and landing on the ground with a soft plop. He crawled backward, wincing at the rustle of brush from the movement, until he sat once again crouched behind the tree.

Sarina grinned at him, and he smiled in return. Turning to his left, he spotted Max watching him from between two trees and nodded the order to retreat to the ship. The order was relayed with silent signals and the men moved as one, emerging onto the beach to discover the missing crewmen waiting for them, swords drawn.

Jonathan eyed James suspiciously. "And where have you been?"

He sheathed his sword. "Managed to get away when Renard's men moved in and have been trying to avoid them ever since. Kane sent them back to the ships, and I found the others just a bit ago." He jerked his head toward Rafferty. "We were on our way to rescue you, but it appears you're in no need of rescuing."

"Apparently not," Jonathan said flatly, still uncertain about whether he believed Ceron's story. There was no time, however, to debate it.

"Back to the ship," he ordered. "We'll keep two dinghies and sink the rest. No sense in making things easy for Kane and Renard." The men grinned in response. "We need to get away from this island. It's only a matter of time before Kane realizes what we've done."

"What of the prisoners?" Max asked as they got into the dinghies and started rowing toward the ship. Rafferty sat next to him, pulling his oar in a steady rhythm. Sarina studiously avoided his gaze, sitting close to Jonathan. He reached out to take her hand in reassurance.

"Keep them for now. We'll leave them on one of The Dogs perhaps, where they'll be out of the way."

Max laughed. "We're headed to The Dogs, then?"

Jonathan eyed James in the other dinghy, lowering his voice. "Aye. We'll be able to take cover there and see when Kane leaves Virgin Gorda."

Rafferty pulled his oar in steady rhythm with Max and spat into the water. "Then what?"

Jonathan grinned. "Then we find the treasure."

Rafferty's black smile lit up his face. "Aye. A fine plan, Cap'n."

"Tell me, Rafferty," he said, again glancing toward the other dinghy. "What do you think of Ceron?" Sarina tensed next to him, but he squeezed her fingers slightly in reassurance.

"Ceron? What d'ye mean?"

"Just hit me as a bit odd that he'd disappear when Renard's men showed up. Did you notice anything?"

Rafferty spat again and shrugged, the movement causing him to fall a bit out of rhythm on his oar. "Dunno, Cap'n. When the fight turned ugly, some of us scattered, thought it better to try and regroup and come back later." He paused, adjusting his rowing to fit Max's once again. "Didn't see Ceron, though. Not 'til about an hour ago."

Jonathan chewed on that for a moment. "So he could have been anywhere."

"I suppose. Although . . ." He glanced toward the other dinghy and swallowed.

"Although?" Jonathan prodded.

"It's probably nothing."

"What is?" Jonathan asked irritably. "Spit it out, man."

Rafferty leaned in slightly. "Now that you mention it, I 'ave seen him about the ship at odd times. On deck in the middle o' the night when he's not on duty, that kind o' thing."

"Perhaps he just couldn't sleep," Sarina snapped, obviously not pleased with the direction of the conversation.

"Per'aps," Rafferty acquiesced with a leer in her direction. His eyes drifted to her open collar, and Sarina shuddered.

"Watch yerself," Jonathan warned.

Rafferty grinned sheepishly. "Sorry, Cap'n. I'm just a man, after all. Can't blame me fer lookin'."

"I *can*. And I *will*."

Rafferty's face paled slightly, and he dropped his gaze. "Aye, sir."

Jonathan sat back, contemplating what Rafferty had told him. He'd thought perhaps Renard was the traitor Charlotte had warned him about, but in fact, he'd never trusted the bastard, and he was in no way close to Jonathan. But Ceron . . .

He glanced at the man again, who was grinning at Sam in the other dinghy as they tried to out-row each other.

James Ceron was another thing altogether. Sarina's defense of the man had started to chip away at Jonathan's distrust, but his disappearance and odd behavior certainly made him a prime suspect.

Sarina squeezed his hand, and he turned to find her watching him with a worried look. It was obvious that she still trusted James and considered him a friend. If he *was* the traitor, she would not take it well.

Jonathan sighed heavily. There was nothing he could do about it at the moment. He had no proof, and Kane was the much greater threat.

So as his men carried out his orders, he watched James Ceron carefully, looking for signs that he was right about him.

All the while, at least for Rina's sake, hoping that he was wrong.

The moon was full, the ship silent as the master gunner made his way up to the deck, stepping nimbly over a discarded rum jug. The men had been celebrating their victory over Kane, and even the captain had indulged a bit, his wench close by and eventually sprawled on his lap. The captain kept a close watch on her, of course. The men were unrestrained at the best of times. Add some rum and ale to the mix, and any wench was a temptation, even the captain's.

Rafferty emerged into the fresh salt air, eyes scanning the deck with devastating purpose. He spotted Crawley near the bow and approached him with a relaxed stride.

Crawley nodded at him. "You here for the next watch?"

"Aye. Anything to report?"

Crawley shook his head, looking out over the water with a deep breath, then lifted a spyglass to his eye. "Nothing. No sign of the *Lady* or the *Curse*."

"He must think Cap'n Tremayne will be back. Waiting 'im out."

"Aye. Most likely." Crawley snapped the spyglass shut and handed it over with a yawn. "You need anything before I turn in?"

"No. Go ahead." He spat over the gunwale. "Quiet night. Everyone must be sleeping off the grog."

Crawley laughed. "Should be a sight when the sun comes up." With a rough pat on Rafferty's back, he headed belowdecks to his hammock.

Rafferty strolled idly about the deck, coming to a stop when he spotted James Ceron looking out over the stern, a hand resting on the main boom. Rafferty gritted his teeth before approaching the man with a determined stride.

"Couldn't sleep?" he asked, spitting on the deck and rubbing at it with the toe of his boot.

Ceron jumped slightly, as if he'd been lost in thought. "Oh. Aye. Lot on my mind, I suppose."

Rafferty's eyes narrowed. "Oh?"

He shrugged. "Just wondering what the captain's up to. And with Kane and Renard on our stern, not to mention Stanton—"

"Cap'n can handle it."

"I'm sure he can." Ceron reached up to stretch his arms over his head. "Well, I suppose I'll turn in. Tomorrow's sure to come quickly."

"Aye. Best get some rack time."

Ceron nodded and headed belowdecks without another word. Rafferty watched him go, black eyes watchful and appraising. Tremayne seemed suspicious of the new addition to the crew. It appeared the captain thought Ceron might not quite be what he seemed.

A slow smile lit his face at the thought, and he spat on the deck again, wiping his mouth with the back of his hand. James Ceron was proving to be a convenient distraction for Tremayne, and one that Rafferty planned to take advantage of.

He retrieved a lantern from the quarterdeck and resumed his position at the bow once he confirmed he was alone. He opened the spyglass and lifted it to his eye, peering toward Virgin Gorda. He saw nothing, but it didn't matter. He knew someone was watching.

Striking a match, he lit the lantern, watching with satisfaction as the flame grew and glowed.

Raising and lowering the lantern, he relayed his message. Twice. Then a third time. He extinguished the flame and raised the spyglass to his eye again, smiling when he saw the signal his message had been received.

Yes, Ceron was a happy accident. Because while Tremayne was focused on him, he'd fail to see what was right under his nose.

And by the time he discovered it, it would be too late.

Rina opened her eyes as the first rays of sunshine drifted through the portholes in Jonathan's quarters. She was warm, even after kicking the blankets off her legs, but it only took a moment to remember why. Jonathan was pressed against her back, an arm wrapped tightly around her waist and his nose buried in the hair at her nape. Their legs tangled over the sheets, his rough and hairy, yet still pleasant against her skin.

She fought the urge to stretch, unwilling to wake him yet, and took a moment to enjoy the feeling of his body against hers. He still wore his drawers, but his chest was bare against the thin fabric of her shift. They had both indulged in a bit of rum the night before and had fallen into bed too exhausted from the day's activities for more than a few soft kisses and gentle touches before they drifted off to sleep.

Jonathan had left firm orders that he not be disturbed unless Kane or Renard were seen sailing away from Virgin Gorda. Since they'd had an uninterrupted night of sleep, Rina could only assume the bastards were waiting for Jonathan's inevitable return. She had no doubt they'd be disappointed. Jonathan, she'd come to realize, could be very patient when he chose to be.

"You're up early, Smith," he mumbled against her neck, his breath raising goose bumps along her skin.

"Did I wake you?"

He chuckled slightly, low and raspy in a way that sent a surge of heat straight through her. "You were thinking too loud again."

She rolled over to face him. "Well, *somebody* has to."

He squeezed her side in what he'd discovered was a ticklish spot. "Cheeky, aren't you?" When she tried to roll away, he held her fast, pulling her close so he could kiss her. A soft brush of lips first, but then deeper, hotter, until Rina whimpered in his mouth, throwing a leg over his hip before she even realized what she was doing. Jonathan drew her closer, his hand sliding down her spine to curve over the fullness of her thigh, holding her firmly against him.

If someone had told her a month ago that she would be lying in a pirate's bed, nearly naked, she would have been too shocked to laugh. It was ridiculous, scandalous, but Rina no longer cared about propriety. Especially when Jonathan was kissing her like this—all hot and wet, alternating between licking into her mouth and sucking lightly on her tongue until her whole body quivered.

Jonathan pulled away abruptly, a bit breathless, and Rina chased after his mouth with her own. He groaned, giving in for a moment, but then pressed her down against the mattress, holding himself above her with a determined look.

"What's wrong?" she asked.

"Sarina . . . I . . ." He rolled away and sat on the edge of the bed, facing away from her.

"Jonathan?" She reached out to run her fingers down his spine. He shivered at her touch and sighed heavily.

"I can't be the one to take your innocence," he said finally.

"My innocence?" She got up onto her knees and moved to his side. "Isn't that my decision?"

He refused to look at her, gaze focused on the floor. "You deserve more—"

"I *said,* isn't that my decision?" When he failed to answer, she reached for his chin, pulling his face toward her. Reluctantly, he met her eyes. "What is this really about?"

"I can't give you what you need!" He jumped to his feet to pace across the floor.

"What I need?"

"A husband! A family!" He threw his hands up into the air to emphasize his words. "Bloody hell, Smith, if you were to become with child . . ."

"Is that what you're worried about?" she asked. "A child?"

"I could never be a father!" he shouted. He took a deep breath and rubbed his hands over his face before lowering his voice. "What could I give a child, Sarina? A criminal as a father? No. It can't happen. I won't let it."

Rina watched him for a moment, realizing she would have to handle this situation very carefully. In truth, the idea of having Jonathan's child, although terrifying, also gave her the smallest twinge of excitement. Not that this was the ideal situation, of course, but to have a child—someone part her and part Jonathan— a piece of him once he left her . . .

Well, she would have been lying if she said the idea didn't have some appeal.

Of course, she would never do that to him, not knowing how he felt about it. Such a thing would be a tremendous betrayal. Still, she wanted to be with Jonathan, here, now, and knew she'd have to tread lightly.

"Jonathan, come here," she said quietly, patting the bed next to her.

After a moment, he obeyed—much to her surprise—but said stiffly, "You're not going to change my mind." Which was not as surprising.

Stubborn man.

"Let me ask you a question," she said, reaching out to take his hand. "What we've done together so far . . . kissing . . ." She leaned in to press her lips to his neck. ". . . touching . . ." She brushed her fingers over his chest, blushing, but pushing through it. "Could that give me a child?"

Jonathan snorted in surprise. "What are you on about, Smith? Of course not."

"Mmm hmm . . ." She scooted closer to him, resting her chin on his shoulder and wrapping her arms around his waist. "So there's no real reason we couldn't continue with that, is there?"

He glanced at her out of the corner of his eye. "Aye. I suppose not," he admitted slowly.

She mouthed at his shoulder, planting wet kisses against his skin. She felt him stiffen as she brushed her fingertips across his stomach. "And are there . . . other things we could do that might be equally pleasurable, but without the risk of pregnancy?"

He turned toward her then, a slight smile lifting his lips. He eyed her carefully for a moment, then one hand slid to her knee and up—ever so slowly—under the hem of her shift.

"Aye," he said, voice low with promise. "Many things."

"Interesting," she murmured as he leaned in to kiss her. "Then I just have one more question."

He tilted his head, nibbling and sucking at her neck as his fingers brushed her upper thigh. "Yes?" he whispered against her throat.

She shuddered, fingers tangling in his hair. "What are you waiting for?"

With a barking laugh, Jonathan picked her up and threw her onto the pillows.

"Saucy wench," he muttered, just before he lowered his mouth to hers.

Rina still felt a bit dazed as she made her way to the deck some time later. Jonathan had left her with a deep kiss. "You do have some brilliant ideas on occasion, Smith," he said before heading to take over command, whistling along the way.

He was right. She was brilliant.

And Jonathan? Jonathan was a *master*.

He'd played her body like a fine instrument, his fingers drawing pleasure and whimpers in equal measure. Sarina had learned a few things, too. She'd asked how to give him pleasure as well, and Jonathan had proven to be a more than willing teacher amidst heady kisses and whispered praise.

She spotted him at the wheel as she stepped out onto the deck and blushed when he caught her eye with a wink and a teasing grin. She realized the deck was busy with preparations to get underway and stepped quickly to Jonathan's side.

"What's happening?"

"Kane and Renard left Virgin Gorda about an hour ago. It's our turn."

"How do you know they're not watching for you?"

Jonathan shouted an order to a boy carrying a coil of rope before turning back to her. "We don't. All we can do is come at the island from the opposite direction. If he's nearby, hopefully we'll see him before he sees us."

The ship began to move, and Rina braced her legs as they navigated out of The Dogs and into open water. Her eyes darted across the horizon constantly, on the lookout for any sign of other ships. Of course, the boy in the crow's nest was probably much more capable, but she couldn't help herself.

As they picked up speed, she began to relax a bit and let her mind wander. She touched the coin at her neck, rubbing it idly as she stared across the channel at Virgin Gorda.

*A coin to give sight.*

How could a coin give sight?

*Jesus saith unto him, I am the way, the truth and the life. No one cometh unto the father, but by me.*

Rina couldn't help but think they were missing something. There had to be a connection, didn't there? Between the poem and the Scripture? Why else would Mellick include them both?

*I am the way . . . no one cometh . . . but by me.*

*The way.*

The way to what? To the treasure, of course. What else could it be?

*A coin to give sight.*

Hesitantly, Sarina pulled the coin from her shirt, a quick glance ensuring nobody was paying attention to her. Jonathan was distracted talking to Max a few feet away, and everyone else was attending to their duties. She eyed the coin, rubbing over it with her thumb.

*The dastardly pirate kept it close at all times, because peeking through the hole gave him unbelievable power.*

*What kind of power?*

*To see other worlds—worlds of adventure and treasure.*

Her heart pounding, she lifted the coin to her eye and peered through the hole in the center. She gasped as everything suddenly fell into place.

"Jonathan!" She hurried over to him, excitement racing through her.

He held up a finger as Max asked, "So you think we should walk across Virgin Gorda, rather than risk laying anchor where Kane did?"

"He'll be expecting that," Jonathan replied. "We'll need to be careful."

Rina bounced on her toes, unable to wait another second. "No, we don't!"

They looked at her in surprise. "What are you on about, Smith?" Jonathan asked.

"We don't need to worry about Kane, because the treasure's not on Virgin Gorda," she said.

Jonathan eyed her skeptically, crossing his arms over his chest. "Well, where is it then?"

"I'm not sure yet, but I'll know soon."

"And how do you expect to do that?"

Rina grinned widely as she held up the coin. "Because *this* is going to tell me."

*It is done. The treasure is secure.*

*Some may call me a monster for what I have done, but those who knew too much could not be allowed a chance to reveal that information.*

*I know God may not forgive me my sins. It is the price I must pay to protect my child's future. And if any others would stand in the way of that goal, I would not hesitate to cut them down as well.*

*- The Journal of*
*Simon Alistair Mellick*
*22 April, 1666*

"Are you certain this is the right spot?" Rina asked as Jonathan stood next to her on the bow of the ship, examining the sketched copy of the half of the map Kane had stolen. Unfortunately, the original had not been in the bag with the rest of the relics, and neither had the other half. Max and Hutchins hovered nearby, but Jonathan had snapped at the rest of the crew to get back to work so they could focus on the task at hand.

"As certain as I can be," he replied, handing the map to Max. "Now what?"

Rina pulled the chain holding the coin over her head and held it out to him. "If I'm right, the positioning of the coin on the map is important. I think if we're in the right spot, looking through the hole will show us the way to the treasure."

"*A coin to give sight*," Jonathan murmured.

"Yes, and my father told me the story about the pirate looking through it to find treasure. I think he suspected the purpose of the coin all along."

Jonathan took the coin and held it up to his eye. "Which one do I look through?"

"I don't know," Sarina said with a frown.

Max examined the map. "The orientation must be important," he said. "Since it's at the bottom of the map, we need to be facing north with the coin held as it's drawn here."

Jonathan looked through it again, then muttered to himself and pulled out his spyglass. He fitted the coin into the eyepiece and once again peered through it.

"Bloody hell," he muttered.

"What is it?" Rina bounced on her toes, heart beating wildly.

"See for yourself." He handed her the spyglass and she lifted it to her eye. Sure enough, with the coin in the spyglass, the smaller hole was filled with Virgin Gorda, but the larger hole circled a smaller island to the west.

"What island is that?" she asked, removing the coin so she could get a better look.

"*Isla Diosa.*"

"But the natives call it *Erzulie Freda*." James appeared at that moment, leaning back against the mast as he crossed his arms over his chest. "Is that where we're headed then?"

Jonathan glared at him, and Sarina quickly interceded. "Are you familiar with the island, James?"

He nodded. "I'm familiar with most of the islands around here. I was born not far away."

"Well, that's perfect," she said with a cheerful smile. "You'll be a big help, I'm sure."

Jonathan grumbled something she couldn't quite make out, then gave the order to set sail for Isla Diosa.

The crew was tense when they made it onto open water, everyone on watch for a sign of another ship. Once they arrived at Isla Diosa, to avoid drawing attention, they used the confiscated dinghies to get to shore, with Jonathan, Rina, Max and James in one, Sam, Crawley, and a couple of mates she couldn't remember the names of in the other. Rafferty, much to her delight, was left in command of the ship. If Kane and Renard showed up, the master gunner would be needed more on the ship than on shore.

She didn't miss the hostile glances Jonathan shot at James, and she knew he'd taken what Rafferty had told him to heart. She'd tried to talk him out of it, explained that James could have many reasons for being on deck at strange hours, and that it made perfect sense that he'd gone into hiding when Kane had attacked—after all, hadn't many of the men? But Jonathan would not be swayed. He trusted his crew more than this man whom he'd only known for a short time, regardless of who his father was. In the end, Rina tried to play peacemaker as much as possible and stayed true to her conviction that James would prove loyal and valuable in this quest.

Isla Diosa was smaller than Virgin Gorda, its most impressive feature a large volcano near the center of the island, surrounded by jungle and large mounds of scattered boulders. They came ashore on a wide beach with unfortunately no place to hide the dinghies. They overturned them, tossing handfuls of sand over the hulls to disguise them as much as possible before heading farther inland.

Rina glanced back as they left the beach to see the *Arrow* in the distance, en route to Virgin Gorda—a ploy, should it be needed, to buy them time if Kane did indeed return.

She hoped it would be enough.

They trudged through the sand and into the shade of a grove of palm trees. Jonathan eyed the surrounding area and consulted the map once again.

"Now what?" Max asked.

Jonathan crumpled the map slightly, letting out a groan of frustration. "We must be missing something."

"Aye," Hutchins said wryly. "The other half of the map."

"I'd hoped once we were here things would become a bit more clear, but . . ." Jonathan took off into the trees, pacing back and forth. The men settled in, sitting on the sand or leaning against a handful of large boulders, waiting for their captain to work things out. Rina took a deep breath and did a bit of pacing herself, exploring the surrounding area. Through the trees, she could spot the rise of a hill to the west, the base littered with rocks but curving upward into a high bluff.

"Perhaps we should climb up," she suggested, pointing to the bluff. "Get a better perspective of the island?"

Jonathan followed her gaze, considering the suggestion. He shrugged. "Good an idea as any, I suppose. Hutchins, you come with me. The rest of you—"

A loud crack had them all whirling in the sand, swords drawn. Jonathan and Max exchanged a tense glance as the foliage rustled from the direction of the beach. Had Kane found them already? If so, how? And what of the *Arrow* and her crew? Rina's fist tightened around the hilt of her sword, and she braced her feet, holding her breath as she waited.

Low voices came closer, filtering through the breeze, the words indistinguishable.

Then . . . a laugh.

A *female* laugh.

Another glance between Jonathan and Max—this one of amused relief as they sheathed their swords. "Avast!" Jonathan called out to the men. "'Tisn't Kane."

Rina gaped at him in surprise, still tense and watching. "Who is it, then?"

He smirked as a flash of blue appeared between the trees, and Rina made out a group of people moving toward them. She breathed in relief when she recognized one as Jenkins . . . then Thomas and Allegheny . . .

"How in the world?" she murmured.

Max laughed. "How do you think?"

The men came forward with grins and handshakes, and Rina finally realized there was a fourth member in their group hidden behind their large frames, a hat with a large blue feather peeking out between their shoulders. Jenkins approached the captain, and Rina squealed when the fourth person was revealed.

"Charlotte?"

"Hello, Rina. It's good to see you again," she replied, stepping forward with a grin. "What do you think?" She twirled around, and Rina had to laugh in response. Charlotte was dressed as she was, in breeches and boots, a dark blue coat brushing at her knees and the blue feather curving proudly from her hat.

"You look wonderful! But what are you doing here? How did you find us?"

Charlotte laughed. "Well, that's kind of my job." She turned to Jonathan, sobering slightly. "Not long after you left, I felt that you needed me—or you *would* need me. I saw your men here going ashore and set off to intercept them."

"It sounded a bit daft, but your sister can be quite convincing, Cap'n," Jenkins added. "We caught passage on the *Agua Clara*. Captain Harry says hello."

Jonathan absorbed it all with an amused half smile, then pulled his sister into a hug. "I'm glad you're here," he said. "I was just hoping for someone to point us in the right direction."

Charlotte beamed and reached out for Max's hand. "Well, then," she said. "It appears I've arrived just in time."

Jonathan watched impatiently while Sarina showed Charlotte the journal and the map. He'd tried to do it himself, but after a few minutes, his sister had not-so-politely told him to leave her alone.

She said he kept staring at her like he was waiting for something to happen. He had to admit he was. Jonathan still didn't have a full grasp on how Charlotte's visions worked, even after all these years, and he could occasionally try to push her a little too hard.

Charlotte snapped that she wasn't a horse you could train to jump with a click of the tongue. She could help them along to a certain extent, but the visions generally came when they came.

Jonathan wasn't particularly fond of that aspect of Charlotte's gift.

They decided it was best all-around if Sarina explained what they'd learned so far about the treasure. Max stayed nearby, of course. The man could never be too far from Charlotte when she was within reach. But he kept silent, allowing the women to pore over the documents undisturbed.

Jonathan hadn't been quiet, which was why he'd been banished to the boulder on the other side of the palm grove. He'd sent the rest of the men—save Ceron, who sat across from him in the sand, tearing a leaf to bits—to survey the area and keep watch for Kane. Jonathan, meanwhile, sat staring at Charlotte and Sarina, willing them to come up with something—anything—to help them move forward.

He also found himself smiling softly whenever his gaze rested on Sarina, remembering their extraordinarily pleasant interlude in bed, and the way she had calmed him down when he'd bolted. He didn't know what he'd expected when he'd revealed his concerns, but it definitely wasn't that Sarina would convince him to experiment with *other* means of romantic pleasure.

The woman was definitely full of surprises.

He watched her now, head bent close to Charlotte's as they studied the journal, gesturing with one hand to make a point. He hadn't lied when he'd told Sarina this was all new to him. What he *hadn't* said was it wasn't simply the fact that she was a lady. True, his experience with women in the past had been limited to those of the professional variety—an exchange of lust and fun for coin, and nothing more. But it wasn't the fact that Sarina was different that had him so nervous—even terrified, at times.

It was the fact that *he* was different.

He found himself longing for things he had no business longing for, hoping for things that could never be. And his panic about the possibility of a child was not solely because he feared becoming a father. It was that—for a dizzying moment—he realized he *wanted* it.

He wanted her, and not temporarily. Jonathan had to admit, if only to himself, that he loved her, and that was the most terrifying thing of all.

Feminine laughter drifted toward him, and he smiled before he realized what he was doing. He was a scoundrel of the worst sort, he admitted to himself, to take what Sarina offered when he could offer nothing in return. But when she adamantly insisted that it was what she wanted—that *he* was what she wanted—he couldn't resist her.

A scoundrel indeed. Pathetic and weak. But then again, he'd never claimed to be otherwise.

With a heavy sigh, he tried to shake off his unproductive thoughts and focus on the task at hand. He caught sight of Ceron and his jaw tightened. Now this was a problem he could deal with.

James, however, beat him to it. "I know you don't trust me," he said, tossing pieces of leaf to the sand. "Although I've given you no reason not to. In fact, I've only tried to do my part since I came on board the *Arrow*."

Jonathan schooled his expression, giving nothing away. "I trust few men."

"But me less than others," he said, his jaw clenched tightly. "I see the way you watch me, as if waiting for me to turn on you at any moment."

"Will you?"

"Of course not!" He got to his feet and brushed the sand off his clothes. "What could I possibly have to gain from that?"

Jonathan watched him carefully, trying to read his expression. "Men will do many things for the right amount of coin."

James laughed humorlessly. "I have no need of coin, other than to feed my belly. I have no desire for riches. And despite what you may think of me, I am not without honor." His accent grew thicker in the heat of emotion. "I do not betray my friends."

"I'd hardly call us friends."

"Rina," he snapped. "*Rina* is my friend. I would never betray *her*."

"Everything all right, gentlemen?" Charlotte interjected, looking from one to the other warily. Jonathan hadn't noticed the two women approaching.

"Fine," he said gruffly. "Any luck?"

"Not really," Sarina said, offering James a sympathetic look before turning back to Jonathan. "Although Charlotte does feel we're on the right island, at least."

"Well, that's something."

Charlotte sighed. "I thought maybe James here could tell me a little about it. I understand it's called Isla Diosa—Goddess Island, is that correct?"

James spared Jonathan one more hard look before turning his attention to Charlotte. "Aye, that's what the foreigners call it at least. It's always been uninhabited because of the volcano, although it hasn't erupted in—"

"The foreigners?" Charlotte tipped her head. "What?"

"You said foreigners call it Isla Diosa."

James nodded. "Aye, Columbus named it that. The natives still call it Erzulie Freda, though—named for the mountain."

Charlotte froze. "Did you say *Erzulie Freda*?"

"What is it, Charlotte?" Jonathan asked.

She ignored him, waving Sarina forward. "Let me see the journal again." Sarina handed it to her, and she flipped quickly to the torn back page. "*Seek Aphrodite's kiss, whence light doth play. And the sword will lead the way,*" she read, slapping the book shut with a beaming smile. "*Aphrodite's kiss!*" she exclaimed.

"Bloody hell, Charlotte, what are you on about?" Jonathan stood with his hands propped on his hips.

Charlotte rolled her eyes, but the smile didn't fade. "Erzulie Freda," she said, enunciating carefully, "is a Vodou goddess."

"Aye." James nodded, stepping away from the tree. "The island was thought to look like her lying on her back in the sea—the volcano, her face. It's where the name came from."

Jonathan huffed. "But what has that got to do with—"

Charlotte held up a finger. "Among other things, she's the Vodou goddess of *love.*"

It took Jonathan a moment, but when he made the connection, a slow smile lit his face. "Aphrodite."

Charlotte grinned. "Aphrodite."

"I think," he said, "that we're heading for the mountain."

They followed an overgrown path through the thickening jungle, palm trees blocking out the sun overhead to create a cool canopy as they trudged through the underbrush. Eventually, the trees thinned and the ground became rockier, large boulders delineating the base of the inactive volcano. They split up, leaving two mates on guard duty along the path, the rest spreading out along the base of the mountain, searching for anything unusual.

Jonathan wasn't certain what, exactly, but he really didn't see any other option.

"Perhaps we're making this more difficult than it needs to be," Sarina said after a while. "May I see the map again?"

Jonathan unrolled the parchment and handed it to her. "What are you thinking?"

She knelt on the ground, spreading out the map and pointing to the sketch of the coin. "I was just thinking that maybe this shows us more than we thought." Looking around, she picked up a couple of thin sticks from the ground and placed them carefully on the map. "If we draw a line from this hole to Virgin Gorda . . . and the other to this island . . ." She looked up at him. "Shouldn't this point to where we should go?"

"Well, if we drew the map correctly, yes," he admitted. "It makes as much sense as anything, I suppose."

Unfortunately, Isla Diosa was not depicted on the half of the map they'd been able to reproduce, and for the next few minutes, a heated discussion erupted as to exactly where on the island they were and where on the map they should be. Finally, James stepped forward and picked up another stick. Without a word, he dropped to a knee and drew an outline of the island in the sandy ground along the edge of the map and a slightly lopsided circle to show the base of the mountain. He reached down and adjusted Sarina's stick slightly, then turned to examine the rise of the volcano behind him. After a moment, he pointed to the right.

"Over there," he said. "Somewhere by those big boulders."

Jonathan still didn't trust James, but seeing no alternative, they moved to the area that Ceron indicated, facing a high wall of solid rock about fifty feet long. They spread out to search for a sign—a cave entrance perhaps, or a marker showing where the treasure might be buried. They ran their fingers along cracks in the rock, pushed against boulders, scraped away at the gravel and rocks covering the ground, but after an hour, they gave up in frustration. They pulled out some food and drink they'd brought along, passing around bits of hardtack and dried beef and skins of water.

No rum this time. Jonathan thought his men needed the focus. Unfortunately, it didn't seem to be helping. Hutchins and Crawley continued to examine the wall, moving beyond the area delineated by James. Ceron, for his part, sat studying the map and muttering to himself. Jenkins, Allegheny, and Thomas set off to check on the mates on guard duty. Charlotte and Sarina spoke in quiet tones as they ate, and Max sat against a boulder, staring at the wall and tossing rocks against it with a frown.

"Don't you see anything, Charlotte?" Jonathan asked in frustration. She sipped water from a skin and wiped perspiration from her forehead.

"I'm trying," she said, just as frustrated. "All I can see is darkness. I can't make anything out."

"That's because there's nothing to make out," Max snapped. "If there *is* a treasure, we're obviously in the wrong place." He ripped off a piece of beef to gnaw on and threw a few more rocks.

"This has to be the place," Jonathan retorted. "We've followed the map . . . the clues . . ."

"Clues?" Max snorted, picking up a larger rock. "Is that what you call them?" He threw the rock with a little more force, and it broke a small piece off the wall before falling to the ground. He nodded a little in satisfaction and grabbed another. "Rantings of a madman is more like it." He tossed another rock, breaking off another piece of the wall.

"That's not helpful, Max," Sarina said shortly. "If you don't have any better ideas, maybe you should be quiet."

"Sarina," Charlotte protested. "We're all feeling frustrated. There's no reason to take it out on Max."

"Well, his attitude is not productive."

"Nobody is being productive at the moment," Max grumbled, throwing another rock. "I believe that's the point."

"All of you, stop it!" Jonathan ordered. "I need to think."

The bickering cut off, and Jonathan began to pace, the only sound his quiet footsteps and the steady chink of Max throwing rocks.

"Perhaps the top of the map isn't north, after all," James offered.

Jonathan sighed. "It has to be. There are no matching land masses if we change the orientation of the map.

"Perhaps you misaligned the coin? Chose the wrong island?"

Max threw another rock and a large chunk dislodged from the wall. He lifted his arm to throw another and froze.

"It's not the wrong island," Jonathan replied, trying to remain calm. "The name makes too much sense. The mountain has to be where we start. We're obviously just in the wrong spot on the mountain."

"Maybe we need to climb up?" Hutchins suggested.

Max ignored the conversation, stood quietly, and approached the wall, running his finger along the long crack now visible from the ground to just above his head. He scanned the ground and picked up a sharp rock, chipping away at what was apparently not rock, but dried mortar of some kind. The crack continued horizontally for a couple of feet, then down again . . . almost like . . .

"Captain?" he called out. "I think I found something."

They gathered around him, scrutinizing the wall with eager eyes. It was Sarina who gasped first. "Is that a door?"

"It appears so," Max replied.

With no further instruction, the men picked up rocks and began to scrape and chisel away at the mortar, excited murmurings replacing the frustrated grumbling from before. After a few minutes, they stepped back to examine their handiwork with wide smiles.

It was indeed a door carved into the rock, and if that wasn't enough to convince them they were in the right place, the letters *S.A.M.* carved into the stone halfway up the right side would have proven the fact.

Hutchins stepped forward, slipping the tips of his fingers into the crack along the edge of the door. The muscles in his forearms tensed as he tried to pull it open. "Help me out here, Crawley," he muttered, and the two of them put their shoulders to the door, trying instead to push it.

"Men," Charlotte muttered to Sarina. "Always with the brawn instead of the brains." She flipped to the last page of the journal. "*A key for the door,*" she read, loud enough for the rest to hear. "Obviously, it won't open without the *key.*"

Jonathan frowned, mainly to cover up his aggravation that he hadn't been the one to realize that. He reached into the bag for the chest and pulled out the locket, eyeing the door skeptically. He stepped closer, then bent down to examine the initials, rubbing his fingers over the engraved letters.

"I think there's a hole here," he said quietly, picking up a rock to scrape at the stone below the letters. Everyone stepped forward, silent and tense, as a piece of stiff mortar chipped away, revealing a thin rectangular hole in the door. Right where a keyhole would be.

Jonathan examined the locket, the emerald on one side, the Latin engraving on the other.

*Behold, I stand at the door and knock.*

Drawing a deep breath, he pressed the locket into the keyhole. Or at least he tried to.

It didn't fit.

"Perhaps if you open it up?" Sarina offered.

He nodded, opening the locket until it lay flat. The group held their breath as the metal slid easily into the keyhole this time. Now to turn it. Jonathan could feel his heart pounding as his fingers tightened on the edge of the silver locket.

"Don't break it!" Hutchins cautioned loudly, making them all jump.

"Bloody hell!" Jonathan snapped. "I'm not going to break it!"

Hutchins shrugged sheepishly but said nothing else.

Returning his focus to the key, Jonathan inhaled deeply and turned it—ever so carefully—to the right.

With a loud click, the door shook and swung inward, a cloud of dust revealing a dark passageway draped with cobwebs.

"No wonder I couldn't see anything," Charlotte murmured. "It's black as pitch in there."

Jonathan felt a gentle squeeze and realized Sarina had taken his hand. He looked down to see her grinning up at him.

"We've found it," she said, bouncing slightly on her toes. He couldn't resist lowering his head to kiss her soundly.

"Not quite," he replied. "But soon." He straightened and stepped toward the opening, not releasing Sarina's hand.

"Crawley, light the lanterns!" he ordered. "I think it's time we found us a treasure!"

Pay heed to the Word
'Twill be your true guide
Quench thirst with the cup
A coin to give sight
A key for the door
A mind for a map
Then cross the bridge to bridge the gap
Seek Aphrodite's kiss, when light doth play
And the sword will lead the way

- The Journal of
  Simon Alistair Mellick
  Date Unknown

Rina swept a cluster of cobwebs away from her face, grimacing in the murky darkness. Jonathan was right ahead of her, carrying a lantern, the rest of the men following behind as Crawley took up the rear with a second lantern. The path led into a low-ceilinged cave, barely tall enough for Hutchins to walk upright and wide enough for two to walk abreast. James explained that volcanoes in the islands often housed miles of such winding caves. She did not find that the least bit reassuring.

Still, she was excited. The discovery of the door—and the fact that the key Mellick described actually opened it—sent a thrill through her, and she couldn't help but believe that they were on the right track. Anticipation buzzed along her skin as she followed behind Jonathan, making the cobwebs almost tolerable.

Almost. She brushed another one aside and Jonathan reached back to take her hand. Rina smiled slightly at the gesture as he pulled her along, eager to get wherever they were going.

Of course, she had no idea where they were going, and she had a feeling Jonathan didn't either. They followed along where the cavern led, curving back and forth until it descended sharply, the steep angle forcing them to grip the damp stone walls to keep their balance.

"We must be deep below the surface," Max said after a while, his voice echoing sharply against the walls.

"Aye," Jonathan agreed. "I wonder how much farther—" He came to an abrupt stop, and Sarina bumped into his back, stumbling a bit.

"What is it?" she asked.

Jonathan held up the lantern, illuminating the path before him. Or rather, the lack of path. The floor fell away into the darkness, and Rina could just make out the edge of the other side of the chasm in the dim light. It was much too far to jump.

Max stepped forward and picked up a rock, tossing it lightly over the edge. They were silent, listening for the sound of the pebble hitting the bottom, but the faint *plink* after a full five seconds proved it was farther away than they'd hoped.

"Perhaps a rope?" Max suggested.

Jonathan called Crawley forward so they could examine the area with both lanterns, but there was nothing to which they could tie a rope in order to swing across the gap.

"There's no way across," Jonathan muttered to himself. "We can't climb down and climb back up again." He looked up, examining the smooth stone walls as far as the lantern light reached. "But there must be a way."

"Maybe it's like the key and the door," Rina offered, unwilling to give up. "We need to find a way around or over. This must be part of the puzzle."

Jonathan nodded in agreement. "Spread out," he ordered. "Look for anything that seems out of the ordinary."

It was Charlotte who found what they were looking for: a small alcove, hidden behind a corner they'd missed at first, the opening barely noticeable in the darkness. Jonathan pulled Rina into the niche with him, Charlotte peeking around the corner curiously. The others waited out in the main passageway.

A stone platform about waist high stood in the center of the little room, cylindrical in shape, with a narrow lip running around the upper edge. Jonathan held the lantern close to the platform, and Sarina smiled when she made out the initials *S.A.M.* engraved in the center.

"I guess we've found it," she murmured, running a finger over the letters.

"Aye, but now what do we do with it?"

"Well, you've already used the coin and the key," Charlotte interjected. "It doesn't seem like the cutlass is the best option here, perhaps the cup?"

Jonathan opened the bag and pulled out the cloth-wrapped cup. He examined it in the lantern light, reading the inscription aloud. *"Pones coram me mensam ex adverso hostium meorum inpinguasti oleo caput meum calix meus inebrians."*

"What does it mean?" Charlotte asked.

"It's from the Psalms," Jonathan replied. *"Thou preparest a table before me in the presence of mine enemies: thou anointest my head with oil; my cup runneth over."* He held the cup in his hand for a moment, eyeing the platform with a slight frown, then carefully set the cup into the indentation on top of it.

It fit perfectly.

Rina held her breath, waiting for whatever was going to happen.

Nothing did.

Jonathan stepped around her to poke his head out into the main passageway. "Anything?" he asked.

"Not yet," Max called, his voice echoing in the cavern.

Jonathan re-entered the small room, moving quietly to circle the platform, his gaze focused on the cup.

"We're missing something," Rina muttered, crossing her arms over her chest.

Jonathan raised a brow. "Aye."

*"Quench thirst with the cup,"* she murmured to herself, staring at the cup. *"My cup runneth over."* She started slightly, looking up at Jonathan, who was watching her with a slight smile.

"What?" she asked.

"You're right, of course."

"Right about what?"

"The cup!" He crossed to the doorway again, calling out. "Bring me a skin of water!"

"Jonathan, what are you talking about?" Rina glanced at Charlotte, who smiled knowingly.

"If a cup is to satisfy your thirst," Charlotte said, "it needs to be full, doesn't it?"

"Aye," Jonathan added, taking the skin from Max and crossing to the platform. "In fact, it should *runneth over.*" With that, he tipped the skin, pouring water into the cup until it trickled over the rim. The center of the platform dropped an inch, a loud click echoing through the alcove as more water sloshed over the rim of the cup. They heard a screeching sound, followed by excited shouts, and Jonathan and Rina exchanged a quick glance before hurrying out into the main passageway.

They came to an abrupt stop behind the gaping others, tilting their heads to follow their line of sight. At first, Sarina couldn't see a thing, despite the fact that both Jonathan and Crawley held their lanterns aloft. Then, more scraping sounds . . . a slight movement.

"What is that?" Hutchins asked quietly.

No one responded, all eyes focused above as the sounds got louder. They stepped back, nervous and unsure, as something large and rectangular descended slowly toward them. As it drew closer, gaining illumination from the lanterns, Sarina could see it was made of thick wooden panels, bound together by iron pins and suspended by heavy chains.

"It's a bridge!" she exclaimed.

Indeed, after a few minutes, the wooden platform came to rest across the gap with a thud and a cloud of dust. The last of the screeching echoed through the cavern until they stood in silence once again.

"Remarkable," Jonathan muttered, still trying to see farther above them. "Pulleys and counterweights, I'd imagine, much like a capstan."

"Mellick certainly had a flair for the dramatic." Rina moved forward, examining the bridge before stepping onto it. "Well, I suppose this is the *cross the bridge to bridge the gap* then. Shall we cross?"

They walked slowly across the bridge, a little uneasy at first, but it seemed quite solid. Max reached out for a handrail, testing its strength. "I wonder how he built all of this."

Jonathan grimaced slightly. "Well, he had significant coin. He hired local help."

"Seems a bit risky for someone so paranoid about keeping a secret."

Rina glanced from Max to Jonathan. She'd read the journal, so she knew how Mellick had handled that problem.

Jonathan shrugged. "He kept the workers blindfolded on the way to and from the caverns," he explained. "Only a couple of men knew the true location." He paused, raising an eyebrow at Max, his face shadowed in the lantern light. "They did not live long enough to share the information."

Max swore under his breath.

"If I'm right," Jonathan continued as he stepped off the bridge and back onto the stone floor, "they're somewhere in here, hidden with Mellick's Gold."

Rina shuddered at the thought.

They continued in silence for a while, the path narrowing until they could only walk in single file. She noticed that they didn't appear to be in a tunnel any longer—at least not a naturally occurring one. The walls were definitely man made and at least twelve feet tall. Every now and then they'd come to another high wall and have to turn either left or right. Jonathan wouldn't pause before turning to the right every time.

"Do you know where you're going?" she asked, quiet enough so the others couldn't hear.

Jonathan's lips lifted slightly. "No idea. But we're bound to get there eventually."

Rina shook her head. "Excellent plan, Captain. Let's hope we don't get lost in the bowels of this mountain for all eternity."

"So macabre," he replied with a grin. "How about some positive thinking, Smith? We haven't come all this way to fail now."

"There's no logic to that whatsoever."

"Logic is overrated. Besides, I think—" He came to a stop at the entrance to a room, approximately twelve feet square. It was surrounded by more high stone walls with a half-dozen doorways appearing at random intervals. In the center of the room stood another platform similar to the one in the alcove but rectangular in shape. Jonathan cast Rina a victorious look. She ignored him and walked toward the platform, the others following her to gather around it.

"Curious," she said, smiling at the familiar initials carved in the center. "It looks like a maze of some sort."

She ran her fingers over the raised areas on the platform, and indeed they did seem to be the walls of a maze. She ran her finger along the path, frowning as, time and again, she'd find herself blocked by a wall, or ending up back where she started.

"What do you think it means?" she asked Jonathan.

"Maybe we're in the maze," he suggested. "And this is a map."

"*A mind for a map,*" Rina mused.

"But a map to where?" Charlotte frowned, leaning in for a better look. "It doesn't seem to lead anywhere."

Jonathan examined it closely, looking up to compare it to the layout of the room. "Hutchins," he ordered, pointing toward one of the doorways. "Try that one. Go left at the first fork, then right . . ." He squinted, following a path on the map. "Then right again. Come back and tell us what you find." He turned to Crawley. "Take Ceron and try this other doorway." He pointed out a path for them to follow, and the two set off with the other lantern. The rest of the group waited in the now dark room, the only sounds a faint dripping of water and their own breathing. Rina felt Jonathan's fingers twine around her own and squeeze gently.

After a few minutes, Hutchins reappeared in the same doorway he had disappeared through.

"Well?" Jonathan said, eyeing each in turn. "What did you see?"

"Nothing," Hutchins replied. "I followed your instructions, but it led me right back here." The other two men returned a few minutes later with the same response.

"That's odd," Jonathan muttered, turning back to examine the map of the maze again. "This map is all wrong. It's like there's a piece missing."

Rina bent to look closer, a twinge of excitement racing up her spine. "Or a *gap*," she offered. *"Cross the bridge to bridge the gap."*

"But we already crossed the bridge," Max pointed out, rubbing a hand over his forehead.

"Or maybe Mellick was referring to something else altogether."

"The cross," Jonathan said softly.

"The cross." She smiled widely. "I can't believe we didn't even consider it was part of the puzzle."

Jonathan quickly pulled the chest out of the oilskin bag and opened it to retrieve the carved wooden cross. He examined the engraving. "Seems so obvious now," he said. "From the Gospel of Saint Matthew: *If any man will come after me, let him deny himself, and take up his cross, and follow me."*

"So what?" Hutchins asked. "Is it a key, like the locket?"

"No . . . No, I don't think so," Jonathan murmured, turning the cross this way and that as he eyed the maze. *"Cross the bridge to bridge the gap."* He slipped the cross into an empty space in the center of the maze, and it clicked softly.

Rina grinned, tracing the newly revealed path with her finger. "That's it! That's the way to go!"

"Aye," Jonathan agreed, taking the lantern from Hutchins and studying the map carefully before leading them toward one of the tunnels. "Try to keep up, men. It looks like we're almost there."

It only took a few more minutes for them to navigate their way out of the maze, and Jonathan couldn't keep the smile off his face.

They were close. He could feel it.

But though it was exhilarating that they were closing in on the treasure, and he was grimly pleased he would finally get his vengeance against Kane, he also couldn't deny a pang of loss at the thought.

The reason walked right next to him.

He knew with every step closer to the treasure, he was taking one farther away from Sarina.

As if she knew his thoughts, she reached out at that moment to take his hand, and he slowed slightly to match her pace.

"The cutlass has to be next," she said, and Jonathan could hear the excitement in her voice.

"Aye, there's nothing else."

"How do you think we'll need to use it?" She looked up at him, eyes wide and glimmering in the lantern light, and he couldn't resist lifting her hand to his lips to plant a kiss on the back of it. He wondered what she saw in his expression that made her brow crease, and he forced a smile, unwilling to diminish her enthusiasm.

"I've no idea," he said. "But I'm sure we'll figure it out."

Sarina nodded, gripping his hand a little tighter as they rounded a corner and entered a cavern, one much larger than the last room. It was also lighter, and he could see why when he looked up to the soaring ceiling, which peaked at a large hole off to one side, open to the blue sky beyond. The floor was littered with rocks of various sizes. They stepped tentatively into the cavern, splitting up to wander around the huge area. Jonathan ran a hand along the cool stone wall, gaping up at the opening in the ceiling—perhaps a hundred feet up, maybe farther.

"There's no platform," Sarina noted, indicating the center of the room.

Jonathan nodded and walked across the room, kicking a rock across the dusty floor. "Search the walls and floor then," he ordered. "There must be something here."

Max, naturally, began to throw rocks at the wall. At Jonathan's wry glance, he shrugged. "It worked last time."

"I don't know," Ceron said as he ran his hand roughly over the wall. "It seems this Mellick of yours isn't one to repeat himself. I'd doubt it's to be so simple."

Max snorted. "There's been nothing *simple* about any of this."

They continued in silence for a while, Max continuing to half-heartedly throw his rocks while the rest of the men examined the walls for any signs of a door or passageway. Other than the one they had come through, however, there didn't appear to be one. Charlotte, meanwhile, took up residence under the hole in the ceiling, the light surrounding her with a diffuse glow. Her eyes were closed, and Jonathan assumed she was trying to access her gift. Everyone kept as quiet as possible to avoid distracting her.

Sarina came to stand next to him in the center of the cavern. "Any thoughts?"

The corner of his mouth lifted wryly. "Plenty. Nothing helpful, however."

She kicked at a rock and frowned as it bounced into another. "I keep thinking over the poem; *the sword will lead the way.* I just can't figure out how it can lead us anywhere." She kicked another rock.

"Perhaps it's another key?"

"That would make sense, I suppose." She kicked at another rock and winced when it didn't move.

"Are you all right, Smith?"

She rubbed her toe on the calf of her other leg. "Yes. I just stubbed my toe."

"Need a kiss to make it better?" He winked.

Sarina smirked. "Are you asking to kiss my toe?"

"Among other things."

"Cheeky."

"Always."

She stretched out her foot to prod at the unmoving rock, then bent to examine it more closely. "That's odd," she said. "This rock has a crease in it."

"A crease?" He crouched next to her, brushing the dust off the rock to reveal a crack about four inches long. He looked up at her. "There's more than a crease, Smith."

Sarina smiled when she saw what he meant, reaching down to trace over the now familiar engraving on the rock: *S.A.M.* "We've found it," she murmured.

"Aye, it appears so." He retrieved the cutlass from the bag and removed it from its sheath. "Stay alert, everyone!" he called out as he stood. "I'm not sure what's going to happen next."

The men gathered around, and Charlotte opened her eyes as Jonathan slowly slid the cutlass into the crack in the rock. It locked into place, sticking out about halfway, and Jonathan could tell the others were holding their breath as he was. He looked up, gaze darting around the cavern.

"Well?" he muttered. "Come on, then."

The men turned to look for a newly revealed hidden doorway or trap door or anything, but found nothing.

"I don't understand," Sarina muttered, frowning in frustration. "Maybe you put it in wrong?"

Jonathan removed the cutlass and tried re-inserting it the other way. It wouldn't lock in, however. "No," he said. "It has to be this way." He replaced the cutlass again, wiggling it slightly for good measure.

Charlotte stepped forward, eyes open but slightly glazed. "You have to wait," she said quietly.

Jonathan straightened, taking a step back from the sword. "Wait for what?"

"It isn't time yet," Charlotte said, her voice a deep drone, and Jonathan realized she wasn't looking at him, but seeing something else. "You must wait for the light." She blinked several times and shuddered slightly, focusing completely on Jonathan.

"What do you mean?" Sarina asked, touching Charlotte's arm lightly. "Do you mean from the Scripture?" She pointed to the engraving around the hilt of the cutlass—*And God said, Let there be light, and there was light.*

"I'm not certain," Charlotte admitted. "I just know you have to wait for it. The light is . . . coming, somehow." She looked up again, frowning at the hole overhead. "James, you said this island was thought to look like Erzulie Freda lying in the sea."

"Aye, that's correct," James replied.

She pursed her lips, tapping them slightly for a moment before pointing at the ceiling. "And that peak. What part of the goddess do you imagine that would have represented?"

James moved to stand next to her, crossing his arms over his chest as he considered the hole. "Hard to say for sure. We've been going round and round in these tunnels so I'm not certain where exactly we are anymore.

"There are three peaks on the island," he explained. "One is said to be her knees, one her . . ." He coughed, glancing at her sidelong in embarrassment. "Err . . . her . . ." He held his hands in front of his chest.

Charlotte smirked. "I get the idea."

"What's the third?" Sarina asked.

James cleared his throat, looking up at the ceiling again. "Her mouth."

Sarina gawked at him, and Jonathan saw that Charlotte was doing the same—only not as much gawking as looking rather satisfied.

"Or her *kiss*," Charlotte said smugly.

James looked at her in surprise. "I suppose."

By that time, all of the men had joined them in the center of the room, and as one they looked up as a flash of light appeared in the hole. The sun edged into the opening, dust motes appearing as its warm rays streamed into the room. The beam grew stronger as the sun moved and filled the opening. They moved back as the rays cut through the air of the cavern.

"*Seek Aphrodite's kiss, whence light doth play,*" Jonathan murmured, watching the beam as it moved ever so slowly across the floor. "*And the sword will lead the way.*"

As if on cue, the light hit the cutlass, flashing bright as it slid slowly up the blade until it glinted against the sapphire in the hilt.

"Look," Sarina breathed.

The sapphire focused the beam against a spot on the far wall of the cavern. Jonathan stalked over to the spot, touching it gingerly where the stone glowed with blue-tinted light. He pushed it with his fingertips and felt it give slightly.

"Bloody hell," he muttered, pushing the spot harder. A rectangular block of stone, about the size of a brick, moved back into the wall, grinding a bit against its tight enclosure. Jonathan continued to push it until his arm disappeared up to his elbow. The sun moved past the opening in the ceiling and the cavern dimmed slightly.

"Nothing's happening," Sarina said, moving to his side.

"I think . . ." Jonathan groped around a bit and felt empty space on the left side of the hole. "There's a gap back here," he said. "I can't reach in, though. It's too tight."

"Let me try," Sarina said, gripping his arm with excitement.

Jonathan pulled his arm out and Sarina quickly reached in, her much smaller arm navigating the space easily.

"Do you feel anything?"

"Give me a moment."

"It's to the left."

"Yes, I'm aware of that, Jonathan. My arm is in the hole."

"Just trying to help, Smith."

"Well, stop trying, please."

A ripple of laughter had them both turning to glare at the group that had gathered around them. The men exchanged amused glances, ignoring Jonathan's pointed look.

"See?" Charlotte told Max. "They're perfect together."

"If they don't kill each other."

"If you don't mind," Jonathan snapped. "We're attempting to find a treasure here."

Max held up his hands. "Apologies, Captain. Please, carry on."

Jonathan ignored the resulting snickers and turned back to Sarina.

"I think I feel something," she said, eyes squinting in concentration. "Yes. It's a lever I think."

"Can you pull it?"

"I'm trying," she said through gritted teeth. "It seems to be a bit stuck."

"Come on, Smith," Jonathan encouraged. "Put your back into it."

She glared at him, and Jonathan felt a smile quirk at his lips. Here she was, a proper lady, groveling around in caves in breeches and boots . . . groping into secret nooks and ready to take a sword—or a rum jug—and fight by his side.

Charlotte was right. She was perfect for him.

Good God, he loved her. And until that moment, he hadn't realized exactly how much. The thought staggered him, and he almost reached out to take her in his arms in the heat of the moment.

Then she squealed.

"I've got it!"

A loud click echoed through the cavern, and the adjacent wall began to shake. Sarina pulled her arm from the hole, stumbling slightly, and Jonathan caught her around the waist to steady her. They watched wide-eyed as a large section of the wall broke away, pivoting on a center point and swinging back to reveal a dark passageway beyond.

"Well done, Smith," he murmured into her ear, pressing a quick kiss to her neck. She gasped, and he couldn't resist doing it again. Sarina wriggled out of his grasp but grabbed his arm to pull him along.

"Come on, Captain," she said with a sunny smile. "Let's go see what we've found, shall we?"

He laughed, following her to the opening, the men and Charlotte close behind them. They came to an abrupt stop at the stone door.

"Lantern," Jonathan ordered, holding out a hand. Jenkins passed it on without a word, taking the other from Crawley. Jonathan held the lantern aloft, reaching for Sarina's hand as he stepped through the doorway.

"Oh my," Sarina whispered as they stepped into another cavern, roughly the size of the one they'd left behind. But where the first room was empty, save a creased rock in the center of the floor, this one was not.

It was full.

Of gold.

Mounds of coins spilled from chests into piles on the floor, ropes of necklaces and bracelets twisted together among them. A pair of solid gold thrones sat against one wall, the tall backs carved with Aztec symbols and inlaid with gems in various colors, a golden mask lying on the seat of one of them. A low table sat next to the thrones, covered with more coins, and against the far wall, a golden statue standing on a rock platform kept watch over the treasure.

A whoop of joy echoed through the chamber, quickly joined by others, and before long all of the men were dancing around the room, trying on necklaces and masks and dipping their fingers into the piles of coins before letting them clink back to the floor. Hutchins took a seat in one of the thrones, waving a golden scepter. Jenkins and Allegheny tossed coins to each other, trying to catch them in their pockets. Max slipped a golden chain with a large engraved pendant over Charlotte's head and ducked in to kiss her lightly.

Jonathan turned to find Sarina examining the statue—a man wearing a mask, sitting cross-legged on a high golden platform.

Jonathan noticed that other than the mask, he wore only a loincloth, his legs and chest both bare. He moved to Sarina's side and slipped an arm around her waist.

"Bit skinny, don't you think?" he teased.

Sarina giggled. "I'm simply admiring the workmanship." She smiled up at him, eyes sparkling in the lantern light. "Can you believe we actually found it?"

Jonathan sighed, tucking a strand of hair that had escaped her queue behind her ear. "Couldn't have done it without you, Smith."

"Damned right you couldn't."

"Such language, Miss Talbot!"

Sarina tried to look affronted and failed, the smile forcing its way back almost immediately. She turned back to the statue, trailing a finger along the intricately carved platform as she slowly circled it. "So, how do you plan to get all of this out of here? Even though he's skinny, I'm sure this fellow is pretty heavy—" She gasped, stumbling backward as she reached the back of the platform.

"What is it?" Jonathan hurried to her side.

With a trembling finger, she pointed to the floor, and Jonathan grimaced at the sight before him. There, mixed in amongst the pile of coins and jewels, lay a human skull, jaw hanging open as the black hollows of its eyes stared sightlessly in their direction. Once he lifted the lantern, he could make out another skull . . . and another, the skeletons held together only by rotting scraps of clothing. He pulled Sarina toward him, turning her face into his chest.

"Well, it seems this is where Mellick kept all his secrets," he muttered, turning to lead her away from the gruesome sight and into the shadow of another smaller statue. Sarina looked pale, her eyes huge and shocked, and he gripped her shoulders, ducking down to meet her stricken gaze.

"Buck up now, Smith. You're not going to swoon on me again, are you?" His teasing words had a soft edge, made even more so by the finger he brushed across her clammy cheek.

She swallowed visibly and took a deep breath, straightening her shoulders. "I'm not going to swoon."

He half-smiled. "Good, because it's a long walk out of these caves, and I'd hate to strain my back carrying you."

Her eyes narrowed. "Are you calling me fat, Jonathan?"

Jonathan fought a grin, glad to see her color returning. "Not fat so much as . . ." He played at considering his words carefully. "Ample."

"Ample?" She bristled, shoving at his shoulder.

"No? Healthy, then? Plump? Robust?"

She smacked him harder with every word. Jonathan laughed and pulled her close, lifting her to her toes as his lips nearly brushed hers.

"Ah, I've got it," he murmured against them. "Comely."

"Comely?" Sarina said breathlessly.

"Aye. Ye'r a comely wench, Smith." He caught her smile in a heated kiss, his tongue tracing her lips before delving deep. Sarina clung to his shoulders, a slight whimper vibrating against his mouth, and he lifted her higher, her breeches making it easy to wrap her legs about his waist. He pressed her against the statue, and Sarina slid her hands higher, tangling them in his hair and scratching lightly at his scalp as she arched forward to meet him.

A recognizable click cut through the haze of lust and want, and Jonathan stilled, fingers tightening on Sarina's hips as she whimpered in disappointment.

"Well, isn't this touching," a chilling voice said from behind him. "I have to say, *Jack*, you do know how to have a good time."

Jonathan let Sarina slide to the floor, her tense jaw and panicked eyes telling him all he needed to know. He turned around slowly, hands held up, and stood blocking Sarina, facing his worst enemy with a frozen glare.

"Kane."

"Aye," the man said with a sneer. He motioned with his extended flintlock for Jonathan to move from behind the statue, and he complied, keeping himself between Sarina and that blasted pistol the whole way. His men were in similar states, disarmed and on their knees with Kane's men standing over them, swords drawn. He locked eyes briefly with Max, then Hutchins, and each nodded slightly. They all knew that if they didn't fight, they were dead. They just needed to seize the right opportunity. His sister watched with wide eyes, clinging desperately to Max's sleeve. He wished he could ask what she saw of the coming few minutes, but wasn't certain he really wanted the answer.

Kane waved his free hand while keeping his eyes focused on Jonathan. "I appreciate you finding the treasure for me, *Jack*. I would have done it myself, but this was just so much more fun, don't you agree?"

"How did you find us?"

Kane tilted his head, his smile growing wider. "You haven't figured that out by now? And here I thought you were a rather clever fellow." He looked pointedly to the left. Jonathan followed his gaze, his jaw tightening when he saw Rafferty step out of the shadows to casually lean against one of the golden thrones. The man wiggled his fingers in greeting before spitting on the floor, and Jonathan's hand flew to his sword in reflex.

"I don't think so, *Jack*," Kane warned, sharp as steel as the flintlock pressed against Jonathan's temple.

"You bastard," he heard Sarina hiss, although he wasn't certain if it was aimed at Kane or Rafferty.

Jonathan gritted his teeth and lifted his hands up once again, his gaze focused on Rafferty. "What did he offer you to betray us?"

He shrugged nonchalantly and moved to sit on the throne, crossing an ankle over one knee as he relaxed. "The *Arrow*, of course. And a larger portion o' all o' this than I'd ever get from the likes o' you."

Jonathan laughed. "You actually think he'll give you the *Arrow*? I knew you were dim, but I'd never thought you an idiot."

"Shut your gob!" he snarled, leaning forward slightly, his black teeth clenched in anger.

Jonathan ignored him. "There's a reason he's called Kane the *Merciless*, you lice-infested scalawag. You're only worth something to him when you have something to offer. And you, you scurvy, mutinous bilge rat, are of no use at all anymore!"

"Mutinous bilge rat?" Sarina murmured from behind his shoulder. "Nice."

"Y'don't know what yer talkin' about," Rafferty snarled, glancing at Kane. "Tell 'im, Cap'n. Tell 'im 'e's wrong."

Kane rolled his eyes. "I don't have time for this nonsense."

"No!" Rafferty shouted, standing and stalking toward them. "Tell 'im I'm a cap'n now. The *Arrow's* mine, as it should be. Tell 'im."

"Watch yerself," Kane warned with a glare. "Ye'll get what I give ye and be glad about it."

"But . . . the *Arrow*," he protested. "You told me—"

"Avast!" Kane shouted. "Don't push me, boy!"

Jonathan glanced at Max and could see his muscles tense, even across the room. He reached back discreetly to touch Sarina's hand and felt her stiffen.

"I helped you!" Rafferty snapped at Kane. "You'd never have found the treasure without me!"

Without warning, Kane hauled back and punched Rafferty in the face, his flintlock never wavering from Jonathan's head.

"I said, don't push me," he snarled. "Now go sit down and shut up."

Rafferty wiped a spot of blood from his lip, then spat on the ground as he glared at Kane with hate-filled eyes. "Yer not going to give me the *Arrow*, are ye?" he asked quietly.

Kane laughed. "Ships are for *captains*," he said as if that explained everything. Rafferty's jaw tightened and his hand flew to his sword, drawing it as he lunged toward Kane.

He didn't get two steps.

Without blinking, Kane swept his arm to the side, firing his flintlock and hitting Rafferty between the eyes. The *Arrow's* master gunner—*former* master gunner—fell to his knees, wide-eyed, a shocked gasp escaping his lips before he collapsed in a crumpled heap amidst a pile of gold coins.

The room stilled in shock, but Jonathan didn't wait for Kane and his men to recover. He drew his sword, shoving Sarina backward as he swung it in a wide arc toward his enemy. Kane caught sight of the movement quickly enough to shift his weight, and Jonathan's sword clanged against the still-smoking barrel of the flintlock.

Jonathan's men hadn't waited, either. They sprang into action, kicking out at their guards and scrambling for their weapons. He could hear the sound of battle all around him and grinned in satisfaction, stepping over Rafferty's lifeless body to swing again at Kane. The blackguard dropped his pistol and drew his sword just in time to intercept the blow, and Jonathan spun, coming at him again from another angle.

Their swords caught, crossed between them as they leaned in with matching grimaces.

"You can't win, *Jack*," Kane snarled.

"We'll see," he replied, shoving Kane back and jumping onto a table to gain a height advantage. He spotted Sarina across the room, sword drawn as she hurried to James' aid. Ceron was fighting two of Kane's men at once, and Jonathan spared a moment to regret ever doubting the man. Barton spied Sarina and started toward her, but before Jonathan could act, Kane came at him again, sword flashing in the dim light of the cavern.

"Smith!" he shouted as he jumped over Kane's sword, then parried with a quick turn. "On your flank!"

Sarina whirled about just in time to duck under Barton's swing. She ran past Jonathan and jumped up onto the statue's platform. "Are you watching my flank again?" She kicked one of Kane's men in the face, grimacing slightly.

Jonathan laughed as he leaped from the table to the platform to stand beside her. "It's a nice flank."

Barton had turned his attention to Max, who fought side-by-side with James across the room. Hutchins shouted victoriously as he sliced the leg of one of Kane's men, who fell to the floor with a shriek before the master rigger turned to take on another. Jonathan wondered how many men Kane had brought with him. They were already outnumbered, but the size of the room leveled the playing field a bit. There were only so many people who could fit inside, and Jenkins and Allegheny moved to the door, effectively striking down anyone else who tried to come in.

"Look alive, men," Jonathan shouted, sword held high. "If any of these scurvy bastards leave these caves to bring back reinforcements, I'll have ye lights and livers!"

His men shouted in agreement, fighting with increased vigor, and Jonathan saw Kane shove off Crawley, his glittering black eyes focused on Jonathan as he started toward him.

"All right then," Jonathan muttered. "Come and get me."

Rina's arms ached, but she forced herself to hold her sword aloft. She winced as she spotted Charlotte across the room, taking a blow to the head before she crumpled to the floor. Max shouted her name and bent over her, touching her neck gently. He whirled around to fight again, and Rina sighed with relief when she saw Charlotte's chest expand with breath.

Jonathan jumped off the platform, fighting his way toward Kane, and Rina's heart raced with worry. She didn't have much time to dwell on it, however, before the man she'd kicked in the nose got to his feet with a ferocious glare. Rina gulped and wished she had a rum jug.

"Ye'll pay fer that, wench," he snarled, wiping his nose with the back of one hand as he raised his sword with the other. She stepped back, eyes scanning for a means of escape. Her size was a disadvantage in a face-to-face fight, and her mind raced to even the odds. She spotted a gold-plated shield leaning against the back of the platform and saw her opportunity. As the man lunged at her, she jumped backward, stumbling and landing inelegantly on her backside with a loud, "Oof!"

The man leapt up onto the platform with a leering grin. "Don't worry, wench. I'll make it quick."

Rina kept her eyes firmly on him as she reached out for the shield, her fingers scrabbling on a pile of coins. A wave of despair clutched at her as she realized the shield was too far away. The man advanced, looming over her, and she stretched farther, finally touching something round and hard, half-buried beneath the coins.

A rock. It could be her only chance. Around her, the fighting intensified with swords clashing and shouts of victory and pain, but behind the statue she was hidden from anyone who might help her, hidden from Jonathan. She clutched at the rock desperately as the man jumped off the platform and bent to sneer at her, his sword pointed at her throat.

"Or mayhap I'll make it slow," he said, rank breath and spittle spraying her face as his gaze drifted over her body.

Rina feigned paralysis, widening her eyes and willing him closer. Her fingers found a hole in the rock, and she tightened her grip. She held her breath as he stepped forward and dropped to his knees, straddling her. Her heart raced as he turned the sword so the flat lay against her neck and she struggled, only to freeze when he pressed the blade more firmly into her skin.

"I do like 'em feisty," he muttered, licking his lips.

Rina grimaced, her stomach roiling with nausea when he ran his nose down her cheek. The sword clattered to the floor as he replaced it with his hand, and she swallowed, feeling his fingers tighten around her neck.

He lifted his head. "Fight gone outta you?" he mocked, his hand sweeping down to tear at her shirt. "'At's a good wench."

Rina muttered, "Well it's not a rum jug, but . . ." She swung the rock with all her strength at the man's still-oozing nose. He howled as blood flowed more freely, joined by a stream from a newly-split lip. He rolled onto his back, pressing against the new wounds with both hands. She sprang to her feet and wasted no time kicking the man hard between his legs, anger and terror giving her a surge of strength. He screamed, curling up into a ball as she kicked him again for good measure. She lifted her hand to throw the rock at his head but made the mistake of looking at it first.

It wasn't a rock.

Her fingers gripped the eyeholes in the human skull of one of Mellick's assumed workers. The jaw was missing, and the grisly half-grin turned Sarina's stomach yet again. She shrieked and threw the skull to the ground, hitting the pirate in the head, despite her lack of aim. She stood over his body, trembling and breathing in harsh pants, when Jonathan bounded over the platform with his sword held high. He took in the scene with amusement, until he noticed Rina's trembling and the tear in her shirt. His face darkened with fury, and he turned slowly to the man lying on the floor. He lowered his sword until the tip barely touched the man's neck. Her attacker froze, then rolled onto his back, hands held by his head in deference. Jonathan pressed a little harder with his sword, until a drop of blood bloomed at the point and mingled with the trickle from the man's nose and mouth.

"You dare," Jonathan hissed. "You *dare* to touch my woman?"

Rina watched in shock and horror, finally jolting out of her stupor to say weakly, "Jonathan?"

He ignored her. "She is *mine*," he spat through gritted teeth, his voice low and deadly, "and you will pay."

She swallowed a wave of nausea. She'd seen Jonathan angry before, but never infused with such a single-minded, frigid rage. She had no doubt he was about to kill a man right before her eyes. To her surprise, he lifted his sword slightly, then kicked the pirate's own sword toward him.

"Pick it up."

The man blinked in surprise, but the look on his face quickly melted into fear as he took in Jonathan's icy determination. He picked up his sword, though, and shakily got to his feet. His knuckles whitened as he gripped the hilt firmly in both hands and braced his feet for Jonathan's attack.

In the end, though, his preparations mattered little. Like an avenging angel, Jonathan advanced, sword flashing in the reflected lantern light. It took only one blow before his opponent's sword went flying yet again, but Jonathan didn't relent. He whirled about, and Rina clenched her eyes shut, only opening them moments later when she felt his arms encircle her.

"It's all right," he murmured quietly into her hair. "Did he hurt you?"

She shook her head, unable to speak when she saw the body lying on the floor behind him, the man's shirt covered with blood. She spun around to bend over with her hands on her knees as she breathed deeply, fighting the compulsion to vomit. Jonathan's shout drew her attention, and she looked up to find him once again on the platform, fighting another of Kane's men. No . . . *two* of Kane's men. Kane, himself had been detained by Allegheny, much to Jonathan's apparent irritation.

Rina swallowed, purposely avoiding looking at the dead body beside her. "Now's not the time, Smith," she muttered to herself, bending to pick up her sword. "You can fall apart when the fight is over." She jumped up onto the platform and deflected the blow of one of Jonathan's attackers. Jonathan glanced at her, relief evident on his features.

"Nice of you to join us."

She reached down for the shield she'd spotted earlier as Jonathan parried with first one man, then the other. She saw James approaching, fighting off his own opponent.

"I couldn't let you have all the fun," she said, swinging the shield with both hands at one of the men Jonathan was fighting. A loud clang echoed through the chamber over the shouts and clashing of swords. The man blinked, stunned, before falling first to his knees, then flat onto his face.

"Aaahhhrrr!" Sarina shouted down at his inert body, all the anger and fear of the past few minutes erupting at once.

"Did you just say *Aaahhhrrr*?" James asked as he struck down his own opponent and jumped up onto the platform to catch his breath. He and Jonathan exchanged an amused glance, but Rina raised her chin stubbornly.

"It's what pirates say, isn't it?"

Jonathan kicked at his opponent, then looked at James again. The two men shrugged and turned to jump back into the fray.

They both shouted, "'Aaahhhrrr!" on the way.

Rina gripped her shield and jumped down to follow Jonathan. He fought his way toward Kane, and she used her shield to both deflect blows and deal a few of her own. The fight had seemed to turn in their favor, with more of Kane's men lying on the floor than standing and fighting. But Rina knew there was only one fight on Jonathan's mind. It was the same one on her's. Anger burned in her chest when she caught a glimpse of Kane's face, mouth twisted in a grin as he spotted Jonathan coming toward him.

"I think it's time we end this once and for all, *Jack.*"

Jonathan elbowed another man out of his way before answering, "For the first time, we agree, old man."

They came together in a frenzy of sword clashes, evenly matched in both skill and motivation. Rina watched, heart in her throat, as first Jonathan seemed to prevail—the tip of his blade slicing across the older man's ribcage —then Kane, who created a similar wound along the length of Jonathan's thigh. Kane pressed his advantage, forcing Jonathan back against a table with three quick slashes of his sword. Jonathan rolled over the table, springing to his feet on the other side and ignoring the blood trickling down his breeches. Barton elbowed one of the *Arrow's* crewmen in the face and started toward Jonathan, sword at the ready, but Kane stopped him with a shout.

"No," he said, climbing over the table. "Tremayne is mine." He attacked with no further warning, his blade cutting through the air. Jonathan deflected the blows but retreated, stumbling backward on his injured leg. Rina saw too late the obstruction in his path, and just when she opened her mouth to shout a warning, Jonathan fell backward over Rafferty's lifeless body, his sword falling from his fingers.

Kane laughed, moving to stand over Jonathan as he lay sprawled amidst the coins and carnage. "When will you learn that you can never win against me, *Jack?*" He grinned, gloating as Jonathan reached for his sword. Rina gulped, eyes darting about for a way to help and landing on the table behind Kane. She moved quietly toward it as Kane placed the point of his blade against Jonathan's neck.

"Such a pity. You really showed so much promise," Kane said, shaking his head mockingly. "But I really have no more time to waste on you. I do have a treasure to collect, after all." His blade drifted down Jonathan's chest, coming to a stop with the point above his heart.

Rina climbed up onto the table behind Kane. Nobody paid her much attention, each focused on his own fight. Barton watched Kane's actions carefully, jaw tight as his fist tightened around the hilt of his own sword.

"I'm afraid it's time to say goodbye," Kane said, placing his free hand flat on the hilt, preparing to force it down.

Rina stood, grasping the shield in both hands as she lifted it over her head. The movement caught Barton's attention, and he leapt for her while shouting a warning at Kane. She didn't wait for him to react. With all her might, she swung at Kane's head, the resounding clang echoing through the chamber as Kane collapsed bonelessly to the floor. Jonathan stared up at her, blinking in surprise, but Rina couldn't spare another moment. She raised the shield again to smash it against Barton's head, but the pirate raised a hand in defense, and the resulting blow knocked him to his knees, but didn't rob him of consciousness. He stood, face twisted in anger, and descended on Rina with his sword held high.

He didn't make it two steps. He faltered, mouth dropping open in shock as Rina cowered, her shield held up against her chest. She watched in awe as blood blossomed on his shirt, spreading outward from the tip of a sword protruding from his chest. With a sickening gurgle, more blood bubbled out of his mouth as he fell to his knees, revealing Jonathan standing behind him, his sword buried in Barton's back to the hilt. He pulled it free as Kane's first mate crumpled to the ground, and Rina looked away quickly from the blood stained blade. It took a few moments for her to realize that the room had fallen into stunned silence. She looked around, surprised to find the fighting over. Kane's men were on their knees, the crew of the *Arrow* standing over them, awaiting orders from their captain. Jonathan wiped his sword on Barton's back before sheathing it. He stood over Kane, fists on his hips, then looked at Rina with a slight frown.

"Blast it, Smith," he grumbled, prodding at Kane with the toe of his boot. "How am I supposed to kill a man who's unarmed *and* unconscious?"

She bristled. "Would you rather I'd let him skewer you on his sword? Really, is it too much to expect a little gratitude—" Her eyes narrowed as Jonathan's lips quirked, and she realized he was *trying* to bait her, most likely to get her mind off the grisly scene she'd just witnessed.

It worked.

She jumped down from the table, carefully stepping over the dead bodies littering the floor without looking directly at them. "You certainly do make a mess, Captain," she said, forcing a note of nonchalance into her voice. "I do hope you're planning to clean up after yourself." She was unable to hide the rush of dizziness that hit her when she neared him, however, and reached out to grab at his shoulder to steady herself.

"Damn," she muttered. "I really do have to get a handle on the swooning, don't I?"

Jonathan wrapped an arm around her waist, encouraging her to lean on him. "I think a bit of fresh air is in order. Hold on, Smith. I'm a wounded man. You're not going to make me carry you, are you?"

Rina forced a laugh, breathing deeply through her nose. "I'll do my best."

Jonathan shouted for the men to bind their prisoners, leaving Jenkins, Crawley, and Allegheny behind to guard them while he and the rest of the crew set off for reinforcements from the ship to secure the treasure. Surprisingly, he'd lost no crewmen in the fighting, although James and Max were both wounded. Despite his injury, Max insisted on carrying Charlotte, cradling her gently in his arms.

"Is she all right?" Jonathan asked, reaching out to touch her forehead carefully.

Max nodded. "She's breathing steadily. We just need to get her someplace quiet where she can rest."

They set off for the surface, retracing their steps through the maze and tunnels and retrieving each of the relics along the way, just in case. Rina felt better when she spotted the door leading outside, even though it was closed—apparently by Kane—and it took several minutes for Jonathan to figure out how to open it from the inside. Charlotte moaned, shifting in Max's hold before her eyelids fluttered open.

"Should have seen him coming," she muttered, her words slurred.

Max pressed a kiss to her forehead. "Don't worry about that. Kane's no threat any longer."

Charlotte shook her head, the motion causing her to moan again. "Not Kane . . . the King . . . the King's man . . ."

Before she could say anything more, the door swung inward, fresh air from outside reviving them all as they stepped into the late afternoon sunshine. Buoyed by their success, the crew of the *Arrow* emerged, laughing and shoving at each other good-naturedly.

Only to freeze at the distinctive sound of a flintlock being cocked. Rina looked around, eyes wide, unable at first to comprehend why there were at least twenty men surrounding the entrance to the cave.

Until she recognized the one who stepped forward. He was dressed in civilian clothes instead of his naval uniform, but his haughty demeanor and icy blue eyes were the same.

"Commodore Stanton," she murmured in shock.

He tipped his head, touching the brim of his hat with the barrel of his pistol. "We meet again."

Jonathan cursed, loudly and colorfully. He glanced at Max as Stanton addressed Sarina, hoping he understood the significant look he cast his way.

He did, apparently, and surreptitiously tucked the bag containing the relics into the underbrush next to him.

"I'm actually surprised you didn't catch on sooner, Tremayne," Stanton said, turning his attention to the captain. "I couldn't understand why Kane and Renard were traveling together and what it all had to do with you. Of course, once I caught Renard, the answers came a bit more easily." He gestured with his hand, and a couple of his men stepped aside to reveal Renard and several others sitting on the sand, their hands bound behind their backs. "It's quite a victory for me, I'm certain you can imagine," he said with a smile. "To capture two of the most notorious pirates in the Caribbean and a treasure, as well? Yes, quite a victory."

He tipped his head curiously. "Where is Kane, by the way?"

Jonathan's mind raced. He'd been so close, and now he stood on the cusp of losing everything. Stanton would stop at nothing to destroy him and claim the treasure for himself. Of course, he had no idea how to find it, but at the same time, Jonathan still had men inside, and he couldn't leave them trapped inside the mountain. He glanced at Sarina . . . then Max . . . Hutchins . . . Ceron. His men trusted him. He owed them so much. If there was only something he could do.

"Did you kill him?" Stanton asked. He shrugged. "No matter. You're enough of a prize, I suppose. Certainly enough to garner me quite the reward. Combined with the treasure, I'll be back in London in no time, leaving these godforsaken islands for good."

Jonathan inhaled sharply, an idea coming as if out of nowhere. Perhaps there was a way. Perhaps he could save his men, if not himself.

"He's not dead," he said, glaring at Stanton.

"No? Well, where is he? Turn him over and perhaps I'll ask the hangman to tie the knot properly so you don't suffer too much."

Sarina snapped, "You bastard!"

Stanton raised an imperious brow. "Such language! Of course, I should expect as much from Tremayne's whore."

Jonathan stepped forward, but Stanton stopped him with a jerk of his flintlock. "I don't think so, Tremayne," he said with a grimace of distaste that quickly turned speculative. "You have feelings for the girl, then?" He slowly moved his arm until the pistol was pointing at Sarina. "Bad move, Captain. Never give away your weakness. I'd have thought you'd have learned that by now."

Jonathan fought down his fury, knowing it would do Sarina no good. "The girl is not involved in all of this. If you want Kane, you'll need to deal with me."

"What if I just take him?"

"You can't. You can't find your way to him, or to the treasure, without my help."

Stanton laughed. "And why would you help me?"

Jonathan held out his hands. "I'm interested in an exchange. One I think will be mutually beneficial to both of us."

The commodore looked at him curiously. "What kind of exchange?"

Jonathan cleared his throat. It was time to lay his cards on the table. "Kane and his men. Plus half the treasure. In exchange for a pardon for me and my men."

"Half?" Stanton laughed again. "Why in the world would I settle for half?"

"Because you'll never find it without my help," Jonathan replied. "It's well hidden, as is Kane."

Stanton started to pace, considering. "Half, you say?"

"Still enough to make you a very rich man."

Jonathan could see the battle going on in Stanton's mind. His hate for Tremayne on one side—his unbridled greed on the other.

"Think of it," Jonathan prodded. "You'd return one of the wealthiest men in London." The gleam of interest in Stanton's eye told him he was getting through. "Not to mention, one of the most powerful."

"Not powerful enough to garner a pardon for One-Eyed Jack Tremayne," he retorted. "You're infamous, Tremayne. I might be able to help your men, but you? There's no way."

Jonathan considered that. "All right then. My men, then. Any who wish to leave the *Arrow* will be left alone."

"No!" Max shouted. "No, it has to be all of us!"

"Avast!" Jonathan snapped. "Mind your place, mate!"

"But Jonathan," Sarina said quietly. "You'll still be a fugitive."

He saw the anguish in her eyes, felt it himself. There would be no future for them. But then again, he'd never really expected one. He turned stiffly back to Stanton.

"What is your word? Do you accept?"

"If I do, how do I know you will honor your part of the bargain?"

Jonathan stiffened. "I will."

Stanton tapped his chin. "I believe I need a bit more than that." He turned to Sarina. "Take her," he told his men.

"No!" Jonathan bellowed. "Leave her out of this!" He watched in horror as two of Stanton's men took Sarina by the arms, leading her away. To his surprise, she didn't fight back, instead looking at him sadly.

"It's all right, Jonathan," she said. "Just give him what he wants and this will all be over."

"That's right," Stanton said, summoning his men with a jerk of his head. "We'll be waiting on the beach. The rest of your men will be released to help you retrieve the treasure. I expect a full accounting to ensure you aren't cheating me, Jack. Do so, and your little wench here will pay. Don't doubt it for a moment. Deliver half, along with Kane and his men, and I'll see to the pardons for whatever members of your crew wish to leave the pirate life behind. As for you, I'll give you a head start before I inform my commanding officer of your last known location. Once I'm in London, I won't spare you or any of this a second thought."

Jonathan looked into Sarina's eyes and saw her willing him to accept. "Let me do this," she said quietly. "It's all right."

With a heavy sigh, Jonathan nodded, sending Max and Hutchins with Stanton to fetch the rest of the crew and get help for Charlotte. Once they were out of sight, he ordered his men back into the caves. It would take days to bring out all the treasure.

With Sarina's freedom at stake, Jonathan planned to cut that time in half.

*Two Weeks Later, Charles Towne, South Carolina*

Rina stood in the shade of a twisted oak tree, wiping tears from her eyes. A few feet away, Jonathan knelt before a carved headstone, his fingers tracing the name idly.

*Elisabeth Jacobs Tremayne, Viscountess Coffey*

His mother.

He had brought Rina here, saying simply that he needed her. When she'd seen the small graveyard on the edge of the Tremayne property, she had faltered, surprised that he would share something so personal with her. Jonathan hadn't pressed her forward, instead leaving her by the tree as he approached his mother's grave and fell to his knees, speaking quietly in the stillness. Rina couldn't hear his words, only the low rumble of his voice mingling with the song of the birds in the treetops.

To be honest, she was amazed she was there at all.

Stanton had kept his word, and no one was as shocked by that as Rina. She'd half suspected when he took her away that she would be bound in chains and turned over to be hanged. She'd felt she had to at least try, however. Do her part to help the others— Max and Charlotte . . . James . . . everyone on board the *Arrow*. It had taken a day and a half for the crew to bring out all of Mellick's Gold, and Rina had a sneaking suspicion Stanton had ended up with more than half. He'd returned her to Jonathan, however, along with written pardons for the members of the crew who wanted to leave the ship. There had been surprisingly few, in the end—Max, of course, and James . . . a handful of others—but most had no desire for a normal life. They'd packed away their part of the treasure and were ready to start off again on another adventure.

They'd stopped in Charles Towne to finally deliver Max to his new home. When they'd set foot on Tremayne land, Charlotte had turned to Jonathan with tears brimming in her eyes.

"Thank you," she'd said, enveloping her brother in a hug. "Thank you for freeing him."

Jonathan had flushed and shrugged, finally bending to kiss Charlotte on the cheek. "Be happy," he'd said, repeating the words to Max with a manlier slap on the shoulder.

Charlotte had looked from Rina to Jonathan then, saying simply, "Sometimes things don't happen as we'd hoped, Jonathan. It doesn't mean we can't have what we want."

Jonathan's brow had creased in confusion. "What on earth does that mean?"

Charlotte laughed. "It means that you should take your own advice." She reached out to take him by his upper arms, squeezing gently. "Be happy, Jonathan."

Max and Charlotte wasted no more time and were married before they'd been back a full day. They'd disappeared into a small house near Grace's and hadn't been seen much since.

Rina smiled at the thought.

As for James, he disappeared one night without saying goodbye. Rina was a little hurt that he'd left with no word, but she hoped she would see him again someday. Even more, she hoped he would find what he was looking for.

Hutchins, on the other hand, opted to stay on the ship, although he planned to use his part of the treasure to go into business with Pearl and expand the *Red Pearl*. He hadn't said it in so many words, but Rina knew he hoped his influx of coin would mean Pearl could stick to managing the business rather than actively participating in it. She hadn't spent much time with Pearl, but after seeing the two of them together for even a short time, she thought Pearl might feel the same way.

Jonathan reached for his dagger, bringing Rina out of her thoughts. She watched him curiously as he lifted it to one of his braids and sawed through it, close to his scalp. He placed the twisted locks on his mother's headstone, before he kissed his fingers and pressed them to her name, bowing his head for a moment before he stood and turned toward her, wiping at his own tears.

"Are you all right?" she asked quietly.

He nodded, taking her hand and lifting it to his lips. She reached out with her other hand to touch the spot on his head where he'd cut off his hair, her gaze questioning.

Jonathan cleared his throat, looking back at his mother's grave. "When she died, I vowed not to touch a blade to my hair until I avenged her," he said, his voice a gentle rasp. "Every time I saw my reflection in the glass, it served as a reminder of my purpose."

Rina swallowed more tears, twisting her fingers into the shining length of his hair. "So you'll cut it now?"

He shrugged. "The vow has been fulfilled."

She nodded, turning to walk away from the graveyard, her fingers entwined with Jonathan's. Kane's death had not come at the point of Jonathan's blade as he'd hoped—nor at hers—but at the end of a rope. He'd been hanged only a day after Jonathan had turned him over to Stanton, as had all his surviving men. A short time later, the commodore had set sail for England, and Rina had no doubt he would end up with a title as well as wealth, no matter how much the idea turned her stomach.

She tried to put it out of her mind and focus on Jonathan. Their future was a bit more muddled. Jonathan would return to the *Arrow* by sundown. He dared not risk staying on land any longer. Stanton was no longer a threat, but Jonathan was still a fugitive, and it was only a matter of time before the Crown tracked him down yet again. Rina, however, was no longer considered a criminal, a fact that should have relieved her, but instead filled her with a quiet sense of dread. Jonathan had secured a pardon for her as well, and she could only take that to mean that he believed it was time they parted ways.

His actions seemed to belie that, though. Since they'd left the island, he'd been a constant presence at her side, touching and kissing her frequently. He seemed hesitant to let her out of his sight, and Rina wondered if he was storing up their moments together as she was—counting down the days, the hours, until they would finally say goodbye.

They ended up on the shores of the creek, once again looking out over the rushing water. The sun was low in the sky, casting gold and red into Jonathan's hair. Rina faced him, reaching out again to touch it.

"I don't think you should cut it," she said.

He tilted his head, the corner of his mouth lifting. "No?"

"It suits you." She swallowed a sob, turning away from him quickly.

"Smith?" He reached for her, but his hand fell short, drifting to his side. "Sarina, it's all right. It's all over. You can go home. Have the life you deserve."

And with that, something snapped inside her. She turned on him, eyes flashing. "I don't want that life. I want you."

Jonathan jerked as if he'd been struck. "Don't be ridiculous. You'd have no life with me."

"Don't call me ridiculous."

"Well, then, don't *be* ridiculous, Smith. You need to go home. Find a nice man. Have a family."

"I don't want a nice man!" she shouted. "I want you, you stubborn, arrogant—" she searched for a proper insult "—lily-livered son of a scurvy sea dog!"

Jonathan blinked, his mouth hanging open, and Rina took no little pride in having struck him speechless. Then he started to laugh.

"It's not funny, you bastard!" she snapped. Jonathan bent over, hands propped on his knees as he gasped for breath. Rina huffed in annoyance and turned to stomp away.

Jonathan stopped her with a hand on her arm, whirling her around and gathering her close. "Oh, Smith," he said, his eye still twinkling with mirth. "I fear I've ruined you for any other man. Who else would have such a foul-mouthed wench?"

Rina struggled against his hold, still annoyed, and it took a moment for her to recognize the significance of his words. She looked up at him, heart pounding in her chest. "What are you saying?"

Jonathan took a deep breath. "Damn it, Smith. I should let you go, but I'm a selfish bastard, aren't I?" He looked away.

"Jonathan. What are you *saying*?" She reached up to turn his face back toward her.

He looked into her eyes, his gaze softening. "I'm saying I love you, Smith. God help me. I don't want you to go anywhere if it isn't with me."

Rina gasped.

Jonathan laughed. "If I knew it would get you to stop talking, I might have told you sooner."

She smacked his arm. Hard.

Jonathan ignored the blow, laying his palm on her cheek. "I can't offer you a normal life, Sarina. I wish I could, but I can't."

"I don't care," she whispered. "I love you, too."

Jonathan closed his eye, a soft smile on his face as he tilted his head back, the setting sun casting it in shadow. After a moment, he looked back down at her, the love evident on his face. "I will protect you, Sarina. I *can* promise you that." He lowered his head until his lips brushed hers briefly. "I will do whatever I can to make you happy. And I can also promise that our life together will never, ever be boring."

Rina giggled, joy bubbling up in an uncontrollable surge. "I believe that." He tried to kiss her again, but she pulled her head back, forcing a serious look as she thought of Charlotte. "You won't leave me behind, then. Pining away here while you sail off to who knows where?"

Jonathan sighed. "I wouldn't dream of it. No, you belong by my side. I need someone to watch my flank, after all."

She grinned. "It's a nice flank."

He laughed, tightening his hold, and she relaxed against him, feeling his warmth . . . his strength.

*Home.* He was her home. What she'd been searching for all along.

"So, what say ye, wench?" he asked with a smirk. "Will you let me make an honest woman of ye? Well, somewhat honest, at least?" He smiled widely at Rina's laugh. "Marry me, Smith. Marry me, and let's go have an adventure or two."

Rina thought it was to her credit that she didn't make him wait for an answer. She smiled up at him, twisting her hands in his hair and tugging it lightly.

"Aye, Captain," she said. "That sounds like a good bit o' fun."

# EPILOGUE

## THE LEGEND OF ONE-EYED JACK

Legends conflict as to the fate of One-Eyed Jack Tremayne and his first mate, Wild Rina Talbot. Some say the pair was captured and hanged, exchanging a passionate kiss before joining hands to face the afterlife side by side. Others say the duo was killed when the *Black Arrow* went down in a vicious hurricane somewhere in the Caribbean islands.

Still others, however—in stories told in hushed whispers around campfires late at night—say that Captain Tremayne and his woman faced no such violent demise, but slipped from sight to live a quiet life among a group of natives in the islands after befriending James Ceron, a local man with apparent blood ties to the chief. They say Tremayne and Talbot were married, had a child . . . grandchildren . . . and lived out their days together. Some stories say the duo got the occasional itch to return to the sea and set out to find treasure or pillage the cargo of another pirate vessel.

"Just to keep sharp," Tremayne was quoted as saying.

The fate of Tremayne's family was a little more clearly documented. His father, Lord Tremayne, married his second wife, Lady Grace Eaton Tremayne in the spring of 1749. Lady Tremayne's daughter, Charlotte Eaton Baines and her husband, Maxwell, former first mate of the *Arrow,* had three children of their own and, despite their advancing years, adopted two more, orphaned in the Revolutionary War. Baines himself was credited with organizing a small group of spies believed to have been largely responsible for thwarting a British attack on Charleston in 1779.

Sam Hutchins, master rigger of the *Black Arrow*, took a brothel owner as his wife, and the two quickly built something of an empire in the islands. Their descendants now own several prosperous vacation resorts, including the original *Red Pearl*, which has been preserved as a historical monument.

Lord Lucius Stanton, who returned to England a wealthy man, boasting of having discovered Mellick's Gold single-handedly, died of consumption less than a year after he claimed his title. Ironically, London's cool and misty weather exacerbated his condition, and doctors speculated if he'd stayed in the Caribbean, he might have added years to his life.

He never wed and had no children. His lands and finances were seized by the Crown to pay outstanding gambling debts.

As for the rest of Mellick's treasure, it was divided amongst the crew of the *Black Arrow* and handed down through the generations. Captain Tremayne and his Sarina stashed their portion of the treasure—not only Mellick's Gold, but all the treasure they'd collected over the years—in various places. They hid caches in caves, buried it beneath trees, and left clues for their children and their children's children to be able to find it.

Why, you ask? Well, your guess is as good as mine, but I suspect Tremayne thought it would be fun. In my research, I've learned that the captain was often motivated by such things.

Most historians believe all of Tremayne's treasure has been discovered, much of it donated to museums over the years. But I believe there is one more cache out there. And I think I've discovered its location. My crew is ready, and I am confident we will discover what may be the greatest pirate treasure ever found.

So, yes, I believe that One-Eyed Jack and his Sarina—his *Smith*—lived a long and happy life together. I believe they plotted together to provide a bit of adventure to those who would come after them. And I believe that somehow, somewhere, they're looking down and smiling as I embark on this journey.

Tomorrow, I set sail in search of Tremayne's last cache. The call of the sea is difficult to resist. The call of a treasure even more so.

I would know, after all. I have the blood of pirates singing in my veins.

*- The Journal of Elisabeth Ann Tremayne, Ph.D.*
*University of Florida, History Department*
*August 7, 2017*

# ALSO BY TAMI FRANKLIN

Coming Soon - The **Love in Holiday Junction** Series

Subscribe to Tami Franklin's Newsletter at **tmfranklin.com/SweetSubscriber** for more information, and get a free copy of the sweet and funny story, **Drive Me Crazy** as a thank you.

**Second Chances, A Magical Holiday Romance**
**Visions of Sugar Plums: A Magical Sequel to Second Chances**

**How to Get Ainsley Bishop to Fall in Love with You**
*"Looking for a sweet first love tale? This is your book. You won't be sorry."*
*- Laurie A., Amazon Reviewer*

**A Piece of Cake**

**FANTASY ADVENTURES BY T.M. FRANKLIN**

**The MORE Trilogy**
*"Reminiscent of the Mortal Instruments Series... only better!"*
*- Penny Dreadful Reviews*

MORE
The Guardians
TWELVE

**The New Super Humans**

Super Humans
Super Powers
Super Natural
Super Heroes

**Unscheduled Departure**
Subscribe to T.M. Franklin's Newsletter at
**tmfranklin.com/Subscribe** and get a free copy!

# ACKNOWLEDGMENTS

This book has been a long time in coming, and there were many people involved along the way. Special thanks to Kate, Tracy, Elena, Sarah, Susana, Annie, Brenna, Kelly, and the many others on Twitter who encouraged me to write this story down.

Also, thank you to everyone who read and reviewed this story online before it was published, including Sille, Denise, Margey, Tiffany, Judy, Melissa, Sherissa, Alanna, Tracy, Colleen, Melinda, Jolanda, Marigel, Laraina, Trisha, Nikki, Angela, Chandrani, Amelia, Lisa, Emily, Martha, Kelly, Alexandra, Amanda, Jenny, Simone, Michal, Belle, Karla, Julie, Brandy, Cheryl, Jackie A., Reeti, Ronnie, Kandy, Melissa, Vinney, Myra, Courtney, Caitlin, Sarah, Shannon, MichelleSB, Pimm, Irene, Gemma, Lisa, Bernadette, Shristi, Lindsay, Rhonda, Hayley, Aneta, Opi, Stephannie, Mireille, Sri, Haley, Dee, Jennie, Grace, Nimisha, Savannah, Carolina, Gemma, Rebecca, Anna, Krisztina, Stacy, Shannon, Emmy, Cintia, Melany, Jennifer, Juanita, Trisha, Erika, Nancy, Trayce, Tara, DeJean, Rochelle, Linda, Caroline, Nichole, Rita, Cassandra, Kate, Sharon, Jiff, Lori, Hafsa Jalal, Katy, Chris L., Diane, Tonya, Rae, Chao, Candace, Sherrie, Carey, Katie, Mina, Sheryl, Jayne, Kristine, Michelle, Tiffany, FSMeurinne, Dusty, Amanda, Daisy, Elaine, Julie, Sara C., Nic, Kat, Pam, Christy, Sue, Tina, Jeanetta, Abby, Rel8tivity, Sarah, withany, Peetah, Alexandra, Susana, Ashleigh, Funmbie, Michelle, Carey, Cozmo, Kim, Marcy, Anastasia, Paige, Joanne, Becky, Nikki,

Krista, Glinda, Remmy, Jecca, Becca, Sami, Nan, Starla, Jennifer, Brandi, Patricia, Jess, Cared, Melissa, Judy, Amy, Jo, Lizettee, Isabel, Jill, Michele, and others along the way. Your support means everything to me.

Many thanks to my wonderful editor, Kathie Spitz, my proofreader, Amy at Rose David Editing, and my pre-reader, Jess Molly Brown. I would never feel comfortable putting my words out into the world without your help. Thank you to Lindsey Gray for her wonderful job formatting this book and making it so beautiful.

Thanks to Jeanne McDonald and the wonderful and supportive authors of Enchanted Publications: Jami Denise, Carrie Elks, Lindsey Gray, Jiffy Kate, Jennifer Locklear, Sydney Logan, Melanie L. Moreland, Ayden K. Morgen, Jo Richardson, Cara Dee, and Alexis Riddley. Go check out their books!

And finally, thanks to my wonderful family who supports me in everything I do. I couldn't do this without you.

# ABOUT THE AUTHOR

Tami Franklin writes sweet and wholesome romance that will sweep you away. A former TV news producer and freelance writer, she now enjoys sharing stories about people destined to be together... they just might need a little help getting there.

Franklin also writes contemporary and YA fantasy under the penname T.M. Franklin.

Connect with Tami at her website: www.TMFranklin.com.
Or for all the latest news on upcoming releases, giveaways, and exclusive content, subscribe to Tami Franklin's newsletter at **TMFranklin.com/SweetSubscriber.**